CW01210198

Twin Soul Series Omnibus 1

Winner Twins
and
Todd McCaffrey

Books 1-5

WINTER WYVERN Copyright © 2018 by Brianna Winner, Brittany Winner, and Todd J. McCaffrey. Second Edition.

CLOUD CONQUEROR Copyright © 2018 by Brianna Winner, Brittany Winner, and Todd J. McCaffrey. First Edition.

FROZEN SKY Copyright © 2019 by Brianna Winner, Brittany Winner, and Todd J. McCaffrey. Second Edition.

WYVERN'S FATE Copyright © 2019 by Brianna Winner, Brittany Winner, and Todd J. McCaffrey. First Edition.

WYVERN'S WRATH Copyright © 2019 by Brianna Winner, Brittany Winner, and Todd J. McCaffrey. First Edition.

TWIN SOUL SERIES BOXED SET: BOOKS 1-5 Copyright © 2020 by Brianna Winner, Brittany Winner, and Todd J. McCaffrey. First Edition.

All Rights Reserved. No parts of this publication may be reproduced, or stored in a retrieval system, transmitted in any form or by any means, electronic, mechanical, photocopying, recording or otherwise without prior written permission of the publisher.
Cover art by Jeff Winner

Books by The Winner Twins and Todd McCaffrey

Nonfiction:

The Write Path: World Building

Books by McCaffrey-Winner

Twin Soul Series:

TS1 - *Winter Wyvern*

TS2 - *Cloud Conqueror*

TS3 - *Frozen Sky*

TS4 - *Wyvern's Fate*

TS5 - *Wyvern's Wrath*

TS6 - *Ophidian's Oath*

TS7 - *Snow Serpent*

TS8 - *Iron Air*

TS9 - *Ophidian's Honor*

TS10 - *Healing Fire*

TS11 - *Ophidian's Tears*

TS12 - *Cloud War*

TS13 - *Steel Waters*

TS14 - *Cursed Mage*

TS15 - *Wyvern's Creed*

TS16 - *King's Challenge*

TS17 - *King's Conquest*

TS18 - *King's Treasure*

TS19 - *Wyvern Rider*

Books by The Winner Twins

Nonfiction:

The Write Path: Navigating Storytelling

Science Fiction:

The Strand Prophecy

Extinction's Embrace

PCT: Perfect Compatibility Test

Poetry Books by Brianna Winner

Millennial Madness

Books by Todd McCaffrey

Science fiction

Ellay

The Jupiter Game

The Steam Walker

Collections

The One Tree of Luna (And Other Stories)

Dragonriders of Pern® Series

Dragon's Kin

Dragon's Fire

Dragon Harper

Dragonsblood

Dragonheart

Dragongirl

Dragon's Time

Sky Dragons

Non-fiction

Dragonholder: The Life And Times of Anne McCaffrey

Dragonwriter: A tribute to Anne McCaffrey and Pern

Map

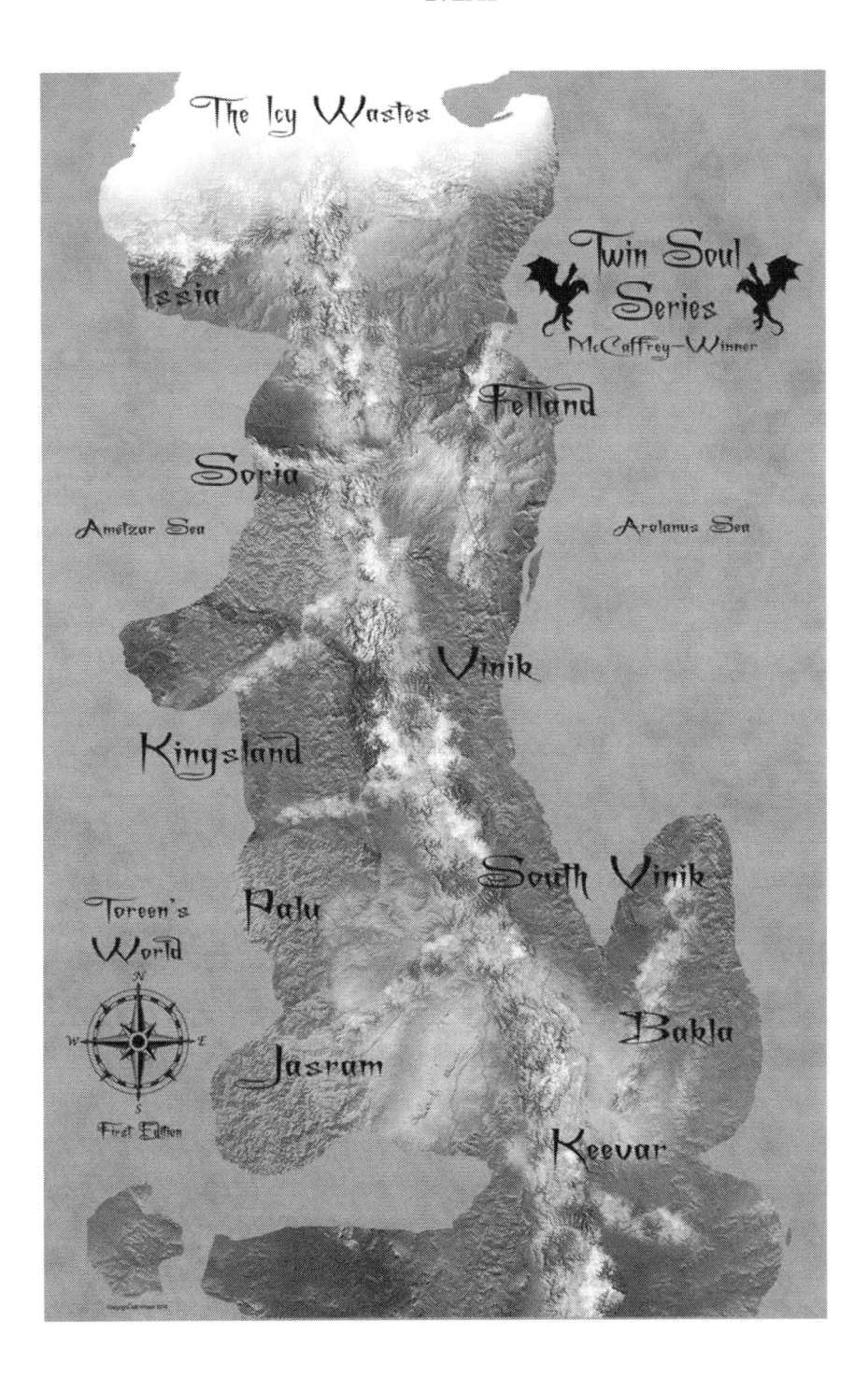

Contents

Twin Soul Series	1
Map	6
Winter Wyvern	10
Chapter One: The Gift	11
Chapter Two: Home Again	16
Chapter Three: Something Lost	18
Chapter Four: Into Town	20
Chapter Five: The Shaman	22
Chapter Six: Hat Pin	24
Chapter Seven: The Fire	25
Chapter Eight: More Tea	27
Chapter Nine: The Thief	29
Chapter Ten: The Docks	31
Chapter Eleven: Hello Krea	33
Chapter Twelve: King's Jail	35
Chapter Thirteen: The Fugitive	37
Chapter Fourteen: Fire Within	39
Chapter Fifteen: The Edge	43
Cloud Conqueror	47
Chapter One: The Airship Spite	48
Chapter Two: The Crown Prince	51
Chapter Three: A Cannon's Fire	54
Chapter Four: A Bitter Triumph	62
Chapter Five: The Young Apprentice	67

Chapter Six: A Wyvern's Corpse	70
Chapter Seven: Captain of Nothing	73
Chapter Eight: A Grave Revisited	77
Chapter Nine: Meeting The Mechanical	81
Chapter Ten: Talent Of Mine	87

Frozen Sky   91

Chapter One: Half a Wyvern	92
Chapter Two: Demands	98
Chapter Three: First Flight	101
Chapter Four: Action Overhead	105
Chapter Five: Prize Money	108
Chapter Six: Payment Made	110
Chapter Seven: The Bitter North	118
Chapter Eight: A Witch's Brew	125
Chapter Nine: Ophidian's Coal	132
Chapter Ten: The Frozen Man	140

Wyvern's Fate   147

Chapter One: Flight	148
Chapter Two: Meetings	151
Chapter Three: Wymarc	155
Chapter Four: The Chore	158
Chapter Five: Wandering	163
Chapter Six: The Bite	167
Chapter Seven: Krea's Room	172
Chapter Eight: Terric's Words	175
Chapter Nine: Gifts	179

Wyvern's Wrath   184

Chapter One: Find Your God	185
Chapter Two: Whole New Body	191
Chapter Three: The Frozen God	196
Chapter Four: Fountain of Air	198
Chapter Five: The Wyvern's Shriek	202
Chapter Six: Let Them Die	205
Chapter Seven: Have A Heart	208
Chapter Eight: House of Life and Death	212
Chapter Nine: Crown Prince Nestor	216
About The Twin Soul Series	218
Acknowledgements	219
About the Authors	220

Winter Wyvern

Book 1

Twin Soul series

Chapter One: The Gift

Krea was bored, and when she was bored bad things always followed. The last time she'd been bored she tried making a sword to prove that she could be a blacksmith just like her father. But, as she hammered the red-hot metal, it jumped out of her tongs, flew into the kitchen and nearly burned the whole house down. The only good thing that had come of that was Smudge, the cat, who'd been so frightened that it had raced out of the barn and right into Krea's arms, where it promptly bit her.

"Serves you right," her father had said later. "At least the cat's not poisonous."

The time before that she decided to take a poisonous spider as a pet, which bit her and — if not for the help of the local shaman — would have killed her in a matter of days.

The year before, on her fifteenth birthday, she'd taken a hammer and smashed anything that might reflect her face. That was at the end of the same day that several villagers, when her hat had blown off, taking her dark glasses with it, revealing her white hair and skin. Shocked, many of the newer villagers and tourists gawked and shunned her. Though this wasn't the first time, it hadn't happened for many years, and it shook her to her core.

Krea decided that she never wanted to see herself again. She hated most that she'd shattered the marvelous pan that her father had made her mother as a wedding gift all so many years ago.

Rabel, her father, had locked her in her room for a week after that. Not long after, he took on Angus as his apprentice. They had taken to talking together outside at the forge for long hours. Occasionally, Rabel would look at Krea and shake his head sadly. Other times he'd point to his daughter, say something and Angus would turn bright red. Angus hardly talked to her and when he did, he stammered. But when he thought she wasn't looking, he'd stare at her.

On the eve of her sixteenth birthday, Rabel had pronounced himself satisfied with Angus' work and told Krea that she would wed Angus the next year. In the months since, Krea had alternately grown more alarmed at the future forced upon her and more intrigued with the young man who would soon be her husband.

When she was sure he wasn't looking at her, she'd stare at him. He was strong, and well-built but sturdy in his face – not ugly but not handsome, either.

Rabel was out with Angus, selling horseshoes to the farmers at the market in town, a good hour away by horseback. Winter was coming so they wanted to sell as much as they could before the snows hindered their travels. Her father had forbidden her from going into the woods surrounding their home. He had made her swear on the names of every god that she would stay inside.

She'd promised that she'd make the evening meal and had dutifully prepared a shepherd's pie — father's favorite. She finished preparing and had it ready for the oven. She tidied up the kitchen, and cleaned up all the dishes with the steam-powered cleaner. She made up all the beds. Swept up all the floors.

And then she was bored. She relented to Smudge's insistent crying and gave her one last scrap which the cat ate with much gusto and loud purring. Once Smudge had confirmed that there were no more treats, she flicked her tail up in a huff and left the kitchen, probably seeking out any mice in the barn.

With a sigh, Krea sat back on the kitchen chair. She realized that everything she'd done she'd soon be doing again every day for the rest of her life… with Angus.

She went up to her room and to the altar she had for the gods. Everyone had an altar. Some had just a few gods waiting but Krea, because she was young, had a full set of figurines. She smiled as she picked up the figurine of Ametza — the sea goddess of their ocean-side kingdom.

Ametza stood for faith, fidelity, and all things feminine. A goddess of life, protector of human sailors and those who lived off her bounty. Ametza could be fickle, fearsome, and demanding. But she was also supportive and kind. Krea held the figurine in her hands.

"Mother Ametza," Krea said. "It's me, Krea." She felt the figurine grow warm in her fingers. The warmth told her the goddess was listening. "I'm bored. And I don't want to stay inside." She glanced out the window. The sky was clear and windy leaves were whirling, the trees were nearly bare. Winter would come any day.

"You understand, don't you?" Krea said. "I'm to be married soon and then I'll never get out. You don't mind, do you? I just want to visit mother's grave." She felt that perhaps the mother goddess understood. With a reverent nod, she placed the figurine back among the others.

She dressed with the utmost care, telling herself that it was in penance rather than admitting it was to ensure that the sun didn't burn her. She secured her wide-brimmed cream colored hat with her longest hatpin made of swirled silver and pearls— the only treasure from her mother. Her oval silver-rimmed sunglasses were secured with a loop of black velvet ribbon, her hair firmly tucked up inside her hat so that no stray wisps might snag and betray her. Her deep green day dress covered her calf-length walking boots so there was no danger of her being seen as improper if any prying eyes should chance upon her progress.

Dark things lay in the woods, and they liked to eat young women, her father had said. Krea was certain that he was wrong. Nothing terrible had happened to her— at least anything since she'd broken her leg racing away from strange noises in the woods when she was seven.

Carefully, Krea looked out from the door of their small brick cottage and peered to either side. She could tell by the sun she had just enough time to walk there and back, before her father returned and the sun set. He would never know. No one was around. The forest was silent. Now was her time to escape.

She gained the cover of the forest and paused to savor her triumph. Father was wrong! There was nothing to fear!

A loud noise from above startled her and her heart beat nearly out of her chest, her blood rushing through her veins. A shadow crossed over her and Krea looked up, shrinking back against a tree trunk to hide. A royal airship crossed over her, new and deadly, silent except for the puffs of steam driving its propellers. Dark smoke trailed from it — had it fired its guns? Were they practicing or had they shot at something?

Krea waited until the airship was out of sight before venturing out from the shade of the tree. She plotted her path away from the airship, back to wherever it had been, her notion of visiting her mother's grave forgotten with the thrill of the moment.

Her path led her by the stream next to her home. Krea rounded the corner. She could see flowers ahead. These were not just any flowers. They were Wyvern flowers. Wyvern flowers were light blue, with wide petals, and a honey scent. Krea halted, taking in the view.

Wyverns were the sort of things the King's airship had been built to fight. But the wyverns loved these flowers so much they now bore their name. The thought of real, living, red-eyed wyverns terrified but also excited her. Krea had no hopes that she would see one this day: it would be impossible for a wyvern to survive an encounter with the royal airship.

The wind changed and the smell of the marvelous flowers overwhelmed her. She smiled as the rich honey scent filled her lungs. The surrounding forest was silent. Krea's smile grew and she threw caution to the winds, rushed into the field, bent down, and inhaled deeply.

The stalks were up to her waist and the small buds flowered in every imaginable shade of blue. She glided her hands over their soft petals. She was now far from the stream, and was deep into the meadow surrounded by thick green trees. She sat down. Laughing, she grabbed a bunch of flowers and deftly wove them into a wreath that she placed over her hat. Her body tingled, and her eyelids grew heavy. She would just close her eyes for a minute, she decided.

Or perhaps... five minutes. Just a little while...perhaps a short nap.

Soon, the honey scent wafted her into a deep dreamless sleep.

#

A loud noise woke her. She opened her eyes to find the sky was orange, and the sun was about to set. Her throat tightened and she hopped up, ready to run home.

She froze when a shadow covered her. Above her was a wyvern, its eyes widened in curiosity.

Krea found herself seeing every detail of the creature. It had golden scales with swirls that seemed carved into them. Its neck was long and sinuous, its body thin and wiry. It crouched on two powerful legs. Tall horns of ivory bone twisted on either side of its head. Its lower face, spine, and the barbed end of its tail were blood red. Its large red slit eyes scanned her up and down. Then, in an exhausted huff, the wyvern lowered its head into its wings.

Krea had heard in the village that like dragons, wyverns destroyed towns and ate humans.

Krea eyed the wyvern, wondering when it would pounce. Or perhaps the villagers were as wrong about it as they were about her?

There was blood on the blue flowers surrounding the creature. The wyvern was breathing heavily, and bleeding in huge spurts.

The creature lifted its head again and stared at her. Krea knew that her father would want her to run, to scream, and race back toward home and safety. But Krea saw the blood, saw the gold scales, and looked beyond them, raising her gaze to peer into the creature's eyes.

There was pain there, much. And sadness, too. And something more — kindness.

The wyvern howled in agony and lowered its head.

Krea made up her mind: no being should suffer alone, unaided. The pool of blood under the wyvern was growing larger by the minute. She stood up and moved toward the winged beast. "Can I help you?"

There was a huge gash in one of the wyvern's legs. The wing on the same side was torn — as though a cannonball had crashed through it and had crushed the leg. The smoke from the airship — it must have fired at this wyvern!

"Why would you help me, human? What do you want from me?" The wyvern was female, she had a deep silky voice. The voice sounded familiar to Krea, but she could not place it.

"I don't understand," Krea said. "Don't you want help? You're in pain! I hate to see you suffer!"

The creature narrowed her eyes and bared her teeth. Was she angry?

She has no right to be angry! Krea thought. Aloud, she said, "I won't stand here and watch you die!"

The wyvern lowered her head, and at first Krea thought she was laughing. As moments passed she realized that the creature was sobbing. Tears misted Krea's eyes. She took another step forward: toward the fangs of the dying beast. She peered up at her, "Let me do something, I want to help you!"

"Child, there is nothing you can do," the wyvern said. "Do you not know why I came to this meadow?"

Krea bit her lip: as soon as the wyvern had spoken, she'd guessed the answer. The wyvern's eyes held hers.

"We come here to die amongst the scent of honey," she said. "To die with the blue flowers that bear our name. That is why I'm here."

In that moment Krea realized why the wyvern's voice was so familiar: it sounded like her mother's. Krea's eyes filled with tears, her lips creased tightly in pain as images of her mother's pale gaunt body forced its way into her mind. Not again, she thought.

She ran forward and wrapped her arms around the wyvern's thin, scaled neck. The scales were soft, almost silky.

"I will not let you die alone."

The wyvern, first stiff and unmoving, lowered her face next to Krea's.

Krea peered into the blood red eyes and held her breath. She forgot the sharp claws, the tearing fangs, and embraced the dying wyvern with body and soul.

"You are kind," the beast told her, "I shall be happy to have you stay with me until the Ferryman comes."

"The Ferryman will come for you?" Krea asked in surprise. The Ferryman came to take souls to be reborn, she had assumed they only came for the souls of humans. No one had ever told her otherwise.

"The Ferryman will come for both of us," the wyvern said. She was silent for a moment, except for her labored breathing. "Or perhaps not."

"I can't have the Ferryman to come for me," Krea said, her chest tightened. "I'm to be married!"

"Really? And this will bring you happiness?"

Krea winced, "My father will be happy. As for myself, I cannot say."

"If you wish, then, I can give you a gift," the wyvern said. "This gift will let you speak to the gods themselves. Accept this gift, for your kindness —" She coughed and gasped in pain. When she recovered, she said, "You shall become something different altogether, and if you accept this gift, and you will save my life."

"I can save you?" Krea cried in joy. "I do not want you to die!"

The wyvern shook her head, "No, I will die... Just answer me this: Are you satisfied with the life your father has chosen for you? Or do you want something different?"

Krea thought of her father: Rabel was a good man, a kind man, but he was getting sickly and frail. If she didn't marry Angus she had no way of taking care of him and, worse, no one else would marry her.

"My wishes do not matter," Krea said, pulling a strand of her white hair, the hair so many thought of as a curse. "I have to marry my father's apprentice or die in poverty. I cannot accept your gift."

"You did not answer my question," the wyvern said. "Tell me true, for yourself and no other, is that the path you desire?"

The truthful answer needed no thought: "No."

"Then you should accept my gift," the wyvern said. A bout of coughing wracked her body. "Chose quickly, while I still breathe!"

The wyvern gasped for air. Her head lowered to the ground, her eyes wide and imploring. She was dying.

Krea's eyes widened in fear and then, impulsively, she cried out: "I will take your gift!"

The wyvern's head dropped to the ground; the life in her blood red eyes faded away.

Pain ripped through Krea's body. She felt like she'd been burned from the inside out.

She screamed and dropped to her knees. Tears rained down her cheeks. She clenched the blue Wyvern Flowers with her hands. The image of the field and the wyvern around her swam in her eyes. Krea fell forward to the ground, and the flowers' honey scent pulled her into a deep and peaceful sleep.

Chapter Two: Home Again

Krea's eyes opened to see Angus's face peering down at her. His expression was stern. His black eyes were narrowed, his thin lips and chiseled jaw only inches away from her face. She saw no sign of her father. She knew where she was: in her bedroom, on her bed. She could not recall how she'd got there.

Angus' face was so close that Krea could not sit up. She felt odd with Angus' brooding silence so sinisterly close to her skin.

"Angus, where is my father?"

Angus lowered his broad shoulders with a sigh, "Thank the gods!" He lowered his face to hers. "We thought you wouldn't come back to us."

He stroked a hand across her cheek: warm and calloused. Krea jerked away.

He gripped her shoulders tightly, pulling back to peer deep into her eyes. With a growl, he said, "If you ever pull a stunt like that when we are married, I will lock you into a room and never let you out again, do you hear?"

Krea started to tremble. Angus released her and stepped back, raising his hands, palms out in a gesture of apology.

"Where is my father?" Krea repeated.

"Asleep in his room. He has been watching you all day," Angus said. With a pleading look, he added, "Please let him sleep, he is exhausted. This day was hard on him."

Krea knew he was talking about her journey through the woods and to the meadow. A wave of guilt washed over her. He was right, and she hated it. "I didn't mean to! If it wasn't for —"

"You are no longer a child, Krea," he said over her words. "I know you haven't had an easy life. And after this…" his words petered out. Abruptly he declared, "Your father and I agreed. We shall be married before the week is done."

Krea's jaw dropped. Angus wasn't a bad man but Krea didn't love him. He was not for her. She wanted to travel, to see the beauty of the goddess's gifts, to have adventures… none of the things that Angus desired.

Around Angus, Krea felt lonely and small: like he was a hole in her world.

"Angus —"

"You'll feel differently when we're wed," he said, guessing at her worries. "It's best that it will be soon. Your father is a kindly man but he is getting sickly. We should both be worrying about him and caring for him." The corners of his lips lifted up. "This time next week, we'll be together and you'll be Mrs. Angus Franck."

"Angus, what happened? How did I get here?" She remembered the meadow, the bleeding wyvern, but nothing more.

Angus' jaw tightened in some strange emotion. For a long while he was silent. Finally he said, "It doesn't matter now. You are safe."

Krea considered this answer. "I'm an adult now, right?" Angus nodded.

"Then you cannot keep from me what happened." She saw the look in his eyes and grew frightened. "You must tell me!" When her strong words didn't get an answer, she pleaded, "Please.

Angus swallowed hard. He bit his lips before responding, "You were found in a field of wyvern flowers unconscious."

What about the wyvern? How could he leave that out? He was hiding things from her — she knew it.

"What else?" she asked. "What aren't you telling me?"

Angus' jaws worked as he searched for the right words.

"There was a woman next to you —"

"A woman?" Krea shook her head. There was no woman. Just the wyvern.

Angus gripped her hand, eyes full of regret, "Krea, the woman next to you was murdered."

Her jaw dropped. She wanted to tell him about the dying wyvern, about the gift, and the pain. But she stopped herself. *He will think I am insane. He will never let me leave this room.*

"What do you remember?" Angus asked with a worried look.

Krea took a deep breath and lied: "I remember nothing."

Chapter Three: Something Lost

Krea told Angus she was tired and pretended to sleep until Angus left the room. She clutched her pillow and sobbed silently, not from sadness but from rage.

As her rage subsided she considered the wyvern's words. A gift that would allow her to speak to the gods themselves — that would save the wyvern's life and change hers? Also, where did the wyvern go? And who was the murdered woman? None of it made any sense.

What was that searing pain? The moment the wyvern's head fell — dead — to the ground replayed itself in her brain. The wyvern had offered her a gift. Krea had taken it. And then what?

Krea stood up. She went to the window, opened the curtains and let the sunlight flood in. Her room looked to the town, not the forest. The sunlight burned her eyes, and she squinted. Krea sighed. She needed answers. She wanted to go back to the meadow and retrace her steps, but knew that neither her father nor Angus would allow it.

Krea backed away from the window, turned and knelt to the altar below. Of Terrene, the mother goddess who molded the Monde, their world, and created her children, all the holy beings who ruled and watched over it. Which would understand her problems? She searched through the dozens of antique carved wooden figurines, picking them from among candles, lace, incense, and sweets. This was a feminine problem, the wyvern was a woman, she was a woman now — as odd as that sounded to her — and marriage was her dilemma.

So she brought out Ametza, her figurine wore a long dress made of fish-like scales of a bluish green, its skin was made of delicately carved pearl, her hands stretched protectively upward holding a golden trident in one hand and a star in the other, with tentacles for hair that seemed to move on their own under a golden crown.

Krea lit the candles and incense. She prayed for forgiveness and understanding to the scent of cinnamon. The door creaked open, and in momentary rage she peered back to Angus's face. Some things had to be private, to be hers and hers alone.

He smiled at her. She frowned in return. With a look of alarm, he shut the door and ran down the stairs.

After a moment, Krea turned back to the goddess. She clasped her hands again and prayed. Nothing happened. There was no feeling of warmth through her hands — the sign the god or goddess was listening — no illumination from the figurine. The goddess refused to hear her! Krea gasped, her heart beating so hard that she heard it in her ears. What had she done?

Why had the goddess refused her prayers? How had her connection had been lost? Ametza always listened!

With trembling hands, Krea searched through the holy figurines. She had never been refused before. Was it because of what happened in the meadow?

She was shunned. In growing desperation she tried every god in her personal pantheon, all the other patron gods of humans. Nothing.

Do all the gods hate me? Krea thought fearfully.

Finally, at the back of the altar she found a lonely figurine: Ophidian, the dragon-headed god. A figurine leftover from generations past when she had discovered in the set. He stood for freedom of choice, rebellion, and irreverence. He was the fire in all being's bellies that humans were taught to ignore. She was told that he was dangerous and never to be contacted. He was the enemy of all her gods.

She had his image because she had to have all the images of the gods. His was a dusty, unloved figure. Secretly, in her wildest dreams, Krea had wondered what would happen if she'd prayed to him. Would he free her, or would he trick her with false words and evil laughter?

She put the figure on a small wooden pedestal above the others and surrounded him with lit tea candles. To the scent of cardamom, she clasped her hands together, and prayed for forgiveness, illumination, wisdom, and answers to her deepest questions.

Her hands tingled and the figurine started to glow. Ophidian answered her call.

Thank you most holy one, she thought. Within her mind's eye, Ophidian's red eyed gaze burnt into her, and the tingling began to expand to every part of her body. Then she saw his face, with his green scales and large sharp smile. He wasn't just hearing her, he was seeing her. He speared her with a godly look: she couldn't move even if she'd been foolish enough to try.

A god had recognized her. Only a few were so privileged. Most never knew the presence of a god until the Ferryman came to bring them to judgement at the end of their life. The pain from the day returned, but her body wouldn't let her scream. The god's head tilted.

"Hello, Krea," he said. Then his eyes closed. His grasp on her vanished; the pain disappeared; and she was left oddly calm.

Chapter Four: Into Town

Her home was her mother's pride and joy. Krea used to hate to clean, and really do any of the feminine arts. But when her mother died the house was all that was left of her.

Krea from then on cared for every inch of it with unstoppable compulsion, one that baffled even her father. The floors were always swept, fresh food always brewing on the stove, dishes were always steam-cleaned, and newly embroidered pictures with red thread — redwork — hung from the walls.

No matter what happened, Krea still had her home. Not Angus's home — regardless of the way her father treated him.

She placed her large-brimmed hat on her head, her dark glasses on her face, and her lace parasol in her hand.

"Be back by sunset, love, I worry about you," her father said, as he hugged her. Rabel was not usually an affectionate man. Occasionally, he would slap Angus on the back, or smile and laugh with him, but not Krea — not since her mother had died.

She could feel her father's frail arms trembling to hold her. Behind him, Angus was staring at her.

"I love you, too," she told her father.

Rabel grasped her tighter. "I know you don't feel ready to be married but you shouldn't worry. Marriage is a sacred bond, a gift from the gods. We are supposed to grow with our partner."

Krea nodded, not even attempting to give him a smile or look of understanding. She could feel the fire well in her chest, and shifted her eyes.

Angus put you up to this, she thought.

"Your mother felt the same way when we were married, she was the same age as—"

"Mother never told me that," Krea said, turning towards the door.

#

Angus drove her to the town in their buggy. Lilly, their mare, was slow and nearly as old as her father. Krea was silent. Usually, she couldn't keep quiet.

"Making me suffer, eh?" Angus asked.

Krea gave him no answer. She didn't even wave to the passengers on the train as it puffed by them on its way from the outlying villages into town.

"I'm not a bad man, you know," he said. "I think most men in my place would have run away and —"

Krea shot him a murderous look but bit back her words, thinking of her father and his aching bones.

Angus raised his hands in a pacifying gesture. "I'm merely saying I care about you, and that I could be a good husband if you gave me a chance."

Krea shifted her eyes to her feet. Her stomach heaved in protest. She was getting married! No, it is too early!

"You don't have to be afraid of me, Krea," Angus said, laying his hand over hers.

She wanted to move her hand, but thought of the years to come. Did she want their marriage to start out with him angry? She knew she wasn't ready but she was given no choice in the matter. Like it or not, she could not forget her father, his bent back, his thin hair, his frail frame — without Angus' help, he would soon be too poor to eat. Krea couldn't do that to her father. She couldn't dishonor him without also dishonoring the memory of her mother and all that they had done for her.

She nodded, and expected him to move his hand away. They held hands for the next hour.

The wyvern had promised her something different — she had never said it would be good.

Chapter Five: The Shaman

Their first stop was the temple. There they separated, Krea joining the young maidens and Angus joining the young men. The small kingdom was known for this temple. It was almost as large as the Castle in the town's center. It had to be to encompass all the gods and their places of worship, but this temple didn't simply have a line of statues like others, each god had their own room or rooms dedicated to them.

The King had declared the temple was a reflection of their dedication to Ametza. Its large arched white doorways and windows of colorful stained glass were meant offerings to the goddess herself, a show of their love and faith.

Krea and the other girls were led to a room near the great knave. There, the shaman would introduce them to the sanctities of marriage.

The room was open, with large arcs providing no barrier to the grassy cliff and stormy sea below. In the middle of the large room. The shaman stood in the massive hand, a statue of Ametza's hand. The shaman's eyes were yellowed and bloodshot, and her skin a blue, a symptom of excessive harnessing of power of Ametza.

Krea's hand itched, she hid it in her dress. She sat along with a small group of young women on cushions in the stone temple, and tried to scratch as quietly as possible.

The other girls were a few years older — mostly eighteen — they were all to be wed within the week.

"You all have a sacred duty to fulfill, "the older woman said, "For the night of your wedding will start the beginning of a sacred act." She paused dramatically. "Marriage."

Krea's stomach lurched. This was not supposed to happen — not now. She shouldn't be here: she wasn't ready to get married.

The shaman, by some instinct, snapped her head around and locked eyes with her. With brows furrowed, she said, "Krea, you should be grateful you will be able to perform this sacred and selfless duty. People like you rarely have a chance."

The other girls looked at Krea and giggled. Krea's cheeks turned bright red. But her embarrassment turned to rage, and she knew exactly what to say. "Tell me Most Holy One, have you performed this most sacred and selfless act?"

"Or course not!" the blue-skinned shaman swore. "I chose to serve our goddess," she continued hastily. Pride swelled her voice as she added, "Indeed, there was never another option for me. I was fated for this."

Krea clasped her hands and bowed her head. "Of course, Most Holy One, refusing so many offers had to be a test for you, was it not?"

"That is enough!" The shaman barked, her blue face beginning to glow red.

All the girls were laughing now, but Krea was not. Krea looked straight into the shaman's yellowed eyes, and scratched hard at a new itch on her finger.

"Forgive me Most Holy One, I felt the goddess urge me to ask questions today, so I had to obey," Krea lied.

The older woman took a deep, calming breath. "Of course," she said. But the look she gave Krea was one of pure loathing.

Before full dismissal, each girl got a chance to speak to the Ametza one by one, kneeling in the giant feminine hand, as if they were literally in the goddess's palm itself.

Krea felt a chill, as if she was pressed against cold metal. Different than the gusts of ocean air. She knew she was no longer welcome here. A fire began to burn in her belly. Rage, lust, longing — for what, she did not know. She took a deep breath and pretended to pray.

The itch wouldn't go away. It got worse and worse. Her finger began to sear. In terror, she pulled off her glove. Her skin was coming off her finger like the peel of an orange but she felt no pain. She could see the muscles and nerves underneath pulsing and pounding. Her stomach knotted.

She should have never gone to wyvern's flowers: she should have never accepted the gift. She had done the unimaginable. She heard the sounds of the girls behind her and quickly put back on her glove, breathed in deeply, and stood. She bowed shakily to the large statue of Ametza before walking out the door.

From the corner of her eye she saw the shaman standing behind the statue, her eyes creased, with a dour look on her face.

She had seen Krea's finger.

Chapter Six: Hat Pin

Krea left the temple without waiting for Angus. She was afraid that if she did, the shaman would talk to them. She didn't want Angus to know about her hand. The air was colder than it had been and clouds were coming in. Perhaps it would snow later.

Krea's right hand began itch, and as she walked over the uneven grey cobblestone streets of the town, the stares from the townsfolk didn't even bother her. The fire in her belly grew. No matter how hard she tried, no calming breath could soothe it.

Krea wondered if this is what it felt like to no longer be protected by the goddess. The world is harsh, she remembered the shaman saying, the goddess is our protection from its endless cycle of misery.

But this didn't feel like misery. Krea liked this feeling, she liked it far more than she should have liked.

As she walked through the crowd, she saw on a balcony above them the prince waving down, as young women screamed and people cheered. On his neck he wore an amulet, a symbol of protection from Ametza, and it glowed blue.

A man bumped into her, and she tripped over the cobblestones beneath her feet. Her world spun, and she fell into his arms.

"I'm sorry—" she began. His eyes stopped her. They were open a little too wide. The man, nearly the same age as her, had long wild hair and a tight grip.

He tilted his head, peering down at her. She realized that the crowd could not see her, and, if she screamed, no one would hear.

"You're not like them," he said, not loosening his grip.

The fire in her belly burned hotter. Her fear was replaced by rage.

"Let me go!"

He smiled at her, his eyes gleaming with their own light. "I know what you are."

He pulled her toward him to get a tighter grip. She surprised him by moving even closer, breaking his grip as she pushed off his stomach. She pulled her hatpin out of her hair. He moved his hand toward her once again.

"I —" he started to say, but she didn't let him finish. She stabbed directly into his wide open palm. He howled in agony.

"Never touch me again!" she roared. As he grasped his injured palm with his other hand, she raced away, losing herself in the crowd. She buried herself in it, certain of safety.

Chapter Seven: The Fire

The crowd engulfed her and Krea felt safe in it. If only her hand would stop itching! She turned to get her bearings just as —

"Fire!!" A man screamed from the edge of the crowd, and hundreds of hot sweaty bodies slammed into her from every direction in their panic. She held on to her glasses and with her other hand slammed her parasol against the crowd. She worked her way to one side of the crowd and was just about free when she felt a large man slam into her back and her parasol and glasses went flying.

Her eyes began to sting as the air became thick with smoke. A thick hand grabbed her waist from behind. It pulled her through the crowd, which seemed to part for whoever held her. Krea gasped for air, coughing and flailing with the force of her rescuer's motions.

The cloud of smoke thickened and her vision darkened. She could feel the crowd part, then subside, then finally she felt no more bodies at all. The screams became fainter and fainter in the distance. Clean air began to fill her lungs, and she choked it in.

A door opened and closed behind her. She was inside. The hand then released her and she fell onto a bed. She tried to look around, but the light was too bright and she had to close her eyes once again.

"Where am I? Who are you?' she asked.

"You could've died out there, lass," said a voice that she immediately recognized.

"Oh, Ibb!" she cried in relief.

Krea had known Ibb all her life. He was the one who got them the marvelous steam cleaner that Krea used in the kitchen. He bought horseshoes from her father, for reasons he never disclosed. He was a traveler, calling no one place home. Many did not associate with him because he worshipped another god, and belonged to an ancient people who believed in transferring their souls into the cold cogs and gears of machines rather than going with the Ferryman to judgement and rebirth. His tall, stocky metal body was topped with a metal head: a mixture of gold and brass, cogs, with two glowing red gems for eyes and thick expressive metal eyebrows.

He was one of the few people she knew that never paid attention to her, good or bad. To him, she was just a normal girl, which was one of the few reasons she loved accompanying her father to town.

Her eyes burned, and she grasped her head in pain. "The light —"

"Rest them," Ibb said. "You are safe in my workshop now, far from the fire."

Krea began to cough. Ibb's large mechanical hands reached out and grasped hers. She flinched away. Her father could not know about her finger.

"You are rubbing your eyes with gloves covered in smoke, best to take them off!"

Krea didn't answer, couldn't answer. Her heart beat louder and louder. What could she say? He was right. She was helpless.

She heard his feet stomp in the other direction, and the familiar squeaking of a tea kettle.

"What are you hiding, Krea?"

Blood pounded in her ears. Anything she told him he would repeat to her father and Angus. But how could she hide her finger from Angus?

Ibb didn't worship her gods: maybe he would understand. Perhaps he was her best hope.

She took off her glove. He gasped and took a loud, clanging step backwards.

"Oh, lass! What have you done?"

Chapter Eight: More Tea

"Your shaman is right, Ametza protects you here, but I think she holds on to you a little too tight," Ibb said after Krea had told him of her encounter at the temple.

Ibb poured her a cup of tea and guided her healthy hand to it. The tea was sweet and spicy. He told her it helped with opening lungs. He said that he used to drink it back when he was in his human frame.

"My mother is dead," Krea said. She took a moment to wonder what mother she meant: her own, or the goddess? Or both?

"What happened to your finger?"

Krea took a deep breath. "I don't know," she said. "I made a choice and this may be the consequence."

Ibb snorted, "And what choice was that?"

"I accepted a gift," she said, "from a wyvern."

Ibb stared at her in silence.

"Ibb," she asked in a small voice, "am I going to die?"

The mechanical being stood still for a very long time. Finally he said, "Did anyone see your finger?"

"I think the shaman did," Krea said miserably, trying to find him in the glare of the room. It hurt her eyes. "Ibb?"

Ibb moved in a blur of speed. Krea gasped as a pair of goggles were placed on her head. Suddenly, she could see. Her eyes stopped hurting.

"Anyone else?" Ibb asked, glancing down at his handiwork and nodding to himself. His bright eyes were unwavering.

Krea wanted to tell him about Ophidian but found she couldn't say the words.

"There was a man on the street, he seemed to recognize me," she said at last.

Ibb sighed, "You are no longer protected by mother Ametza. I think you are safe here no longer."

"What about my father?"

Ibb shook his head, "People in these parts don't like those who don't worship their gods, Krea. Whatever is happening to you is beyond me. And I know many things I shouldn't."

"What will happen to me now?"

"You didn't make a mistake Krea, you chose for yourself," Ibb said reassuringly. "There is a difference."

"I was being selfish," Krea confessed miserably. "I never thought of my father or Angus."

"Perhaps," he said with a wave of his hand. "But it was your choice. Being able to make a choice, and to experience the good and bad that come from it, is what makes us adults."

He gestured for her to drink more tea.

"I've never felt like this," she said. "I feel so sick with myself."

Ibb shrugged, a strange clanking of metal going back and forth. "You have to learn to live with your actions," he told her. "Good and bad aren't that easy. Sometimes no matter how hard you try, it isn't enough."

Krea began to cough again.

"You should sleep — stay on the cot in here. If you need me, I shall be working in my office across the hall."

"All night?" Krea asked. Her brows furrowed in curiosity. "Don't you have to sleep, too?"

"I am no longer flesh and blood, so the answer would be: no," he said, as he clanked toward the door.

"I wish I didn't sleep."

Ibb turned in the doorway, "If you can't sleep, you can't dream."

Chapter Nine: The Thief

Krea woke at the sound of Ibb's heavy footsteps moving steadily toward her. She saw that he carried a tray with a cup and a pot of tea. The workshop was made of carved woods, and painted brass flowers. Small handcrafted bells hung from the ceiling. A large grandfather clock stood in the middle.

It was decor from another place and time, and wherever that was, Krea had always wanted to visit. Krea got up from her bed and met Ibb at the table. He passed her the cup. Krea was delighted to see that it was delicately painted with yellow flowers. On a matching plate was placed a large, cold jellied eel.

"Forgive me, since I no longer eat, I have no kitchen, and I did not have the time to gather anything finer," he told her.

Krea did not mind, going into town was always a rare treat and jellied eel was a treasured pleasure. Ibb watched her eat in silence. She could not read the expression on his face, since he was not human, but the slight tapping of his foot made him seem anxious.

"What aren't you telling me?" Krea asked when she'd finished eating.

In response, the massive machine man lifted the teapot, "More tea, lass?"

Krea raised an eyebrow. "That bad, eh?"

Ibb poured the tea, and nodded. The movement of his mechanical head sounded like her father's hammer forging iron on his anvil. Krea smiled.

"While you were asleep I had created a plan to get you to safety, but something has come up which will make it far more difficult."

Krea sank back into the overstuffed chair and grasped her tea.

"You are no longer protected by Ametza. The shaman knows this. They are looking for you." Ibb clasped his hands, "If this was the only problem we faced, it could be overcome."

Krea leaned forward, "What does that mean?"

Ibb stood up, walked to his office, and then back again. He held in his hands a new pair of gloves, a boy's shirt, trousers, a bulky jacket, boots, a broad black hat, a pair of black-glass goggles, and a leather pouch. It was standard apprentice garb.

"It means I cannot go with you." he said. Krea lowered eyes to hide her sorrow. He snorted when he saw her look. "But that does not mean I won't try my best to help you. If you dress in this —" he held up the bundle of clothes "— people will mistake you for a boy. If I come with you, they'll know who you are no matter how you're dressed. Besides, there is much I do not know."

"Know?" Krea repeated.

"About your condition," Ibb told her. "There is much that troubles me."

"I cannot return, can I?" she guessed, looking up into his mechanical eyes.

"No, you can never return to this city," he said, clanking mournfully as he shook his head. "In fact, to be safe, I would avoid any place that Ametza can see."

"Where do I go?" Krea asked, shocked. More questions came to her in a rush. "How do I get there? What about my father and Angus?"

"You must go north, into the mountains," Ibb told her. "My driver will find you and take you."

They heard screams outside, the sound of running feet.

"There has been a robbery; the amulet of the crown princess has been stolen. That fire was set to create a distraction."

Krea remembered the man with the wild eyes. "Did anyone see his face?"

"Yes, actually," Ibb replied. "The man had shoulder-length black hair, black eyes and —"

"That's the man who stopped me!"

Ibb leaned back, "Does he know what is happening to you?"

"Yes!" she said. "I saw it in his eyes."

"Normally, I would say a feeling such as that is something that to be ignored, but from my limited dealings with wyverns, or any of Ophidian's children, I know they can connect with the essence of another in a way we cannot."

"You are saying my feeling is correct?"

"I am saying this man most likely knows something, and that he is very dangerous. If I were you, I would not look for him."

Krea gave him a fuming look. She was surprised that Ibb didn't remember that the best way to get her to do something was to tell her that she couldn't.

"I know that expression!" he said with a snort. Shaking his head so that it clanked, he told her, "I can't make your decisions for you. What you must do is change immediately, go to the docks, and when night falls my driver will come for you. Take these shillings in case you need them."

Krea opened her mouth to protest but before she could speak, someone pounded on the outside door. "Open up, you clanker! We got questions for you!"

"Just a moment!" Ibb called. He turned back to Krea, gesturing her toward the back door, saying in a low voice, "Go!"

The front door burst open just as Krea ducked behind the back stairs — and before she could reach the door.

Quickly, Krea hid under the stairs. She heard men rushing in and stamping about the room. At first she shook in fear, but then she felt rage. How were these men acting so horribly to Ibb? He'd done nothing wrong! They were being mean just because he was different.

Her anger threatened to engulf her, she wanted to rush out and beat on the intruders. Never before had she felt this way. She gripped her hands tightly together to control herself. They stung horribly, like they'd turned into burning nettles. She heard a sound as something fell to the ground in front of her. She moved her foot, and kicked something: it rolled away from her. Startled, she kicked it again. It slid away from her, further into the dark corner under the stairs. After a moment, she reached for it, searching. She found it. It was thin and long.

Her stomach lurched in protest as she brought it up to her face. It smelled awful. Vomit rose in her throat and the back of her mouth. She inched closer to the light shining through the wooden planks and finally confirmed her worst fears: It was her finger.

Chapter Ten: The Docks

Krea vomited as quietly as possible. Pain seared all of her limbs. It felt as if her blood flowed like the molten metal her father created in his forge. She clutched her finger in one hand and the side of a floorboard in another. Her eyes burned and nostrils seared as undigested eel projected onto the floor. It felt as if her internal organs had detached from each other and had begun to slide out of her throat and mouth.

"What is that, it smells awful!" A man screamed.

"Something I've been working on. Gentlemen, let us move this conversation outside, or soon the fumes will become toxic for your lungs," Ibb replied.

"Fine, but your house will be inspected whether you like it or not. By order of the Crown Prince, all legal scoffers such as yourself must be searched," a gruff voice returned, adding piously: "It's nothing personal."

She heard the men leave. After waiting until all was quiet, she peeked out from behind the stairs. Heart racing, still clutching the finger, she rushed out the back door to the docks.

The lower docks were seedy, unkempt, rundown, and haunted by groups of people moving in small, tight knots. Krea made her way past, her head and eyes covered with hat and glasses. No one looked her way. She made her way toward the market.

The market was filled with men and women who worshipped many different gods – and many who didn't worship any god at all. The traders at their stalls sold tea, coffee, jellied eels, trotters, and other street food. The smell of the food nauseated her. The people didn't smell much better. She focused on moving forward.

Ibb said she should go toward the mountains but she had to meet his driver here. First, Krea thought, I have to clear my head. She went to a stall, gave the woman a half-penny, got a glass of ice-water, and gratefully drank it.

She moved on. Behind her, the crowd parted oddly. She turned and caught a glimpse of a shadow flitting further into darkness: Krea was being followed. She knew who it was: the man who had grabbed her, the thief. The one who had stolen the Crown Prince's amulet. Her breath came faster as she recalled Ibb's warning.

She wanted to hide, to lose him. Quickly. She peered around the docks: where would be the last place a self-respecting young woman go?

The answer came to her in an instant and her lips turned up in a quick grin — the Inn of the Broken Sun.

Krea took a deep breath as she knocked on the gaudy door. A large woman wearing nothing but a corset and stockings opened it, her face white with makeup and lips red with rouge. "Hello sweetheart, what can I do for you?"

"A room would be nice," she said, swallowing her revulsion. Ibb had given her a lot of money. She slipped the woman a shilling. The woman grinned, "You have found the right place!"

The woman beckoned her inside. In the large front room, men sat around tables, drinking spirits and playing cards, with all sorts of women arrayed around them. The smell of smoke and thick perfume was gagging.

"This way, then." The madame led her upstairs and to a room on the right-hand side. The room was dirty. Krea saw thick dust on the furniture. The whole room reeked of alcohol and smoke.

"Can I get you anything else?"

Before Krea could answer, there was a knock on the door. The madame turned around, her brows lowered thunderously, and yanked it open. A young woman curtsied and beckoned her close, a look of worry in her eyes. The two women whispered to each other in a hurried exchange. When they were done, the young woman disappeared and the door closed.

The madame flashed her a fake smile, "I will be back in a moment." She gestured to the bed. "You can settle yourself there."

Krea sat on the bed, relieved to be alone. She dropped her head in her hands.

She looked at her hand again. There were only three fingers. The fourth she'd hidden in her trouser pocket.

"Hello there," a man's voice called from the doorway. Krea hastily dropped her hands to her lap, then moved and sat on them.

She knew the voice. It was the thief.

Chapter Eleven: Hello Krea

"Hello Krea," the man said. Krea jumped up and reached for her hat pin.

The man raised both of his hands, "I come in peace."

"How do you know my name?"

"It's easy enough to learn," he said with a smirk, "if you know who to ask."

Krea clenched her fists under her legs, glad that he couldn't see them. Her face burned with anger. She felt the rage course through her veins like fire. She wondered why she wasn't scared or frightened — the rage consumed her as much as fire consumed wood.

"What do you want?"

"I only want to talk," the man said, hands still raised. He stepped toward her.

"I don't want to talk to you. Get out of here!" Krea started to move further back on the bed, remembered her hands and thought better of it.

The man's smirk turned into a grin. "I'll leave if you show me your hands."

"Why?" Krea demanded. He made no move, so she continued, "There's nothing wrong with my hands! They're cold, I see no reason to show them to you!"

"So only one finger fell off?" He asked, watching her jerk in reaction. He laughed. His grin broadened. "Just wait until the rest of them go!"

"How do you know that?" She wanted to punch him, but she knew she was weaker than him, he would easily overpower her.

"What do you —" she began. He cut her off.

"You and I are a lot alike."

"I don't even know who you are!" Krea said.

"I'm Jarin," he said, extending a hand toward her. Krea did not take it. "Oh, I forgot! You don't have any hands!"

She glowered at him. He looked at her a moment longer, shrugged, and said, "So what do you know?"

"About what?"

"About yourself, about what's happening," Jarin told her. Loud shouts from outside distracted him. "You help me, I help you."

"How?"

"Get into bed with me," he said, moving toward her.

"Never!"

"If you don't, you'll die," he said, jumping onto the bed beside her. He threw her toward the headboard and scuttled up beside her, reaching for the bedspread with his other hand. He got underneath it and threw it over the both of them just as the door burst open.

"In the King's name!" a guard shouted at the door.

"Keep these safe on you, I'll come back for them," Jarin said, thrusting a packet toward her.

The door burst open and two guards rushed in.

"That's him!" one shouted.

"You're under arrest, by order of the King," the other said. They looked contemptuously toward Krea, dressed still in boy's garb.

"You lad, do you know this man?" the first guard demanded.

Krea shook her head, eyes wide with fright.

"He's a thief," the guard said. The two pulled Jarin out of the bed roughly. With one taking each arm, they marched him out of the room.

Jarin turned back at the doorway long enough to catch her eyes and shake his head: say nothing. Krea was too frightened to consider speaking.

A long moment later, the madame returned to the room. "I'm terribly sorry," she said. "He paid me more than you."

"And so you prosper," Krea said with a bitter look.

"You're a girl!" the madame exclaimed.

"What I am is no concern of yours," Krea shot back. "If you've any sense, you'll forget you ever saw me." She jumped out of the rumpled bed and headed past her, through the doorway. She turned back and said, "Where are they taking him?"

"The jail, no doubt," the madame said. Her eyes took on a calculating look. "For a shilling, I'll have someone bring you to him."

"I've already paid," Krea snapped.

The madame seemed to consider this and then, wordlessly, nodded. She started down the stairs, gesturing for Krea to follow her. At the front room she signaled a young girl and spoke to her in low tones. The girl gave Krea a quick look, nodded once, and motioned for Krea to follow her.

Krea grabbed the girl's arm as they left the inn. "If anyone asks, I'm your brother from out of town. Someone stole something from me and I'm trying to find them."

The girl gave her a measuring look, brows furrowed, then nodded. "This way."

Chapter Twelve: King's Jail

The King's Jail was a musty stone building set at the worst part of the dockyards. Here, the smell was fouler than anything Krea had encountered. The girl stopped outside and pointed before darting off, lost from sight in a moment as she flitted from one shadow to the next.

Krea hovered at the outskirts of the jail, wondering what to do when the guards marched through the gates with Jarin still between them. At least she didn't have to worry about finding him.

Ibb had told her to find his driver. She didn't know how long he would wait. But Jarin had said she would die and that he knew what was happening to her. How?

He'd told her to keep his packet. She felt in her jacket and pulled it out, careful not to dislodge her dead finger or hurt the stub on her hand. The packet was a small, red purse of fine velvet. The laces were gold. With a sense of growing dread, she opened it. Gold gleamed back at her. At the very top of a large pile of jewels and coins was the Crown Prince's amulet. If anyone found her, she'd be jailed for certain.

A grubby child came rushing out of the jail, looked around, smiled grimly when he spotted her, and rushed over to her. Krea quickly hid the packet as the boy approached. His eyes were sunken in a starved face and he smelled.

"He said you'd give me a penny," the child said.

"Who?"

"He'd said you'd know," the child replied. He held out a grubby hand. "A penny for his message."

Krea fished in her pocket for a penny from the coppers Ibb had given her. She held it tightly in her good hand, "What did he say?"

"He said to meet him, he's just inside in the first cell," the child said. "The guard will let you in for a shilling."

Why is everything a shilling? Krea wondered as the child grabbed the penny and scampered away. She took a deep breath and crossed the street to the jail.

Her lungs burned inside her like she was breathing the heated air of her father's forge. Father! she cried to herself. What would happen when she didn't come home? How would he survive if she didn't marry Angus?

"What do you want?" a guard called out from an alcove. Krea looked up, startled.

"Pl-please," she stuttered. She remembered what she was supposed to say. "My brother. I've come to see him."

"No one can see the prisoners," the guard said, jerking his head toward the exit.

"I can pay," Krea said pulling a silver shilling out of her pocket.

The shilling disappeared into the guard's large hand. "You have five minutes."

Krea nodded and rushed away, looking for the first cell and trying not to vomit at the horrible smells that assailed her senses.

"There you are!" Jarin cried, rising up from the straw strewn across the hard-packed floor. "You took your time!"

"I came as soon as I could," Krea replied in surprise.

"After you had a drink or two, you useless knave," Jarin roared back angrily. "Come here, let me smell your breath, prove that I'm wrong!" He beckoned her forward. When she hesitated he gave her a large wink of the eye furthest from the guards.

With a sigh, Krea moved forward. Jarin grabbed her arms and dragged him right up to the bars.

"Here, here, enough of that!" the guard barked.

"Ach, you're a liar, just as I said!" Jarin shouted, thrusting Krea away. "Get you gone! You're no use to me and I've no use for you either."

Krea gave him a shocked look — then realized he was just acting. But when would he share his secrets with her?

"Go on, go on, you useless knave!" Jarin shouted, reaching down and throwing dirtied straw at her. Instinctively, Krea ducked away.

"You heard the lad, away with you!" the guard said, moving toward her.

Head bowed, Krea left.

Outside the jail, she turned back in bewilderment. What was she going to do now?

Chapter Thirteen: The Fugitive

Was Jarin telling her true, that he knew something she didn't? Or had he just used her for his own ends? And if so, what were they? And how did he know about her hand? Had the shaman told him? How was that possible?

Krea stood there, lost in thought for a long moment until a motion from the jail caught her eye. It was the guard looking at her suspiciously. She realized that if she stayed much longer, he might come after her.

She could go find Ibb's driver, go to the cold north. She shivered. Even here it was already cold enough. Fall was slipping into winter and, from the chill in the evening air, she guessed it would be a fierce one. She turned back toward the docks, toward the meeting place Ibb had described to her, not far from the inn. She hadn't taken more than two steps when a shout came from behind her. Before she could turn or do anything, a hand gripped her elbow tightly.

"Run!" Jarin cried, pushing her along in front of him. The noise behind her grew louder as more guards added their voices to the alarm. "Over here!" Jarin pulled her down a side street.

The next few minutes were a bewildering rush of twists and turns. Krea cried out in pain at his insistent jerking on her elbow — it burned so much that she feared it, too, might come off just like her finger. A moment later he pushed her through a back door. They were in shadow and silence.

"Why aren't we running?"

"We're safe, they'd never expect us to return," Jarin told her. Krea sniffed and recognized the awful perfume of the Inn. "And, if I know you, you've got our escape all planned out."

Our escape? Krea thought angrily. "Why should I do anything more for you?"

"Because you'll be wanted by the King's men, for your part in my escape," Jarin said, his teeth gleaming in the darkness.

"Why?" Krea asked, her brows narrowing. "They think I'm a boy."

"How many boys use hatpins?" Jarin asked. Krea's eyes widened. "How do you think I escaped?"

"You thief!"

"And you have my jewels," Jarin said. "So we'd best escape quickly before the king's men decide to return here." He paused for moment, then asked snarkily, "So, once again I ask you: what's your plan?"

Krea snarled at him, wishing she could bite his head off.

"Careful!" Jarin said, raising his hands. "You'll burn us all in your rage!"

Krea realized that she could see. The darkness seemed lighter like someone had lit a lamp. She glanced down and saw that the light was coming from her.

"Calm yourself," Jarin said.

"What's happening to me?" Krea asked. She closed her eyes, wishing the horror would end. She felt Jarin's arms enfold her.

"Shh, shh, it's a good thing," Jarin told her quietly. "Just calm yourself, and it will be all right."

Angrily, Krea pushed him away. "I told you, don't touch me!"

Chapter Fourteen: Fire Within

Everything had changed. Everything was different. Krea didn't know what was happening.

"I'm to be married," She said in the darkness.

"I don't think so," Jarin said. She sniffed in anger. He held up his hands soothingly. "You made a choice, you are seeing the consequences."

"What are you talking about?"

"Later," Jarin said. "This is not the time."

"Tell me now or I'll give your jewels to the guards," Krea said, shoving a hand into her jacket.

"They'd kill you," Jarin said. "We need to escape, go somewhere cold before too much happens to you." He grabbed her shoulders. "What is your plan?"

"You'll get nothing until you tell me," Krea said. Impulsively, she added, "And you owe me a shilling and a penny."

Jarin laughed. "Oh, that's rich! You're threatening me!" She could feel him shaking his head back and forth. "You even think to threaten me and you don't know what you are!"

"Why, don't people threaten you all the time?" Krea said. "You are a most annoying man, I can't see why they wouldn't."

"I'm not a man," Jarin told her.

"Well, boy, then," Krea replied. He seemed to have not much more than her own sixteen years.

Jarin's laugh grew louder. He dropped his arms. "Boy! You think I'm a boy!"

"What, are you a girl in disguise?"

"Ha!"

Krea burned with anger.

"Calm down," Jarin said, suddenly serious. "I've no desire to get burnt with you."

"What do you mean?"

"You made a bargain, didn't you?" Jarin said.

"A bargain?"

"Don't be coy," he said. "You made a bargain with someone dying."

"It was a wyvern," Krea admitted.

"What did she say to you?" And Jarin's words were now like frost on the ground or ice over a river.

Krea was slow to answer. Finally, she said, "She offered me a gift, a chance for a different life."

"And when was this?"

"Yesterday," Krea said, surprised at the urgency in his tone.

Jarin took a step back from her. Then he turned, grabbed her arm and rushed them back out the door. His hold on her was so tight that she couldn't pull away no matter how hard she tried. It was like her arm was in a vice.

They reached the docks and the piers before he slowed down. Krea was breathless.

"I —" he began.

"What —" she demanded at the same time.

He glanced upwards and gestured. Snow was falling, small flakes at first, then larger clusters.

"Good," he said. "That should help if things go wrong." He lowered his gaze to her. "Where are the jewels?"

Krea's hand went toward her pocket before she stilled it, her eyes flinty. "You were going to tell me."

"You should be dead," he said, looking at her with pity in his eyes. "Why aren't you dead?"

"The wyvern —"

"Annora," Jarin said.

"What?"

"Her name was Annora," he replied. "Annora Wymarc."

"The airship shot her down," Krea said.

"No."

"I saw it."

"Did you?" Jarin challenged her.

"Well…" Krea recalled what she'd seen. She'd seen the airship, the dissipating smoke, she'd found the wyvern.

"She died saving me," Jarin said. "They fired at me and she pushed me aside." He glanced at Krea. "She didn't tell you, did she?"

"She was dying," Krea said, as if that was all that mattered.

"And she offered you a choice," Jarin said. "You say it was yesterday?"

Krea nodded. Jarin looked at her critically.

"You should be changed by now," he told her. "I thought this was your first day. It only takes a day unless…" he broke off and gave her another, longer critical look. Finally, he said, "What happened, afterwards?"

"What?"

"When you woke up next to the body," Jarin said, his voice catching on the last word.

"I…" Krea's brows furrowed in concentration. "I didn't," she said. "I woke up in my bed."

"So someone found you and brought you back," Jarin guessed. "Who?"

"Angus," Krea said. She saw his eyebrows rise and explained, "He's my father's apprentice."

"And what is he to you?"

"We're betrothed," Krea said. She turned from her head, looking around in the dark night, wondering where Angus was and what he was thinking at that very moment.

"And you don't want him," Jarin guessed. Krea snapped her head back, her flashing eyes meeting his. Her anger ebbed as she noticed a look of … pity? … fear? … coming from him. He gestured for her to answer.

"I… my father is getting old, I can't take care of him by myself," Krea found herself stammering. "Angus is a good man."

"Whom you don't want to marry," Jarin said. Before she could respond, he added, "When is the date?"

"We're supposed to be married today," Krea admitted. Again, she darted her head around, peering toward where the Temple might be, wondering if Angus was waiting for her there.

"Ah!" Jarin said, nodding to himself. Krea looked back to him. He leaned down to bring his eyes level to Krea's. "You are in a very grave dilemma: you are torn between two oaths." He shook his head. "And you must choose one before the sun sets this evening."

"And if I don't?"

"You'll die," Jarin said. "Horribly."

"Like when I lost my finger?" Krea asked.

"Much, much worse," Jarin told her. "I've only seen one person refuse the call." His lips tightened into a thin line and he looked away from her to some distant memory before he turned back. "That is more than I ever want to see."

"The woman," Krea asked, "was she special to you?"

"She was half of special," Jarin told her. Krea gave him a questioning look. Jarin sighed. "What do you know of the twin souls?"

"Twin souls?"

"Some bodies are only big enough for one soul," Jarin said, giving Krea a pitying look. He pointed a finger at himself. "I am not." Krea's eyes widened. "Annora was not."

"Two souls in one body?"

"Which is why there was only a woman's body left behind," Jarin said. His eyes grew wistful. "Oh, Annora, you saved her!"

"How?" Krea asked bluntly. "You said she was dead."

"She is," Jarin agreed, further confusing Krea. She arched a brow at him half in inquiry, half in demand for answers. "One soul is dead." He told her. "But the other lives on in you."

"In me?"

Jarin moved close to her, grabbed the fabric of her sleeve. "Slide it back, I want to look."

Krea made a face and slid the sleeve of her blouse up.

Jarin's touch on her skin made her jump. It didn't burn but it felt... like nothing she'd ever felt before. She looked at the lines his fingers traced on her skin. The lines grew brighter, fading slightly when his fingers left them but remaining visible where before they were not.

"You must be in great pain," Jarin said with much feeling in his voice. "Wymarc, I am so sorry."

Krea pulled away from him, angrily rolling her sleeve back down. She met resistance where the lines on her skin tugged at the fabric.

"If you choose your new life, you will save more than one soul," Jarin told her with feeling.

"If I choose as you wish, my father will die," Krea told him.

"And if you don't choose, all will die," Jarin warned. He held up his hand. "And now that I've told you, my jewels, please?"

"How do I know I can trust you?" Krea replied. "You're nothing but a common thief."

"I have already told you that is not so," Jarin said. He gestured toward her arm. "And you saw the markings yourself."

"If you're not a common thief, then what are you?" Krea demanded. "And why did the wyvern carry you —" Krea broke off, something about his words did not match what she was imagining. Before she could resume, Jarin broke into a long, loud laugh.

"Carry me?" he chuckled, bending over and pointing at her. "Carry me?"

"You're small enough!"

"Small enough!" Jarin's laughter redoubled and he was laughing so hard he was nearly bent in half. "Annora could never carry me! Not in all her golden glory."

"So you're a wyvern?"

"No," Jarin snorted. "Don't insult me."

"Then what are you?" Krea demanded.

"I'm nothing as modest as a wyvern," Jarin told her.

"So —"

Jarin stopped her with a raised hand, rising to his full height once more. "That is all I'm willing to say where other ears might hear."

"But —"

"Just know that I am not a wyvern and ask about it no more," Jarin told her.

"So what you are some strange thief," Krea declared.

"Not a thief," Jarin told her. "I merely got my just amends for the harm that the King and his lackeys caused me and my friends."

"Alms for the dead?" Krea guessed.

"Something like that," Jarin agreed. His lips twitched. "And a little extra for pain and suffering."

The snow was coming down heavily now. Krea saw that it did not land on Jarin but it was already covering the ground. She glanced at her clothes. They were wet — like she'd been in the rain. She watched one snowflake falling toward her and jumped when it melted into a droplet of water.

"We're melting the snow," Krea said in awe.

"Yes, we are creatures of fire," Jarin agreed. "It is part of both of us. Twin souls burn brightly."

Chapter Fifteen: The Edge

"Krea!" a voice called from the distance, muffled by the snowfall.

"Angus?" Krea replied, turning toward the voice. Angus came stomping toward her, broke into a run to close the distance and stopped dead just short of her arms. Behind him was Ibb, who seemed to be purposely slowly his strides. Angus looked at Jarin. "Who is this?"

"Who are you?" Jarin demanded in return.

"I'm Angus," the apprentice said, drawing himself up to his full height. Jarin's lips twitched as it became apparent that Angus' height was half a head shorter than his. Angus dismissed Jarin with a glare and turned back to Krea. "Where is your dress? What happened? Your father and I have been searching all over for you." His eyes narrowed as a thought came to him and he turned back to Jarin. "You're the thief they've been talking about." To Krea he said, "Grab him! There's a reward!"

Jarin ignored Angus completely "You're Ibb? I have heard about you!" Jarin in surprise. He pointed to Krea. "Do you know her?"

"Yes," the two said in unison.

"What does she know?" Ibb said to Jarin when they recovered from their surprise. To the thief, he added, "I heard from my man that she missed the meeting just as I'd finished going through the old scrolls."

"How did you find me?" Krea asked.

"It's a talent of mine," Ibb told her, then signaled to Angus, "I brought him. He needs to know what is happening."

"Know about what?" Angus said, taking a step closer to Krea and further from Ibb. Krea gave him a sad look — she hadn't realized that Angus was one of those who feared the gentle mechanical.

"What old scrolls?" Krea said to Ibb.

"He's the one you've promised to wed?" Jarin asked Krea. Angus threw him a dirty look even as Krea nodded in confirmation.

"The scrolls about the twice sworn," Ibb said to Krea.

"Twice sworn?" Krea asked.

"There's no time to explain," Ibb said. He waved at them. "You need to flee. They're going to find you!"

"Who?" Krea asked.

"How?" Jarin demanded.

A howl rent the night and was answered by a chorus of voices.

"The king's men!" Ibb said. "And there's a reward for both of you — dead or alive!"

"What?" Angus bellowed. He waved at Krea. "Is that why you're dressed as a boy?"

"How?" Jarin said to Ibb, ignoring Angus entirely.

Ibb answered by turning to Angus. "They found the woman's body." He pointed to Krea. "They're calling her a witch and him her familiar... and the both of them thieves!" He made a shooing gesture. "Run!"

As they moved off, Ibb called, "And Krea? If you make the choice, your love must kill you! Stab you through the heart!" Krea stumbled as the words hit her ears. She paused to turn back to the mechanical man but he gestured her to flee. "Go!"

"Where?" Angus bellowed. Jarin grabbed Krea's arm and dragged her away before she could hear Ibb's response. She turned back to see Angus moving toward the growing mob. "Go!" he called. "I'll find you!"

She spotted Ibb darting toward a hiding spot — the mechanical would be a natural target for the mob.

Krea felt a stab of pain in her side as they ran away, upwards, to the cliff on the far side of the docks. Her lungs were burning, her chest heaving in pain.

"They'll see us!" she said to Jarin as they broke out from the last of the buildings and into the clear, snow-covered hillside.

"Let them!"

"But they'll kill us!"

"You're dying already," he told her. "All that matters is how."

He stopped and glanced around. Krea looked around with him. They were at the very edge of the cliff, a good fifty feet from the raging sea below them. Jagged water broke over the rocks below. For Krea, the sight was strangely compelling.

"My father will die," Krea said. "He'll die because of me, because I wouldn't marry Angus."

"All things die," Jarin told her. "And the Ferryman will come and life will begin anew."

Krea gave him a hard look which he returned with equal measure.

"You have a choice," he told her. "A hard one either way." Angry shouts came from below and Jarin pointed toward the approaching crowd.

"We could still run away," Krea said, pointing toward the other side of the hill.

"No, Krea, you can't," Jarin told her. He pointed to the sun. "Your hour has come."

"You knew this would happen," Krea said.

Jarin nodded. "The moment I found her body, I knew there would be a hard choice."

"You found her body!"

"I had to know," Jarin said. "Others needed to —" he broke off. "I have said too much."

A rustling through the bushes startled them. It was Angus.

"Quickly!" he called. "I've drawn them off; we can escape down the other side!"

"There is no escape," Jarin said, shaking his head sadly. "Oaths were made."

Angus' eyes grew wide with understanding. He moved toward Krea. "Marry me!" he told her. "Marry me and I'll tell them that it was not your fault. That, as your husband, I made you —"

Krea felt her heart melt at his kindness. And then pain doubled her over and she shrieked in agony.

"It's happening," Jarin said, moving toward the blacksmith's apprentice. "She is changing."

"Changing?"

"She took two oaths, Angus," Jarin told him. "One to honor the fallen and the other to honor her father." He shook his head sadly. "She must choose one or die."

"I'll die either way," Krea said, raising her head to look at them. Her face was pale, her red eyes burnt with an inner brightness. She looked to Angus. "If I become your wife

— even if we live — I will die with my vows." And she turned to Jarin. "And if I honor the fallen, I'll — what will become of me?"

"You'll live," Jarin told her with great feeling. He looked to Angus. "She'll live for many lifetimes, touch the minds of the gods themselves."

"I've already seen the eyes of one god," Krea said in a low voice. Angus' eyes widened. Jarin jerked his head around to meet her gaze. "Ophidian."

"The god of choices," Angus breathed in awe. He looked at Krea with wide eyes. "What choice have you made?"

I have a choice! Krea thought, her heart leaping. I have a choice!

"It can only be yours," Jarin told her. He glanced to Angus. "No one can force her."

Krea's heart pounded in her chest as time seemed to stop. Either way, someone would die. Who would it be? That was her choice. Her only choice.

Choose life. Krea thought. Time lurched forward once more and her heart slowed. She could hear the outraged sounds of the villagers in the distance.

Krea turned to Jarin, pulling the bag of jewels from her pocket. "I'll give you half if you give me my hatpin."

"I could take it all," Jarin said. He gestured toward the town and the mob rushing towards them. "I'll be lost in the shadows before they know it."

"No," Krea said. Jarin jerked in surprise. "You want me to change. To honor the fallen. This is the deal."

"The hatpin?" Jarin asked.

"It was your mother's, wasn't it?" Angus said.

"Here," Krea said, pouring half the jewels from the purse into Angus' hand. To her surprise Jarin didn't even flinch, and instead gave a nod of approval. He was far more interested in Angus's reaction. "Hide this. Take care of father."

"I don't need this, and you can't buy me," Angus told her, pushing her hand away and shooting a look toward Jarin. "Your father is now my father."

Krea shook her head. "I can't marry you, Angus," she told him, surprised at the tears that suddenly sprang in her eyes. She pulled up her sleeves and showed him the markings on her arms. Markings that were transforming into white scales even as they watched.

"You've made your decision," Jarin said in an approving tone. "Good. I will find you, after." He placed the hatpin in Krea's outstretched hand and took the bag now only half-full of jewels. He turned to Angus. "You heard Ibb, are you willing to do your part?"

"My part?" Angus repeated. He looked to Krea who pressed the jewels on him once more. He pocketed them with a frown. She passed him the hatpin.

"Do this," she said, "pierce my heart, free me from my vow, and you save our father."

"I can't!"

"Do it and you save more than one life!" Krea told him, pressing the hatpin into his hand.

"You're burning!" Angus cried, as he caught sight of her clothes. "Your clothes are on fire!"

"Stop!" a guardsman ordered. "Stop in the name of the King!"

"Save my father," Krea begged, moving toward the man who would marry her.

With a sob, Angus thrust the hatpin into her heart. Blood burst forth and rained down the hatpin, covering his hands, drenching his sleeve. Tears poured down his face as the one girl he'd ever loved fell, lifeless, backwards over the cliff.

Krea felt the pain, felt the blood rushing out of her, felt herself falling. She was on fire. She was burning. She was dying.

Here child! A voice called out to her. Take this!

Krea reached to find something bright, shining, and hot inside herself. Something she'd never felt before. Something that felt wrong and right at the same time.

And then she was no more.

With a loud cry she was reborn, alive, fiery, proud, and glowing. She stretched her arms out — and flew!

The snow melted upon her and covered her scales with their soft coldness. She reveled in the feeling, in the flying, soaring up over the mob of humans staring blankly at her from the cliff's edge.

She was all clad in white, her scales brilliant in the night sky. Her heart, torn no longer but beating with the strength of two souls, pounded within her and she roared with triumph — only to stop as she saw one brawny man move toward her, arms outstretched, a gleaming hatpin in his hand glowing red.

He fell to his knees, his eyes never leaving her. Angus!

The winter wyvern screeched in triumph.

And soared into the heavens.

Cloud Conqueror

Book 2

Twin Soul series

Chapter One: The Airship Spite

"Strangest ship I've ever seen!" someone swore in the crowd nearby. The comment, however rude, was not without merit. The ship had a hull but no rudder, a bowsprit but no masts.

"'Tis not a ship, fool! It's an *air*ship!"

"An airship?"

"It flies in the clouds!"

"There are no masts, only those large balloons!" There were ten large balloons straining at their bonds to the ship, trying to flee into the sky above, arranged into two rows of four with the final two perched atop.

"They lift the ship into the sky!"

"Shh, the Queen approaches!"

Queen Arivik, accompanied by Crown Prince Nestor, walked gingerly down the steps and up the gantry set by the prow of the strange vessel. Both dressed in a expensive green silk and wore crowns made of white coral, both rare materials said to have been gifts given by Ametza, their patron goddess.

Captain Ford, as befit his station, walked three steps behind the last noble, even if it was his ship in the first place.

#

"You'll be getting the most powerful ship ever!" the first minister, Mannevy, had told him.

"I'll be losing my livelihood," Ford had replied grumpily.

"You'll be a King's man!"

"I already *am* a King's man!" Ford replied. "How many pirates have I brought to his throne, how many ships have I sunk, all under his letter of marque?"

"And that's why the King chose you for this!" Mannevy replied as he adjusted his monocle.

Ford had known enough not to protest too wildly: money had changed hands: Captain Ford had changed coats — although he much preferred the functional nautical garb to this… this affront to all his senses. Still, he wore the feathered cockade as required, worked his way around managing the long plumage on his blue jacket — and the gold braid on his sleeves was more rank than he'd ever imagined.

His skin told a story of years in the sun. Ford's blonde hair was tucked back in a ponytail, and he wore a gold earring in each ear. His weathered look contrasted sharply with Mannevy, whose ebony skin was soft with no wrinkles and whose dark hair was tightly coiled hair and cut short.

"The first among many, and you'll be the admiral!" the first minister had promised in a rich bask voice. Ford had known the King — and his promises — long enough to know to take *that* with a large grain of salt.

#

"In the name of my husband, good King Markel —" the queen's words brought Ford back to the present "— I commission this ship the royal airship *Spite*."

Ford couldn't help smiling to himself: up until a month ago, his ship had been the good ship *Sprite* but in the aftermath of dealing with the Crown Prince, his mother the queen, and the shadow of the man that had once been a proper King, he'd decided in the dead of night to change the name to something more appropriate.

The queen splashed the holy water on the prow and everyone applauded, some only for the joy of the occasion, others because it meant they could go off to their afternoon meal. Crown Prince Nestor, turned his pale face back toward Ford, brows furrowed in a demanding look. Ford bit back a harsh retort — the child pretending to be a man! — and turned to the end of the gangway.

And now I command His Majesty's Airship Spite, Ford thought to himself. He surveyed the length of what had once been a very jaunty two-masted brig and bit back an oath. The masts were gone. In their place were ten large balloons filled with a magical air that could raise the ship from the ground. At her rear, where the proud rudder had once been mounted was nothing. At the stern, instead, were two large upright spars with large furled vanes of strong cloth. *It looks like a two-tailed peacock*, Ford thought ruefully to himself.

"Ship's crew, man your stations!" Ford barked, moving up the walkway to take his place at the helm. A rush of feet followed behind him and took their places, although Ford knew full well that some were already aboard, stoking that never-to-be-sufficiently-damned coal burner set just before the wheel to provide heat and steam for the thaumaturgy that would propel his ship into the sun-drenched sky.

"Stations manned and ready, sir!" Boatswain Knox bellowed from his place by the wheel.

"Prepare to release mooring lines!" Ford called. He turned toward the infernal machine not ten paces in front of him. "Mage, prepare the lifting spells!"

"How many times, Mr. Ford, must I remind you, I'm a thaumaturge —"

"It's Captain Ford and if I call you a mage on my ship, then a *mage* you shall be, sir!" Ford roared back, drowning out the thin young man dressed in purple robes. The mage looked ready to argue so Ford took a step forward and gestured upwards commandingly.

"Aye sir," the mage said in a smaller voice, "at your command."

"Are we ready?" Ford said in a lower voice to the boatswain. Boatswain Knox looked around to all his people and nodded. The Boatswain was short and muscular, with thin black hair beginning to thin. Like Ford, Knox's skin was withered, and wore a gold earring in each ear.

"Wait!" a voice called from the prow by the gantry. "I shall join you on this magnificent journey!"

"Oh, cripes, it's his nibs," Knox muttered.

"That's *Prince* Nestor, Knox," Ford growled. "Never forget that. If he heard you call him 'his nibs', he'd have you flogged."

He turned back toward the Prince.

"We would be delighted to have you on this most dangerous voyage," Ford called down the length of the ship. "Crewmen, help your prince aboard."

"Look at him, he's turning green already," Knox muttered as the Crown Prince paled at the words: 'most dangerous.'

"If he pukes, you'll be cleaning it up, Knox," Ford warned the man.

"He'll have the best view at the bow, sir," Knox replied, waving forward. "I'll let Doyle know to escort him there."

"You do that," Ford agreed with a half-smile. He scanned the length of his ship and called, "Single up all lines!" He waited while one set of ropes securing the ship to the docks were pulled away. Then he said to the mage, "Prepare to lift ship!" He turned to the mechanic, "Prepare to deploy propellers!"

"Aye, sir!" Mechanic Newman said, saluting smartly.

"I already said I was —" the mage started irritably.

"Release all lines!" Ford shouted. He turned then to the mage, "Lift ship!"

With a heavy sigh, the purple-robed mage turned toward the bow and raised his arms upwards in the lifting incantation.

"Check all rigging!" Ford shouted to his idlers. He didn't need one of the lifting balloons to come loose.

Slowly, with great reluctance, the good ship *Spite* floated upwards. Ford looked down below him waiting until the keel was clear of the highest spire before turning to the mechanic, "Deploy propellers!"

On either side of the stern the large booms lowered and locked in place. The feather-like cloths unfurled and turned to lock, one at each corner of the compass to form giant four-bladed propellers which began turning, slowly at first, until they provided the airship with a steady forward thrust.

"Adjust for level sailing!" Ford ordered, wondering just *how* his mixed crew would respond. It was the first time he'd issued the order for effect — all other times it had been on a ship that was being fitted out for the King's latest venture.

"Check the rigging!" Knox added to the idlers who scurried about, checking to ensure that all the ropes holding the balloons were taut and none were chafing.

"Oh, my goodness!" a voice wailed from the bow. "We're ever so much higher than I'd imagined!"

"He's fainted!" Doyle called in alarm. "You lot, come help me bring him below!"

"Apparently His Majesty has become a bit overwhelmed with excitement," Ford remarked tartly to the boatswain.

"Indeed, sir!" Knox agreed. "Fortunately, we've lost naught in the change!"

"What heading sir?" the helmsman asked.

"Take us toward the coast, lad," Ford replied. "I'd like to see how she handles a real wind."

"Aye sir!"

"I'm not sure how the prince will fair it," Knox muttered loudly enough for others nearby to hear and grin.

"It's the way of all landlubbers to wobble a bit when finding their feet," Ford allowed diplomatically, casting an eye on the mage, Reedis. The other must have sensed his gaze for he turned back and bowed deeply.

"Carry on mage, carry on!" Ford called to him with a half-bow of his own. The mage might be strange and in purple but he clearly knew his stuff.

"Shall I have us go higher?"

"No, I think we should be close to the ground for now," Ford replied. Mage Reedis agreed with a nod.

Chapter Two: The Crown Prince

The shoreline approached at a leisurely pace, so much so that Ford, called to the mechanic, "Can we increase speed?"

The mechanic nodded toward the coal-blacked sailors — no, *airmen*, Ford corrected himself — who grinned in response.

"We're only running at half pressure, sir," Newman assured him. "Shall we go full out?"

"No, save that for later," Ford replied. "Let's try two-thirds power, if you would."

Newman knuckled his forehead in a salute and turned to the stokers. "You heard the captain, lads, let's see some effort!"

"When we get to the new power level, I'll relieve you if you want," Ford said to the stokers. He knew that stoking a steam boiler was hard work and he prided himself on sparing his men when possible.

In a few minutes the airship noticeably increased speed and the coast rapidly came into view.

A stiff offshore breeze slowed their progress measurably but Ford was still impressed. He glanced to the boatswain who nodded in appreciation.

"We're sailing straight in to the wind," Knox said in awe.

"We're *flying* straight into the wind," Ford corrected him with a twitch of his lips.

"Aye sir, that we are," Knox agreed. "That we are."

"Once we get over the sea, I'll have us reverse course," Ford said. He turned and let his eyes scan the deck from stern to prow. All seemed in order. "Lieutenant Havenam!"

"Sir!" the red haired first lieutenant jogged from his place amidships back to the helm, saluting his captain properly. He has a wiry build and his hair was short and curled.

"Are you ready to take her over, Sam?" Ford asked.

Havenam's face burst into a huge grin for a brief moment before he schooled his expression into a proper officer's stern gaze. "I believe I am, sir."

Ford grinned back at him. "Good! Then, sir, let's be about it."

"Sir, I relieve you," Havenam said in all seriousness.

"Mr. Havenam, I stand relieved," Ford said. The first lieutenant came to attention and saluted his captain. "Mr. Havenam has the watch!" Captain Ford called through the length of the ship. In a normal voice he said, "I'll be below, Sam, if you need me."

"Aye sir," Havenam replied. "Did I hear correctly that we're to reverse course when we're properly over the sea?"

"You did," Ford agreed. "But I'll amend those orders. Steer out to sea, then back to the Westing lighthouse before you turn back to shore. Go full around the Westing lighthouse — show them what we can do — and then back home."

Havenam's eyes widened with surprise and delight. "Aye sir. Out to sea, back to the Westing lighthouse, circle it, and then back to the capital."

"You have your orders," Ford said, exchanging salutes before turning to the hatchway. He turned back to call over his shoulder. "And send the watch below."

"Aye sir!" Havenam replied. "All hands, watch below! First watch, man your stations!"

Ford was in his cabin before the second and third watches came scuttling down the hatchway to their quarters.

#

Ford had just enough time to settle at his desk before someone was pounding on his door.

"Sir, sir! The prince is awake and calling for you!" a sailor — no, *airman* — called nervously.

"Escort him to my quarters, please," Ford replied. "And ask the cook to provide us with some tea."

"Aye sir," the man replied.

Another knock on his door warned him of the prince's arrival. Ford rose to greet the haggard young man courteously but Prince Nestor was having none of it.

"I shall not have it said that I was inconvenienced on this first voyage, Captain!" Nestor said as soon as the door opened.

"Inconvenienced, your majesty?" Ford replied, his brows creased in question.

"I heard your men snickering!" Nestor said, his voice rising in a whine. "I am the Crown Prince, I will be king someday and all shall fear me."

"As they do now, your highness," Ford agreed. "If you heard the men act inappropriately, I assure you it was not directed at you, sire."

"If not me, then who?" the prince demanded.

"Why seaman — or should I say, *airman* — Lubber, your highness," Ford replied. 'Seaman Lubber' was the name given to the non-existent worst crewman. Ford was certain that the Prince — no sailor he, let alone *airman* — was not familiar with the name.

"Airman Lubber?"

"Yes, your majesty," Ford replied. He spread his hands expansively. "I'm afraid I made a poor choice in him, your majesty. Only he was an orphan and now he's got a wife and she's expecting so I took pity on him when he applied — even though I'd been warned that he'd heave his guts—" Ford noted with enthusiasm the way the prince turned slightly green at the phrase "— at the first opportunity."

The prince started to reply just as lieutenant Havenam ordered the ship to turn to port and the airship heeled in the wind. "What's that?"

"We're turning, your highness," Ford replied. "I don't doubt that the wind's pushing us over a bit as we're going broadside to it."

The prince stared at him wide-eyed just as someone knocked on the door.

"If you'll be seated, your majesty, I sent for tea," Ford said.

"I'm not thirsty," the prince said, even while taking his chair.

"Would you permit me, I'm rather parched," Ford said. Prince Nestor gave him a jerky nod. Ford waved the crewman inside and nodded politely as the tea was placed on the center depression in the table.

"When you get a moment," Ford said to the crewman, "please inquire after the mage and see if he requires refreshment."

The man gave him a jerky nod in response and Ford thawed enough to add, "He'll probably just want some tea, don't worry."

"Aye sir," the airman returned, knuckling his forehead in acknowledgement.

"Do you think that's wise?" the prince asked as the airman turned away. Ford raised an eyebrow in inquiry. "If Reedis gets distracted won't we all die?"

"Mage Reedis assures me that his magic is contained, sire," Ford said. "He uses it only when we need to go up or down. Other times he is completely at his leisure."

"That's not what he told *me*," the prince said darkly.

"Perhaps he was unclear," Ford said. "I know that I have seen the effect of the spells on the magic air balloons and how they have maintained their buoyancy without his direct attention."

"If we crash, *captain*, I shall have your head," the prince promised.

Ford managed a small nod, raised the teapot and gestured toward the prince's cup. "Are you sure you won't indulge?"

Prince Nestor shook his head with a shudder.

Captain Ford held back a sigh and raised his cup to his lips partly to refresh himself and partly to hide the fact that he had absolutely nothing to say to the man opposite him.

"When were you planning on drilling the guns, captain?" Nestor asked after the silence grew oppressive.

"Why, sire, I had thought on our maiden voyage —"

"My father will want to know that his ship is fully capable of dealing with dragons and other aerial menaces, captain," Nestor broke in frostily. "I'm certain that he'd be *very* disappointed if you could not tell them the state of your weaponry upon our return."

"Sire," Ford said slowly, "we still have not planned on how to arrange targets for our guns —"

"Deck there!" a lookout shooted. "Something in the clouds to port!"

Nestor shot to his feet. "There's your target, captain!"

"Indeed, we'll certainly want a look," Ford agreed, placing his cup on the table and rising briskly from his chair.

Chapter Three: A Cannon's Fire

On deck, Lieutenant Havenam saluted quickly then pointed to the prow. "I have Senten and Marder out on the bowsprit, sir."

"Good," Ford said with a quick nod. "I'll take a look myself."

"Is there anything I can do?" Mage Reedis asked as Ford and the Prince passed him by.

"See if you can bring us to the same altitude," Ford said giving the man an encouraging look.

"Aye, captain!" Reedis replied surprisingly.

"I think I'll rate him mate," Ford said to himself as they continued on their way.

"He should be an officer," said the prince who'd overheard him.

"If I do that it'll go to his head," Ford replied. "No, I think I will warrant him as an airmate, first class."

The prince scowled at him but said nothing as they neared the bowsprit. The ship's original bowsprit had been maintained even though it no longer had the support of the stay lines rigged from the foremast. And there were no sails hung beneath it. The catwalk had been widened and safety nets strung below in a poor attempt at providing the lookouts with a sense of protection from any mishap that might cause them to slip from their perches.

"Are you coming?" Ford called over his shoulder as he started his way out on the broad spar supported only by his nimble feet.

The prince, eyes wide with fright, shook his head once in a quick jerk and stood, transfixed, as Ford waved a hand and continued running down the bowsprit toward the forward lookouts.

#

"What have you got?" Ford asked as he straddled the bowsprit just behind the two lookouts.

"I saw it first to port, sir," airman Senten said, pointing toward a bank of clouds.

"Then I spotted it — or maybe another — down and starboard, sir," Marder added.

"What does he mean 'starboard'?" the prince called from the safety of the deck.

"Starboard is the side of the ship that's on the right when looking from the stern toward the bow," Boatswain Knox explained, coming up to the prince's side. "'Port' is on the left as you're looking forward."

"Why not say left and right, then?" the prince asked petulantly.

"Because, sire, left and right depend upon where you're looking," the boatswain said patiently, "while port and starboard always mean the same thing."

"Another?" Captain Ford asked the lookouts, shaking his head in dismay at the prince's ignorance.

"It was smaller, golden, and very fast," Marder said. "Wasn't the same as the first one."

"And the other?"

"It was a dragon, sir," Senten said, "I'd stake my life on it."

"Let's hope you won't have to," Ford said. He turned around, hopped back up on top of the bowsprit and raced his way back to the deck, calling, "All hands, man the guns!" He lifted his cockade hat and waved high above his head in signal to Havenam at the far end of the ship, shouting, "Battle stations!"

"Battle stations, aye sir!" Havenam shouted back to him. He turned to the ship's boy and shouted, "Beat to quarters!"

The little boy grabbed his drum and started rattling on it with his drumsticks. From below airmen boiled up, racing toward the guns and the gun tackle. Powder and shot were brought up and slow matches lit from the boiler's fire. The entire ship's crew, thirty-six strong, were now on deck or at their stations.

Spite was a small ship. She carried only eight six-pound cannon, four on each side. Each cannon took a crew of four — so the ship could only man one side of guns and still sail.

On the sea, Ford had never needed more than that because his brig had been quick on the stays — she'd turn around in less than a ship's length — and he'd trained his crew to perfection. Up here in the air, he wondered if he should split his crew to allow him to have guns manned on both sides. He was about to order it when he looked to starboard and realized that his home town was sprawled below him. Any shot to the right of the ship would land on the town.

He crossed to the port side of the ship and nodded as second lieutenant Jens touched his hat and reported, "All guns manned and ready, sir."

"Very good," Ford said, returning the salute. "Be on the lookout, and be ready to fire on my command."

"Aye sir."

And then they waited. Ford returned to the bow to question the two lookouts.

"What color and size were they?" Ford asked them. "And about how far off would you say?"

"I'm new at guessing distances up here in the air, sir," Marder replied slowly, "but if they were on the sea, I'd say they were within a league of us, maybe less."

"One seemed gold with bits of red — that was the smaller one, sir," Senten reported. "It seemed a fair bit faster, too." He frowned before adding, "It seemed to me like they were cavorting, sir."

"Cavorting?"

"Playing, sir," Marder added in support of his fellow lookout. "And the big one was black also had tinges of red — near about half the size of the ship, certainly the size of a good house."

"So not the size of a brig," Ford replied. "But half." He could see the two men relaxing as the difference in size relieved their worries. He smiled at them, "Nothing we haven't beaten before, then."

"No, sir," Marder agreed. "At least, as a ship on the sea."

Ford waved a hand at the air and clouds around them. "This is our new sea now, lads."

"Aye sir," Senten said in a wary tone.

"Keep a good lookout," Ford said, turning back to the stern of the ship. "I think we'll see if our cavorters can be encouraged to visit us."

"Sir?" Marder asked.

"It's time to drill the guns, I think," Ford said. He raised his voice to carry the length of the ship as he called, "All hands, prepare to fire guns!"

Lieutenant Jens ran over to meet him. "What target, sir?"

Ford came to the port side and looked about. Finally he pointed to a cloud in the distance. "Aim for that," he said, "let's see what we can smoke out."

Enlightenment dawned on the young man's face. "You're hoping to attract them to us, then, sir?"

"Indeed," Ford said. He waved to the gun crews. "We're going to see what a broadside in the air sounds like, men."

The crew gave a cheer but it was half-hearted.

"What about the dragons?" the prince called. "What are you going to do about them?"

"I'm hoping to get their attention, sire," Ford told him with as much calm as he could muster. *Really!*

The prince thought about it and nodded. To the gun crews he shouted, "You men! A guinea to the first crew who hits the dragon!"

That brought a much louder cheer from the crews.

"Fire in succession," Ford said, turning to lieutenant Jens who nodded.

"Gun number one, set bearing," Jens said, walking back to the aftermost gun. "Ready, fire!"

The gun captain lit the fuze and stood back just as the little six-pounder roared and reared back against its moorings. Black smoke billowed from its muzzle and captain Ford drew his telescope to train it on the flying ball in the distance.

"Stop your vents!" the gun captain roared to his crew. "Swab her out!" an airman rammed a wet swab down the barrel. "Charge the weapon!" A bag of powder was placed into the barrel followed by a wad of cloth. "Ram home!" The swabber rammed the cartridge down. The gun captain went to the touch hole with his long pricker and pricked open the powder bag. "Home!" he called, followed by, "Load shot!" The six-pound shot and another wad of cloth were loaded in. "Ram home!" A moment later, he shouted, "Run out!"

The men strained on the tackles to pull the gun back to firing position. Satisfied, the gun captain turned and saluting lieutenant Jens, said, "Gun number one ready to fire, sir!"

"Very good, Marsters," Jens said. He turned to the second gun. "Gun number two, prepare to fire!"

"Captain!" Senten called from the bow. "I see them!"

"Hold your fire!" Ford shouted to the gun crew. "Senten, whereaway?"

"Fine off the starboard bow, sir!"

Ford turned to the indicated direction, squinted, and then nodded. He turned back to Jens. "Fire the second gun."

"Sir?" Jens asked.

"What are you doing?" the prince shouted. "The dragon is over there, shoot it!"

"So is our town, sire," Ford replied with all the calm he could muster. "Our shots will fall down regardless of what they hit first." The prince looked at him in confusion. "Do you believe the king will thank us if we shell his town?"

"So why fire, then?" the prince demanded.

"I intend to give them a good target," Ford replied. The prince's brow rose in consternation, so Ford pointed his finger to the deck, saying, "Us." He turned back to Jens. "Fire number two."

"Aye, sir!" Jens called, knocking off a quick salute. "Gun number two, fire when ready!"

"Aye sir!" A short time later the second gun barked, hurling itself inwards and its shell out toward the distant cloud and the fields below.

Ford frowned and gestured for the first lieutenant. Lieutenant Havenam came at a trot and saluted, even as his sides heaved from his exertion.

"I regret our lack of masts," Ford said to him. Havenam gave him a surprised look. "I wish we could get a look from higher up."

"Two thoughts, sir," Havenam replied after a moment. Ford gestured for him to say more. "I could climb to the top of the highest balloon. That would give us a better range." Ford nodded and gestured for him to continue. "Later, if we have time, we could perhaps rig an independent balloon to carry a man aloft."

"Good suggestions, both," Ford agreed, clapping his lieutenant on the shoulder. "Let's do the first now, and talk with our mage about the second at a later date."

"Aye, sir," Havenam said, grinning. He started toward the ratlines that girded the sides of the ship and attached her to the balloons raising them into the air. As he started to climb, he called back to his captain, "I've been itching to do this for quite some time!"

"Well, enjoy it then," Ford called back. "As soon as you demonstrate the joys of riding on the tops of balloons, I've no doubt that we'll have more than enough volunteers to replace you!"

Havenam grinned again and scrambled up and over the top of the nearest balloon.

"And Sam?" Ford called after him. The first lieutenant looked down at him. "Don't fall, it's bad form!"

"Aye, sir!" Sam Havenam agreed with a laugh. A moment later he was out of sight, obscured by the balloons.

Ford sought out Reedis. "That will work, won't it? Having one of our men at the tops of your balloons?"

"It should be safe enough, provided they don't puncture them," Reedis allowed. He made a face, then added, "Although it might be wise to bring up a spare from the holds just in case."

"And how soon can you make it ready when we bring it up?"

Reedis pulled on his chin in thought. "Five, maybe ten minutes," he allowed. He waved at the ballon above them. "Mind you, it'll take a lot out of me. I won't be good for more magic for another fifteen minutes or so, after."

"Even with the help of the gods?"

"That's counting on their help," Reedis replied. "And their good will, too."

"Then we shall do all in our power to retain their goodwill," Ford promised, clapping the man on the shoulder. Reedis looked at his shoulder where Ford had touched it with an odd expression. For a moment, Ford wondered whether the mage would take offense but then the man grinned up at him.

"If I may, sir," Reedis said, emboldened, "it might not be best to offend Ophidian, given that we are here in the sky."

"Ah, but we're over Ametza's realm and our ship is powered by steam," Ford countered. "And you know how Ametza feels the other gods."

"I do," Reedis replied. "Still, we might do our best to avoid Ophidian's wrath."

"The King has commissioned us to keep the wyverns and dragons from raiding his lands, mage," Ford told him sternly. "In that, we will not fail."

"Deck there!" Lieutenant Havenam shouted from above. "I see them! They're coming this way!"

"Jens, fire gun number three!" Ford commanded, turning away from the mage and back to the business at hand.

The third gun barked and its smoke blew back across the deck. Ford turned to the mechanic, "Mr. Newman, how quickly can we get more speed?"

"It'd be best if you relieved the stokers, sir," Newman replied. "After that, five minutes and we can be at full power."

"Very well, make it so," Ford said.

"Do you think that wise, captain?" the prince asked.

Ford shrugged. "We've got to know our best speed sometime, sire. And with luck, we'll be faster than the beasts we're chasing."

The prince thought on that for a moment and nodded. "One thing, captain."

"Sire?"

"When it comes to shooting at the beasts, I shall be the gunner," the prince said.

"Sire," Ford spluttered, "with all reverence, you've not the experience!"

"And this is how I'll get it," the prince said. "When we kill the beast, the blow shall be mine."

Nestor the Dragonkiller, Ford thought to himself, *with that title he'll have no trouble taking the kingdom.* Ford wasn't so sure that he liked the idea of Nestor as king.

"We may not be able to time the shot, sire," Ford temporized.

"It shall be *my* shot, sir, depend upon it!"

"On deck! The beasties have come around and they're heading our way!"

"Let's give them something more to consider," Ford said. He shouted back to the boatswain, "Bring us ten degrees to starboard." To lieutenant Jens he said, "Fire number four when we're on the new course."

"Aye, sir!"

Ford grabbed his telescope and moved starboard to peer over the side in the direction Lieutenant Havenam had indicated. He looked and scanned and then — "I have them!"

Bang! Gun number four blasted the air to port.

"Jens!" Ford shouted. The lieutenant turned toward him. "I want a skew elevation — gun one down, gun two steady, and gun three pointed up — and be prepared to broadside on my command."

"Aye, sir!" Jens replied, bellowing orders to the three guns that were ready while the crew of the fourth hastened to reload their weapon.

"Mr. Reedis!" Ford called, promoting the mage with his words. The mage looked toward him from where he was supervising the unfurling of a spare balloon. "How quickly can you lower us?"

"Sir?" Reedis said, confused.

"The beasties are about to cross under our hull," Ford explained. "I want to let them and drop to their level where I'll fire a broadside."

"How far below us?"

"Not more than a hundred feet, I'd say," Ford said, peering through the lens of his telescope to confirm his estimate.

"I can get us down a hundred feet in less than a minute," Reedis allowed.

"And can you do more, after?"

"I'll be a bit drained for probably the next several minutes," Reedis admitted. "The spells take energy and thought."

"Very well, be prepared on my command," Ford said.

"Aye, sir," Reedis replied. Ford began to think that he might actually come to like the purple mage. Always, leadership was about learning how to inspire, he reminded himself.

"They're closing," Ford now called, his voice in unison with Lieutenant Havenam from the balloons above. "Steady, steady… Now! Reedis, lower us! Jens, fire when sighted!"

Spite practically fell from the sky. For a moment captain Ford feared that the mage had lost his abilities and they were going to plummet to their deaths. But the ship seemed to find its footing, even as several airmen lost theirs at the sudden maneuver. From above, Havenam let out a surprised cry and Ford looked up to see his first lieutenant flailing above, reaching for a handhold before climbing back up, clearly unprepared for the fall.

"Targets in sight!" Jens called. "Steady, steady… fire!"

The three guns roared out and pushed *Spite* sideways in the air with their recoil even as Jens' gun captains bellowed, "Stop your vents!"

"Number four gun, ready, sir!" the gun captain of the fourth gun shouted.

"Fire as you bear!" Ford called back, turning to watch the shot and the dragons — no, the white one was smaller and hand only two legs, not four… a wyvern, then.

"We're going to hit the black one!" someone cried.

The prince ran forward. "No! No, that's *my* shot!"

Ford ran to the port side, following the one ball that had been aimed level as it tore through the air straight toward the large black dragon.

But the smaller gold wyvern turned in the air and practically jumped up in the path of the ball — *crack!* — even from the hundreds of yards distance, Ford could hear the bones on the wyvern shatter. The wyvern pierced the air with a dying cry and crumpled, falling like nothing more than an old sack of cloth toward the ground.

The black dragon roared with anger, first diving toward the stricken wyvern and then, in an instant, turning back to roar at the *Spite*.

And that was when it opened its jaws and let out a burst of flame.

"Reedis, drop the ship!" Ford ordered as the dragon rose to their level, its jaws opened to spew another gout of flame in their direction. "Idlers, man the buckets! We've got to wet her down!"

The four idlers, who'd been pressed into helping with the gun crews, grabbed their buckets and started dousing the sides of the ship to give it what little protection against flame that they could.

At the same time, Reedis closed his eyes and waved his arms — and *Spite* fell from the sky.

"Steer towards the water!" Ford shouted to the helmsman. "We stand a chance if we can make the harbor!"

The sudden drop had surprised the dragon who seemed to pause in mid-air before diving down to the tops of the balloons, roaring in fury. A desperate shout matched it and Ford turned to see Lieutenant Havenam falling from the balloons above.

"Sam!" Ford cried as his long-time friend fell toward the side of the ship. He had just a moment to meet his friend's eyes before Havenam bounced sickeningly off the side rail and fell toward the ground below. In the distance, Ford saw a field of blue. The white of the wyvern's crumpled form was visible against the blue of the flowers in the field. *Wyvern flowers.*

"Gunners, another broadside for that bastard!" Ford shouted.

"I shall take a gun!" the prince cried, running to push lieutenant Jens aside and taking a place at gun number two.

Spite was still falling.

"Newman!" Ford shouted. "Full speed!"

Spite had turned and was bearing toward the coastline even as she fell from the sky.

"Mr. Reedis!" Ford shouted. "We can't hit the ground!"

"Aye, sir," Reedis said, his whole body trembling. "I'll do my best."

"If you don't, we'll all die," Ford warned him.

A ghost of a smile crossed the weedy mage's lips before he answered, "Then I'll do my best, sir."

"Cook!" Ford called. "A tot of rum for the air mage!"

A head popped up from the hatchway, eyes wide with fright and surprise.

"I don't think he drinks, sir," the cook allowed.

"Then some tea, and be quick about it," Ford said. "And get a tot of rum for all the stokers."

A cheer went up from the coal-blackened men surrounding the boiler that seemed to glow bright red above the steel plate that protected the ship from its fiery contents.

"Mr. Newman," Ford called, "we've got to make the harbor before we hit the ground."

"The lads are stoking flat out, sir," Newman replied. "This is as fast as we go."

Ford turned to look for the dragon but it had disappeared from his sight. "Marder! Senten! Where away the dragon?"

A moment later the two lookouts called back, "No sign of it, sir! It disappeared over the town!"

"If it sets the town alight, captain," the prince growled, "you'll pay for it with your head."

Ford thought for a moment. "If we turn, we can give chase but we'll be firing our guns over the town, sire. We may end up doing more damage than good."

The prince glowered at him. "If we get beneath it, we can fire up."

"The balls, even if they hit him, will still fall to the ground, sire," Ford replied slowly, using the same tone he'd use with a foolish child.

The prince turned red. "Needless to say, I wish us to land at our proper dock," the prince said. "Our mother will be waiting for us and there are laurels well won." He paused for a moment. "I killed a wyvern, as *all* will attest!"

"Begging pardon, sire," said the captain of the number two gun, "but what about our guinea?"

The prince took two quick steps toward the man and slapped him hard on the face. "There is no guinea! It was *I* who took the shot, —" and he hit the helpless airman again "— *I* who killed the creature —" another slap "— and *I* who will wear the laurels!"

He turned to Ford and shouted, "Really, captain, what sort of a crew do you keep?"

Ford locked his jaws and turned his head away to avoid replying to the tyrant in front of him.

Nestor turned from him to shout at Reedis, "We're landing at our dock!"

"Ease off on the boiler," Ford said to Newman. "Helmsman, come about and head us to the docks."

"Aye, sir," the helmsman said, turning the wheel that caused the port side propeller to stop turning while feeding more power to the starboard propeller, causing the ship to turn to port in a leisurely manner. "Bow! Report when you have our dock in sight and lined up!"

"Aye!" came the cry back from Marder. "Dock in sight. Another twenty degrees and we'll be straight on."

Ford took a look around the deck and gestured for Jens to join him. When the lieutenant was within earshot he said, "Secure the guns, dowse the matches, and prepare for docking."

"Aye, sir," Jens said.

"I'm going below," Ford told him. "You have the ship."

"Aye, sir, I have the ship," Jens said loudly.

Without another word, Ford turned to the hatchway and climbed out of the sunlight and into the cool darkness below.

Chapter Four: A Bitter Triumph

Twenty minutes later, he was called back to the deck. In the intervening time, Ford had sat at his chair, writing what he could in his log, and trying to forget the dying scream of Sam Havenam as he fell to his death.

"Ah, you're back," the prince said when he spotted Ford rising to the deck. "We've managed quite well without you."

"I'm glad, sire," Ford replied, ignoring the jab.

"I've had some time to consider our next actions," the prince said even as the ship lowered toward the dock below.

Ford waved a hand palm up, before turning to the mechanic. "Mr. Newman, prepare to feather the propellers on my mark."

"Aye sir, on your mark," Newman agreed.

Ford looked beyond him to the mage. "Mr. Reedis, how are you?"

"I'm well enough, captain," the purple-robed mage allowed. "Could do with a rest, truth be told."

"Doubtless you'll get it and much rewards from the King," Ford assured him. He glanced forward and toward the ground below. "Is our descent steady now?"

"Aye, sir," Reedis replied. "We're going down at about —"

"Twenty feet a minute, by my guess," Ford interjected.

"Aye, sir," Reedis agreed.

"Good," Ford said. Raising his voice, he called, "Mr. Newman, feather the propellers and prepare to stow them!"

"Aye, sir!" Newman called back.

"You know, sire, no one has ever docked an airship before," Ford remarked calmly to the prince who was pacing nearby.

"I'm sure you'll do well at it," the prince allowed. "When we get docked, I'll want you take a party —"

"A party, sire?" Ford repeated, brows drawn in a frown. He'd planned on securing the ship, making sure that the balloons were safe and not punctured, emptying the boiler, clearing the ash from the firegrill, and ordering more coal to be brought aboard.

"You know where that beast fell," the prince said. "I want you to find it and bring it back so that I can show everyone what I've done."

"Sire?" was all that Ford could say.

"Get the beast, bring it to the castle, and we'll have a triumph," the prince said tartly. "Then everyone will be able to *see* what I've done."

"Surely, your word is enough —"

"And then I'll have it gutted and stuffed," the prince continued, ignoring Ford's words. "Perhaps we can eat the meat, Mother and I. I'm sure dragon meat conveys strength and health."

"It was the wyvern we hit, sire," Ford reminded him gently. He'd had enough time to reflect that the only way to treat this prince — his future king — was very carefully.

"*I* know what *I* hit, captain!" the prince growled. "And it's your job to make sure that everyone on this ship, everyone in this kingdom, knows it as well!"

"As you say, your highness," Ford replied. He glanced toward the ground below and said, "If you'll excuse me, we're about to land."

"Have our pennants raised, break out the victory signal," the prince commanded.

"We've no masts, sire," Ford protested, "so we packed no pennants."

"An oversight you'll correct as soon as we make landfall, captain," the prince said.

"I could have our ship's boy man the drums," Ford suggested, "that'd get everyone's attention. But I don't doubt that reports of our encounter have preceded us."

"Hmmph," the prince allowed. "I suppose you're right. But *do* get your boy drumming just in case."

Ford gestured for the ship's boy who ran off to grab his drum and, as the drummer beat a steady tattoo, the crew lined the railings to drop lines to hands waiting below and the ship was pulled down into its dock.

The gantry was raised up from the ground and secured.

"Sire, yours is the honor," Ford said, gesturing to the gantry amidships. The prince nodded in acceptance of his due and made for the planks that led to the ground beside them.

"Behold! I return in triumph!" Prince Nestor shouted from the top of the walkway. His white pasty skin was now red from the sun and covered in soot, and his brown hair was now wind blown and frizzy.

"I, Nestor, Crown Prince, have slain the wyvern! I have frightened the dragon away from us! Never again shall our kingdom have to fear the air over our heads!"

Queen Arivik rushed up the gantry and grabbed the prince in her arms, crushing him against her. She was cadaverous, her cheek bones prominent under her bronze skin. Her brown hair was braided around her coral crown.

"Oh, my son, my son!" she cried. She glared at Ford. "How could you let him get into such danger?"

"I followed the prince's orders, your Majesty," Ford said.

"I must go tell father," Prince Nestor said, pulling his head back from his mother.

"He shall order a triumph!" the queen agreed, turning to head back down the gantry, the prince's hand clasped tightly in hers. "He'll have no reason to doubt you now, my son."

Nestor reddened and turned his head to catch Ford's eyes. "You have your orders, captain."

"As you wish, your highness," Ford said with a deep bow. He waited until the prince turned away again before rising upright. At which point, he called to the crew, "Three cheers for the Prince!"

The crew cheered half-heartedly.

The prince and his mother mounted the royal carriage and were whisked away in the direction of the castle.

"Jens, I'll need a horse immediately and a wagon to follow," Ford said. "Secure the ship, see to the men and then find me."

"Aye sir," Jens said, saluting sharply. "And Mrs. Havenam, sir?"

Ford sighed. "I'll tell her when I can," he said. "He'd want me to tell her personally."

"Aye sir," Jens said in a tone which did not hide his relief at avoiding the odious task.

"Mage Reedis?"

"Captain?"

"Are you up for a ride?" Ford asked the purple-robed mage. Reedis swayed on his feet and shook his head. "Hmm," Ford continued, "perhaps you'd best make use of the bunk in my cabin and get some rest."

"If it's not too much trouble, captain," Reedis agreed, tottering toward the hatchway.

"Mr. Newman," Ford said, looking for coal-grimed mechanic. Newman bobbed up beside him. "Will you see to your gear, douse the fires, clear the ash, and get more coal aboard?" Newman looked at him in confusion. "I can't say when we'll next need to fly, so I'd like us to be ready."

"Of course, captain," Newman agreed. "After, can I let the men take leave?"

"Of course," Ford agreed. "I would be surprised if we're called to action again this day."

"I'm glad to hear that, captain," Newman replied.

"I'll leave you to it, then," Ford said, moving toward the plank gantry and to the ground below. He could see a seaman leading a pair of horses. He turned back and shouted, "Mr. Knox?"

"Sir?"

"What would you say to a ride in the country?"

"If it's to see where that devil fell, I'd relish it, sir," the boatswain returned, moving to follow his captain off the ship. He glanced over his shoulder. "My mate can manage here."

"Aye, no problem," the boatswain's mate, Needles, called back, easily. "And then I'll join the others ashore."

Ford waved his assent to that and jerked his head to Knox, to hurry him up to the horses.

They mounted and found the easiest way out of the cobblestoned streets and into the roads outside the city proper.

"Did you get a good bearing on where the beastie fell, sir?" Knox asked as they eased their mounts into a slow trot.

Ford nodded and held up a hand, pointing. "That way."

"And Mr. Havenam, sir?"

"Also that way," Ford replied. "That's part of the reason for the wagon."

They rode for a while in silence before Knox said, "Did you understand what her majesty said, about the king and her son, sir?"

Ford grimaced. "I've heard a rumor or two." He glanced at the older man. "And you?"

"There's many a tale told about the queen," Knox allowed. "And not so many about the king before he married her."

Ford's lips twisted upwards. "I'd heard something like that myself."

"There's some that say that the prince is not the king's natural son."

"He's the prince, Knox, and it will never do to forget that," Ford said reprovingly.

"Aye, sir," Knox agreed in a low voice. "I won't."

They rode for many minutes in silence. Captain Ford spent the time thinking. He was the first airship captain, he doubted he'd be the last. When he'd sailed on the sea with a letter of marque from the King he'd made a good living, taking the ships of warring nations and selling them and their cargo at good prices. He'd made a name for himself: a fair rise for an orphan child whose first memories were of the hard life at sea. What sort of money would he get ridding the skies of dragons? Particularly if the Prince would claim them as his own?

And what would have happened if the dragon had managed to flame their ship? There was no convenient, if raging, sea in which to fall — merely thousands and thousands of feet of thin air. Havenam's death made it clear that falling from an airship was fatal.

Ford felt trapped. He couldn't just give up his ship: he was tied to it. Without it, he was merely a penniless seaman with a few good tales to tell. He'd hitched his fortunes to king and kingdom, he would pay the price or fail utterly.

Which meant, Ford's mind reasoned on, that he would have to find a way to work with the prince — who would one day be King — and work well enough that he kept his head on his shoulders and food in his belly. More than that would be asking too much, he feared.

A whistle in the distance startled him out of his reverie and he looked up to see a train passing by them on the way out to the outlying villages. He waved at the fireman and the passengers who looked out at them. And then the train turned northwards while he continued toward the west.

They crested a hill and saw a farm not too far in the distance and several fields.

"There," he said, pointing toward a valley full of blue flowers. "That's where it fell."

Knox grunted in acknowledgement and the two of them turned their horses toward the valley.

It was a large valley and the flowers were tall. Ford had expected to see the gold of the wyvern easily and was surprised when he didn't. He and Knox rode all around the valley, scouring it for any sign of the dead beast. Captain Ford was just beginning to wonder whether the beast had been as injured as they'd assumed — perhaps it had slunk off to some lair and was licking its wounds — and wouldn't *that* be the sort of news he'd hate to deliver to the Prince — when Knox called from uphill and waved him over.

"What is it?" Ford asked when he neared enough for his voice to travel the distance to the other's ears.

"There," Knox said, pointing toward a mound of newly-turned earth.

Captain Ford peered down from his mount at the mound. He frowned and jumped down from his horse to examine the ground close up. "It's too small for something that big."

"Maybe," Knox allowed. He glanced around the far end of the field and pointed. "There's the wagon, maybe they've got a shovel." He pointed to another spot. "And look here, sir! There's crushed flowers like something large fell and there's a path from it to this mound."

"You think to dig it up?" Ford asked. "It looks like a grave, fresh dug."

"Dug today, I'm sure," Knox agreed. "If it's not the wyvern, whoever dug this would know where to find it, wouldn't they?"

Ford thought about it and nodded. He pointed to the large depression with its crushed flowers and said, "That looks about where the wyvern fell." With a frown, he added, "But I didn't see it land. I was too busy watching Havenam's plunge."

"And the best way to find out who dug this is to find out who's in the dirt," Knox said.

"You're a ghoul, boatswain," Ford grumbled. With a deep sigh, he added, "But I suppose we've little choice, the prince is expecting a triumph."

They shouted for the wagon and saw that it was manned by Marder, the lookout.

"Came as soon as I could, Captain," Marder said as he pulled the wagon to a halt.

"Have you got a shovel with you?" Ford asked.

"I do," Marder replied. "I figured we'd want to do the honors for the lieutenant." He pointed at the mound. "Is that him? Did you find him already?"

"It could be," Ford allowed with a shudder. "But we found this mound, we don't know what's in it."

"A body, I imagine," Knox said. He gestured to Marder. "Throw us that shovel and we'll see."

It took them twenty minutes to dig down to the corpse. It was a woman. She was naked except for a cloth someone had laid over her.

"We should cover her back up," Marder said after a moment. "It's not the lieutenant and it isn't a flying beast, either."

"But look at her," Knox urged. "See how she lies." He pointed toward her leg. "Her leg's been shattered and she was bleeding when she was put here."

"Over here!" Marder called to the others. "There are tracks here," he said, peering down and pointing toward a line of footprints. "A girl's."

"And a man's here," Ford said.

"They weren't together," Knox said. "The grass is recovering from the girl's tracks, she was here just over an hour ago, I'd say."

"Just when we were fighting the wyvern," Ford noted. He pointed toward the grave. "So who is this person?"

"Magic got us in the air, sir," Knox said. "Perhaps magic is at work here, too?"

"If you look at her legs, she's injured just about the way the wyvern was," Marder said.

"So you're saying this woman was the *wyvern?*" Captain Ford said.

"Maybe," Knox said. "It would explain the tracks. The body was dragged from that great depression — where the wyvern might have landed — to this spot where the woman was buried."

"The Prince is not going to accept a corpse for his triumph," Ford said sourly.

"Perhaps we should look for poor Lieutenant Havenam?" Marder suggested.

"There's a farm nearby, we should go there first," Captain Ford said.

Chapter Five: The Young Apprentice

They were met by a surly young man who insisted that he hadn't heard a thing.

"I was in town," he said. "I'm the apprentice here and my master is resting now. He won't wish to be disturbed."

"Did he see anything?" Captain Ford asked.

"No," the lad said, shaking his head firmly. "He was with me."

"Was there anyone else who stayed here?" Ford asked.

The lad's eyes widened fractionally but he shook his head in vigorous denial. "No one saw anything."

"We found a body," Ford persisted. "A woman's body. She was recently buried."

"That can't be anyone from around here," the lad declared. "I've heard of no one sick in these parts for the past sennight."

"Very well," Captain Ford said. "We thank you for your time in the name of the Prince."

The lad's eyes flared quickly. "You work for the Prince?"

"I'm the captain of the royal airship," Captain Ford replied. "This is my boatswain, Knox."

The lad gave Knox a quick look and nodded at Ford. "I think I saw your ship flying, earlier."

"Indeed," Captain Ford said. "We fought a dragon and a wyvern."

"We hit the wyvern," Knox added. "We thought it had fallen near here."

"And we lost a man," Ford said, "one of my lieutenants. We're looking for his body."

"That's why we dug up the grave," Knox said, feeling the need for an explanation.

"Oh," the lad said.

"If we need to talk with you again, who should we ask for?" Captain Ford said.

"Angus," the lad replied. "My name is Angus Franck."

"And your master?" Knox asked with a nod toward his captain. "What is his name?"

Angus gave him a sour look. "He's not to be disturbed, he's old and the day took too much out of him."

"Give us his name," Ford ordered.

"Zebala," Angus said in a surly tone. "Rabel Zebala. He's a smith. I'm his apprentice."

"He works with Ibb, the mechanical, does he not?" Ford asked.

Angus gave a jerky nod in response.

"I know Ibb," Ford said, his tone half-warning.

"We saw him earlier," Angus said. "Now, if you'll excuse me, I've got chores."

"Of course," Ford said, turning away from the door. "Thank you for your time."

Angus watched as they walked away and then, when they turned back toward him, hastily shut the upper and lower halves of the split kitchen door.

Ford gestured for Knox to head toward the horses. They mounted and rode down the path back toward the main road. A short while later they pulled up their horses beside an abandoned cart.

Marder sprang up from a clump of underbrush and waved at them.

"What did you learn?" Captain Ford asked the man as they pulled up to a halt.

"There were two sets of tracks led to that farm," Marder said. "And there's a forge in the barn —"

"The man's a smith, works with Ibb," Ford said.

"— crazy ol' clanker," Marder muttered.

"Captain likes him," Knox warned.

"What else?" Ford prompted, motioning for Knox to leave off.

"I found a shovel, it was dirty, like it had been used to dig sometime today," Marder said.

"Did only one set of tracks come back?" Knox asked. He glanced at the captain. "Perhaps they buried the girl we found."

"Then why deny it?" Ford asked. The other two shook their heads in puzzlement.

Marder gave him a sour look. His skin was jaundiced, and eyes bulged from his skull. He had a silver earring in both of ears.

"The tracks of the man, the one that came back, they were heavier than the ones on the way to the field."

"He was carrying something?" Captain Ford wondered.

"Or someone," Knox suggested.

"None of this gets us nearer to our missing wyvern," Ford said.

"It seems like the King ought to look into this," Marder suggested. The other two looked at him like he was crazy. "Well, aren't we supposed to get the King's justice?" He pointed back toward the field of blue flowers. "And doesn't that poor soul deserve some of it?"

"Are you saying she was murdered?"

"She's dead," Marder replied. "That's all I'm saying." He chewed his lip for a moment before adding, "And she was injured just like she took our cannonball."

"We should look for Lieutenant Havenam's body," Captain Ford said after a moment's thoughtful silence. "Maybe we'll find the wyvern, too."

"He might be only the next field over," Marder said hopefully. Captain Ford nodded and turned back to mount his horse.

"Follow us," Ford ordered Marder as he and Knox set their horses off to a slow walk.

#

They found Lieutenant Havenam's body two fields over, in a small forest of trees.

"It looks like he landed in the trees, then fell through them to the ground below," Marder said as they bent over the ruined remains of the handsome officer.

"Mmm," Captain Ford agreed, moving further into the trees and hoisting himself up. He climbed swiftly and found himself out of the foliage with a good view of the land around.

"What do you see, Captain?" Knox shouted up from the ground below.

"I've got a bit of cloth, sir, I can cover Mr. Havenam up and put him in the wagon, if you'd like," Marder added.

"Do that," Ford said. "Mr. Knox, please join me."

"I'll help Marder first, if that's okay," the boatswain replied.

"Of course," the captain said. "Marder, if you're in for a climb after all your exertions, you are welcome to join us."

Marder made a noncommittal noise. From below, Captain Ford could hear the two men lifting the body into the wagon and the sound of harsh fabric being drawn over. He hadn't the heart to do it himself — or rather, his heart would burst if he had to cover his friend's ignominiously destroyed body. He and Havenam had been midshipmen together on old Seneer's *Retribution*: they were close. So he kept his gaze off to the distance where the scarring of the field beyond showed the destruction of the wyvern's flowers as a patch of brown in a field of blue. And beyond it he could see trampled flowers leading toward the dark brown of the grave they'd found.

A sound from below alerted him to the ascent of his two crewmen. A moment later, their heads appeared beside him and he gestured silently into the distance. Knox and Marder followed his hand and gazed at the same torn ground he'd been watching while they were busy with the body.

"Whatever fell there was dragged to the grave and buried there," Marder said.

"Aye, I'd say the same," Knox agreed.

"So what do we tell the prince?" Captain Ford said. "He's expecting a wyvern's body and a triumph."

The other two shook their heads in silence.

"Mrs. Havenam, should see her first?" Knox asked, dodging the question.

Captain Ford jerked a nod. By unspoken agreement they started back down the tree and to the wagon waiting below.

"We should go then, shouldn't we?" Marder asked, gesturing toward the town. "It'll be full dark when we return."

"Aye," Ford agreed.

Chapter Six: A Wyvern's Corpse

"I promised my father a wyvern's corpse, Mr. Ford!" Crown Prince Nestor roared when Ford met him hours later. "How am I to receive a reward, if I can't show the body?"

"It's Captain Ford, Sire," Ford said. "We looked for the body and found nothing."

"Except maybe that strange woman," Knox put in feebly. The boatswain had offered to accompany the captain after they'd paid their respects to Mrs. Havenam.

"I have heard enough about that nonsense!" Nestor snapped. "How can you expect my father to believe that the woman was the wyvern?"

"Sire, I know very little of magic and I haven't had a chance to talk to Mage Reedis," Ford replied. "Perhaps one of the court magicians would know something more?"

"If you'd wanted their opinion, why didn't you bring them the body?" the prince demanded.

"We thought it might not be a good idea to bring a woman's corpse to the royal palace, Sire," Ford said.

The prince bit back a violent retort as the image formed in his imagination. "No," he agreed, "that might not be the best of ideas."

"We can bring one of your mages back to the site," the boatswain offered.

"First, perhaps, we could just ask?" Ford suggested.

"Not possible," the prince said, shaking his head violently.

Ford's brow creased in question.

"They are a bunch of tattering old women," the prince explained. "If I ask them, you can be certain my father — and the whole kingdom — will know of it in no time."

"And..." Ford said, reflecting his confusion.

"Could you imagine how it would get out?" Nestor demanded. He changed his voice to something that sounded remarkably like his royal father. "'The prince killed a woman and wants to say she was a monster!'"

"I hadn't thought of that," Ford confessed.

"Get Mage Reedis and have him confirm it," the prince ordered. "I'll have him brought to father to confirm."

"That should do, he saw it," Knox murmured to Ford.

"I don't expect you back until the morning," the prince said, waving them away with a look like he was conveying a great favor.

Ford and Knox bowed their way out of the room.

#

Captain Ford sensed trouble even before he pulled his horse to halt beside the *Spite*. The normal hustle of a ship's crew, even just a watch crew, was absent.

"Ahoy the ship!" Knox yelled as he jumped down from his horse. He grunted as he shook out his legs and gave Ford a look that mirrored his own. Knox raised his voice and called again, "Ahoy the ship!"

Ford moved quickly toward the gantry, crossing the distance between wharf and ship in scant moments.

A shape appeared on the deck in the darkness. "Did someone call?"

Ford recognized the voice of Newman, the mechanic, his voice coming from the stern of the ship near his steam engine.

The soot covered man was a good head taller than Ford. His thick black hair was tied back, and his red beard had begun to go grey.

"Indeed we did, Mr. Newman," Ford said. "But we didn't mean to disturb your labors. We were expecting one of our men to be on watch."

Newman snorted and shook his head. "They're all gone!"

"What?" Ford said, glancing around, hoping his eyes would prove the other a liar. "I said that there was to be a watch kept, that only some were to go on leave."

"Well, sir, it seems they didn't listen, did they?" Newman said with a sour look. "It's not just your men, my men scarpered as well."

"What?" Knox said. "You're the only one left? What about lieutenant Jens?"

"He was the first to leave," Newman said, spitting in derision. "Said there was no good staying on a cursed ship with no hope of pay."

"Pay?" Ford repeated angrily.

"I can't say I don't see their point," Newman said. "The prince promised a guinea and then welshed on it. They said if he couldn't pay a guinea, why should they believe that he could pay a pound?"

"So where are they?" Knox asked. "Let me find them —"

"Lieutenant Jens has shipped out on the *Warrior*," Newman said.

"What? When?" Knox asked. Captain Ford couldn't speak, he was so dismayed.

"He left first, took four seamen with him," Newman said. "Then the rest took off." He added bitterly, "And then my stokers when my back was turned."

"So there's no one left?" Knox said.

"Indeed."

"Where is the mage?" Ford asked.

Newman pointed up the road. "He went for a bite to eat, last I heard. He was gone when all this happened."

"Let's find him," Ford said, turning back toward the gantry.

"Should I stay here, sir?" Knox asked.

"Yes, wait for Marder," Ford replied.

#

"Reedis?" Ford said, sitting opposite the purple mage.

"Captain?"

"Are you almost done?" Ford said, eyeing the dishes overflowing the table. "The prince has asked me for your opinion on something of import."

Reedis motioned for him to continue while helping himself to another mouthful of meat.

"We found a body of a woman near where we found where the wyvern must have fallen," Ford said.

"But no wyvern?"

"No," Ford said. "But the woman was injured in a manner that seemed to match the wyvern's injuries."

"And you're wondering if the woman was the wyvern and somehow magically transformed?" Reedis guessed, stabbing another forkful of meat.

"Yes."

"I don't know much about wyverns. I know they look to Ophidian and I've heard that they're twin-souled," Reedis said after a moment spent blissfully chewing and swallowing his morsel. Ford wondered how the man could be so thin and eat so much.

"Twin-souled?"

"Indeed," Reedis said after swallowing once more. "They burn so brightly that two souls are required to create them."

"How is that possible?"

Reedis shrugged, stabbing carrots and parsnips with his fork and shovelling them into this mouth.

"Could you tell if someone was magically transformed?" Ford asked, waiting for the other man to swallow.

"No," Reedis said. "But there might be some up in the King's court who could."

"The prince prefers not to ask them," Ford said with a sour look. Would the man never stop eating? Ford had been hungry when he'd entered the tavern but, now, his appetite was quite gone.

"They're a bunch of old women," Reedis said after swallowing his next mouthful, "doubtless they'd spout off to everyone in the kingdom, the king included."

"Doubtless," Ford agreed, hiding his surprise in finding the mage in agreement with the prince. "But without a body, I've got a problem."

"You mean the prince has a problem," Reedis said, laying his fork down on his now empty plate.

"Which means that *I've* got a problem," Ford agreed with a sigh.

"So, where is this body?"

"In a grave not far from where the wyvern fell," Ford said. "It's too dark now to look for it."

"Indeed," Reedis said, rising from the table. Ford rose with him. "I'm staying here this evening."

"Shall I call for you in the morning?"

"You may," Reedis allowed. "But not too early, I'm quite fatigued from all the exertions of the day."

"The sooner the better," Ford said.

"I can't do magic without rest," Reedis said. He paused to think. Finally, he nodded to himself, saying, "Noon. I should be able then."

Ford bit back an angry retort and forced himself to say instead, "Very well, I'll see you then."

Chapter Seven: Captain of Nothing

Captain Ford spent the night aboard the Spite, alone. He woke shivering the next morning, wishing that the cooks hadn't deserted along with the rest of the crew. He made his way to the galley, started the fire and warmed himself a cup of tea. When he'd finished that, he went on deck.

A fog had engulfed the airship and for a moment Ford feared that perhaps the ship had lifted skywards in the night but then a gust blew the fog into tatters and he found himself looking at the buildings around him and the gantry amidships.

"Ahoy the ship!" a voice called from a patch still hidden in darkness. It was Knox.

"Come aboard!" Ford called back. The boatswain swarmed over the wooden gantry and knuckled his forehead in a salute to the captain. He glanced around the ship and spit sourly at the lack of men.

"I was hoping some of the lads might have come back," Knox said.

"I'm afraid that their assessment was too accurate — if the prince would welsh on a guinea, what hope had they of their pay?"

"Well," Knox said with a shrug, "they'll never know now."

"True," Ford allowed. He gestured to the street. "I'm supposed to meet mage Reedis at noon and we'll go see the woman's body once more."

"To see if it's the wyvern?" Knox guessed.

"To see if his magic might tell us if it is," Ford said.

"Good enough," Knox said. He glanced around the ship and then added, "Will you need a hand?"

Ford shook his head. "I need you to stay here and guard the ship. See if you can get any of the lads to return."

"I'll try, captain," Knox said, his tone doubtful.

"That's all I can ask."

#

Captain Ford found Reedis at the same table, busily ingesting a half dozen eggs and countless slices of bacon. *Perhaps he has worms.*

"Ah, good morning, captain!" Reedis called, gesturing for the other to join him at the table. "I trust you had a restful sleep?"

"Well enough," Ford allowed. "And you?"

"The same," Reedis said, stuffing his mouth with a whole egg.

A maid came by and served Ford with a glass of water, delightfully chilled. Ford eyed it in surprise and Reedis pointed a finger at himself. "I did them a favor with some cold magic, and they let me stay here whenever I want."

"That's some magic," Ford agreed.

Reedis leaned forward and whispered conspiratorially, "It won't last, of course. So I'm eating as much as I can before the spell fades."

Ford raised an eyebrow in surprise. His face creased into a frown as a sudden thought occurred to him but Reedis answered his unspoken question with a dismissive wave of his hand, "It's not quite the same magic as the balloons, I assure you."

"Those spells won't wear off?"

"Oh, no! They'll wear off, sure enough," Reedis said with a bark of laughter. "But not while I'm still aboard!"

"So the *Spite* can't fly without you?"

"Surely you knew that already, Captain?" Ford said, chasing his egg with a handful of bacon.

"I did," Ford said. A moment later, he asked, "And does the King?"

"I worked mostly with Her Majesty and the prince," Reedis said. "The King would have nothing to do with me because he's sworn to Ametza."

"And you're not?"

"A mage that makes fire magic?" Reedis asked, his eyes dancing. He shook his head. "No, the goddess of water is not my patron."

"Nor is Ophidian, I imagine."

"Indeed," Reedis agreed. He made a face. "Ophidian's a fickle god, I wouldn't want to trust my life to such."

"So who do you serve that your magic provides hot and cold?" Ford asked.

Reedis placed a finger alongside his nose to show that Ford was being too nosy to ask.

"No offense," Ford said quickly. He needed this man.

"None taken," Reedis said. "But the less you know of magic, the better."

"Hmm," Ford considered that. "Actually, I think I should like to know enough that I wouldn't have to rely on you."

Reedis' eyes widened at that admission and Ford continued quickly, "Not that I don't appreciate your efforts and company but just in case something rendered you incapacitated and I needed to power the ship by myself."

"Captain," Reedis began in a gentle tone, "you not only have to know my magic but also how that fireman Newman manages his flames."

"Are you saying he's a mage, too?"

"No," Reedis said sourly. "Of course not. But he's worked with them — and me, even — in the past to get his infernal engine to behave the way it does." Reedis paused, nabbed another slice of bacon and chewed on it thoughtfully before continuing, "No, just as you were dependent upon sailmakers and shipwrights when you were captain of a seaship, you are dependent upon Newman for the steam engine and me for your lifting balloons." He gave Ford a genial nod. "If I might be so bold, I'd recommend that you stick to doing what you know rather than trying to master such arcane arts."

"I see," Ford said. After a moment, he said, "But when on the sea I had the chance to throw myself on its mercies if the ship or the sails failed me. I don't have the same choice up in the air."

Reedis nodded and gave the captain an attentive look.

"If the dragon had flamed our balloons, there would have been nothing you could do to save us," Ford guessed. Reedis winced at the notion then, reluctantly, nodded. "I was wondering, however, if there might be a way to build a special spell that could be used quickly. A spell that would inflate a spare balloon or two so that men could escape on them earthwards to safety, just as we do with a life jacket."

"A life sphere?" Reedis joked, cocking his head at the notion. A moment later, he nodded. "You know, I *do* believe it could be done!"

"I was thinking of it last night, thinking of how we could have saved poor Havenam," Ford admitted.

"How was his widow?" Reedis asked somberly.

"She was furious," Ford said. "She threw things at me, cursed me."

"She did?" Reedis was surprised.

Ford nodded. "You see," he said, "I'd convinced Havenam to join my crew by convincing *her* that it would be safer up in the air than on the sea."

"Oh," the other said sympathetically.

"And now the crew's deserted," Ford continued, encouraged by the understanding of the other. "They said that if the prince could welsh on a bet, he'd welsh on their wages, too."

"Quite probably," Reedis agreed.

"Does that not worry you, too?"

"The prince and his mother were the only ones who considered the advantages of an airship," Reedis said. "It was through their patronage that I am where I find myself this day."

"Riding out to view the corpse of a woman in hopes that she's the wyvern?" Ford asked in bitter humor.

Reedis snorted in amusement. "Well, not quite *that*, perhaps, but certainly the first of my breed."

"Your breed?"

"I'll make a fortune when it comes time to take apprentices," Reedis said with a smug look.

Ford leaned back in his chair, startled by the novel concept. "I suppose you will, at that."

"But," Reedis said, raising a hand in caution, "before I can do that, I must first prove the efficacy of our airship against flying creatures."

"Like this wyvern?"

"Indeed," Reedis agreed, laying his fork on his plate and pushing back from the table. "So, Captain, shall we go see this body?"

Ford rose with him, a smile on his face.

"Mr. Reedis," he said, extending his hand, "I believe this is the beginning of a beautiful relationship."

"Indeed," Reedis said, taking his hand and shaking it firmly. "I had thought we were probably in the same boat." Ford snorted in amusement. Reedis' smile broadened. "As it were."

#

Mage Reedis needed no instruction in horsemanship even if he had a bad seat and tended to saw on his mount's reins. He and Ford made good time. Captain Ford had obtained a shovel, assuring the mage that he knew where they could get a wagon if the need presented itself.

They rode in companionable silence, sweating with the sun beating down upon them.

"If you get too hot, let me know," Reedis said as he adjusted his hat against the sun's glare.

"Why? Do you have a spare hat?" Ford asked, regretting that he hadn't brought his with him.

Reedis smiled. "Better, I'm a mage of hot and cold." He waved his hands and suddenly Ford found himself cooled by a small but steady cold breeze.

"I can't see how you couldn't make your fortune with just *that* magic," Ford said as the sweat evaporated from his head.

"It's moment magic," Reedis said. Seeing the other's confusion he explained, "I can only make it in the moment, I can't prepare the spell ahead of time."

"Whoever could do that would be rich, then," Ford said.

"It was partly as a result of this simple magic that I convinced the queen to fund our airship," Reedis said.

"A hot day and you provided the wind?" Ford guessed.

"Indeed," Reedis agreed with a smile. "That and the wind covered the sounds of a rather indecorous liaison the queen was having."

"Ah!" Ford said. He gestured to the left at the fork in the road and they moved down it. A moment later he pulled up and pointed to the field of wyvern's flowers. The field was full of the blue, pungent flowers.

"I see," Reedis said, scanning the field and finding the scar of a fallen beast. "They say that wyverns seek these flowers when they're about to die."

"Really?" Ford said in surprise. "I hadn't heard that."

"So you've learned something this day," Reedis said with a smile. "Let us go to this gravesite and see what else we can learn."

"Indeed," Ford said, taking the mage's favorite word for his own.

Chapter Eight: A Grave Revisited

Reedis pled the fragility of his bones when it came time to exhume the grave for the second time in as many days, leaving Captain Ford to strain with the shovel, cooled by Reedis' occasional magics.

When the body was revealed, Reedis peered down and examined it with a hand to his face.

"She was no beauty, that I'll say," the mage said as he took in the woman's face.

"I think she looked better yesterday," Ford said, finding his hand rising to protect his nose as well. The decay was beginning to take stronger hold. "I think this night in the dirt has altered her features." He glanced up from the dirt to the mage. "Can you tell if she was the wyvern?"

"No, she wasn't," Reedis said. "She'd only be half of the wyvern at best."

"So why is she a woman and not a beast?"

"I think that this was the human half of the beast," Reedis said with a frown. He raised his hands and moved them in a widening circle, muttering a spell under his breath. A moment later the spell burst over the corpse and the two jumped back as they saw a larger, shadowy creature in the grave. It had white and gold scales. It was the wyvern they'd shot from the skies. "Yes," Reedis said in a fainter voice, "this is the human half of our twin-souled wyvern."

The image faded and Ford rocked back on his heels. He glanced at the woman once more and then leaped out of the grave.

"So where is the *other* half?" Ford said when he was at the same level as the mage.

Mage Reedis shook his head. "I can't possibly say."

#

"Sire, it's true, I saw it myself," Reedis said to the prince as Captain Ford recounted their adventure in the fields two hours past.

"So you are saying that I killed only *half* of the wyvern!" the prince roared. "Captain Ford, can you imagine me asking my father for *half* of a triumph?"

"Sire," Ford began slowly, "Mage Reedis is of the opinion that perhaps the other half of the wyvern is still alive and looking for a human host."

"A host?" the prince repeated, the fire of anger dimming in his eyes. He turned to Reedis. "And if so, what then?"

"They'd form a new wyvern, sire," the mage said in a small voice.

"I can *not* allow that to happen!" the prince said. He turned to Ford. "You cannot allow that to happen, captain."

Ford groped for something to say in reply.

"At the moment, sire," Reedis spoke up hesitantly. The prince turned a stony gaze to him and Reedis swallowed nervously before continuing, "At the moment, I — and Captain Ford — are willing to swear that the wyvern was hit —"

"By me," the prince interjected.

"Sire?" Reedis asked.

"The wyvern was hit by me," the prince said. "It was my excellent gunnery that hit the beast while the other shots flew wide."

"Um, yes," Reedis said. "Although honesty compels me to admit that my attention was directed in keeping our airship flying, sire."

"If I wanted honesty, mage, I would ask for it," the prince told him with a gleam in his eyes. He chuckled, apparently amused at his own words. A moment later, more seriously, he said, "What I need, *Captain*, is for you, the mage here and all your crew to stand in the presence of my royal father and declare the truth to him and his court."

"Ah, sire," Ford began slowly. The prince's gaze hardened angrily. "I'm afraid that the crew are not available —"

"What?" the prince howled.

"I let them take leave, sire," Ford temporized, "and I'm afraid they're in no condition to swear before the King." *Condition, location — all much the same, isn't it?* Ford thought to himself.

The prince glared at the two men then nodded. "Very well, I'll explain that they are busy getting ready for our next conquest."

Reedis glanced nervously toward Ford.

"Next conquest, sire?" Ford asked.

"Well, we certainly can't tell my father that we're going after the *same* wyvern, can we?" the prince said. He clenched a fist and raised it between them. "If I am to swear that the beast is dead, I'd best make certain, shouldn't I?" He lowered his fist and in a more moderate tone, almost to himself, continued, "And that way I'll be able to claim *two* of the beasts."

"I see," Reedis said in the awkward silence that descended after that pronouncement. "You know, sire, there's a chance that the wyvern half of this twin-soul has found another human here in our fair kingdom."

"Perhaps even in this town," Ford said in quick agreement.

"Then why have we not seen it?" the prince demanded.

"The form left in the grave was that of a woman," Reedis said. "So I must imagine that the wyvern half is looking for — maybe even now has found — a suitable partner." The prince gave him a confused a look. "A woman."

"A woman?" the prince repeated. Reedis nodded. The prince frowned. He drew a deep breath. "Very well, prepare yourselves for the royal presence and then, after, you shall go hunting this beast."

#

"Well, *that's* over," Ford said as he and Reedis found themselves back outside of the palace, waiting with the crowds at the triumph balcony, watching the prince waving and smiling broadly and waving the glowing blue amulet of Ametza that hung from his neck to the crowd below. Every second wave or so, he'd raise a large red velvet bag that was overflowing with gold and gems — his added reward.

"It would have been nice if he'd given us more than a thank you," Reedis said, gesturing to the royal purse in view above them.

"What, *Sir* Reedis, do you not revel in your royal appointment?" Ford said mockingly.

"I do not see you doing the same, Sir Ford," Reedis replied with a touch of frost in his voice.

Ford sighed and shrugged. "The honor doesn't put food on the table or crew on my ship."

"Didn't the prince give you full rein to raid the royal goal?" Reedis reminded him.

Ford snorted. "Indeed, and how well will you, Sir Reedis, sleep at night with my crew of cutthroats and thieves guarding your rest?"

Reedis replied with a sour look and started to speak but before he could someone in the crowd shouted: *"Fire!!"*

And the crowd scattered in fear and confusion. Ford kept a hold of Reedis despite the buffeting and dragged the mage back to the tavern where they sought rest and refuge.

"You!" the tavern-keeper shouted when he caught sight of the mage. "What did you *do?*"

"Me?" Reedis cried in surprise. "What are you talking about?"

"My food! It's all *ashes!*" the tavern-keeper said. "That cooler of yours turned into a fireball not twenty minutes ago!"

"I had nothing to do with that, I can assure you!" Reedis cried in surprise. "I was with the King, receiving a knighthood."

"Well you can take your knighthood elsewhere, sir knave, your company is not welcome here," a woman's voice — the tavern keeper's wife — shrieked. "Be gone before I find a mage of curses and spite you!"

Ford pulled Reedis out of the tavern and they stood on the cobbled street, wondering what to do next.

Finally Ford said, "There's food on the *Spite*, not great fare, but something."

"And your cook?"

Ford gave him a sour smile. "Perhaps Knox can cook for us."

Reedis shrugged and gestured to Ford. "Lead on, Sir Ford, and we shall have our repast on your royal airship."

"Indeed, Sir Reedis," Ford said, "My ship shall be proud to have the royal ballooneer grace its timbers with his presence."

The two laughed, locked arms and strolled back toward the ship and the gantry.

Knox was still there but eager to leave them as, "I've got to get home to the missus. There was a disturbance and a fire and she's right worried."

"Go!" Ford said, waving his last crewman off. "We'll talk in the morning."

Knox seemed reluctant to leave but knuckled his forehead in a salute and trotted quickly off the ship and down the street.

"Do you think you'll see him in the morning?" Reedis wondered.

"Aye," Ford said. "But whether he'll stay when he learns about our new crew…" his voice trailed off. He shook himself and jerked his head toward the hatchway. "I've a bottle in my quarters, and Knox swore he kept the galley fire going."

"If he didn't," Reedis said, "I know someone who can magic a fire to life."

#

The galley fire was dead in the morning and Reedis could do nothing to revive because they were out of wood to burn.

They drank brackish water and regretted that they'd finished not just one but *two* bottles of wine between them. They were just motivated enough to search for some place that might feed them when a royal messenger clambered — loudly! — up the gantry and shouted for them.

"Sir Reedis! Sir Ford! His Royal Highness requires your presence!" the page bellowed in proper form.

"Ahhh!" Reedis said, raising his hands to his ears. "Can he not do it more quietly?"

"I'll bet you wish you were a mage of sound, right about now," Ford added grimly. He waved to the page and asked in a quiet voice, "And does his royal highness have transport for us?"

"I have two horses with me," the page said.

"Wonderful!" Reedis groaned. "Hooves on cobblestones! What a charming sound so early in the morning!"

"It is not early, sir," the page replied stiffly. He glanced upwards to the sky. "The sun is nearing noon, if you'd see."

"Ahh, I'd prefer not, if it's all well enough with you," Reedis replied. Ford jerked his head toward the gantry, regretted the motion, and gestured with one hand for the page to lead them away.

#

"She's here!" the prince bellowed, stomping down the hallway toward them as soon as they alighted their horses. "The shaman at the temple said that she'd seen her!"

"What?" Reedis asked in puzzlement while wincing in pain from the prince's voice. "Who?"

"The girl?" Ford, whose seaman's life gave him a better tolerance for wine on an empty stomach, guessed.

"Yes, indeed!" the prince said. "She wouldn't give us the name, saying some rubbish about oaths to Ametza —" the prince caught himself and glanced nervously toward the port and the sea beyond, hoping not to gain an inundation in response for his inopportune words — "but she *saw* the girl. She was about to be married, can you imagine?."

"Imagine her husband on their wedding night," Reedis muttered to Ford. The comment caused the other to splutter in amusement.

"What?" the prince said. "Do you doubt me?"

"No, sire," Ford said quickly. "I was just wondering — where is your amulet?"

The prince's face clouded in pure loathing. "Stolen! It and my jewels were stolen!" He frowned in memory. "We couldn't catch the thief, he got away when some idiot shouted 'fire!' at the ceremony."

"We were there!" Reedis exclaimed.

"Well, why didn't you catch him?"

"We didn't see him, sire, we were overwhelmed by the crowd," Ford explained.

"So were my guards," the prince grumbled.

The two newly knighted royals exchanged looks: they both wondered how hard the guard looked and whether the soldiers were as well-rewarded as Ford's sailors.

"What do you desire of us, my prince?" Ford said, going down on one knee.

The prince wiggled his fingers in indication that Ford should stand. "Do?" the prince said. "Why find her, of course! Kill her and show her the King's justice!"

"Don't you mean show her the King's justice and then kill her?" Reedis asked.

"I meant what I said!" the prince roared, waving them away. "And don't come back until she's dead!"

Chapter Nine: Meeting The Mechanical

"Well, that was a help," Reedis muttered when they were safely back on the street. "What do we do now?"

"Can you use magic to track her?" Ford asked.

The mage shook his head. "I'm a wizard of hot —"

"— and cold magic," Ford finished in unison with him, shaking his head bitterly. "So we'll have to see what we can do on our own." He started walking.

"Where are we going?"

"Back to the ship," Ford said. "At least we'll get a cup of tea."

"We'll have to get more water first," Reedis warned.

Ford shrugged agreement and picked up his pace, noting sourly that the prince hadn't seen to offer them horses for the ride back. "Perhaps Knox will have an idea."

Knox did, indeed, have an idea. He helped them get water and make tea and the three sat at the small table in Ford's captain's quarters.

"That apprentice, didn't he seem shifty?"

"He did," Ford agreed, worried that he would find himself making another trip out of town. "Why do you ask?"

"Well, he mentioned the mechanical, Ibb, didn't he?"

Ford nodded.

"So, you know this Ibb, don't you sir?"

"Are you suggesting we talk with him?" Ford guessed. He grimaced as he mulled the notion over then knocked back his cup in one gulp and rose. "Come along then, let's see what Ibb knows."

"He's a mechanical?" Reedis asked, rising himself and looking worried.

"He is," Ford said. "Many people don't associate with him because he worships a different god. They say the mechanicals were an ancient people who decided that they could cheat the Ferryman by transferring their souls into the cold cogs and gears of machines rather than frail flesh."

"What's he look like?" Reedis asked.

"His soul is in a tall, stocky metal body topped with a metal head that seems a mixture of gold and brass, with cogs, and two glowing red gems for eyes. He's got metal eyebrows, too." Ford shrugged. "His voice is deep, like it comes from a cave, but after a while you don't notice."

"How long have you known him?"

"I knew him from years ago when he first came here," Ford said. "In fact, we rescued him when my ship, the *Sprite*, took the corsair that had captured him. He helped us by giving us a list of improvements for our rigging — we got three knots more speed after that."

"Ah!" Reedis said, encouraged. "So he's in your debt."

"I'd count him more a friend than a debtor," Ford said as they made their way back onto the street. Ford set a good clip.

"Mechanical men have peculiar loyalties," Reedis said cautiously.

Ford raised an eyebrow. "Swindled one, did you?"

"Sir Ford! I must protest your language!"

"Well, how else do you describe that fire box that so infuriated your late benefactor?"

"Fire box?" Knox asked, glancing between the two. "And why does he call you Sir Ford, sir?"

"The King seems to have a particularly dark sense of humor," Ford explained. He pointed to Reedis. "He knighted us last night."

"Knighted!" Knox exclaimed. A moment later, he said shrewdly, "And did he pay you by any chance, captain?"

"As I said," Ford replied, shaking his head, "he has a dark sense of humor."

"So the lads were right," Knox said to himself.

"I don't know about that, boatswain," Ford said. "We're not due our wages 'til the end of the month and that's a fortnight yet."

"There's much that can happen in a fortnight," the boatswain muttered darkly.

"Bad *and* good," Ford reminded him. They entered a broad street and he picked up the pace.

Minutes later they turned down a side street and came to a well-appointed but old building. Ford strode forward and wrapped on the door, calling loudly, "Open up, you clanker! We got questions for you!"

"Just a moment!" a mechanical voice called back. Ford glanced at the others and crossed his arms, waiting. Some moments later, the door opened and the mechanical man gestured them inside.

Knox came in slowly but Ford rushed in, going from one thing to the next, rushing about the room in excitement. Reedis, inspired by the captain, was no less inquisitive.

"What have you been doing lately?" Ford asked, slapping a hand — carefully — on the metal man's shoulder. He'd sprained his wrist years back so he knew that the metal was hard and unyielding.

"Many things," Ibb replied. "I heard you are flying an airship these days." The mechanical man clanked as he shook his head. "I think you were safer on the sea."

"Aye, safer!" Ford agreed heartily. "We lost Havenam. You remember him, my young midshipman from all those years back?"

"Is he still young?" Ibb asked. "And a — a mid-ship-man?"

"He's dead," Ford said sourly. "A dragon toppled him from the tops of the balloons and he fell to his death."

"That is sad." Ibb said, his voice emotionless. Ford knew that the mechanical had trouble with emotions, having not had any for hundreds of years or more.

"It is," Ford said. "His widow cursed me when I brought his body home."

"Was it a good curse?"

"The words were powerful," Reedis spoke up for the first time, "but she hasn't a drop of magic in her."

Ibb rotated to look at Reedis. "And you are?"

"I'm sorry, where are my manners?" Ford apologized. Before he could continue, Ibb said, "I do not know. Have you misplaced them?"

"Probably," Knox muttered, his eyes dancing with amusement. To Ford he said, "I'd forgotten what a corker Mr. Ibb is!"

"This is mage Reedis," Ford said, ignoring the boatswain. "He is responsible for the hot and cold magic that raises the airship."

"And Mr. Newman is responsible for the air propellers that move it," Ibb said, nodding gravely. A moment later, he asked, "And where is Mr. Newman?"

"Cursing his luck," Knox said in a low voice.

Ford ignored him. "He is well and with the ship, my *Spite*."

"I thought your ship was named *Sprite*," Ibb said.

"It was, until the King took it into service," Ford said. "Then she was renamed."

"A good practice," Ibb said. "Although there are air sprites, I'm given to understand that this ship is to be the spite of flying fire beings."

"Indeed," Ford said. "Which leads me to our journey here."

"How so?"

"We shot a wyvern," Ford explained. "The dragon we were shooting at got away, after killing poor Havenam."

"Only we didn't find a wyvern's body when we went looking," Knox spoke up. "We found a woman's body."

"Did you find her in a field of wyvern flowers?" Ibb asked.

"Why?" Ford said, his brows narrowing. "Do you know something of this?"

"I know that wyverns like to die in wyvern flowers," Ibb said. "And that they're twin-souled, part human, part soul of fire." He turned slowly, first toward the back door and then around to them. "I could inquire of more."

"What can we tell you?"

Ibb clanked backwards a step, then moved to the right, reaching for something by the door. Ford followed him with his eyes and saw a coat rack with an umbrella sticking up. The mechanical reached for it.

"I would not inquire of you," Ibb said, moving toward the door. "I would inquire of those more knowledgeable, naturally."

His progress was interrupted by another loud knocking on his door. "Open up! In the King's name!"

Ibb turned to Ford. "What is this?"

"There was a theft, the prince's amulet and jewels were stolen," Ford said. "They're looking for it."

"Indeed!" Ibb said. "They will doubtless impede my journey." He gestured toward the back door. "Perhaps you will not want to handle this delay. If you go that way, please open the barrel just by the door."

"What's in it?" Knox asked.

"Something to persuade guests not to linger," the mechanical replied. Ibb started rumbling in the rusty noise that was his version of a laugh.

Ford smiled at him and nodded. "We'll be on our way then."

"Safe journey!"

"And more knowledge," Ford said, completing the farewell of the mechanicals. The three moved to the back and, at Ford's gesture, Knox lifted the lid on the small bucket by the door. Instantly, he turned a horrible shade of green and rushed past them out the door.

#

"What was that?" Ford asked as he joined Knox and Reed is safely away from the horrid smell. "I don't know," Knox said. "Smelled like someone vomited something horrible." He shuddered. "I think I saw a bit of eel, too."

Through the back door they heard someone bellow: "What is that, it smells awful!"

"Something I've been working on," Ibb's mechanical voice replied. "Gentlemen, let us move this conversation outside, or soon the fumes will become toxic for your lungs."

Ford smiled and gestured to the others. "Come on, let's go!"

"Where to, sir?" Knox asked.

"We're going to the goal, of course," Ford said.

"Whatever for?"

"To pick up more crew, no doubt," Reedis muttered darkly.

Ford raised a hand. "I'm hoping it won't come to that."

Catching the look of relief on Knox's face, he added in vile humor, "Perhaps we'll just get some stokers for Mr. Newman." He was rewarded with a look of ill-repressed horror from the boatswain.

"If not crew, then what, Sir Ford?" Reedis asked.

"Answers," Ford replied. He picked up his pace forcing the others to follow in silence.

The jail was in turmoil with guards clattering about, seeming in great spirits.

"What is it?" Ford asked as they approached.

"For a penny, I'll tell you," a small child said, approaching with a hand held out.

"For less, my mage will freeze you to death," Ford growled. He'd been dealing with urchins all his life, having started out as one himself.

The small child's eyes widened in horror as she took in Ford's expression, saw the purple robes of the mage and the rough features of the boatswain.

"They - they caught the thief," the child said, pointing toward the jail. "Caught him in the inn, of all places! The madame turned him in!"

Ford frowned, reached into his pocket but, before he could pull a penny as a reward, the child scampered off as quick as her thin legs could take her.

"What now?" Reedis asked. "They've caught the prince's thief."

"We still have to find the girl," Ford said darkly. He headed to the jail. "We should talk with the thief."

"And scout for crew," Reedis muttered.

"Possibly," Ford said. He asked the mage, "How soon could you lift the ship again?"

"I'm ready enough now," Reedis said. "Although there's one thing I'd like to do, first." Ford gave him an inquiring look. Reedis glanced briefly to the boatswain before replying, "That little project you mentioned."

"Oh! Oh, yes!" Ford said. "It might be useful." He gestured to jail. "This first, I think."

The King's Jail was a musty stone building set at the worst part of the dockyards. Ford had known it of old and avoided it as much as he could.

"What do you want?" the guard at the gate asked them in surly tones.

"Respect, for a King's knight, for one," Reedis replied, drawing himself up to his full height.

"For two," Ford said, his lips twitching as he pointed to himself.

"Captain Ford?" the guard said, brows narrowing.

"It's Captain Sir Ford these days," Ford corrected airily.

"I'd heard you'd gone and blown away in a gale," the guard said.

"I blew back again, Sykes," Ford said, his tone becoming harder. "You've prisoners and I've a writ from the prince to inspect them."

"A writ?" the guard repeated. He glanced at Reedis and Knox, whom he recognized with a nod. Knox responded with a growl of intense dislike. "Well, I suppose that's all right then," Sykes said. "I'll need a shilling from each of you."

"You'll need to hope the mage doesn't get in a temper and boil your skin off your worthless bones," Ford snapped, moving past the guard as though he didn't exist.

Sykes took a step backwards frightened, eyeing the mage warily. "H-he could do that?" he asked Knox.

"Worse," Knox replied striding past.

The three stopped a pace later, their hands going to their noses.

"You get used to the stench!" Sykes called to their backs in grim humor. "We don't call them the scum of the earth without reason, you know!"

"Come on," Ford said, regretting the breath the words required of him. Having breathed, and finding that he could still breathe, regardless of the foul odors which assailed him — worse than Ibb's bucket of vomit — he called to Sykes, "Where's the thief?"

"Second on the left!" Sykes called back. "We keep the ones the King wants to hang close by the door."

A shape darted to the bars as they approached and Ford thought the look on the thief's face was eager, expectant almost, until he saw them.

"Who are you?" the thief growled. "What do you want?"

"Manners, at least," Knox rasped back, drawing his dirk and banging it, flat-bladed against the thief's fingers wrapped around the bars. The thief was too quick and jerked back with snake-like speed, leaving Knox's weapon to clatter loudly against the metal.

The thief smiled at Knox's discomfort. "You have to have manners, first, dog." He glanced toward Ford without recognition but his eyes flared as he took in Reedis' purple robes and he slammed against the bars once more. "You! Murderer!"

"What?" Reedis said, stepping back in surprise.

"You burn and you freeze," the thief said. He laughed bitterly. "I saw what you did at the tavern. You can be sure I put a fix to *that*."

"What?" Reedis said again.

"What are you?" Ford said, his eyes narrowing as he examined the thief carefully, as though looking for something else.

"Nothing your ears will hear," the thief snarled lowly. He cocked his head at Ford, considering. "Are you the captain, then?"

"Captain Sir Ford commands the king's airship, and you'd best not forget that," Knox said supportively.

"Ah! So it was you who killed her," the thief said.

"What's your name?" Ford asked conversationally. "I'd like us to at least speak civilly."

"My name is Jarin and I've no need to speak to you," the thief spat. "I don't talk to carrion or the dead."

"The woman in the wyvern field? You knew her?" Ford guessed, startled by the thief's reference to the dead.

Jarin jerked back as if struck. He was silent for longer than usual before replying, "I don't know what you're talking about."

"We're looking for a girl," Reedis said. "Have you seen her?"

"I've seen many a girl," Jarin replied with a leer. "You'd have to be more specific."

"What do you know of wyverns?" Ford said. "Why did you steal the prince's amulet?"

"Ametza's bauble?" Jarin replied with a snort. "It means nothing to her, you know. Nor me."

"So it was the jewels," Ford guessed. "You stole them."

"They were owed me and mine," Jarin said. "I stole nothing."

"The King thinks differently," Knox muttered.

"The King thinks that *boy* is his son," Jarin snorted. "He is ignorant, lazy, indolent, and soon to lose all that he values."

"You'll lose your life before that," Ford said, although noting that no one would gainsay his words.

"I shall dance on your grave," Jarin said, eyes glinting. "I am just waiting —" he cut himself off and shook his head. "I'm tired, I shall rest now." He turned away from them and went to one of the dark corners of his cell.

"Come on," Ford said, "we'll get no more from him." He motioned them to move on. "We need to inspect the others that are here."

"For crew?" Knox asked in astonishment.

"At least we know where they *are*," Ford said mildly, moving toward the back of the jail.

They spent another twenty minutes in the jail. Ford identified four men he'd known of old — they were good workers when sober — and found another eight who might do in a pinch. That left him short four regular crew and four stokers. The thought of continuing the search in that horrid stench was too much for him and he jerked his head back to the entrance in a wordless order. Neither Reedis nor Knox objected.

Chapter Ten: Talent Of Mine

Outside, Reedis said, "So what now?"

"Now, we find ourselves a warm meal and wait," Ford said, nodding toward the jail.

"What?" Knox said.

"We wait," Ford said. "And we keep a careful eye on the jail."

"They won't take our prisoners, sir," Knox said, "they've got nowhere to take them."

"Our thief made a mistake," Ford said. Knox and Reedis looked confused. "He said that he was waiting." He shrugged. "So we wait."

"What for, sir?"

"For whatever he is waiting for," Ford replied. Reedis gave him a dubious look. "The King will have his head this evening but our thief does not seem fearful. Clearly he expects something to aid him before that time."

"There's an inn just down the road," Knox offered. "The food's not great but it's warm."

Ford gestured for him to lead. "By all means, boatswain, let us feast!"

The inn proved lively. It was run by a woman who was referred to as "the madame." The food was good but Ford suspected he'd be happier sleeping aboard his ship — and would be less likely to wake up with lice or worse.

"There's a huge crowd here tonight," Knox said, "more than usual."

"Why don't you see what is happening?" Ford suggested. Knox smiled and rose, heading off to a table at the far side of the bar. Ford followed him with his eyes and then stopped — rising precipitously from his chair.

"What?" Reedis asked from over his large, full plate, a fork poised just before his mouth.

"Stay there," Ford said, "I just want to check on something." He had spied a small child enter the room, an urchin. She looked like the one who'd begged for a penny.

She spotted him as he approached and tried to sidle away but he called out, reaching into his pocket, "I just wanted to pay you."

"Sir?" the little girl said, glancing about for safety.

Ford showed her the copper penny. He pulled another from his pocket and showed it to her, too. "This other one is if you do something for me."

The girl sidled away, suddenly more wary than before. "What?"

"I need you to go back to the jail and keep an eye on that thief," Ford said.

"For that I'll take a shilling," the girl said boldly.

"Tuppence, no more," Ford countered. She thought about it, nodded, and put her hand out. Ford's eyebrows rose in astonishment. "I'll pay you when you've got news, not before!"

"So pay me," the girl said, with a hungry grin, "'cuz I've got news!"

"Sir, did you hear?" Knox came rushing over at that moment. "The thief's escaped!"

The girl's face fell.

"That was your news?" Ford guessed. He passed her the two pennies. She took them but gave him a look of confusion. "The first is from before. The second is half of what you would have got if you'd done the job."

The girl's face twisted as she considered this, then she nodded and clasped the pennies, turning in the same moment and vanishing into the crowd.

Ford turned to Knox. "How did he escape?"

"The door was wide open," Knox said, shrugging. "There are those who suspect magic."

"What about a simple pick?" Ford asked. Knox allowed that possibility with a shrug of his own.

"They say there was a girl who visited not much before and they ran off together," the urchin, who Ford had believed long gone, offered up shyly. "There's a reward, the prince says that they killed a woman in a wyvern field."

Ford sighed, reached into his pocket and pulled out two more pennies. "Do you know where they went, by any chance?"

"Pay me first," the girl demanded. With a heavy sigh, Ford put the pennies in her hand. She made them disappear into her thin shift, smiled at him and shook her head. Ford smiled again and she laughed, a light, airy laugh that seemed totally at odds with her situation. When she finished, Ford gave her a dark look but she just laughed again, saying, "Where does anyone go to escape?"

"Oh!" Ford said in sudden understanding. The others looked at him in surprise. "Come on, Knox, we're going to the docks!"

#

"My feet are killing me, is it much further?" Reedis complained as they spied the masts of ships dimly visible in the fading light. He glanced upwards. "What's that?"

"Snow," Ford said, following his gaze and catching sight of the first flakes. "An early fall but not unexpected."

"I'm going to freeze!" Reedis whined.

"Use one of your warming spells, then," Ford said with little sympathy.

"You cannot imagine how *difficult* it would be to warm anything in this cold," Reedis responded.

"Shh," Ford hissed. "Listen!"

"Krea!" a voice shouted in the distance toward two people not two hundred paces from them.

"That's the apprentice!" Knox said to Ford in surprise. His brow furrowed, "But who's Krea?"

"Shh!" Ford said again. Knox was right, it was Angus, the surly young apprentice they met earlier. Softly, he added, "If we are quiet, we may well find out." Ford gestured toward an overturned rowboat nearby and indicated that they should take shelter there.

A clanking in the distance, near the shout of the apprentice, alerted them to the presence of a mechanical man. Ford needed only one glance over his shoulder to determine that the mechanical was Ibb himself. Reedis saw him too and started to exclaim in surprise but Ford put a hand over his mouth warningly.

They reached the rowboat and their shadows blended with it. They listened. The light breeze brought some words toward them.

"How did you find me?" the girl, Krea, asked.

"It's a talent of mine," Ibb replied, trying to keep his booming voice quiet. Ford saw him wave in the direction of the apprentice. "I brought him. He needs to know what is happening."

The breeze took the next several exchanges away from them except for a few snippets.

"Is that why you're dressed as a boy?" the apprentice asked. Ford realized that the girl was dressed in pants.

Reedis tugged on Ford's sleeve and Ford turned to give him an irritated look only to find that the mage was pointing into the distance. There were torches moving towards them. Many torches.

The mob had found the thief.

"Go!" Ibb bellowed, his voice carrying clearly in the night. Lower, he added, "I'll find you!"

Three darks shapes sprinted away, leaving the looming bulk of the mechanical to stand before the mob.

"Come on!" Ford called, urging the others to their feet. He started toward the mechanical man.

"Shouldn't we go after *them?*" Reedis asked, pointing at the fugitives.

"He said he'll find them, didn't he?" Ford said, not hiding his exasperation. Understanding dawned on the faces of the other two. "He can't do that if the mob tears him apart!"

He rushed to Ibb's side and raised his arms above his head and called to the approaching torches, "Stop! In the King's name, stop! Your quarry is that way!" He pointed after the fleeing thief and the girl. The mob paused and seemed about to disregard him but he caught sight of a mounted guard. "You there! I need your horse!"

"Two of them!" Reedis shouted, pointing toward another mounted guard. "Hand them over now, in the King's name!"

"And who are you to be using the King's — oh! It's you!" Sykes, the guard, said in a resigned tone.

"Us, indeed!" Ford cried. "Now get off your horses! Guard this mechanical and hold him — he knows something and I mean to learn it."

Reluctantly the two guards relinquished their mounts. Ford and Reedis climbed up in their stead. Ford looked down to Knox, saying, "Look after Mr. Ibb, if you would. We'll find you when we can."

"Aye, sir," Knox replied. "I'll be sure that nothing untoward occurs."

Ford sketched him a salute and urged his mount into a trot after the vanishing mob.

"However does he command so much loyalty?" Ibb rumbled in surprise to Knox.

"He doesn't," Knox replied. "His whole crew's deserted."

"Hmm," Ibb rumbled in response.

#

They were too late. Ford pulled up his reins as he heard a shrill screech and looked upwards to see a brilliant white wyvern — much younger than the one which had fallen to *Spite's* broadside — rise high into the air, crying in triumph and disappearing northwards into the night.

"Come on!" Ford called, urging his horse into a gallop and turning it back to the town.

"Where are we going?" Reedis cried in surprise, turning to follow him.

"To the jail!" Ford called back. "We're going to need a crew!"

"What?"

"We've got to follow that wyvern or the prince will have our heads!"

With a groan of pained agreement, the purple mage followed.

Far ahead, the winter wyvern flew on into the growing snowstorm. All too quickly she was lost from sight.

Frozen Sky

Book 3

Twin Soul series

Chapter One: Half a Wyvern

"So you're saying that you killed half a wyvern?" the King shouted from his throne to the assembled group, his eyes singling out his son, Crown Prince Nestor for particular disdain.

King Markel was the second of his line. His father, Alavor, had won the kingdom through some pact with the sea goddess Ametza. King Markel was not a man cut from the same cloth; he lived a large life of indolence tempered with a certain vicious practicality that mostly included appeasing the goddess.

He continued now, acerbically, "And, having killed only the half, you let the wyvern reform, taunt my entire kingdom and fly off — unhindered — in complete freedom?"

It was morning. Only two days before Captain Ford and his gallant crew had first flown the royal airship Spite — expressly commissioned to rid the skies of flaming dragons and wyverns. They'd been successful, having shot a golden wyvern out of the sky. After that, things did not go well.

The prince leaned toward Captain Ford to surreptitiously nudge him in the side with his elbow. Ford glanced at him and saw the prince cut his eyes toward the throne, clearly indicating: say something.

"Sire, in our defense we were woefully ignorant of the nature of wyverns and dragons," Captain Ford said, bowing his head. "We had to exhume the female body twice to understand what had happened. And by then we only knew to look for another female. We had no understanding of the time it took for a wyvern to assimilate a new human and become reborn."

Ford remembered how the newly-made wyvern had screeched in triumph as she had flown northwards through the blizzard of snow the night before, soon lost from his sight.

"And now I have a murderer on my hands!" the King griped, his eyes turning toward the downcast form of Angus Franck. The lad was apprenticed to the wyvern lass' father — an aging smith — and had been promised the girl's hand in marriage. Instead, he'd burst her heart with a hatpin — which, according to Ibb the mechanical, had been necessary to complete the transformation. Ford intended to have a good long talk with the mechanical man, now safely the newest addition to the King's jail, as soon as he could. He considered the cold metal immortal a friend, of sorts.

"I'll take him, sire," Ford said, looking at the sad-faced apprentice, "I could use a good hand."

"And many more, too!" the King snarled. "Really, Captain, what good is a ship without a crew?"

"There was some confusion over pay, sire, which I could not put to rights in time," Ford explained.

"Well, at least with the scrapings of the jail, you won't have that problem!" the King said.

"Indeed, sire," Ford agreed, suppressing a shudder. "And Mr. Newman, our steam engineer, and mage Reedis have both agreed to stay on as well as my boatswain whom I will rate first mate for his loyalty."

The King waved these concerns away with a bored hand. "What matters to me, Captain Ford, is that my royal airship be seen to pursue and destroy this menace."

"Indeed, sire," Ford agreed.

"So when can you leave?"

"I can depart as soon as my crew is settled aboard," Ford said. He hesitated, adding, "If you could spare them, I would like some of your jailers as guards."

"Afraid of getting your throat slit while you sleep?" the King murmured. Ford nodded jerkily. The King leaned forward on his throne to confess, "Mind you, Captain, some of those guards are worse than those they're guarding."

"I know, sire," Captain Ford replied. "I've had dealings with them before."

"Indeed?"

"When leaving my past captives in their care," Ford said, reminding the King of his years' of service as a privateer.

"They didn't stay long," the King murmured. "Mostly we ransomed them off in due course, as I recall."

"To our great profit," first minister Mannevy chirped up from his place just below the King.

"Haven't made a penny on this yet," the King said, his long grey and brown beard swaying as he looked at Mannevy.

"The plan, sire, was to ensure that we could keep our profits and please our goddess at the same time," Mannevy reminded him.

"As you say," the King said, waving the issue aside and turning his attention back to Captain Ford and the others. "So, again I ask you, when can you capture and destroy this beast?"

"I can set sail — I mean lift ship — a week after I get my crew, sire," Ford said.

"A week!" the King said. He shook his head. "You have four days, Captain. From now." The King looked over to his minister. "See to it, Mannevy."

"As you wish, Your Majesty," the first minister replied. He got up from his chair and beckoned for the rest to follow him out of the royal receiving room.

"The murderer will stay behind," the king said as the others shuffled out.

"Sire?" Captain Ford asked, wondering if he needed to up his crew requirements by one more.

"I want to speak with him in private," the king replied. He glanced toward the mage. "And, later, I shall want to speak with you, Sir Reedis."

Reedis gave Ford an alarmed look but the captain merely shrugged, nodding, pointedly, toward the king.

Reedis licked his lips nervously, "As you wish, your majesty."

The king waved them out of his chambers, leaving a very nervous Angus Franck in attendance.

#

"You may approach," the king said to Angus Franck, gesturing with one languid hand.

Angus took a few hesitant steps towards his king, he had a chiseled jaw, black eyes, calloused hands.

"Young man," the king said, "I wish to speak for your ears alone."

Angus' eyes grew wide. He walked right up to the throne. King Markel rose, he wore a grey silk robe and a white coral crown. Angus bowed in fear, head downcast. He was surprised when, a moment later, a hand tapped his shoulder. He looked up and saw that the king was standing right in front of him.

"Get up," the king said, "I have a very special mission for you alone."

\#

The doors to the throne room opened and a wide eyed Angus Franck gestured to Reedis. "The king wants you."

Reedis gave him a worried look but Angus gestured once more and the purple mage moved forward with a jerk.

"Good luck," the young apprentice murmured as the purple mage moved into the throne room.

\#

Reedis turned at the sound of the doors closing behind him. Nervously he turned back to the throne and, clearing his throat to soothe his nerves, stepped forward.

The king was nowhere to be seen.

"Your majesty?" Reedis said tentatively, entertaining a faint hope that the apprentice was teasing him and that he wouldn't have to face the king — the king and many potentially troubling questions, such as: "And how well do you know my wife?"

"How well do you know —" the king began from a distant corner.

Reedis jumped and squeaked in surprise. "Sire?"

"— nervous sort, are you?" the king asked, beckoning him forward. Reedis trotted over. The king was in an alcove to the side of the throne. Reedis guessed the alcove was a place where the king could rest or engage in quiet conversation. Reedis bowed when he put himself before the king.

A tall page in full court livery stood beside him either for protection or to fulfill his needs, Reedis couldn't say. The page alarmed Reedis because his features were so obviously Sorian: the copper skin and thin, pointed goatee were practically a hallmark of the kingdom to the north.

"Sit, sit!" the King commanded.

Reedis sat.

"As I was saying," the king said when he was satisfied that he had the purple mage's attention, "how well do you know your magic?"

Reedis nearly cried in relief at the question. The king gave him an expectant look and Reedis quickly marshalled his thoughts.

"I have been practicing this brand of magic for many months, your majesty," Reedis said, trying to sound calm.

"I see," the king said. He smiled. "I'm very interested in everything to do with these airships. I believe that they could prove a great boon to our kingdom. Please tell me everything you know about them. I need assurances before I decide to commit to a fleet."

"A fleet?" Reedis asked, casting a nervous glance to the page who was listening intently.

"A dozen ships at least," the king said, his eyes gleaming. "Perhaps two dozen." Reedis' eyes widened.

"Sire, this is momentous news," Reedis said, imagining a whole school of eager young — and rich — apprentices hanging on his every word and filling his pockets with gold. He glanced nervously at the page. "Is this secret?"

"From Tirpin?" The King asked, snorting. "He is new to the court but I assure you his loyalty is not in question." Reedis stiffened, wondering if perhaps the King questioned his loyalty instead. Nervously, Reedis gave the king an understanding nod.

Satisfied, the King continued, "I was wondering, though, why do you use so many balloons? Why not one?"

"For safety, your majesty," Reedis replied easily. "The smaller balloons are easier to build and easier to enspell. And, of course, we'd never tried before so it was easier to get small balloons made."

The king motioned for him to continue.

In the end, with the king's skilful questions, Reedis found himself talking for over an hour, telling the king every little thing he could recall about how he'd discovered the magic, perfected it, and ensured that it was safe.

Finally, King Markel stood. Reedis stood with him.

"Thank you," the king said. "You have been very helpful." He pursed his lips, then added, "Just one thing."

"Your majesty?"

"Who else knows all this?" the king asked. "Have you started training apprentices?"

"No one, your majesty," Reedis said. He continued, "I'm hoping to start training some apprentices immediately."

"Wait until your return," the king advised. "You'll know so much more then."

"If your majesty so wishes," Reedis said.

"I do," the king said, turning toward his chambers. "You have been most useful." He gestured toward the double doors at the entrance. "Please see yourself out."

Reedis bowed and the king waved him away, smiling affably. Under his breath, Reedis blew out a sigh of relief.

#

Inside his office, Mannevy waved Ford to a chair. "Sit, sit!" he pulled a cord as he went to his plush chair behind a huge parchment-covered desk and said to the air, "Tea for two!" A moment later he added, "And some snacks!'

"The help here is marvelous," Mannevy said as a tray appeared on a side table with a pot of piping-hot tea and several scrumptious snacks. He stood and moved toward the table. "Please, Captain, take your fill!"

Ford rose from his seat and joined the minister.

"My crew wasn't paid," Ford said, going straight to the point.

"They were due wages at the end of the month," the first minister replied immediately, putting a few snacks on a plate. He lifted the teapot and gestured inquiringly to Ford who nodded. Mannevy filled a cup for the captain then another for himself.

"And Lieutenant Havenam died in the King's service," Ford added.

"He is due a pension, or at least his widow," the first minister decided, moving back to his plush chair and placing his teacup on the huge marble topped desk before seating himself.

"The rest of the crew are due wages for the time they worked," Ford said.

"They're mutineers, they were under the King's service, they should be rounded up and hung," the first minister replied smoothly.

"The prince promised a guinea to the crew and then skipped on the payment," Ford said. "After that can you not understand why they feared for their wages?"

"The prince shot the beast himself," the first minister said, raising his cup to his lips once more. "Why would anyone earn that guinea?"

"You know very well, Mannevy, who is telling the truth," Ford growled. The prince had not shot the wyvern but had insisted on this retelling of events for his own ego. He took a sip of his tea. The tea was hot and it burnt on the way down. He glared at the delicately painted blue cup and put it down, away from his sight.

"I do," the first minister agreed glumly. "And I know who will sit on the throne one day."

"'Makes two of us," Ford returned with a frown. He raised a brow. "You ever think of emigrating?"

"I am sworn to the King!" the first minister replied stiffly. His brows thundered down as he added, "And so you are!"

"This King, yes," Ford agreed mildly.

"I… see," Mannevy said. "But your loyalty is wavering now, I take it?"

"If you mean to say that I don't look forward to fearing for my life on a daily basis from my crew… yes."

"And how can we remedy this?"

"Pay my crew," Ford said. He raised a hand to forestall the first minister's ready retort. "They earned half a month's wages, pay them and be public about it."

"Half of them are at sea!"

"Book the amount and record it on the docks," Ford said. "They'll know that they'll get it when they come back."

"But they mutinied!"

"Pardon them," Ford said. With a sour look, he added, "There's enough blood spilled already."

"Just a girl's!"

"Two girls," Ford corrected. "The one in the grave and the one that's flown away."

"Not a girl anymore, surely!"

"Tell that to the other's grave," Ford said bitterly. "Better yet, dig her up and have a look yourself."

Mannevy shuddered.

"Why are you so squeamish?" Ford asked. "You must have more than your share of blood on your hands."

"Always for the King."

"This is another," Ford said. He shrugged, dismissing the issue. "Pay my crew, pay the gunners their guinea, and pay me."

"How much?" Mannevy asked, his eyes hooded to hide his delight. Now they were getting somewhere!

"Three month's wages and half again as bonus," Ford said quickly. He saw the way the first minister ducked his head and knew that he'd asked for too little. "In advance," he added. "And when the deed's done, an earldom with appropriate rents and lands."

"Done," Mannevy said, rising from his chair, hand outstretched.

Ford waved him off, adding, "And prize money for the crew."

"Prize money?"

"Anything they capture and a bounty for the wyvern," Ford said promptly.

"But they're all going to be prisoners!"

"And their freedom, all charges dropped, royal pardon," Ford pressed on. He made a face. "If I can give them that, they'll think twice about sticking a knife in my ribs while I'm sleeping."

"But they were sent to jail for a reason!"

"And they'll be pardoned for another reason," Ford said. He rose from the chair and turned toward the door. "Those are my terms." He started toward the door, calling over his shoulder, "Take them or my title and commission."

"Wait!" Mannevy called, coming around his desk. Ford turned back to him. Mannevy extended his hand once more. "Deal."

"And the King's writ on all this," Ford added. "I don't trust the prince."

"All under the King's seal," Mannevy agreed. "To be delivered when you return in triumph."

"Delivered then but signed and witnessed before I leave," Ford said.

"Of course," Mannevy said, licking his lips and looking like he had meant that to start with. Ford kept his smile to himself: it was obvious that the first minister had hoped to welsh on the deal when he returned.

"Deal." Ford shook the other's hand with a cold, hard grip. "And the prince stays behind."

"If the King agrees," the first minister temporized. He smiled at Ford and twisted their hands to remind the other of their agreement. "We have a deal, captain."

Chapter Two: Demands

The King did not agree. He looked up as he signed the agreement Ford had hammered out with Mannevy and smiled, passing the signed forms to the prime minister. "There," he said, "that's done."

"Sire," Ford said, bending his knee and bowing. "You are most gracious."

The King waved for him to rise. "I only want results, Sir Ford," the King said, reminding Ford of his new-won title. "Results," the King continued with a languid smile, "and one other thing."

"Sire?"

"The prince," the King said. Ford gave him an inquiring look. "He shall go with you."

"Sire —"

"He shall go with you, Captain," the King repeated and there was an iron resolve in his voice. Ford accepted the royal order with a jerky nod. The prince was a coward, a braggart, and the man who had lost Ford his hard-trained crew. The King's eyes glinted as he continued, "He shall go with you. But I do not expect him to return."

"Sire?"

"You are no fool," King Markel snapped. "I have spoken plainly enough. If he returns, you'd best not." He waved them away with a dismissive gesture.

#

"Well," Ford said as they left the royal receiving room, "that was unexpected!"

"Captain!" a woman's voice called from the far end of the hallway. Ford turned even as the first minister standing beside him tensed. It was Queen Arivik, dressed in orange silk with a white coral crown, almost identical to the crowns King Markel and Prince Nestor wore. "Your Highness?" Ford said, turning toward her. The queen bustled up to them quickly and looked them up and down with a frown.

"To what do we owe this honor?" first minister Mannevy said in a fawning voice.

"You!" the queen snapped at him with a jerk of her chin. "You are to blame for all this!"

"What, your majesty?" Mannevy asked, looking very much like a whipped dog.

"You told me that this airship would convince Markel to accept Nestor!" the queen hissed. She glanced to Ford. "You told me that this man was amenable! That he would listen to reason!"

Ford shot Mannevy a hard look and the first minister winced.

"Your majesty, the planned worked," Mannevy said. "Everyone agrees that the prince shot down the wyvern —"

"He killed a girl!" Arivik cried in disgust. "And now what?" she jerked her head to the royal chambers. "What did he say?"

"His Majesty has determined that Prince Nestor shall increase his glory," the first minister said. "Captain Sir Ford has agreed to journey under the Prince's command." Ford did his best not to wince at this phrasing. "They shall journey to the north, destroy this wyvern and return covered in triumph."

Arivik's nostrils flared and her eyes flashed in fury. "He said that?" she looked to Ford. "And you agreed?"

"His Majesty was kind enough to agree to my terms," Ford told her.

"I hope you set a high price," the queen said.

"It was a fair bargain," Mannevy said.

"You would know," the queen told him sourly. She glanced back to Ford. "Very well," she said. "You and the King have terms. Hear mine."

"Your Majesty?"

"My son goes with you to glory," the queen said. "And he comes back in glory."

"There will be glory enough for all, I'm sure," Mannevy murmured silkily. The queen dismissed his words with a flick of her eyelashes.

"Come back with my son, Captain," the queen said, "or don't come back at all."

#

"There you are, captain, twelve men, all able and sober," Sykes said as he arrayed the prisoners on deck. The prisoners were chained together in leggings, their arms bound with shackles.

They looked no better in the sunlight than they had in their dank cells the day before. Nor did they smell any better, Ford noted as the wind changed to bring their stench in his direction.

"Lieutenant Knox!" Ford called. "Mr. Newman, Mr. Reedis, if you will!"

The three men so named came to stand beside him. Knox looked resplendent in his new officer's clothing and his face was fit to burst with the grin on it. In fact, the former boatswain had found it nearly impossible to keep his face straight ever since Ford had surprised him with the promotion.

"It's the least I could do," Ford had said to the newly-minted officer.

"I never thought —! Sir, it's the greatest treasure —" here Knox ran his fingers down the dark stripe on his new trousers which marked him as an officer "— I cannot begin to thank you —"

"It won't be easy," Ford had cut across him. "I'm not giving you a simple job, you know."

"Oh, I know, sir! I know!" Knox had assured him. Then his face broke out into a grin. "But I never expected —! Never hoped —!"

"Indeed," Ford had said, suddenly finding himself at a loss for words. "You'd best go tell your wife, I'll need you back here first thing in the morning." Knox brought himself to attention and saluted sharply. Ford returned it with a grin of his own. "Oh! And see the agent at the dock."

"Sir?"

"He'll give you your pay," Ford told him with a grin. Knox's eyes went up in astonishment. "From the King. For the past fortnight as mate and the next month as lieutenant."

Knox's eyes threatened to pop out of his face, he was so amazed. Ford had waved him away with a grin. "First light, Knox! At the goal!"

"Aye, sir!" And then the former boatswain was gone.

Newman and Reedis had been not quite as overwhelmed by their appointments but they'd been grateful and excited all the same.

And now all three officers stood by while Ford eyed the men before them. The worst dozen of the collected scum of the kingdom.

His new crew.

Ford took a deep breath, regretted it for the stench, and called in a loud voice, "You men! You are here at the King's pleasure!"

The twelve looked back at him with an array of expressions: disbelief, hope, incomprehension, and outright fear. Sykes grinned evilly at them until Ford added in a lower voice, "You too, Sykes."

"Captain?"

"You're part of the crew," Ford told him. He patted his pocket and the royal orders it contained. He pulled them out, selected a particular sheet and started to read, "By order of His Most Excellent Majesty, King Markel, I do hereby accept you into the crew of the royal airship Spite. From this moment forth, your care, your health, your lives are bound to this ship until the end of our voyage." He paused for a moment to let the shock wear off. "At the completion of this voyage all past crimes will be pardoned and you will be free men." Some of the prisoners looked at him in surprise. "You will receive pay equal to your work as well as a daily allowance of food and such clothing as you need." Ford had had to fight hard with Mannevy over that last — they were going to the cold north, there was no way these men would survive in the rags they currently wore.

"In three days time we will receive Prince Nestor aboard and shall depart in pursuit of an albino woman formerly known as Krea Zabala and the wyvern to which she is bound," Ford continued. "By the King's commission we are required to return with her body. Dead or alive."

A murmur now from the prisoners as they began to understand the dangers of the journey,. Before they could burst out in protest, Ford continued, "By order of the King, each man, upon our return, who aids in the King's justice will receive a bounty — in addition to regular pay — of two guineas."

"Two guineas!" Sykes burst out. The prisoners were now all looking at Ford, wide-eyed and amazed.

"Two guineas each man," Ford said. "To receive this bonus, each man must obey all orders and be in good standing with the captain and his officers." Some of the crew looked confused, so Ford rephrased himself, "The money will be paid to those who work, not those who shirk."

"Let's hear it for the Captain!" Knox shouted out. "Hip hip hooray!"

He was joined by only four of the prisoners and Jenkins, the other guard. Ford glared at Sykes who glanced to the ground and then up to prisoners. "Let's try that again, shall we?" Sykes said, raising his whip to their eyes. He paused a moment, then bellowed, "Let's hear it for the Captain!"

"Hip hip hooray!" the air shivered with their cheers.

"See?" Knox said, nudging Ford in the ribs, "they just need a bit of encouragement!"

Captain Sir Richard Ford nodded feebly, suppressing an anguished groan.

It would not do to dampen their spirits.

Chapter Three: First Flight

"All hands, all hands!" Knox shouted the length of the ship two days later. "Prepare to lift ship!"

"Are we ready, Mr. Reedis?" Captain Ford asked the purple-robed mage as they strode along the rear of the deck.

"I am," Reedis said, pointing to another man. "I don't know about him."

'Him' was the replacement for Mr. Newman, the master of the steam engine that powered the ship.

"Mr. Newman assures me that his apprentice is up to the task," Ford said calmly.

Reedis shot him a look. "If he's so sure, why isn't he here with us?"

Ford suppressed a sigh. "As you know, he's ill."

"Sick of not being paid," Knox muttered with a sour look.

Ford suspected that the mechanic's 'illness' was not money-related but he was also rather certain that it had nothing to do with his health.

"Either way, Mr. Bennet is now our engineer and we will shortly see how well he performs, won't we?"

"May the gods have mercy upon us all," Reedis muttered. Ford turned to the middle of the ship where the stokers — ex-convicts all — and the nervous young apprentice were gathered.

"Mr. Bennet! Is the engine ready?" Ford called.

"Aye sir, ready when you are!" the young Mr. Bennet called back. He had brown hair that had begun to thin far earlier than most.

"Very well," Ford said. "Mr. Reedis, you may begin the spell." He turned to Knox and nodded.

Knox gave him a momentary look of confusion, then knuckled his forehead in a salute and bellowed, "All hands, single up all lines!"

"Single up, aye, sir!" Sykes called back from amidships. A moment later he added, "All lines singled!"

Skyes would have been considered attractive, if he wasn't so covered in dirt and the stench of the jail. His hair was blonde and his face was pock'marked.

"I can't believe I'm going say this," Mr. Knox muttered sourly to himself before bellowing back, "Very good, Mr. Sykes!"

"Start lifting," Ford called to Reedis who had walked forward to be directly under the ten different colored lifting balloons.

"Lifting, aye!" Reedis called back. He spread his arms under the balloons, closed his eyes, and began chanting his spell.

"Mr. Bennet!" Ford called. "Be ready to deploy the booms!"

"Yes, sir!"

"Mr. Knox?" Ford said.

"Let go the fore line!" Knox called. "Prepare to release the stern line!"

"Fore line released!" an airman called back.

"Ready aye!" called an airman from the rear line. Knox glanced at their forward elevation, glanced over to Ford, and called, "Release the stern line!"

"Stern line, aye!"

Slowly the ship rose into the air.

"Deploy the booms!" Knox called. "Prepare to engage propellers!"

"Boomsmen, to your stations!" Bennet called.

Knox and Ford exchanged winces. The boomsmen should already have been sent to their stations.

"Stations, aye!" the lead boomsman called back.

"Deploy the booms!" Bennet called.

The two large booms at the end of the ship were lowered from their upright position to the sides of the ship.

"Ready propellers," Bennet called. "Prepare to engage!"

"Wait!" Ford called hurriedly. They had not cleared the tops of the buildings.

"Engage!" Bennet ordered.

"Belay that!" Ford shouted, running toward the lead boomsman. He quickly saw that the boomsman hadn't relayed the engineer's order. "Mr. Bennet," Ford called in a lower voice, "please await my order."

The young engineer turned bright red and couldn't speak for his embarrassment. Finally, in a small voice he said, "Aye, sir."

Ford glanced toward the skyline and then toward Knox. A moment later he called, "Someone see to the mage!"

Reedis was kneeling on the deck, clearly exhausted from his efforts.

"Have the cook bring up a cup of tea immediately!" Ford ordered. He turned back to the stern and shouted, "Mr. Bennet! Engage the propellers!"

The four blades of each propeller fanned out from their respective booms, locked in place in large crosses and slowly began to turn.

Presently Spite was moving forward into the crisp morning air.

Ford glanced above and shouted, "Jenkins, how fares the day?"

Jenkins, in his place at the top of the foremost upper balloon shouted back down. "The air is cold and threatens snow, sir! The clouds are scattered and broken!"

"Good man!" Ford called back to the ex-guard. "Keep a sharp eye out!"

"Aye sir!"

Knox came toward him and saluted. "What course, captain?"

Ford gestured to the shore line. "To the sea."

"Sir?"

"We've some mutineers to catch," Ford told him.

Knox looked surprised for a moment then grinned viciously. "Aye, sir!" He raised his voice to the helmsman, "Helmsman, come about, we're heading to the sea!" He raised his voice to the balloons above and shouted, "Jenkins, we're heading to sea! Call out any sail in sight!"

"Aye sir," Jenkins called back.

Ford waited until Spite was firmly on its new course, steaming steadily, before turning his first mate. "I'm going below," he told him. "When Mr. Reedis is ready, have him join me." Formally, he added, "You have the con."

"Aye, sir," Knox said with a broad grin. To the ship he shouted, "First watch below! Mr. Knox has the con!"

Ford smiled in response to the former boatswain's evident delight, nodded once, and went down the hatchway to his cabin in the stern. They were once again in the air and, aside from a few mistakes by the young engineer, all was well.

#

"What I want to know, sir, is where that mechanical man of yours disappeared himself to," Reedis said as he sipped gratefully on his cup of warm tea.

"Yes, he did a rather good job of disappearing from the king's jail, didn't he?" Ford agreed.

Reedis narrowed his eyes at him. "You don't seem disturbed by it."

"I'm not sure what we could have done with him," the captain replied with a shrug, "after all he must weigh several hundredweight."

"I could have lifted him," Reedis sniffed with wounded pride. "After all, I can raise your ship!"

"Indeed," Ford said mildly. "In fact, I'm sure that he would not have plunged through the decks as I've had him aboard this ship before."

"Have you?" Reedis said, his brows rising. "You mentioned rescuing him from corsairs once…"

"I did," Ford agreed. When Reedis implored him with an uplifted hand, the captain shook his head. Reedis gave him a crestfallen look. Ford laughed. "Have you not thought, my good mage, that a large metal man is rather hard to hide?"

"A metal man…?" Reedis tried the words on his lips and then, irritatedly, shook his head. "You can't follow him with a compass!"

"Nothing quite so distractible," Ford agreed. "But I have my ways."

"Your ways?" Reedis repeated. He spent a moment recalling Ford's past ways and then his expression brightened. "You set the little street urchin on him?"

"Her name's Ellen, by the way," Ford said, nodding. "And she told me quite the tale of a pair of large boot prints appearing outside the king's jail with no sign of their maker."

"He used an invisibility spell!" Reedis' brows furrowed as he added, "But why didn't he disguise —"

"It was snowing," Ford said. "Perhaps he forgot about that."

"Or he wanted only smart people to find him," Reedis said thoughtfully.

Captain Ford rewarded him with a smile and a dip of his head.

"Did you find him, then?" Reedis demanded.

"Did you have a good meeting with the King?" Ford asked. At Reedis' blank look, he expanded, "While I was closeted with first minister Manneyy."

"It was quite odd, really," Reedis said. "He wanted to know all about the balloons and my magic. I got the impression he was hoping that they could be deflated or something." He paused for a moment, then added worriedly, "And there was a page with him, listening the whole time. Listening quite intently."

Captain Ford took a moment to digest this news.

"When we return, before we set out north, we're to take on the prince," Captain Ford said. He paused, taking another sip of tea, before saying, "The Queen was most adamant that he return unharmed."

"Understandably, she is quite fond of him," Reedis allowed.

"The King had similar words on the topic."

"Did he?" Reedis inquired with a gleam of his eyes. "And his intent…?"

"Exactly the opposite of the Queen's," Ford said grimly. He saw the way Reedis reacted to the news and allowed himself a slight grin. "Which got me to wondering if the King had as much affection for us as he conveyed with his words?"

"Kill us all?" Reedis asked in a whisper. Ford nodded silently. Reedis' eyes flared in anger. "But he can't! He'd have to have —"

"Help?" Ford finished for him quietly. After a moment, he said, "Did you have any luck with that life-balloon idea of mine?"

"I haven't had time to work on it," Reedis replied brittlely.

"Perhaps you should invest some effort," Ford said.

"I shall, rest assured, I shall," Reedis promised, finishing his tea. "In fact, if you don't need me, I think I'll get to work on it immediately."

Captain Ford rose from his seat, smiling. "I think that's a most excellent notion, Sir Reedis!"

Chapter Four: Action Overhead

"Two sail, dead ahead!" the lookout — neither Marden nor Senten of the original crew — called from his perch on the bowsprit.

"How far?" Lieutenant Knox called.

"A league, maybe less," the lookout allowed.

"Sir Reedis," Captain Ford called from his position by the helm, "you may start our descent!"

"Aye, sir!" Reedis called back, moving to stand amidships, directly below the center of the ten balloons that magically lifted Spite into the air.

"Mr. Bennet, bring us to two-thirds power!" Captain Ford called to the engineer apprentice. He turned to Knox. "Have the port guns manned, loaded and run out, if you please."

"Man the guns port side!" Knox bellowed. His order was followed by the patter of feet as men ran to their stations. "Cook! More rum for the stokers!"

"Only a half-tot," Ford corrected mildly. "We'll give them more when they earn it."

"A half-tot only!" Knox called in agreement. In a lower voice, he said to Ford, "Hadn't considered that."

Ford dismissed that with a wave of his hand. "I'm going forward."

"What's our purpose, captain?" Knox asked before Ford walked too far. Ford turned back and smiled at him.

"You remember our mutineers?"

Knox nodded, spitting angrily on the deck.

"I know where five of them are," Ford said. He gestured below them. "Mr. Newman told us — they're on Warrior."

"He did, didn't he?" Knox said, his expression growing cheerful.

"And you know what they say about mutineers from a king's ship," Ford said.

Knox cocked his head in question.

"Any ship harboring a mutineer is a prize," Ford said.

"It is indeed!" Knox said, his expression growing into a huge smile. Then he frowned. "But that's Warrior, sir! She mounts twelve pounders, we've only got a poor broadside of six pounders!"

"Ah," Ford said, tapping the side of his nose in the universal sign of a man with a secret, "but those guns don't shoot up!"

Knox nodded and chuckled, throwing a congratulatory salute to his captain.

Ford returned it with a grin of his own and turned back to his task. He strode quickly down the deck, clapped Reedis on the back in acknowledgement of his exertions, then nodded to the gun crews who had formed up and were steadily loading and priming their weapons.

"Can you make them out?" Ford called as he started easily down the bowsprit toward the lookout. He turned his head over his shoulder to shout, "And another man on the lookout!"

"Aye sir!" Knox's voice came back the length of the ship.

"There they are, sir," the grizzled old airman said. Ford smiled at him. He knew this man from of old. His name was Quirrel. He was nearing the end of his life as a seaman — airman, Ford corrected himself. He was one of the men Ford had taken from jail. Apparently he'd been trying to drink himself to death but one of his in-laws wanted to speed up the process and there'd been an altercation involving a knife and stitches, and a drunken party of contrition ending with the surprise of waking up in jail. "That's the Warrior nearest us. The other one, don' know but I figure her for some Sorian merchantman." He creased his brow. "Are we at war with them, sir?" A moment later he added, "Because it looks like Warrior is flying the King's marque, sir!"

"If not now, we soon will be," Ford predicted, watching the flash of smoke rise from Warrior's side as she fired a full broadside. He glanced down again, measuring the distances, then asked, "How do you feel about prize money?"

Quirrel smiled, showing his three remaining teeth. "I'd like that a lot, sir. I'd like it a lot!"

"Then let us take some prizes, airman Quirrel!" Ford clapped the man on the back, noted how bony Quirrel was, and started down the bowsprit.

"Mr. Knox!" he called as he strode down the length of the ship. "What do you say to two prizes?"

"Sir?" Knox repeated in surprise before adding enthusiastically, "I'd say that's a good start, sir!"

"All hands, prepare for action!" Ford bellowed.

"All hands on deck!" Knox roared in agreement. "We're going to take prizes!"

The crew roared in approval and moved to their stations with gusto.

#

Captain Nevins smiled to himself as the smoke from his broadside billowed back and he saw the damage to the merchantman's sails. Good, he thought. He'd ordered his crew to fire for the rigging; he didn't want to hull the ship. Makes it harder to tow back.

The Sorian ship staggered as its rigging fell and it lost way.

"Prepare to board!" Nevins shouted. He glanced to Jens and his crew. "You know what to do."

"Aye sir!" Jens, formerly lieutenant Jens, replied with a bob of his head. Jens' head was shaved and his skin weathered from the sun. He wore a gold earring in each of his ears. "Their captain and officers —" he made a throat-slitting gesture with one hand. "Marder! Senten! To me!"

The named crew, also formerly of His Majesty's Airship Spite, along with the two other deserters, rushed to his side.

"Bring up the helm!" Nevins barked. "Prepare to board!"

A shout went up from the crew. Nevins smiled to himself. It was going to be a good day!

A sudden roar from above startled him. Warrior shuddered and staggered as shots hit home. Nevins turned toward the sound, eyes wide with fright and fury. What the hell —?

"Ahoy, Warrior!" a voice called down the from the sky that was shrouded in smoke. "Prepare to strike all sail and surrender!"

Nevins grabbed a speaking horn and bellowed back, "Strike! I'll see you in hell first, sir!"

"Doubtless so," the voice above returned smoothly, "but if you want to avoid the Ferryman today, you'd best strike!"

"By whose orders?" Nevins shouted back, trembling with fury. "I carry the King's mark!"

"By my orders, as a captain of the King's Navy, you cur!" the voice roared back. "Strike now or feed the fishes. Your choice, Captain Nevins!"

Nevins recognized that voice. "Ford? You bastard, you fired on my ship!"

"I'm going to take your ship and the mutineers you have aboard her," Ford told him calmly.

Spite floated out of the sky, still well above Warrior's guns, her cannon run out and manned by grinning seamen. Well, Nevins thought grimly, not seamen.

"And what of my prize?" Nevins bellowed back.

"My prize, you mean?" Ford called back spitefully. "Why, I'll thank you to restrain yourself from further damaging it, if you will." His voice grew harder as he said, "Now strike your flag!"

Nevins looked up at the ship that he'd never seen until it had fired on him. It took him a moment to realize why he hadn't spotted it — it had sailed against the wind! No wonder he hadn't been looking for it!

That enough to convince him. "Strike the flag!" he shouted to his first officer. He pointed his sword to his coxswain. "Arrest those five and hold him for Captain Ford's pleasure."

"And the prize, sir?" first officer Smythe said.

"They're to surrender to Spite," Nevins said bitterly.

"Sir!" Smythe protested.

"Our foremast is gone, we can't fire up to hit him and he can fire down right into our hull," Nevins said sourly. "What do you propose to do, drown?"

"Sir, we can fight when they board," Jens cried from his position surrounded by hostile crew.

"They'll haul off and pound us into kindling," Nevins said, shaking his head. He turned to Smythe. "There'll be other days."

"Sir," Smythe agreed with a sigh. He turned to the crew. "Prepare to be boarded!"

"No need!" Ford called down from above affably. "Just make repairs, and turn about for Kingsford."

"Kingsford!" Nevins called. "Are we to be herded back to port like a dog with our tail between our legs?"

"Yes," Ford agreed heartily, "except you'll be flying my flag as prize."

Nevins grit his teeth. "Very well," he growled.

"And I'm going to lower a line in a moment," Ford said.

"A line?" Nevins called back. "You mean to take us in tow?"

"No," Ford replied, "I mean for you to send me up Jens and my four mutineers."

Nevins heard a struggle from amidships as Jens and the four former Spite airmen fought to break free. He smiled to himself as he heard the hard crack! As the coxswain brought a belaying-pin down on their heads, knocking them unconscious.

"It will be a pleasure!" Nevins called back, smiling to himself. *I didn't like them, anyway.*

Chapter Five: Prize Money

"Sire, sire!" a page called as he rushed excitedly into the royal throne room. "Spite has returned!"

"As well it should," King Markel replied evenly. He frowned, his face clouding. "I see no reason for the interruption."

"She brought prizes!"

"Prizes?" King Markel repeated rising from his chair in surprise. "What ships and how many?"

"There's a Sorian merchantman and a frigate," the page replied. "I was sent by the watch commander as soon as it was reported by the signal towers, sire."

"You were, were you?" the King muttered. The page, wide-eyed and attentive, nodded. The king glanced toward Mannevy. "Have someone send for Captain Ford."

"It shall be done," Mannevy promised with a low bow.

The King looked around the room, frowned and beckoned to another page. "Tirpin, I shall want some lunch," he announced. "You may have it brought here."

#

"March the prisoners to the jail, Sykes," Ford said as the gantry was raised to the ship, "I'm sure you know the way."

"Aye sir!' Sykes replied, knuckling his forehead and smiling to himself.

"Captain Nevins and Master Parvour will accompany me, I think," Ford said. He turned to Knox. "Secure the ship, reload our supplies." He pursed his lips. "Give the men a tot of rum and see about getting fresh food onboard."

"Aye sir," Knox allowed.

"And me, sir?" Reedis asked.

"See if you can help Mr. Bennet with his... problems," Ford said with a sigh. The apprentice appeared much worn by his exertions and went red with shame at the captain's words. Ford glanced to him and started to say something reassuring but couldn't find any words. To Reedis he said, "Perhaps our murderous apprentice might be of use."

"Angus?" Reedis replied in surprise. He glanced toward the younger man and nodded. "He was a smith, I suppose we could do worse."

"It's worth a try, at least," Ford allowed. He finally found something to say to the apprentice engineer. "It's not that you haven't tried, Mr. Bennet. It's just that... well, perhaps an airship isn't the best position for you."

"Sir," Bennet responded feebly.

The lad had done his best but once the ship had fired her guns, he'd run for the depths of the ship's hold and had to be coaxed out by his anguished and ashamed stokers, led by a very angry self-appointed Sykes who'd muttered loudly, "Ain't no coward going to lose me my prize money!"

After that, Christian could only whimper and moan. There was a chance that Reedis or Reedis and the smith's apprentice, might calm the lad but Ford doubted it.

With a shake of his head, Captain Sir Ford parted his ship.

"Your Majesty," Captain Ford said, crouched in a low courtly bow, "I wish to present you the captains of the prizes Warrior and Parvour." He rose and turned to the two captives. "Your Majesty, I have the honor of introducing you to captains Nevin and Martel. Gentlemen, may I make you known to His Most Noble Majesty, King Markel?"

"Mannevy?" King Markel said, glancing imploringly to his first minister.

"Captain Ford was, with your permission, in search of his mutineers, your majesty," Mannevy explained. "He found them aboard Warrior just as she was engaging the Sorian merchantman under your letter of marque."

"So I took them both," Ford added suavely. "Warrior as she was clearly harboring fugitives of your majesty's justice and Parvour as she was a ship of our enemy."

"I haven't declared war on them, captain!" King Markel replied wearily.

"Your Majesty, if that were so, Captain Nevins wouldn't be operating under your letter of marque," Ford replied. "Instead, he'd be a pirate."

"I'm no damn pirate!" Nevin bellowed. He glanced toward the King and wilted when he saw the royal expression.

"No," Markel replied with a sigh, "you're not." His eyes flicked to Ford. "You are correct, we are at war with Soria." He sighed. "Although I had not planned to announce it widely just at this moment."

"Your Majesty," Ford said, bowing deeply in penance.

The King snorted and gestured for Ford to rise. "However, Sir Richard, you've ably proven that your airship can easily take two ships simultaneously." He glanced toward Mannevy. "Award him his prize."

"Your majesty," Mannevy replied suavely.

"Leave the prisoners here, if you would," the King said waving Mannevy and Ford out of the room. As Ford crossed the doorway into the hall beyond, the king called after him, "I presume, Sir Richard, that you are in all respects ready for your next mission?"

Ford turned back and bowed deeply. "As your Majesty commands."

"To the north, then, captain and remember my words earlier," the king said with a final dismissive wave.

Chapter Six: Payment Made

When the double doors shut once more, King Markel turned to the two captains.

"Sire, it was my fault," Captain Martel said with a low bow. "I saw the letter of marque and assumed the worst."

"Jacques," the King said with a wave of his hand. "I understand. I am sorry that you did not trust me at my word, however."

"The letter of marque was a ruse if we were spotted from land," Captain Nevins explained. "Only that… bastard Ford screwed it all up!"

"Indeed," the king agreed sourly. "However," his expression changed, "he has demonstrated rather remarkably the efficiency of my royal airships."

"There's only the one, your majesty," Nevins observed in a tight voice.

"For now," the king agreed with a wag of his finger. A moment later, he added, "I fear that Captain Ford won't be returning from his trip north." He watched Nevins as his expression changed from sour to smiling. "And you are right, Captain Nevins, I will need more airships."

"Your Majesty," Nevins said, catching on immediately and going to one knee in a bow. "I am yours to command."

Beside him Captain Martel also went to one knee. "As am I, Your Majesty."

King Markel rewarded the both of them with a broad smile.

#

"There!" Mannevy said crisply, "Now that we've agreed on the prizes and their cargo, when can you leave?"

Ford gave him a sharp look up from the large bags of gold on the table in front of him.

"I'll need stores," Ford said.

"Done."

"And I'll need winter gear," Ford added.

"Winter?" Mannevy's brows furrowed.

"It's cold in the air," Ford said. "And we're going north."

"Oh! Yes, quite," Mannevy said. He pursed his lips. "Winter gear?"

"Fortunately, Parvour was well-equipped with such," Ford said. "There's enough to fit out my crew." He paused. "The prince, however, might not take to the quality of the clothing."

"The prince's needs will be met by the King," Mannevy said. He rose from his plush chair. "So, captain, when can you leave?"

"Tomorrow at the earliest," Ford said. "We're getting more stores aboard and we want to be sure we've got the bunkers full of coal."

"Of course," Mannevy said cheerfully, "there's no problem with that. Wouldn't want your magic to run out mid-flight, would we?"

"The boilers, you mean," Ford corrected. Mannevy waved a hand, dismissing the distinction as pointless.

"So we'll have the prince prepare for a royal departure tomorrow at noon," Mannevy said. He gestured to the heavy bags of gold. "Where do you want these?"

"I'll bring them with me," Ford allowed. "I know a place to store them."

"We could store them here in the royal vault," Mannevy offered. "Well-protected, of course, and we would insure you against any loss."

"I'll take my chances," Ford said, lifting the heavy bags that he'd tied together and throwing them over his shoulder. "Besides, I'll want to pay the crew."

"And the mutineers?"

"I'll pay them, too," Ford said, nodding curtly to the first minister. His lips twitched as he added, "You can be sure that I'll pay them all that they earned."

Mannevy's brows twitched in understanding. "I'm certain you will, captain!"

#

"Very well, Angus, let us see what you know," Mage Reedis said to the nervous looking young apprentice as they moved to the boiler and the steam engine.

"I watched him pretty carefully," Angus said. Reedis and Ford had singled him out as the most promising candidate to take over the apprentice engineer's position if anything untoward accord — as it had. They'd asked Angus if he thought he could manage and he'd given them a diffident smile and suggested that he spend time observing the apprentice. Reedis was pretty certain that Angus would have been observing even without orders. Now, he gave the mage a wry smile. "I've always had a thing for coal and fire, from when I was little."

"Indeed," Reedis said. "So show us you know how to work this engine, if you please."

Angus frowned for a moment, then glanced to the now-cold boilers. "First thing, you've got to make sure that you've got enough water in the boiler —"

"And if you don't?"

"Well, no steam, that's for certain," Angus said. His brows furrowed. "And I can't imagine it'd do the metal much good to be heated without something inside."

"So the boiler's got water," Reedis allowed. "And then?"

"The stokers start the fire," Angus said, gesturing to the loose coal in a bucket beside the boiler.

"And how do they do that?"

"Well, if they're smart, they ask you," Angus said. "But if your busy they can see if the cook has coals or they can use the oil and a spark to start it themselves."

"So they've got the fire started?"

"They'll need to fan it with the bellows," Angus said, pointing. "Bring it as hot as possible so that the steam gets to the engine."

"And in the engine…?"

"The engine pushes a piston back and forth which turns the sails," Angus said.

"You mean the propellers?"

"If that's what they're called," Angus allowed. The sound of hooves distracted him and they both turned to see Captain Ford gallop up beside the ship, dismount and retrieve two heavily-laden saddlebags.

"All right, Captain?" Knox called from the stern.

"Couldn't be better, Mr. Knox," the captain replied with a huge grin. "How stands the ship?"

"We're ready in all respects, Sir," Knox called back cheerfully, then turned to Angus and Reedis. "Excepting we need a new engineer seeing as how the last one's bolted."

Ford paused on his way up the gangplank and then pressed on.

"Mr. Reedis?" Ford called. He moved to join them. He glanced at Angus. "And how does he fare?"

"He can do the job, captain," Reedis said. Angus gave him a startled look. "We all know he doesn't get sick at heights and he knows his stuff."

Ford nodded and turned his attention to the apprentice smith. "Are you up for this, lad?"

Angus brought himself upright and gave Ford a smart salute. "Ready, captain."

Ford's eyebrows shot up and he gave Reedis one more inquiring look. Reedis met his eyes and nodded.

"We're going to be putting our lives in your hands," Ford told the apprentice in a low voice.

"You're safe with me, captain," Angus promised.

Ford gave him one more look, then nodded in approval. He turned to Knox, "Have the master-at-arms mustered and place these in the safe."

"Sir?"

"Our prize money, Mr. Knox," Ford said. He glanced about. "Who's our master-at-arms?"

"That'd be Sykes or Jenkins, sir," Knox said after a moment's thought.

"Sykes, then," Ford said with a sour look. He turned to Reedis. "What do you know of locks and magic?"

"Sir, I know something about them," Angus spoke up hesitantly.

"And how do you know about them?" Ford asked in a voice that was suspiciously pleasant.

"Ibb, sir," Angus said. "Before he got me set with Master Zebala, he took me in for a bit."

"He did, did he?" Ford said.

Angus nodded. "And he taught me a fair bit about locks."

"Opening them or securing them?" Ford asked with a stern look.

Angus reddened. "Both sir. You can't know one without the other."

Ford pursed his lips. "I see," he said. "And did you learn how to make a lock unbreakable?"

Angus shook his head. "Mr. Ibb never taught me such a thing. And I don't that it can be done."

"It can't," Reedis agreed. "But it can be made very hard."

"Could you add some magic to it?"

"I could but then I'd be the only one able to open the lock," Reedis warned.

Footsteps distracted them as Sykes and Jenkins ran up. "You sent for me, sir?" Sykes asked before Jenkins could draw breath. He glanced at the heavy saddlebags. "Something needing guarding?"

"Only for the moment," Ford said, tossing the sacks so that they landed evenly between Jenkins and Sykes. "Mr. Knox will escort you to the armory and the safe. This is our prize money."

"You've no worries with us," Sykes promised. "We'll keep it safe, sir."

Ford nodded to Knox who led them off. When they were out of earshot he said, "Ah, but from whom?"

"If you wanted it safe, sir, I would have recommended Mr. Ibb," Angus spoke up. Ford turned to him. "He knows ways to keep things safe."

"I've no doubt he does," Ford agreed. "But as he has disappeared from under the eyes of his guards, I doubt we'll be able to call upon his services for the foreseeable future."

Angus said nothing but shook his head. Ford noticed the lad's unsurprised reaction and guessed that Angus had learned quite a bit from the now-missing mechanical man.

Ford jerked his head toward the hatchway. "Go after them, then and see what you can do."

Angus drew himself up and saluted again before darting back to the hatchway and down into the gloom of the ship.

"Mr. Ibb seems to get around," Reedis said to Ford as the lad went out of earshot.

Ford gave him a sharp look. "You noticed that, did you?" He shook his head. "I suspect we'll be seeing our mechanical friend again soon." Then he asked, "And your project, mage, has does that prosper?"

"I've got three of them," Reedis said. He pulled a small belt from around his waist and passed it to Ford. Ford took it in surprise and noticed that Reedis wore a purple belt around his waist. "You put it on."

Ford obliged him and gave him a look. "And then?"

"I've set it so the spell takes just one word to cast," Reedis told him with a wink.

"And the word?"

"Can you read?" Reedis asked, reaching into a pocket in his robes. Ford nodded. Reedis passed him a piece of paper. "Read it but don't say it."

"Can I spell it out?"

"Yes," Reedis said. "You must say it to cast the spell."

"A-L-T-U," Ford read carefully. He glanced up from the paper to Reedis. "And that's it?"

"Hopefully," the mage replied.

"Hopefully?"

"Well," Reedis said with a shrug, "I haven't had time to test it, you see."

Ford gave the belt around his waist a long look, then shook his head. "Let's hope we don't have to use them, then."

"I, for one, shall endeavor stoutly to that end," Reedis agreed.

Ford turned to Knox, eyeing the former boatswain thoughtfully.

"Send the hands to dinner, sir?" Knox suggested.

"Indeed," Ford agreed. He looked to Reedis. "Care to dine with me?"

"I shall be honored," Reedis said with a nod.

"Have our dinner brought to my quarters," Ford said.

"Aye sir," Knox replied, knuckling his forehead. He turned to the ship at large and bellowed, "First watch to dinner! Second watch take stations."

#

"By the gods that smells good!" Reedis exclaimed as an airman bustled in with a tray of food, a bottle of wine dangling from a strap at his side.

"Put it there, put it there," Ford said, pointing to the captain's table. The airman obliged, setting the two plates at either chair and pouring two large glasses of red wine. "That'll do, I'll call when I want it taken away."

The airman saluted and left quickly.

"Must be the cook's mate," Reedis said, seating himself with relish at his place. He leaned in and sniffed his plate. "Captain Ford, sir, I believe you've been deceiving us!"

"What?" Ford asked, laying his napkin in his lap and reaching for his fork and knife.

"I don't recall smelling anything so tempting on our maiden flight," Reedis said before filling his mouth with the mound of food on his fork. "Mmm! It tastes as good as it smells!"

It was gruel, which was a usual dish on any sort of ship. But instead of just wheat or oat flour, this dish also featured spices, and bits of fish, corn, and peas.

Ford eyed the meal suspiciously, raised a small bite to his face and sniffed. His expression changed to one of alarm and he dropped his fork, reached across the table and swiped Reedis' fork out of his hand.

"What?"

"It's charmed, don't eat it!" Ford warned, rising from his seat and grabbing his sword. He raced through the door, muttering, "That witch!"

"What witch?"

"Get ready to freeze someone," Ford said. "And follow me."

Ford led Reedis quickly through the passageway and into the galley. "Everyone out!" he bellowed. "All of you! Out of here, now!"

When the airmen were slow to move, Ford waved his sword at them. "Out of here, NOW!" The cook moved to dart past him but stopped when the point of Ford's sword swung back. Ford looked over his shoulder to ensure that the rest of the airmen had left.

"Knox will be down here soon, no doubt," Ford warned Reedis. He turned to the cook. "I don't have a place for murderers on my ship."

The cook laughed. "You don't? Then what are you going to do with your crew?"

Footsteps came down the hatchway rapidly, followed by Knox's voice. "Captain, what is it?"

"Come here, Knox, and smell the gruel," Ford said, keeping his sword at the cook's throat.

Knox, frowning at his captain, moved to the pot and sniffed. "By the gods!" he swore, turning with a venomous look to the cook. "I thought we'd seen the last of you!" He drew his dirk and stood beside the captain. "Do you want me to kill her, sir?"

"See? Murderers," the cook murmured.

"Her?" Reedis repeated in surprise. "Mr. Knox, the cook is a man!"

"Only when you eat her food," Ford said with a growl. "When you eat her food, she has control of you and you see what she wants."

"You're saying that she's a witch?"

"And a damned good cook, more's the pity," Knox growled. "The crew eat what she's serving and then we're all damned." Knox spat on the deck. "The last time we saw her, we lost all our prize money."

"You didn't lose it," the cook said.

"We gave it to you," Ford said. "You bewitched us."

"But you've done well enough since, haven't you?" the cook asked.

"And we'll do better without you on this ship," Knox said.

"You'll die without me on this ship," the cook replied. "You said it yourself — murderers. How long will you last before your crew mutinies and slits your throats?"

"How long will we last with you, Annabelle?" Ford said.

"Annabelle?" Reedis repeated, glancing at the cook. And then he gasped. "By the gods! It's a woman!"

"It's a witch," Knox said. He glanced to Ford. "And we should kill it."

"Not if you want to live," Annabelle said. She glanced to Ford. "You know what I can do."

"I do," Ford agreed.

"My word is my bond," the witch said. "You know that, too." She looked to Reedis. "Tell him."

Ford raised a hand in warning as the mage drew breath to speak. "Don't say anything, she's got you under her spell."

"Maybe, maybe not," Annabelle said. "He's a mage."

"The last time I believed you, I lost five treasure ships," Ford growled.

"But you ate well!" Annabelle said. "You have to admit that."

Ford shook his head, his sword still at her throat. "Tell me why I shouldn't kill you."

"Or turn you over to the King," Knox added. Ford gave him a slight shake of his head without taking his eyes off the cook.

Annabelle laughed. "The King!" she said, her deep voice rough with amusement.

"What?" Knox said, turning to Ford. "What's up with the King?"

"Later," Ford said. "Right now, we've got her to deal with."

"Deal with me, then," Annabelle said. "Deal with me and I'll deal true."

"Why?" Ford asked.

"You need me," she told him.

"And you need us," Ford guessed. "Who are you escaping from this time, Annabelle?"

"That's my own problem," she said.

"Not if you're on my ship," Ford told her. "You're trouble enough without inviting more."

"I'm not a tenth of your troubles," Annabelle said, eyes narrowing. "And without me, it's not just your crew you'll have to watch."

"She's annoyed the gods, sir, and you know it!" Knox said, shaking his head. "We bring her and there's no telling what we'll face."

"There's no telling anyway," Ford said.

"Trouble's brewing and you need all the friends you can find," Annabelle said in agreement.

"What proof can you give me?"

"You're alive," Annabelle said with a small smirk. "And you would have been well-fed if you hadn't caught my scent."

"You're saying that you could have drugged me so that I wouldn't notice?" Ford asked. "That's your proof of sincerity?"

"I have charms that will protect you," Annabelle offered.

"Even from you?"

"Her blood," Reedis said. Ford cocked his head toward the mage but kept his sword steady. "She gives you her blood and that binds her to you."

Annabelle looked nervous for the first time.

"Just a drop," Reedis continued, "no more."

"A drop?" Ford asked.

"Too much and she'll be bound to you unto death," Reedis said.

"What did you do with our gold?" Ford asked.

"Spent it," Annabelle said.

"On what?" Ford asked, nodding toward the torn clothes she wore. "You could have bought an army with what you stole."

"Perhaps I did," Annabelle said. "Perhaps I learned things, perhaps I lost it all."

"Witch," Knox said. "There's some that died because of that stolen gold."

"And some that lived," Annabelle said. "It's all part of the Wheel, isn't it?"

"This is getting us nowhere," Reedis said. He turned to Ford. "Captain, if it's true that she can keep the crew from murdering us in our sleep, I say we should bargain with her."

Ford's jaw hardened for a moment, then he lowered his sword. He said to Knox and Reedis, "You two, stay here." To the witch he said with a jerk of his neck, "Come with me."

#

Ford led her to his cabin. He opened the door and gestured for her to precede him. With a flip of her hair, Annabelle walked through the door. Ford followed, closing and locking it behind him.

Annabelle was taller than the average woman. Her dark curly hair was highlighted from the sun. She was zaftig — she had a full rounded figure, and her olive skin was littered with freckles. She wore high brown leather boots and a clearly hand-sewn dress of dark green and brown patchwork.

When he turned back, Annabelle threw herself on him. He dropped his sword and grabbed her, meeting her lips with his own. They kissed for a long time. When finally they broke for air, she said, "Gods! I've missed you!"

Ford's lips twitched. "I knew you'd be back."

Annabelle raised an eyebrow and cocked her head. "How?"

"The gold was cursed, of course," Ford said with a chuckle. "You had to come back."

"It had nothing to do with love, did it?" Annabelle asked. "Just cursed gold, nothing more."

Ford smiled at her and she reached for him, wrapping herself against him and begging with her eyes for another kiss. Ford leaned forward and obliged.

"You're in a right mess, you know that?" Annabelle asked as they broke apart once more.

"And you're going to save me?" Ford asked.

Annabelle shook her head and gave a low laugh. "No one could ever save you." A moment later, more seriously, she added, "Not now, certainly."

"So you valiantly decided to come to my aid," Ford teased.

"So your cursed gold forced me to come back," Annabelle replied.

"And what did you do with all that gold?"

Annabelle dropped her head and spoke in a low voice. "Some things I won't talk about, particularly with you."

"The gods love us, don't they?" Ford said, reaching over to lift her head back up to meet his eyes.

"Some gods." Annabelle agreed. She shook herself. "But now that you have made such a huge scene and convinced everyone that we hate each other, tell me why I'm in your cabin?"

"Your bargain, the parts of it that are real, I accept," Ford said.

Annabelle snorted: she had expected nothing else. "And?"

"I need three fire demons," Ford said.

"Spies?"

"Messengers," Ford said. Annabelle arched an eyebrow. "There's a girl —"

"There's always a girl!"

"— an urchin in my employ," Ford finished with a scowl. "Perhaps six years old."

"If she's in your employ, she's in danger," Annabelle said.

"But not of starving to death, now," Ford said. "She helped me find the wyvern —"

"And such great good that did you!"

"And she tracked footprints in the snow from the jail," Ford continued implacably.

"Footprints?"

"But no body," Ford agreed.

"And then?"

"And then the footprints disappeared," Ford said. He did not add that the urchin — Ellen — said that the footprints were replaced by the broad tracks of a wagon, equally invisible. The tracks went north.

"So there's trouble," Annabelle shrugged. "I told you that, already."

"Between Soria and Kingsland?" Ford asked.

Annabelle gave him an intrigued look. "This is news."

Ford's lips twitched. "So my urchin will need two messenger demons before we leave."

"And the third?"

"That's for safety," Ford said.

"For you or for her?"

Ford gave her a quelling look. Annabelle shrugged, saying, "You haven't changed, really, have you?"

"What of the crew?"

"I can handle them," Annabelle said. Ford started to speak but she raised a hand to his mouth. "You cannot be controlled by me, not after the last time."

"And you'd be a fool to try," Ford said.

"And I'd be a fool to try," Annabelle agreed. She leaned in to him again, resting her head on his shoulder, whispering, "Gods, I've missed you!"

Ford answered her with a hug and a kiss on her head. He pushed back from her, meeting her eyes. "So the only question is whether you want to continue to be seen as a man or as a woman?"

"Your crew will not harm me," Annabelle said with certainty. "Not after they taste my food."

"They probably wouldn't hurt you if you didn't put a spell on it," Ford agreed. "Your cooking is good enough by itself to ensure their loyalty."

Annabelle smiled at the compliment.

"But we won't be traveling alone," Ford said. "We're to have a very special, very important passenger."

"The prince," Annabelle said.

Ford nodded.

"He'll be protected against my spells," Annabelle warned.

"Will that be a problem?"

"It depends," Annabelle said with a grin, a slim blade suddenly sprouting from her free hand, "on how much he cherishes his manhood."

Chapter Seven: The Bitter North

"I'm going to miss you so much!" Queen Arivik sobbed as her one and only child, her precious Crown Prince, ascended the gangplank leading to the airship Spite. She spied Captain Ford moving to grab the Prince's hand and shouted, "You take good care of my son!"

"I shall do my best by King and country," Ford called back. "You may depend upon it."

"Mother always gets carried away," Crown Prince Nestor said quietly to Ford. He glanced around the ship. "Is everything ready?"

Ford nodded. "It is."

"Then, please, Sir Ford, let us depart before mother breaks down completely," Nestor said, turning to wave back to his mother, calling, "I'll be fine, mother!"

"Kill another wyvern for the kingdom!" Queen Arivik shouted back.

"Rest assured, mother!" Nestor called back. Under his breath, he said to Ford, "Please, let us leave." He waved to his mother, adding to Ford, "I think she's had a bit too much tea today."

"Tea?"

"It's not just tea, you see," Nestor confessed. "Now, please, by all the gods, let us leave!"

"As your highness wishes," Ford said, gesturing to Knox by the helm.

"All hands, all hands!" Knox called. "Prepare to raise ship."

Hands move quickly to their places and Reedis assumed his position under the balloons. Ford gestured for the prince to precede him as they walked steadily toward the stern.

"The crew seems different," Nestor remarked as he caught a scowl from one particularly repellent specimen.

"We've had some changes," Ford agreed. "I replaced Lieutenant Havenam with my boatswain, Knox."

"So I see," Nestor said, nodding toward the newly-made first lieutenant. "But wasn't your... Havenam... the one who fell to his death?"

"Hence the need for replacement," Ford said.

"What about that one, there?" Nestor asked, pointing to Jens. "Wasn't he a lieutenant?"

"He was," Ford agreed, nodding toward the surly airman. "We had a bit of a falling out, as it were."

"Whatever for?" Nestor asked just as they neared Lieutenant Knox.

"He 'fell' off the ship," Knox explained sourly.

"What? He fell, too?" Nestor asked.

"From virtue only," Knox said. The prince gave him a look of confusion, so Knox explained, "He jumped ship, your highness."

"Jumped ship?" Nestor said, glancing to Ford. "From how high?"

"My lieutenant means that Jens mutinied and signed aboard another ship," Ford said. Ford allowed himself a small smile. "We recovered him on our last flight."

"Oh!" Nestor said, eyes going wide. "The prizes you took!"

"Exactly," Ford said. "If it weren't for Jens here, we would be a lot poorer." The ex-lieutenant gave them a miserable look and returned to his duties, splicing lines.

"And yet you bring a known mutineer with you?" Nestor asked in surprise.

"We were short-handed and didn't have much choice," Knox said, "the jail left us five short."

"The jail?" Nestor exclaimed, glancing around the deck to examine the various crew visible. "You mean they're all convicts?"

"Ex-convicts," Ford corrected easily. "And some guards, too."

Nestor gestured for Ford to come closer and whispered, "I'm not too sure of the guards, Sir Ford."

"I feel much the same way, your highness," Ford replied. "However, 'Needs must when the gods drive', as they say."

"Do they?" Nestor said. "I'd never heard that before."

Knox snorted.

"Perhaps we'd best get you settled below, your highness?" Ford suggested, gesturing to the hatchway.

"No, I'd prefer view our departure from the deck."

"As your highness wishes," Ford said. He turned to peer toward the bow of the ship. "However, I've duties to attend."

"Don't let me hold you back, captain," Nestor allowed. "I'll stay here with Mr. Knox."

"A pleasure," Knox grumbled.

"Hands aloft!" Ford called. "Watchman to the top!"

"The top?" Nestor asked, looking around. "Where's that?"

"The top balloon, your highness," Knox explained. He looked around and barked, "Jens! Get yourself up there and be sure not to spare your throat!"

Jens gave him a surly look but started up the ratlines on the side of the ship, grabbing the netting that held the balloons and climbing out of sight.

"Mr. Reedis!" Knox called. "When you're ready!"

"Ready now," Reedis called, closing his eyes and spreading his arms in the magical gesture that started the ship ascending.

"Mr. Franck!" Knox called. "How fares the steam?"

"We're ready when you need, sir," the young smith called back. He gestured to the stokers, calling, "Marder! Sens! More coal!"

"Isn't that the murderer?" Nestor said, pointing to Angus. "The one who killed his fiancé?"

"Yes," Knox said. "He killed her and made that damned wyvern out of her."

"The one we're chasing," Nestor said.

"The very same," Knox agreed. Knox looked forward and raised his voice to shout, "Lookouts, are we clear the ground?"

"We're clear!" Captain Ford called back. "You may deploy the booms!"

"Did you hear that, Mr. Franck?" Knox called to the smith.

"Boomsmen, deploy your booms!" Angus shouted. "Prepare to engage the propellers."

The appointed men moved to the stern of the ship and pulled on the hoists that lowered the upright booms to the sides of the ship. Satisfied, they lashed the lines around belaying pins and called back to Angus, "Booms deployed and secured!"

"Engage the propellers!" Angus called, moving to the engine and pulling on levers.

A moment later, the furled propellers, like windmill sails, spun around to fan out to four corners, locking in place. Slowly, the propellers began to spin, pushing Spite through the air.

"Booms deployed! Propellers deployed! Making thrust!" Angus confirmed to lieutenant Knox with a booming voice and a curt salute.

"Very good, Mr. Franck!" Knox called back, returning the salute. To captain Ford he called, "What speed and course, captain?"

"North," Ford called back, "and two-thirds power, if you please Mr. Knox."

"Aye sir," Knox called back. "Course due north at two-thirds power."

"Wait a minute," Nestor said, reaching into his pocket for something. "North takes us to Soria, right?"

"Soon enough, your highness," Knox agreed.

"Well, well," Nestor muttered then brightened as he pulled a small envelope from his pocket. "Here it is!"

"Here's what?" Knox asked in barely restrained exasperation. "Your highness."

"Secret orders," Nestor told him.

"What do they say?"

"I don't know, they're secret."

"Captain!" Knox called forward. "The prince has something for you!"

"Can it wait?" Ford shouted back.

"I think not, sir," Knox called, waving frantically and gesturing toward the note in the prince's hand.

Ford frowned but rushed back down to the stern. He glanced at Knox, then Nestor, holding out his hand. "What have you got for me, your highness?"

"Orders," Nestor said, handing him the envelope. "From my father, the king."

Ford took the envelope and started opening it.

"They're secret orders," Nestor said, glancing around at the crew.

"For when?" Ford asked.

"Well now, of course!"

"Then it won't matter where I open them," Ford said.

"But can you trust the crew?" Nestor asked nervously. "Aren't they all cutthroats and murderers?"

"Mostly," Ford agreed with a shrug. "And, for your information, cutting throats is one of the surest way to become a murderer."

"Oh," Nestor said, going pale. He glanced to the crew. "Do they know that?"

"Only the cutthroats, your highness," Knox told him.

Nestor glanced at him in perplexity for a moment, then brightened. "Yes, I suppose they would."

Ford, meanwhile, had ignored the by-play, intent on reading the spidery script of the small note. He read it twice, then folded it carefully, put it back in its envelope and then put the envelope in his pocket.

"New course, Mr. Knox," Ford said. "West to the sea."

"To the sea, sir?"

"West, past the Westing lighthouse and then north," Ford said. "We're to take precautions to ensure that we're not seen by any Sorian vessels or spotted from the coastline."

Knox blinked. "Oh, that makes sense. Keep us from prying eyes as it were."

"Indeed," Ford said. He glanced at the prince, the tilt of the ship, the speed of the propellers, the lump that was the unconscious mage in the center of the ship, then said to Knox. "I'm going below. Have someone take care of the mage."

"I'll do that, sir," Knox said, knuckling his forehead in a quick salute. "And the prince?"

"Have someone show him to his quarters and introduce him to the cook."

"The cook, sir?" Knox repeated in surprise. "Are you sure that's wise, captain?"

"He's got to eat sometime," Ford said airily. With a final, curt nod, Ford left them to their devices and retreated to the comfort of his cabin.

#

"I'm the Crown Prince," Nestor cried when Annabelle told him that his dinner would be in the galley, with the rest of the crew. "I'll eat in the captain's cabin! And when I please!"

"Are you aware of the Articles of War, prince?" Annabelle replied.

"Dealing with pirates?" Nestor said, nodding firmly. "Of course! I've stood with my father at court many times."

"Dealing with the captain and of His Majesty's ships," Annabelle corrected.

"I'm sure they have nothing to do with me," Nestor snapped back. His brows furrowed angrily. He was surprised when she didn't bow in fear at his look.

Annabelle laughed at his expression and said, "I'll bring you a copy of them."

"What? Why?" Nestor demanded. "Where's my dinner?"

"I'll have an airman bring them to you," Annabelle said. "When you're done reading them, bring them back to the galley."

"What? No!" Nestor cried. "When do I eat?"

"After I'm satisfied that you know the articles," Annabelle said.

"What?" Nestor said. "I forbid it!"

Annabelle shook her head, smirked and left — without Nestor's royal consent.

#

Twenty minutes later, Annabelle looked up at a polite cough and was surprised to see Prince Nestor standing before her.

"I read them all," Nestor said, his eyes wide. He gestured for her to lean over and whispered, "Can he really do all of that?"

"He can," Annabelle said. "And has, in the past."

"He can't do it to me, though," Nestor said, looking for reassurance.

"He is the captain of the ship," Annabelle said. "His word is law. You hold no commission from your father, you are merely a passenger."

"But he wouldn't —"

"Break any of those rules, test any of those Articles, and you'll be a very sorry man," Annabelle said, reaching out for the rolled up parchment. Nestor passed them over. "You don't want to make the captain angry."

"I did what I wanted last voyage!" Nestor complained.

"And look where that got you," Annabelle said. "The crew mutinied because of you. Can you imagine how happy the captain is about that?"

Nestor shook his head.

"It's going to be a long voyage," Annabelle predicted. "A very long voyage. And accidents happen. Even to princes."

"What?" Nestor cried, looking around in fear of any accident that might be sneaking up on him.

"If I were you, I'd lay low, make no trouble, keep to myself, and let the crew do their job," she told him.

"I'm the Crown Prince!"

"Not if you're dead, you're not."

#

"What if the wyvern is in Soria?" Reedis asked Ford as they met for dinner. The prince had not joined them: having discovered that his stomach was still unused to the rocking motion of the airship in the sky.

"How do we track it at all?" Ford asked. He glanced to Reedis. "Can you track it as a creature of heat?"

Reedis shook his head.

"And the king's mages didn't offer any advice?" Ford asked.

"I don't think they'd speak with me," Reedis said. "The only one in my meeting with the king was his page, Tirpin."

Ford grunted.

"We're on a fool's mission," Reedis complained.

"At least we've got the fool for it," Ford said bitterly, jerking his head toward the compartment where the prince was resting uneasily.

Reedis snorted in agreement. "But we don't have a way to track the wyvern."

Ford nodded thoughtfully then brightened. He called to his door, "Send for the cook!"

The sound of footsteps clumping away indicated that he'd been heard.

"The cook?" Reedis repeated. "Do you trust her?"

"With my life," Ford said.

"With mine, too," Reedis said sourly, scooping up the last forkful of the amazing meal in front of him.

"We have an arrangement," Ford told him.

"Did you seal it with blood?"

"Something better," Ford said, not meeting the other's eyes. Reedis looked dubious but said nothing — footsteps approached and there was a quick knock on the door.

"Come in!" Ford called. Annabelle walked in and saluted. "You sent for me, sir?"

"Close the door and have a seat," Ford said, gesturing to one of the two empty seats at his small square table. "Reedis and I were discussing our course and our course of action."

"Stay alive, try not to crash, and wish for the best," the mage surmised for the other's benefit.

"We need to find the wyvern," Ford said, getting to the point. "And I think you might know how to track her."

Annabelle said nothing.

"Do you?" Reedis asked her. "Because I'm out of my league."

"In so many ways," Annabelle said, her lips twitching. She glanced to Ford. "You can track anyone by their heart."

"Indeed," Ford said noncommittally. "But she hasn't got a heart, our engineer burst it with a hat-pin."

Annabelle snorted. "You have the engineer, he'll give you the course." She paused. "If you let me."

"Without the engineer we've no ship!" Reedis warned, looking warily at the cook.

"A tracker spell?" Ford asked Annabelle, ignoring the mage's outburst. "Because he loved her?"

"If he killed her with a hat-pin you can be sure that they're bound together," Annabelle said.

"Send for Mr. Franck!" Ford bellowed to the guard outside his door.

"Aye sir," the guard replied, rushing once more to do the captain's bidding.

"Who is guarding your door?" Annabelle asked in idle curiosity.

"Sens or Marder?" Reedis guessed.

"Jenkins, the jailer," Ford told them.

"He'll be listening in," Annabelle warned.

"He'll hear nothing," Reedis said with a small smile. "That much magic I can do." He caught Annabelle's look and continued, "What? Is that beyond a witch?"

"I've always wondered," Ford said," what's the difference between a witch and a mage?"

"A witch or warlock implores the power of the gods and a mage steals through the rules of Terrene laid out for her children," Annabelle said quickly.

"That's not quite it," Reedis said. "A witch is in tune with the gods, using herbs, potions, blood — sometimes all three. A mage works through understanding of the gods and our world."

"Exactly what I said," Annabelle observed with a catty smile.

Ford mulled on their words and asked them, "Would you say, perhaps, that the mages know the minds of the gods and witches know the hearts?"

Reedis and Annabelle exchanged startled looks. "That's a neat turn of phrase, Sir Ford," Reedis allowed. Annabelle nodded firmly in agreement.

The sentry knocked on the door and called, "Mr. Franck, sir."

"Have him come in," Ford said.

Angus Franck, dirty with coal and drooping with exhaustion, brought himself to salute the captain. Ford stood and returned it, gesturing for the smith to take the last seat.

"We were talking about how best to track the wyvern," Ford said. "Annabelle has an idea or two that may involve you."

"The cook, sir?" Angus said, looking at her in surprise. "Your name's Annabelle?" The witch nodded. Angus swallowed and continued, "Isn't that hard luck for a man?"

"I'm not a man," Annabelle said, waving her hands over the smith's eyes, "as you can plainly see."

Angus jerked back in surprise. "You're — you're — you're a girl!"

"Hardly," Reedis sniffed.

"It's been many years since I've been called that," Annabelle said with a bright expression.

Angus looked to Ford. "But, sir, isn't it bad luck to have a woman on the crew?"

"Not the way she cooks," Ford and Reedis said in unison. The mage jerked his head, surprised at his own reaction but Ford merely chuckled.

"It is good food," Angus agreed. He steadied himself. "But you were asking about Krea, sir."

"I was indeed," Ford said. "It's our mission to track her —"

"And kill her," Reedis added. Angus gasped and Ford shot the mage a fuming look.

"— to track her," Ford repeated, glowering at the mage to keep quiet, "and bring her to the king's justice."

"Why?" Angus said, glancing warily around the table. "What did she do wrong?"

"Don't listen to them, Angus," Annabelle interrupted. "They're silly and they don't know what they're talking about."

Angus' brows raised and he pointed to Ford, "But he's the captain!"

"He is," Annabelle agreed in a soothing tone, "but he misspeaks. The king wants to have your Krea and her wyvern half back in the kingdom because he wants to ask her a number of questions." She leaned toward him conspiratorially. "He might even consider recruiting her to his service."

"He might?" Angus asked, glancing to Ford for confirmation.

Ford nodded, not needing Annabelle's prompting boot smashing on top of his foot in warning. Angus was more easily swayed because he was eating Annabelle's food, but it did not completely enchant him.

With a pained glance to Annabelle, Ford told the smith, "And we need your help to find her."

"Oh! Of course, sir," Angus said. He licked his lips. "And when we find her, will the king pardon me?" The others looked confused. "For killing her, sir?"

"Of course!" Ford said. "After all, if she's not dead, you've done no crime, have you?"

Angus nodded, seeming much relieved. "So what can I do to help?"

"I want you to think of her," Annabelle said. "Close your eyes and tell me what you remember of her, of how she looks, and what she smelled like."

Angus closed his eyes. "It was hard looking at her," he said, his voice going soft and dreamy, "she was an albino, so she shunned the sun. She wore hats with flowers in them."

"What sort of flowers?" Annabelle asked.

"Wyvern flowers, usually," Angus said. "She liked the scent. Master Rabel often brought them to her."

Annabelle shot Ford a quick look, then moved her hands towards the smith. She moved them all around his head, as though grabbing something and bundling it up. A moment later, Angus' head bowed forward until it rested on the table and the smith started snoring, lightly.

"What did you do?" Ford demanded.

"I bundled up his memories," Annabelle said. "I can find her now," she told them. She grabbed a fork and wrapped her hands around it. She murmured something under her breath and closed her eyes.

"She's doing magic," Reedis told Ford. "It's strange, different from mine but I can still feel it."

"Shh," Ford said, bringing a finger to his lips. Reedis shut his mouth in a pout.

Annabelle moved one hand from the fork and balanced it on the index finger of the other. Slowly the fork swiveled on her finger, pointing to the north, just slightly east of true.

Annabelle's eyes snapped open. "There," she said, "there's your compass."

Ford took it from her and balanced it the way she had: it pointed to the same heading. He nodded toward Angus. "And what about him?"

"He's exhausted, let him rest," Annabelle said.

"Did you steal his memories?" Reedis demanded, his nostrils flaring angrily.

"No!" Annabelle said. "I would never do anything of the sort!"

"So why is he asleep?"

"Look at him," Annabelle said, pointing to the smith's face. "He's smiling in his sleep." She shot a look at Ford and said, in a quieter tone, "He's dreaming of her."

Chapter Eight: A Witch's Brew

First minister Mannevy knocked on the door to the king's office at precisely one in the afternoon.

"Enter!" the king called. Mannevy hustled through the door, pausing at the threshold to bow before turning to close the door and make his way to a seat near the king. There were five other people in the room but there were still several more empty chairs at the great conference table.

"They're gone?" the king asked as Mannevy found his seat.

"Out of sight these past five minutes or more," Mannevy affirmed.

"Good," the king said, turning to the others. "Captains Nevins and Martel, may I make known to you Mr. Newman, his apprentice Mr. Bennet, and my personal friend, Tirpin."

"Mage Tirpin," the young man said rising long enough to bow to the others. The king allowed himself a satisfied smile at the expression of the others.

"Can you handle hot and cold magic?" Newman asked him.

"My best magic is transformation," Tirpin conceded. He pulled forth a small piece of paper from his pocket, waved his hands and turned it into a small balloon, which hovered above the table. "I trust it will suffice."

"You spoke with that purple-robed fellow, then?" Nevins guessed.

"He was most effusive," Tirpin said in agreement. He glanced toward the king. "He felt it his absolute duty to educate your majesty on all the fine points of his thaumaturgy."

"Indeed he did!" the king replied with a loud guffaw. "Silly twit!" He glanced to Mannevy. "He said something about you promising him a monopoly on his magic."

"On his return, sire," Mannevy said suavely.

The king barked a laugh. "Oh, well said! 'On his return!'" He turned to Newman and Tirpin. "How soon can I have my fleet?"

"I have already started construction on more boilers and engines," Newman said. "Although I must confess that it is taking longer than I had anticipated." The king raised an eyebrow at him, so Newman explained, "Apparently Ibb, the mechanical, failed to impart all his knowledge to me."

"I thought you said you could build them," the king said in a dangerous tone.

"I can, sire," Newman assured him. "But honesty compels me to admit that it may take longer than I had planned."

"How much longer?" the king demanded.

"A month," Newman said. Seeing the king's thunderous look, he amended, "Maybe less, particularly if I can get help."

"That Rabel fellow — the girl's father — is around here somewhere," the king said. He glanced to Mannevy.

"He is a guest in your jail, sire," Mannevy said.

"In jail?" Newman said, his face falling. "But what crime —?"

"He upset me, Mr. Newman," the king said frostily. "Pray that you don't do the same."

Newman shut up quickly and nodded meekly.

"Two ships by the end of the month," the king declared. He glanced to Tirpin. "That won't be a problem, will it, mage?"

"I'll need supplies, sire," Tirpin said, carefully keeping his fears to himself, alarmed by the king's reaction to Newman the engineer.

"You'll get them," the king said, glancing to Mannevy who nodded.

"And ships?" Newman asked. "I'll need access to them, to fit them out."

"I have two in mind," the king said. Dryly he added, "They need some slight repairs but most of their damage was to their rigging."

"That won't bother us," Tirpin assured him, "as we'll be removing masts and sails."

"No," the king said, "leave enough of the main mast to allow for a lookout."

Tirpin's brows rose but he nodded in acceptance.

"Warrior and Parvour are your first ships, Mr. Newman," the king said. "Have them ready by the end of the month." He rose from his chair and nodded as the others rose with him. "I'll have need for them."

#

"Prepare to throw the log," Ford said to Knox three days later.

"Aye sir," Knox said. "Jens, prepare to throw the log."

Jens, the ex-lieutenant, gave Knox an evil look but nodded in acceptance, pulling the strange assortment of wood and canvas from the locker near the helm. He assembled the pieces into a serviceable kite, attached the log line and walked to the stern.

"Turn!" he called as he released the kite held onto the line. Knox turned the timer and eyed it critically even as Jens kept an eye on the line playing out behind them. In five minutes, Knox called out, "Time!"

Jens tightened his finger on the line to stop it playing out, bent down to look at the markings hanging from it and called out, "Seven knots!"

"Secure the log," Knox ordered, moving to the log book to mark the speed.

"Mr. Knox," Ford called out.

"Sir?"

"Add this to your readings," Ford said, "355."

"Aye sir," Knox said. "I'll be certain to add it."

"I'll be in my quarters," Ford said. "Have Mr. Franck report to me."

"Aye sir," Knox called. "Shall I have some food sent your way?"

Ford considered it and shook his head. "See to the crew first, if you would."

"Aye sir," Knox called after the departing captain. A moment later he crossed the ship to find the prince looking over the railings. "Rare sight, isn't it, your highness?"

"I never knew there was so much sea," the prince said weakly.

"Shall I fetch you some food?" Knox asked with malice carefully hidden in a cheerful demeanor.

The prince turned to him, turned green and threw his guts up once more over the side of the ship and into the air below.

"Maybe later, then," Knox allowed affably, sauntering back over to the helm.

#

Down below in his cabin, Ford reviewed his charts with cold satisfaction. Spite was making a solid steady seven knots even against a breeze. In three days, she'd covered over four hundred knots. In another half day, she would have covered the whole length of the kingdom of Soria — all five hundred miles of it.

Soria was a good solid kingdom which had been led peaceably by their king for over forty years. That was in the past. Something had happened three years ago and King Sorgal had been deposed. The new king had come from one of the bordering duchies — independent dukedoms — to the west. The new King, Wendel, had consolidated his position quickly by marrying the queen and accepting her son — and the late king's — as his heir.

The relations between King Markel and King Wendel had seemed good enough to Ford… until now.

Even with good relations, Ford could see why Markel wanted to keep news of his airship a secret. What he couldn't understand was why Markel planned a war with Wendel — and how he could possibly hope to prevail.

Of course, Ford thought, he couldn't understand how Wendel had overcome Sorgal with such ease. Probably he had help.

A knock on his door brought him out of his reverie. "Enter."

Angus Franck marched in and saluted. Ford nodded back to him and gestured to the chair. "Sit."

"Sir," Angus said. Three days at sea had done the young man much good. His sense of ease and authority had grown steadily as he handled the duties of engineer and kept his stokers and propeller-men on task and properly motivated.

"All well?" Ford said.

Angus nodded. "All's well," he agreed. "I was just checking on our coal."

"And?"

"We've enough for three more days," Angus told him.

"And then we're out?" Ford asked. The young man nodded. "So where should we stop to get more?"

"There's the coal mines of Magiron," Angus said. Ford nodded, peering down to his map.

Magiron was one of the northern towns of Soria, just at the edge of the border between it and the colder, sparsely populated, Issia.

"Hmm," Ford said. "How much will we have to pay?"

"I don't know," Angus confessed, "I've never bought coal before." He frowned. "Especially this much."

"How much?"

"Three tons, at least," Angus said.

"How will we get that aboard?" Ford wondered.

"The mage?" Angus guessed.

"Strictly hot and cold," Ford said, shaking his head. "We'll have to hoist it aboard."

"Or haul it in sacks," Angus said. "At a hundredweight a sack, that'd be… six hundred sacks."

"Mmm," Ford said. He gestured at the table, saying, "Excuse me."

Angus glanced down and saw that the captain wanted to roll out a chart. He moved himself away from the table. Ford rolled out the chart, grabbing a pencil and a ruler.

"What do you know of triangulation?" he said to Angus.

Angus shook his head.

"We use it a lot in finding distances, and measuring courses," Ford said, quickly pointing at a point on the chart and reaching for a compass. "We first took a bearing on the wyvern when we were here —" he tapped the point "— and the bearing was just one degree east of north."

Angus tried to look like he understood what that meant.

Ford drew another point from a bearing on the compass and joined it to the original point on the map. He used the ruler to extend the line.

"So we know that three days ago she was somewhere on this line," Ford said, tapping the chart. The line went through Soria, through Issia to the north and further on. "I don't think she's in Soria and I don't she's in Issia," Ford said, drawing a line straight up from the original dot. He measured it carefully and pointed to it. "For the past three days we've travelled this far — five hundred miles." He glanced at Angus who showed no signs of enlightenment. "And now our reading is just five degrees east of north —" again Ford used the compass and drew a line from it, continuing on until it intersected the first line. He leaned back and shot a smile at Angus. "And there is where your friend will be found." He picked up a pair of dividers and set them to the distance they'd travelled — 500 miles. He used the width of the dividers to snap back and forth along the new line until he'd measured four widths. "Which means she is about two thousand miles away from us still."

"That's got to be at the top of the world!" Angus exclaimed. He glanced at the chart. "Are you sure you've got it right?"

Ford nodded. "I've done this before, many times."

"But that means —" Angus gestured for the dividers and Ford handed them over. The young man used the dividers to divide up the distance on the first line — the line from their start to Krea's current position. "— if I did this right, it means that she traveled —"

"Flew, surely," Ford observed mildly. Angus shot him a glance, then nodded.

"She traveled two thousand five hundred miles in a day!"

"As a wyvern? Quite possibly?" Ford agreed. "Although it's possible that it took more time than that."

"It's been — what — six days?" Angus asked. Ford nodded. "So even if it took her the full six days to get there, she'd still be traveling at…" he scrunched his eyes shut, doing the calculations, "…four hundred miles a day or roughly fifty miles every hour if she only flew for eight hours a day."

"And if she made it in just one day, she'd cover at least a hundred miles in an hour, more if she didn't fly non-stop," Ford agreed. He shrugged. "From what I recall, the speed is handily within her abilities."

"How do we know she'll still be there?" Angus asked. "And if it's taken us three days to get this far, will she still be there in the twelve extra days we'll need?"

"If she's not, we'll see it on our fork compass," Ford said, nodding to his pocket. "My question to you is: how much coal will we need?"

"Four times what we have, at a guess," Angus said, confirming Ford's fears. "And don't forget the water for the boiler."

"So how much coal? How much water?" Ford asked.

"How much food?" Angus added, nodding thoughtfully.

"It's going to get colder," Ford said in agreement. He looked over to Angus. "How much coal have we used?"

"We've gone through a ton — twenty hundredweight," Angus said quickly. "And about five hundredweight of water."

"We brought twice that aboard," Ford said. "So we know that we have enough for another three days."

"Twice that if we can refuel," Angus allowed.

"I'll check with Knox but I don't think we can load more," Ford said.

"Even if the mage could lift the extra weight, the propellers would push us slower," Angus said in a agreement.

"So we need to resupply our coal twice before we reach our destination," Ford said.

"And then we'd need to find coal wherever we end up," Angus said dubiously. "Do they have coal up in the bitter north?"

Ford shook his head. "I don't know."

"Unless we find the coal…"

"What else can we burn?" Ford asked. "Wood?"

"Certainly," Angus agreed. "I'm not sure how much we'd need or how well it will heat the boiler."

Ford nodded, stood back from the table and said to the young man, "It's enough to be going on. You've done well. I'll let you get back to your duties."

Angus stood back from the table, gave captain Ford his best effort at a salute and walked briskly out of the cabin.

#

"…so that's where we're at," Ford concluded later that evening to his gathering of officers: Knox, Reedis, Angus, and Annabelle.

"We know that there's coal at Magiron, inland at the north of Soria," Knox said, pointing to the chart.

"And there's another spot at the top of Issia, in the village of Snowden," Reedis said.

Ford gave the mage a look. "You've been there?"

"I've heard tell of it," Reedis said. He frowned in thought. "In fact, I think I heard it when we first started on the airship project." He paused. "One of the king's mages, I think."

"Hmm," Ford said. "The king has been thinking about this for a long time, it seems."

"Clearly," Knox agreed.

"The only question is how do we get the supplies," Annabelle noted.

"Do you have any suggestions?" Knox asked challengingly.

"Do you have any gold?" she shot back.

Knox gasped breath for an angry retort but Ford waved him to silence.

"In fact, we do," Ford said. "Not as much as you'd doubtless like, but not a small amount, either."

"I heard about the prizes," Annabelle said.

"We won't need that much," Reedis said.

"The big problem is how are we going to get it aboard?" Ford said.

"We can't just land!" Knox said in agreement.

"And we couldn't disguise our ship, there's no river that goes up that far in Magiron," Annabelle said.

"How far can a ship go?" Reedis wondered. "Could we land there and disguise ourselves?"

"We've got no masts, no sails, and ten great big colored balloons," Annabelle said, "that's pretty hard to disguise!"

"No one ever suggested we'd need a disguise!" Reedis said in protest.

"No one said a lot of things," Ford said soothingly. "Our mission, now is to find the wyvern. For that we need to get coal. And we need water and food." He turned to the others. "So how do we get it aboard?"

"Steal it," a voice spoke from the hallway.

Ford suppressed a groan and nodded decisively to Annabelle who turned on her heels, slammed open the door and hauled the outsider in before he could react.

"Ah, Sykes!" Ford said without surprise. "So glad you could join us!"

"I thought the captain would never ask," Sykes replied with equal aplomb, going so far as to give the captain a half-bow.

"You've a suggestion to help us overcome our current issue?" Ford said.

"I said steal it," Sykes replied.

"How?"

"There's only one way to steal it," Annabelle said. The others looked at her. "You make people believe you're supposed to have it."

Ford nodded quickly, his eyes glowing. Knox was a bit slower on the uptake but he chortled when he got it.

"Thinking of brewing up a special tea, cookie?" Knox said to the witch.

"I'm sure I could think of something," Annabelle agreed with a sly smile. She glanced toward Sykes. "Do you think you'd do as a tea-seller?"

"Perhaps I could," Sykes agreed.

"Then it's settled then," Ford said.

"One thing," Sykes said raising a hand. Ford raised an eyebrow. "I'll want rank."

"Master's mate," Ford said. "And you'll have to earn it by doing more than this."

"I can do that," Sykes said. "That comes with more prize money, right?"

"From the date of your rank," Ford agreed. "Which is today."

Sykes spat on his hand and held it out to Ford. Ford gave him a look.

"You have my word," Ford said. "I'll not shake a slimy hand."

Sykes wiped his hand on his trousers. "Suit yourself."

"Can he keep a watch?" Ford asked Knox.

"I'll want to see how he does, first," Knox said giving Sykes a hard look. "You do your work and we'll see."

"Fair enough," Sykes said. "So when do I get to deliver this tea?"

"Tomorrow," Ford said. "We're a bit over a hundred miles away from Magiron." He gestured them toward the door. "I'll see you in the morning."

"What about the prince?" Sykes asked.

"Do you want to bring him along?" Knox offered.

Sykes gave him a leer then his expression changed. "Actually, he could be quite useful."

"He could at that," Ford allowed. "I'll tell him in the morning." He gestured toward the door again. "Good night, gentlemen," he nodded toward Annabelle, "lady."

Annabelle snorted at the appellation, bobbed her head and left, followed by the rest — all except Reedis.

Ford waited while Reedis turned and shut the door, pressed his ear to it for a moment to be certain that they wouldn't be overheard, then turned back to Ford.

"Are you sure this is wise?"

"I think wisdom has long since left us," Ford said. "But if we're to complete our mission, we have to have the coal."

"Perhaps we could ask the gods," Reedis suggested.

"Really?" Ford replied. "And which god helps us steal coal?"

#

When he was finally alone, Ford paused to listen at the door. Then he walked back to his bed, a standard ship's bunk bed sturdily contained by high wood sides. He lifted up the mattress and slid open the wooden door cleverly hidden underneath it. He smiled as he pulled out the well-polished wooden box.

He placed it reverently on his table and opened it slowly.

Inside were small carved wooden figures of the gods. Gently he laid out the soft velvet liner. He moved it so that it was on top of his compass card and carefully aligned. He frowned as he spied Ametza. Next to her was a god with a stern but benevolent gaze. He smiled at the figurine and reverently pulled it out of the box, to place it on the carefully aligned liner.

"Arolan, hear my plea," he said. "Show me where you are. Let me aid you."

Ford stared for a long time he stared at the figure of the god. Then slowly, the god's head turned over his left shoulder. His grave, clean-shaven face turned haggard and lined, a beard sprouted from it and, even more slowly, what seemed like frost formed over his head. Ford let out a gasp of amazement then bowed low. He followed the line of the figure's head and marked its position on his compass card.

Arolan's head was pointing five degrees east of north — the same as Annabelle's fork.

"I see, my most awesome god," Ford said. "I shall seek you out." He gently picked up the figurine which glowed with a godly light. "I shall give you all my aid."

The light of the figurine dimmed then went out and the figure of the sea god was once again nothing more than a figure.

Chapter Nine: Ophidian's Coal

The lookout spotted Magiron by the roads leading towards it; the village itself was covered in snow. One road traced the south side of the hills to the north from the coastline which they had followed for the past day; another road lead south from the center of the town. There were several thinner lines of pure white indicating the presence of snow-buried cart tracks and lesser roads. The buildings in the village were mostly obscured by the snow. Where the two roads met in the center of the village there was a dirty spot where carts and foot traffic had churned through the snow to the dirt below.

The coal mine was visible at the far northern edge of the town, marked by its darker smudge surrounded by the white of new snow.

"You can land me and the prince here," Sykes said, when they were still a mile from the town proper. He clapped the prince on the shoulder, saying, "Are you prepared for your part, my prince?"

Prince Nestor smiled at him. "Indeed I am!"

"Prepare to lower the cargo!" Ford called and a crew assembled at the side of the ship. Nestor and Sykes climbed aboard the cargo net and a rope was attached to the capstan. The crew slowly lowered the pair to the soft snow below. Sykes helped the Crown Prince out of the netting, waved to Ford in the airship three hundred feet above, and led the prince away toward the road and the village beyond.

#

Ford would have never guessed that the guard and the prince get along at all, let alone so well. But Sykes had curried the prince's favor with all the tact of a courtesan. His job was made easier by the fact that practically no one spent time with the prince, so he was always lonely and looking for any sign of recognition.

"I've met his type before," Sykes had said when Knox commented on the unlikely friendship, though he gave no further explanation.

The guard had had no problem engaging the prince in his plan. Nestor was terrified of Annabelle — something which the witch encouraged pointedly as she had no time "for useless princelings." So when Sykes explained that the witch had brewed a special tea and that they would use it to steal three tons of coal, and other miscellany, the prince was more than intrigued. He was passionate in learning his lines and thrilled with every bit of encouragement Sykes gave him.

What probably shouldn't have surprised Ford was that the prince was a natural-born actor.

"He'd have to be to survive this long," Annabelle had replied sourly when Ford had commented on it to her. She shrugged. "I don't care how bad he is, really, just as long as they deliver their goods to the mine and make the pitch."

#

The delivery itself was simple. Sykes and the prince would go to the mine, find the first person they could and argue volubly about the prince's royalty. With Sykes continuing to doubt the prince's claim and the prince exclaiming how valuable he was for ransom, they figured the guard and whomever would be easily sold on the next part.

Sykes would swear that he had a truth serum which they could give to the prince. The prince claimed he couldn't be drugged. In their argument they would enlist whoever they met into proving the claims one way or another. Tea would be brewed and all would drink it.

Of course, as Sykes and the prince were already immune to the tea, courtesy of Annabelle 'providing' them with the antidote, only their new 'friends' would succumb.

At which point the guards and personnel would be told of the secret mission to bring the prince to the north in a flying ship created by the god Ophidian just for that very purpose. Sykes would put another set of leaves in a fire burning outside which would turn the smoke green, the signal to Spite that the plot had worked. If it hadn't, Sykes was to try to get a different set of leaves in a fire which would produce red smoke in warning.

#

Fortunately, Sykes didn't need the red smoke.

"Green smoke, sir!" the lookout called to Ford. Ford went forward to see for himself and spied Sykes, Crown Prince Nestor, and five other men rushing about, pulling wagon after wagon out the front gates.

"Land ship!" Ford called. He spied Reedis amidships. "Mage Reedis! You may start the descent!"

"Aye, sir!" Reedis called back, waving in additional acknowledgement.

The airship landed neatly just beside the first wagon.

"Hands to the sides!" Ford called. "Hatches open!"

Several hands, detailed for just this task, leaped over the side to the top of the laden wagon and began to build a human chain, hauling the sacks of coal up to Spite. Another group took the sacks and lowered them into the coal bunkers.

They were finished in less than an hour.

Long before that Sykes and Crown Prince Nestor returned, driving a wagon loaded with food.

"Turns out the local mayor was visiting when we arrived," Sykes said with a grin. "So he provided food and goods for our journey."

Prince Nestor added, "They think much of Ophidian up here, being so cold and all."

"That makes sense," Ford agreed. He looked to Sykes. "And the water?"

Sykes pointed to the snow all around them. "Why can't we just put that in our barrels?"

"What about to drink, man!" Knox replied irritably.

"It will work," Annabelle said from where she was ordering the hands with the supplies. "I can make it work, just as long as it's clean snow."

"No yellow snow, then," Reedis snorted. The witch gave him a dark look through lidded eyes. Reedis shook his head. "It was a joke, witch."

"A bad one," Annabelle agreed. She turned back to her work.

"What are they going to do when they recover?" Reedis said to her, looking at the silly drugged smirks on the guards and the mayor.

"They're not going to recover," Annabelle said.

"What?" Reedis cried. "You're not going to kill them!"

"No, you silly fool," Annabelle scolded. "They're going to live their lives thinking that they aided Ophidian in his quest." She pointed to the wooden deck below them. "They won't forget this ship for a long while."

"Why choose Ophidian? Why not Vorg or Veva?" Reedis asked, referring to the god and goddess of fire.

"They are more likely to turn you into a pile of burning ashes if you evoke their names." Annabelle replied.

"What would Ophidian do?" Reedis asked.

"Nothing if he doesn't find out about it, " Annabelle said.

"And if he does?"

"Hopefully, he'll have a sense of humor," she replied.

"An angry god means a very short life," Reedis warned.

"But — oh! — the profits!" Annabelle joked.

Captain Ford frowned as he listened to this exchange. "I'm not sure the king will appreciate that."

"I doubt he'll be in a position to complain," Annabelle said.

"We were supposed to keep this secret," Ford said. "That's why the king wanted us to keep off shore."

"This is winter," Annabelle said. "How long do you think it will take for a messenger to reach their king all the way south?"

Ford considered the notion dubiously.

"We'll be long gone, whatever occurs," Annabelle said. "And how much do you think they'll believe a report from people who think they were dealing with Ophidian?"

"That depends," Ford said. Annabelle gave him a look. "Don't you believe in the gods?"

"Of course!" Annabelle said with a snort. "How could anyone not?"

"So why not believe that…" Ford stopped, giving Annabelle a look of enlightenment.

"Say it," Annabelle prompted with a smirk.

"… that Ophidian sent an airship on a journey north," Ford completed with a hangdog expression.

"Exactly," Annabelle agreed. "So all king Wendel will know is that Ophidian created a ship that flies in the air."

"That doesn't exactly keep this a secret," Ford said pointing to his ship.

"But it does make it clear that only a god — and one particular god — created it," Annabelle countered.

#

The tea-enspelled inhabitants of Magiron waved excitedly as Reedis caused Spite to rise once again into the sky. Angus Franck performed brilliantly in setting the booms out, engaging the propellers, and speeding the ship on its way.

"Your Highness," Sykes said when they were aloft, "you were magnificent!"

"Do you really think so?" Nestor asked in surprise.

"I couldn't agree with Mr. Sykes more," Ford said to his surprise. "We couldn't have done it without you."

"Just as long as you don't forget that, captain," Nestor replied haughtily.

"I won't," Ford said. He glanced up and then called to the lookout on the balloons, "How fares the weather?"

"It's snowing captain," the lookout called back. "Snowing hard and cold."

Ford could see patches of white fall down from above and looked forward where the sky seemed to turn a forbidding gray with the setting sun.

"Have all hands bundle up tight tonight, Mr. Knox," Ford said to his lieutenant. "Have the cook be certain to make something hot for the men."

"Aye aye, sir," Knox said, saluting.

"It's bitter now," Ford said, glancing at the air around. "It's certain to get worse."

#

Ford was right. In the next three days, as they steamed their way north, having found an easy pass just beyond Magiron through the hills into Issia, the weather grew colder and colder.

"I'm worried about ice, sir," Reedis reported one morning, gesturing to the layer that coated parts of the ship. Only the area around the steam engine was clear, covered instead in a thin layer of water. "It adds a fair bit of weight, you see."

"How much lower does it take us?" Ford asked, trying to gage their altitude.

"Five hundred feet, maybe more," Reedis guessed.

"And how hard would it be to raise up back to our old level?"

"I can do it," Reedis allowed, "but it'll be a strain."

Ford eyed him critically. The mage looked thinner than he had days back, and haggard.

"You should get more rest," Ford told him.

"I'm the only one who can keep the ship in the air," Reedis replied.

"That seems to be an issue," Ford said.

"You're the only one who can captain the ship," Reedis said.

"Not true," Ford said. "Knox would take over if anything happened to me."

"I pray that the gods will let nothing happen to you," Reedis said.

"And I pray even more that the gods will let nothing happen to you," Ford replied.

"I shouldn't worry that much," Reedis said. "My magic will seep from the ship slowly, you'll be able to land without damage."

"That's not reassuring," Ford said. Reedis gave him a look. "Our mission is to find the wyvern or die trying."

"There is that," Reedis agreed. He took a deep breath. "Well, if you don't mind, I'll not raise us back up the five hundred feet."

"And I'll get a detail to chip the ice off the ship," Ford said.

"But not the balloons," Reedis warned. Ford nodded but, even so, the mage felt compelled to mutter, "Chipping ice off the balloons would doubtless puncture them."

"And we don't want that!" Ford agreed. He clapped the younger man on the shoulder and said. "Go! Get some rest." He turned to the stern and called out, "Mr. Knox! I'll have a party of airmen chipping off this ice! It's a hazard in so many ways!"

"We could use salt, sir!" Angus called from his station at the engine. Ford turned to him with a raised eyebrow. "Salt will melt the ice." "It will," Ford agreed. "But I don't think we have enough salt for the whole ship."

"I'll check with the cook," Knox said. "She's got the salt in her supplies."

Annabelle was most firm in retaining possession of her precious salt. "You all need the work, anyway!" she shouted when Knox asked her. "Your lazy airmen can get off their duffs and clean this scow up!"

Ford affected not to notice the insult to his ship, merely nodding to Knox and saying, "I'll be below if you need me."

#

All the warm clothing, jackets, boots, and undergarments were but little against the cold the heights they were at, particularly in the harsh northern winter.

Ford took it upon himself to wake at various hours of the night, grab a flask of something warm from the kitchen and climb up to the heights of the balloons to check on the lookout stationed there. He spent a few minutes chatting with him, then went to the bowsprit to perform the same deed with that lookout before returning aft to check with the helmsman and return to his interrupted slumber.

He did this more often after the night when he woke and found that there was no lookout atop the balloons. A hurried inquiry revealed that the assigned lookout was the old man, Quirrel, and that he was not in his bunk.

"He relieved me, sir, right and proper," the man on the previous watch said when angrily woken by Ford and Knox. "I swear, he was up there!"

The blood drained from Ford's face. He turned to Knox. "Mark him as DD in the roster and have someone collect his things."

'DD' stood for 'Discharged, Dead.'

After that, Ford woke up more often to check on the lookouts and ensured that the ballooneer was secured to the nettings that held the ship with the balloons.

#

Two nights later, Ford woke as the ship lurched. How he made it out the door, up to the deck fully clothed with his boots unlaced and pea-jacket wrapped around him, he could never figure but he was there.

"What happened?" Ford called to the helmsman.

"Dunno, sir," the man replied. "The ship just lurched. She's down in the head, like she took on water."

Ford reflected on that for a moment, then looked up. "The balloons!" He shouted to the helmsman even as he ascended the lines to the balloons above, "Call for Mr. Reedis! Have him on deck! It's an emergency!"

He was up to the top of the balloons before he heard a reply. When he could see enough in the dark night, he shouted out, "Stop right there!"

"Ha!" Jens called back from the ruin of the foremost top balloon. "Not so mighty now are you captain?"

Ford made no reply, lunging for the ex-lieutenant and the sharp knife in his hands — the knife that had already shredded the first balloon.

Jens twisted to meet Ford's attack, his knife at the ready.

Ford reached to his side only to realize that of all that he'd put on, he hadn't put on his belt… or his knife in its sheath.

Jens saw him reach to his side and smiled. "So what'll it be, captain?" Jens said. "Do I cut you or burst another one of your baubles?"

Ford leaped at the man, grabbing onto his collar with his left hand even as Jens swung with the knife. Ford's jacket deflected the worst of the blow, and Ford pulled back his right fist and slammed it into Jens' face. The ex-lieutenant went limp and dropped the blade but Ford continued to pummel him until the man's face was a bloodied mess and he was limp in Ford's grasp.

"I need a man up here!" Ford bellowed down to the deck below.

"I'm here, captain!" Reedis cried. "Oh, my gods!" he said as he caught sight of the burst balloon.

"I trust you've got a spare," Ford said, glancing sourly at the mess.

"I've got a rope," Sykes said, climbing up behind Reedis. "D'you want to hang him now or later?"

"He won't hang," Ford said, releasing the unconscious form to the ex-guard.

"He won't?" Sykes asked in an angry, raspy tone.

"I've got something better planned," Ford told him grimly, brushing past him and starting back down to the deck. "Have him brought down and put him in chains."

#

"So, how bad is it?" Annabelle asked when she came in early the next morning to the captain's cabin with a tray of warm gruel.

"Reedis has a spare," Ford said. "It'll take some hard work to get it placed and harder work still from the mage to get it inflated, but we'll get our tenth balloon back."

"And?" Annabelle prompted.

"Jens will get his due," Ford said. "Best have some rum ready for after."

"What about the prince?" Annabelle asked. "I've heard he faints at the merest mention of blood."

"Nothing to worry about in this case," Ford replied grimly.

#

"All hands! All hands! Stand to hear punishment!" Knox called loudly from amidships. The crew assembled quickly and quietly, looking at the long plank that had been rigged at the side port. A plank that ended in thin air.

"Are the hands ready?" Ford asked a moment later.

"They are, sir!" Knox called back.

"Have the prisoner brought forward," Ford said. He gestured to the Crown Prince who, forewarned, came to his side and stood at attention.

Jens was brought up, shackled and bound, marching between Sykes and Jenkins, the two former guards. They stopped so that Jens was standing just in front of Ford.

"Read the articles, if you please," Ford said to Crown Prince Nestor.

"Ahem," Nestor cleared his throat and scanned the parchment. "Here ye, here ye, here ye! By order of the His Most Noble Majesty, King Markel, hear my words!"

Eyes turned toward him as the crew recalled that the speaker was the king's son and heir to the throne. Nestor continued, slowly but steadily through the articles, his voice rising as he said:

"Article Eleven. Every person in the fleet, who shall not duly observe the orders of his superior officer, shall suffer death."

All eyes flicked toward Jens who lowered his head. Ford cast a warning glance toward the other four mutineers whom he'd recaptured from Warrior. They caught his look and lowered their heads in shame.

Nestor continued on.

"Article Fifteen. Every person in or belonging to the fleet, who shall desert or entice others so to do, shall suffer death."

Again Jens jerked and so did the other four, Marder and Senten going so far as to glance up imploringly to Ford who ignored their pleaful looks.

Nestor continued, his voice rising again as he proclaimed: "Article Nineteen. If any person in the fleet shall conceal any traitorous or mutinous practice or design, he shall suffer death."

All the crew flinched at the force of the words. Jens began sobbing slowly when Nestor read, "Article Twenty-One. If any officer, mariner, soldier or other person in the fleet, shall strike any of his superior officers, he shall suffer death"

Nestor paused for a moment to look at Jens and then, at Ford's prompting continued through to the very end. "Article Thirty-Five. All other crimes not capital committed by any person or persons in the fleet, shall be punished by the laws and customs in such cases used at sea."

"And in the air," Ford added loudly. Nestor gave him an odd look, then nodded, rolling up the scroll carefully and handing to it lieutenant Knox who took it and placed it under his arm.

"Attention to sentencing!" Ford said. The crew came to attention. "Airman Jens, you have the honor to be the first to receive punishment aboard a royal airship," Ford said with no emotion. "You are found guilty of Article Fifteen, Article Twenty-One, Article Thirty-Five, and many more too numerous to mention."

Jens straggled to an upright position, meeting Ford's eyes.

"We weren't paid," Jens said bitterly.

"Ah!" Ford said, he gestured to Knox who moved forward and presented Ford a small velvet bag.

Ford counted out two guineas. "Your prize money," Ford said, holding up the gold so that all could see. "Forfeited by your desertion," Ford said, putting the money back in the bag. He pulled out another coin. "Your two weeks' pay," Ford said, putting the money back in the bag. "Forfeited by your desertion." He pulled the strings on the bag tight, shutting it and tossing it to Knox. "There, you've been paid," Ford said coldly. He waited a moment, getting no pleasure watching Jens swallow hard. "There are other payments due you," Ford continued.

Jens' eyes widened.

"For assaulting a superior officer," Ford said, "the payment is death."

Jens gasped. The rest of the crew were deathly silent.

"For destruction of His Majesty's property in time of war," Ford continued, "the payment is death." He waited a moment, then nodded to Sykes. "Place the prisoner for punishment."

Sykes and Jenkins pulled at Jens' arms, moving him to stand before the plank.

"Mr. Jens, you are found guilty of crimes meriting death," Ford said. He could hear Jens' heavy breathing even from where he was, even over the cold wind. "Shall I show you leniency?"

"P-p-please!" Jens begged in a ragged whimper.

"Very well, Jens," Ford said. "For your past deeds, I shall merely order you off my ship." He gestured down the gangplank. "You may leave. Now."

Jens looked at him with eyes like saucers. Numbly he shook his head. Ford nodded curtly to him.

"You tried to destroy the ship with all aboard," Ford said. "You shall leave it."

He nodded to Sykes who smiled and pulled forth his dirk, the short knife that all seamen — and airmen — carried.

"There is only one question, Jens," Ford said.

Jens could only whimper in response.

"The question is: whether you will walk like a man to your well-deserved fate or will you have to be pushed?"

In the end, Jens had to be pushed. Ford watched with narrowed eyes at the way Sykes took so much glee in poking the terrified man to the end of the gangplank and then off.

Jens' wail slipped away from their hearing and was abruptly silenced.

Ford nodded to Knox who called out, "Attention on deck!"

The crew looked from the gangplank to the captain with varying degrees of fear and respect.

"Dismiss the hands, Mr. Knox," Ford said quietly.

"All hands dismissed!" Knox called. "Second watch on deck!" Knox turned curtly to Ford and saluted him crisply. "Hands dismissed, sir!"

"Carry on," Ford said, moving stiffly toward the hatchway and down to his cabin.

Chapter Ten: The Frozen Man

"Land ho!" the lookout cried three days later as they neared another tall range of mountains.

"Land ho?" Knox cried in dismay. "What in the world is wrong with the man? We've been over land the past three days!"

"I think he's trying to tell us that he's spotted the village of Snowden," Ford guessed. "Pass the word to Mr. Sykes and the prince, if you please."

Knox smiled. "With pleasure, sir!" He raised his voice to shout, "Mr. Sykes! Crown Prince to stations, if you please!"

In twenty minutes they were low enough to winch the two men to the ground. Sykes waved when they crawled out of their cargo net and the two took off at a trot.

#

The Crown Prince had been very somber ever since the punishment of Jens. If Ford had any feelings for the prince, he would have been worried. As it was, particularly given the conflicting sentiments of his mother, the queen, and his father, the king, Ford was ambivalent about the prince's fate.

Sykes, for his part, had done as much as he could to cheer the prince up.

"He was a mutineer, a deserter, and he tried to kill not just his captain but this ship with all of us on it," Sykes had said when the prince brought the issue of Jens' punishment up. "What would you do with such a man?"

"I don't know," Nestor had said morosely. "Maybe we could have given him another chance?"

"Ah, but you see, the captain did that already," Sykes said. "By all rights, Jens should have walked the plank for deserting and the captain took him back."

"He forgave him once, why not twice?"

"Because the captain has to keep discipline," Sykes said. "Who's to say that Jens wouldn't have tried again with the balloons and killed us all?" Sykes shook his head with feigned sympathy. "He couldn't allow that, so he had to do what he did."

"I don't think I like the captain," Nestor said.

"Well that's too bad," Sykes said firmly. "Because he's the captain your father appointed to command this ship and he will be obeyed."

Nestor glowered at the other's words but said nothing.

#

And now they were off again with the special tea and the same con job to try again, this time with the new village of Snowden in Issia. Sykes glanced at the prince as they strode through the thick snow, their breath fogging white the cold air.

"It's so cold it'd freeze the balls off a brass monkey!" Sykes said.

"Whatever does that mean?" the prince asked as Sykes had planned.

"Did you see those bronze triangles up on the deck back on Spite?" Sykes asked. Nestor nodded. "Well we put the cannonballs on them, don't we?"

Again the prince nodded.

"The balls are held in place by dimples in the metal," Sykes said. "But when it gets too cold, the dimples shrink and the cannonballs roll away."

"Oh!" Nestor said in enlightenment.

"You thought I meant something else, didn't you?" Sykes asked with a grin.

"Well… yes," the prince admitted. "And I was wondering why anyone would want a brass monkey, let alone try to freeze it."

Sykes clapped the prince on his shoulder and barked a laugh. "Well now you know!" He glanced ahead to the patch of darker landscape in front of them. "We're nearing the mine, get ready for the act."

"I'm ready," Nestor said, looping his hands inside the coil of rope that Sykes had flung over his shoulder. When the crown prince was finished he pulled back against his bonds, looking for all purposes like someone tied up and being tugged by the ruffian, Sykes.

#

"It's Ophidian's will," one of the smirking guards said as they helped the crew of Spite load up with their coal.

"He needs our help!" the coal-mine's boss agreed with the same silly grin.

"That's right!" Annabelle called from the side of the ship as she supervised the loading of foodstuffs. "Ophidian ordered us here to do his bidding."

"You must be blessed to serve such a god," the guard said in awe. He turned to the other miners. "Let's get this done quickly, as Ophidian wishes."

"Ophidian's wishes must be obeyed," a young boy who'd come along with the others agreed.

"Wise lad," Sykes said, patting the boy on the top of his bare head.

"If he's so wise," Knox murmured for Ford's ears alone, "why isn't he dressed warmer?"

"Be sure to find him something so he doesn't catch his death of cold," Ford said looking at the nondescript youngster. "Can't have them freezing in Ophidian's name."

"Aye sir, I'll do that," Knox said.

#

They waved to the miners below as Spite took once more to the air, this time climbing higher than ever before — for they'd learned that this was the lowest spot in the mountain pass for hundreds of miles and Ford declared that they'd just have to climb above the mountains rather than wasting precious coal — and time — seeking a lower pass.

"Mr. Knox!" Ford called as he spied a small body dressed in warm furs. Knox rushed over to him. "I thought we agreed to get this lad some warm clothes, not bring him aboard."

"We need a ship's boy, sir," Knox said, nodding toward the young lad. "He volunteered."

"Did he?" Ford said, looking at the fur-wrapped boy racing about the deck, peering into this corner and that, all the while muttering low-voiced to himself. Ford heard part of his words, carried on the cold wind. "That's good," the boy said. A moment later, "That's not good."

"Is he daft?" Ford said to Knox.

"Who?" Knox asked.

"The boy," Ford said, surprised at his lieutenant.

"What boy?" Knox said. He blinked as he spotted the small boy in furs. "I thought we were going to give him furs, sir, not take him aboard!"

Ford shot his lieutenant a surprised look and then his expression changed. "What were we talking about?"

Knox shook his head. "I don't know sir," he said, troubled. "Something about the weather?"

"Perhaps," Ford agreed absently. He stood for a moment longer, straining to remember, then shook his head in exasperation. "Carry on."

"Aye sir!" Knox said, saluting and moving about his duties.

#

Ford was quite glad of the little boy — he never got his name — over the course of the next few days because the lad appeared at the most opportune times. Ford would find him holding a hot cup of tea and a warmed flask whenever Ford roused himself to check on the lookouts. He greeted the boy gladly and was thrilled to have him tag along. Sometimes the boy reminded Ford of something he'd forgot — the lad was a veritable life-saver.

Yet, as soon as he was out of sight, Ford would forget all about him. So much so that he never mentioned the lad to anyone else — he just didn't remember.

One night, he forgot to take a reading on the fork compass, only remembering when the boy prompted him.

"Right you are!" Ford cried in surprise. He patted his pockets. "I haven't any paper!"

The lad handed him a slip of paper. Ford wrote down the coordinates, thanked the lad and went happily below to compute their course.

In the comfort of his cabin he forgot all about the boy but when he was plotting his course, he remembered that he'd forgotten to take the reading, that someone had reminded him, and that he had been given a piece of paper. But who?

Ship's boy, the thought came to him and, relieved, he dismissed the issue from his mind again, more challenged by computing their course.

He ran through the numbers three times to be sure.

A days' sailing, no more.

#

"Morning captain!" Reedis called as soon as he spied Ford come up on deck. He clapped his hands together, puffed out a great gout of white breath, and smiled. "Seems a good day for it, whatever it'll be!"

"The ship's moving well today," Ford said, feeling the cold wind on his face and glancing around. He creased his brow. "Did Angus speed us up?"

"We're higher, too," Reedis said, looking around. He frowned. "That's odd."

"How do we get higher and faster if…" Ford broke off. "Mr. Knox! The coal!"

"Coal, sir?" Knox called back, rushing to join them. "What about it?"

"It's our heaviest cargo," Ford said.

"Actually, sir, the water is heavier," Reedis corrected. Ford glared at him and Reedis backed off, saying, "But we're definitely lighter."

"Check on the coal and the water, then," Ford said to Knox. The lieutenant gave him a puzzled look. "Something's wrong! We're too high and too fast and the only way that can happen is —"

"Is if we've lost something heavy," Knox finished grimly. "Sykes! Jenkins! I need you to check on stores!"

"Stores, sir!" Jenkins said, rushing to join them.

"No, need!" Annabelle shouted from the hatchway, pushing the prince up in front of her.

"Unhand me, I told you!" Nestor growled to the witch.

"We might need another plank," Annabelle said darkly. Ford gave her a surprised look. "I caught this one going through our coal locker." She paused, shoving Nestor forward and down to the wooden deck. "What's left of it."

"What?" Ford said. He glanced down to Nestor. "What did you do?"

"I didn't do anything," Nestor whined. "It's not my fault, I swear!"

Sykes spat. "Fat lot of good that'll do us," he said. He glanced to the captain. "I doubt we've got another hour's worth of coal and then we're —"

"Land ho!" the lookout shouted. "Oh my gods! Look ahead, look ahead!"

Alarmed by the lookout's fearful cries, Ford and the others raced to the bowsprit.

"What is that?" Nestor cried pointing to what they all saw.

In front of them, on the starboard bow, a huge shape loomed up out of the icy plains below. Whatever it was stood taller than Spite was flying.

"It looks like a man," Reedis. "Like a frozen man."

#

Indeed, as the huge shaped loomed closer and closer, Reedis proved right. The man was frozen, with his head peering down and over his left shoulder, his long beard encased in ice, his left arm outstretched to prop him up.

"He's got his hand on something!" Knox exclaimed as the morning haze lifted and they could see more details. He turned to Ford, in an awed expression. "That's the wyrm, sir!" Ford nodded. "It's the same wyrm!"

"Wyrm?" Reedis said. "A sea serpent?" He glanced down. "But what's it doing so far inland?"

"Being crushed by a god," Ford said grimly.

"A god?" Reedis said. "Are you saying — that's Arolan!"

"Indeed it is," Ford agreed. He turned back toward the stern and the still sprawling form of prince Nestor.

Annabelle took one look at the frozen god, one look at Ford and shook her head. "So that's why you took this ship."

"It's the only ship that can be on land," Ford said in oblique agreement.

"Well, it won't do any good no matter what," Angus' voice came grimly toward them. "We don't have any more coal."

"And how do you free a frozen god?" Reedis said, glancing once more to the blue shape coming clearer and clearer into view as Spite approached.

"I don't know," Ford said.

"It won't matter, we're never getting to that god," Angus said. "We'll be dead, propellers stopped in another twenty minutes or so."

Ford growled and stalked down the ship toward Nestor. "What did you do?"

"Nothing," Nestor whimpered. "Nothing at all. I just found them, that's all."

"Found what?"

"Nothing," Nestor said quickly, darting his head up to glance at Ford tentatively and then ducking down once more, his head touching the deck in reverse supplication.

"And now is the time to see what will be done," the young boy said, moving to stand beside the prone form of the crown prince and glancing toward Ford. "Will the right thing be done?"

Ford spared the lad an angry look and then shook his head, forgetting him once more. He strode past Nestor, shouting over his head, "Someone hold him!" And then he was down below, striding toward the coal locker.

It was empty. There were only a very few small lumps left. The locker should have been brim full with them. Ford started to turn away when something caught his eye. He turned back and stared. Nothing. He turned away and — there! A gleam of light. He bent down and carefully picked up the small gleaming stone.

Diamond.

"What turns coal into diamond?" Ford wondered aloud. Footsteps came rushing down the passageway and Ford turned to see Reedis and Annabelle.

"What did you say?" Annabelle asked, looking at the empty locker and turning pale.

"We're going to die out here, aren't we?" Reedis said. "Angus said we've got about a half-hour of steam, then we stop. And freeze."

"You can lower us," Annabelle said.

"To the icy plain below?" Reedis said, shaking his head. "Death might be quicker up here but it's death either up or down."

"What turns coal into diamond?" Ford said again, looking at the two.

The two exchanged looks and Reedis pursed his lips before saying, "Only a god can do this."

Annabelle frowned and nodded. "Ophidian."

"Even so, there must be a whole lot more of these little diamonds," Reedis said. "We know that diamonds are made from the same substance as coal only crushed under the weight and heat of the deep earth."

"I know where!" Ford shouted, rushing out of the locker and down towards the cabins. He stopped outside Nestor's, burst the door open and began a quick but thorough search.

"Under the floorboards," Annabelle said as she caught up with him. Ford nodded, already in the process of stooping down. He saw one spot that was different, gave a snort of disgust at the prince's poor hiding abilities, then pulled out the slat and came up with handfuls of diamonds.

"Whatever was he thinking?" Reedis said as he joined them. "There must be a king's ransom here!"

"Or a prince's," Ford said. "That's probably what he was thinking." He grabbed a sack and filled it quickly with all the diamonds he could. To the others he said, "Get the rest."

"Where are you going?" Annabelle asked.

"On deck," Ford said. "I have to tell the crew."

"They'll kill the prince," Reedis warned.

Ford shrugged. He didn't care. He was going join his long-lost god, Arolan, here in the frozen north. For all he knew, he and Spite would sail forever in the frozen sky.

#

On deck, the crew had gathered around the still prone form of the crown prince. Sykes stood over him, not protecting him from the occasional angry kick of the others.

"Men!" Ford shouted, gathering their attention. He heard Reedis and Annabelle come up and join him, their lungs heaving in the freezing air as they carried the sacks of diamonds up to the deck. Angus saw them, frowned, and moved to stand at Ford's side.

"We have been betrayed," Ford said, pointing to Nestor. "The coal is all gone and soon the ship will be stopped, motionless here over hundreds of miles of barren frozen ground."

The crew groaned in shock.

"The prince stole this," Ford said, upending his sacks of tiny diamonds. The crew looked at the sparkling gems, first in surprise and then in growing delight. Before they could react, he raised a hand. "But the prince could not make our coal — our life's blood — into diamonds." He paused to let them consider that. "That took a god."

The men's eyes went wide and then they started nodding and murmuring in agreement.

"I cannot say which god we enraged," Ford replied. "Except for that god, over there." He pointed ahead. The others craned their necks to the distant frozen god, then back to Ford. "That is the god Arolan, king of the sea."

Some of the airmen took a second look, others gave Ford looks of disbelief and doubt. "I know because I was oathsworn to him," Ford said. He pointed to Knox who nodded. "Oathsworn after a wyrm attacked our ship five years ago." He pointed toward the god's feet. "That wyrm, there." He waited a moment. "The sea god was betrayed and we helped trap him here in the north."

"Who can betray a god?" Nestor asked in a small voice.

"Another god," Annabelle said sourly, appalled at the sniveling man's lack of wits. "Who else?"

"Who would betray the sea god?" Nestor asked, rising to a crouch. "I mean, who would be so foolish?"

"Whoever would gain at the sea god's loss," Ford said.

Nestor frowned. "My father?"

Ford pursed his lips. "It's possible," he admitted, then shook his head. "But it doesn't matter." He turned to the crew. "I swore to help the sea god as best I could." He dropped his head. "And now I'll only be able to keep him company, frozen here in the north."

"What about the diamonds?" a boy's voice called out. Ford frowned for a moment, trying to remember something about a boy but his thoughts were drowned out by the din of the airmen's voices in agreement.

"It's our lives," Ford said, picking up a handful of diamonds and throwing them toward the crew, "it's our treasure."

The crew roared in amazement and delight.

Ford raised a hand, and they all stopped racing forward to the gleaming diamonds on the deck.

"We'll divvy them fair and square," Ford said. He nodded to Knox. "See to it."

"Now, sir?"

"Now," Ford said, nodding. "We've not got much time left, might as well let the lads enjoy it."

"We'll be frozen rich, we will," Sykes said, glaring at the prince.

"Who knows what we would have seen," Marder said, "had we gone to the far north." He shook his head, eyeing Knox studiously as the other started to portion out the diamonds, more now that Reedis and Annabelle had dumped their sacks.

"Krea will be safe," Angus said. "And she'll… she'll never know what happened to us."

"Only if the gods don't tell her," the small boy warned. Angus glanced toward the sound of the voice but couldn't spot its owner.

Angus turned to Ford. "What will you do with your portion, captain?"

Ford frowned, lifting a small pile up in his hand and tossing the pretty glints in his palm.

"Dead, these are no use to me," Ford said. He glanced toward the frozen god in the distance. The distance was much closer now. There were near enough to see Arolan's frozen eyelids protecting his frozen eyes. He frowned. "It's been a good life, I have no complaints."

"'Could have lived longer," Annabelle suggested.

It took more time than Ford had guessed to divvy up the diamonds appropriately. When Knox touched finally his hand to his forehead in salute, they were right beside the frozen form of Arolan.

"All done, captain," Knox said.

"Very well," Ford said. He went to the starboard rail and stood looking at Arolan. Finally he raised the hand that held the diamonds in a grim salute. "My god, I salute you!"

And he threw the diamonds into the sky. As they fell, they formed a rainbow on the way to the ground.

"I salute you!" Annabelle said, tossing her diamonds after Ford's.

"Arolan!" Knox shouted, throwing his diamonds far out toward the frozen god.

"To the gods!" Angus said, throwing his share.

"What the hell, to the gods!" Sykes shouted, throwing his lot as well.

One by one, the crew came to salute the frozen god and threw their diamonds to the ground.

A long rainbow streamed behind them falling earthwards.

"Did he get his share?" Ford said, pointing to Nestor.

"He did," Knox allowed sourly. To the crown prince he said, "You're now the richest man on the ship."

Nestor opened his eyes and glanced up at the sailors and officers looking down at him. He rose, helped up by the small boy who appeared at his side.

He nodded to the boy in thanks and continued slowly to the ship's side.

"God Arolan, I salute you!" Nestor shouted, throwing his diamonds high into the air. In a lower voice he added, "I couldn't freeze to death in better company."

Ford looked at him in surprise. "Why, my prince, I've never been prouder of you than in this moment."

Nestor looked over to him and bowed low. "My captain, I am proud to have your praise."

"Look!" Reedis shouted.

"Magic!" Annabelle swore as if in pain. "My gods, the magic!"

Ford looked around at them and then toward where they were pointing.

On their side, the frozen god stirred.

"Arolan!" Ford cried in amazement.

"Arolan!" "Arolan!" "Arolan!" the crew shouted, moving to the side and cheering at the sight of a god slowing wakening, breaking out of his icy cage and stirring in the frozen sky.

"Well," Ford said to Knox, "it was worth it."

"Indeed it was," Knox agreed.

"It is not over yet," the small boy said, laughing. "I advise you all to hold on!"

Ford looked around for the small boy and suddenly moved to grab Annabelle and Reedis. "Hold on!"

The great god Arolan turned his head, pursed his lips —

— and blew the royal airship Spite deep into the bitter north, high in the frozen sky.

Wyvern's Fate

Book 4

Twin Soul series

Chapter One: Flight

With a final triumphant cry, Krea clawed her way higher and higher above the outraged townsfolk, soaring through the falling snow to heights which made her newfound wings ache with joy. She was on fire. So hot that the snow melted all around her. She shrieked in triumph, flinging her defiance not just to the king and the townsfolk but also to Ametza, the town's sea goddess.

Water! What was Ametza's power compared to Krea's burning flame and soaring wings?

Contemptuously, Krea turned north and flew steadily away from the seaside town.

She reveled in her flight. She swooped down and soared back up in the skies, joyful for every new feeling, every wingbeat.

On and on she flew. Minutes became hours. Still the snow fell. And still Krea, with her new wyvern body, with the heat of the "twin souls," flew onward.

The wyvern had given her a gift greater than she could possibly imagine, even if it was at a price more painful than she ever dreamed. Her new heart, the one that had grown after Angus, her betrothed, had pierced the old one, beat strongly, loudly.

She was fire, she was steam, she was boundless.

She was bloody freezing! Suddenly, Krea realized that she was shivering. Her wings were lead weights that she could barely lift one more time. She found herself gliding more, flapping less. And less, and less.

The ground loomed in front of her. There was something wrong with getting too near the ground, Krea thought. But the snow — all that pleasant whiteness — it called to her. She could wrap herself in its soft blanket and be comforted. That notion seemed off, though with each passing painful flap, it grew more and more attractive. She could close her eyes. Rest. Sleep. If just for a moment.

Wham!

Krea woke long enough to realize that she'd hit the ground hard. She'd hurt more than she could ever imagine. And then she knew no more.

#

Bells rang around her. She was moving. Her wings… she couldn't feel her wings! She felt warm, comfortable. The motion was steady, slow. There was no rush of wind in her ears. She was on the ground. On something else that moved.

Krea opened her eyes. She was in a brightly colored caravan, wrapped in a quilt of warm furs. A lantern housed a single candle that gave the whole interior a fuzzy, warm light.

"Don't move," a woman's voice called from beyond the canvas covering at the front of the caravan. "We'll be there soon."

"Where?" Krea asked. And then, "And who are you?"

"I'm Ibb's driver," the voice replied. "I'm taking you to safety."

"The north?" Krea guessed, recalling her conversation with mechanical Ibb before she'd changed from a girl to a flying twin-souled wyvern.

"The house of the north," the woman said in agreement. "You'll be safe there."

The woman made some guttural noise and the caravan slowed. Stopped. A sound of rustling heralded the woman's arrival through the canvas door.

Krea realized she could hear but couldn't twist her head upwards to peer toward the front of the caravan. Her worry was relieved when the woman stepped into her view.

A multi-colored scarf covered her mouth. Her eyes were hazel and warm. Her skin was freckled. Krea caught sight of large boots and a thick brown leather coat. The woman moved out of her view, toward the front of the caravan and rattled some dishes. A moment later she returned with a bowl of something steaming that smelled heavenly.

"You shouldn't move," the woman said, as she knelt beside her. She spooned some of the hot liquid from the bowl, blew on it and drank. Satisfied, she turned to Krea and repeated the process, spooning the liquid into Krea's parched mouth. She kept feeding her until Krea finally felt warm. Somehow, without speaking, the other woman knew for she finished the bowl herself. "You rest now," the woman said. "We've still got a long ways to go."

"Who are you?"

"I'm Lyric," the woman replied, her eyes twinkling. She made a pushing motion toward Krea, indicating that she shouldn't move. "Sleep, we'll be there before you wake again."

#

As if Lyric's words were a spell, sleep engulfed Krea immediately. She slipped into a comforting darkness. In the darkness, two golden eyes opened. Krea knew she was sleeping, but could not wake up. She also knew that this was not a dream, it was something different altogether.

"Are you Ophidian?" she asked, wondering if the god had once again laid his eye on her.

"No, my dear," a woman's voice replied. She recognized it instantly, it was Annora.

"I know you," Krea said.

A face started to appear around the golden eyes. It was a wyvern, similar to the one she had seen only a few days ago. But this wyvern was different, she had white scales and golden eyes. A winter wyvern.

"In a way, yes," the wyvern said.

"But you aren't Annora." Krea replied.

The wyvern nodded its head, her expression grim.

"No, I am Wymarc. My dear Annora has gone with the Ferryman to judgment."

Krea remembered. She was in the field of blue wyvern flowers when she asked Annora how she could help her. When she was offered a gift, one that could let her speak to the gods themselves, she impulsively agreed. But the gift had a price as well as a reward: the price was that she had to die; the reward was that she became a twin-souled wyvern. To complete the transformation, her betrothed, Angus Franck, her father's apprentice, had pierced her heart with her mother's hatpin.

Krea felt the sting of grief, but it was not her grief. It was Wymarc's grief, tears welled in her golden eyes.

"I am sorry for your loss," Krea said, wanting to reach out a hand, and into her vision came one. It was her hand as she remembered it. Pale with thin long fingers, with several scars from her younger impulsive nature.

Her hand touched Wymarc's face, and she smiled.

"My dear, this will not be easy for either of us. Learning to share a body never is."

Wymarc formed changed suddenly, from a face to a magnificent body, white-scaled, with two legs and powerful wings. Swirls seemed to be carved into each of her scales.

Krea realized what Wymarc had meant. She remembered falling off that cliff and transforming.

This form was her. She had become a wyvern.

Chapter Two: Meetings

Krea woke up to see nothing but white and an eerie silence.

Was she dead? She looked closer and realized it was white marble. More pristine than the marble she had ever seen in the temple of Ametza.

She heard a rocking noise, and saw a young woman, about the same age as her, rocking back in forth in an old wooden rocking chair which was painted white to match the room. She wore all white, and her black hair was twisted into a bun. She was knitting a hat out of blood-red dyed wool. A cold chill went down Krea's spine.

"For a moment, I thought I was dead," Krea said to the young woman.

The young woman nodded, and reached next to Krea. Krea flinched, but then realized that beside her was a table made from the same white marble. A dented copper teapot sat on it, next to a pair of circular gold-rimmed sunglasses.

Were those glasses for her?

She took a deep breath. She recognized the tea's scent immediately. Her mother had once served it to her, many years before. It was imported from a land far away.

"Green tea," she said.

The young woman nodded, and poured the tea into a chipped, faded colorful cup, then offered it to Krea. She waited while Krea drank her tea, refilled the cup when Krea had emptied it and waited, still silent, until parched Krea had drunk her fill.

"Who are you?" Krea asked, but before the girl could answer, Lyric walked in. She recognized her by her eyes and freckles.

"Hello, Krea," Lyric said, then turned to the young woman. "Thank you for your help."

The young woman nodded, and then exited the room.

"Can you walk yet?" Lyric asked.

Krea moved her legs and noticed she was wearing a simple white dress.

"Good, come with me," Lyric said as she walked toward the door.

"But I have so many questions to ask you!" Krea said.

Lyric turned and gave Krea a smile, then pointed to sunglasses and a pair of brown leather shoes on the ground next to her bed.

"After all you have been through, you should speak to the gods first. Their wisdom surpasses mine. Oh, and wear those shoes. They were made for you."

Krea slipped into the shoes, the leather wrapped around her feet perfectly. She then put on the glasses. They were molded to her face comfortably, and a strain and low level of eye pain she was accustomed to vanished.

Lyric began to walk out the door and Krea followed.

"Where are we?" Krea asked as she caught up with Lyric. The new shoes fit really well. Krea thought she'd never had such marvelous shoes in her life. She said to Lyric, who nodded in appreciation.

"They owners of this place can be kind, if they wish," Lyric said.

They walked down a long corridor which faded from white marble to yellow marble. There were several corridors branching off to the left and right but they passed them without pause. Krea didn't even have enough time to peer down them in curiosity as Lyric bustled them forward.

The corridor opened out into a large foyer and Lyric slowed. Krea saw that in front of them were a set of steps in a wide staircase leading upwards. The stairs stopped in front of a pair of brilliant silver double doors. On either side of the door large marble hands circled them.

"Are those supposed to be Ametza's hands?" Krea asked.

Lyric chuckled, "Ametza is a young arrogant god. It disgusts me how she tries to make herself seem as if she is Mother Terrene herself."

Krea had been introduced to all the gods in the small wooden set that had been passed down to her by her mother. She mostly worshipped Ametza, the sea goddess of where she lived. All the gods were created by the great mother, Terrene, and she created this world as a way from them to play and grow as she slept.

Terrene was asleep, so no one prayed to her, as far as Krea knew. All she had learned was taught to her in the temple, or in whispers from her father. She realized she may not even a part of the whole truth.

Lyric stopped, gesturing Krea forward. Krea gave her a worried look. Lyric gestured her forward once more, saying, "You must meet the gods alone."

Krea took a deep breath and climbed the stairs. Krea has been shunned by Ametza, and seen by Ophidian, and had survived. Her father always told her if she trusts her own judgement and heart, the gods would respect her. Hopefully they would.

Krea squared her shoulders and pushed both doors open at once. She entered a room which seemed endless and huge. Soft light streamed through the purple stained glass ceiling.

"Wymarc?" Krea asked out loud with worry.

This is your test, my dear, yours alone, Wymarc's voice spoke inside her head.

Krea nodded, took a steadying breath, and stepped away from the doors. They closed silently behind her, cutting off the light that had streamed in.

In front of her, and to her left and her right, were huge statues. Statues of the gods.

"I'm sorry, I don't know you all," Krea spoke out loud, curtsying deeply toward them all and spreading out her arms as gracefully as her awkward self could manage. She held the curtsy for a long while, feeling that the gods were judging her. Finally, beyond the pain of her tired muscles, she stood up and moved forward once more. "I'm only young and I lived in Kingsland all my life," she told them as she glanced from one figure to the next, not sure what she was looking for or even if she was looking for anything at all. "My name is Krea Zebala and my father was Rabel Zebala —" she cut herself off, putting a hand to her mouth in shock. *Was?* Quickly, she spoke again, "Please, please, can you tell me if my father is all right? I worry about him so."

Silence greeted her. She moved forward, keeping a sigh of disappointment to herself. She finally dared to look up at the face of one of the statues. It was a bearded man, his face, eyebrows, beard, every part of him covered in ice. He looked frozen and forlorn. Krea imagined that he was a nice man… god. She wondered why the figure was frozen, did it show her the god as he was now? She turned and saw Ametza, the sea goddess beside the man.

She appeared very similarly to the figurine she had back home. Ametza's skin seemed to be made of pearl and she wore a long dress if fish-like scales of blueish green. Instead of hair, she had long curled tentacles that seemed to move on their own.

Was he her husband? Was Ametza married like the other young elemental gods? Ametza seemed to glare down at Krea. Did she know she was here? Did she know… she was twin-souled?

What did it mean, to be twin-souled? Krea realized she'd never thought of it. She only knew that she'd wanted to help the mortally wounded wyvern, wanted to offer her comfort. And she'd made a bargain without knowing the consequences.

She forced herself to move onward, past the frozen god and the frowning Ametza. Two more gods loomed up. They were glowing and fiery. Their skin seemed to be carved from coal, and their eyes were small orbs of fire. They both wore robes of what looked like melting lava.

Krea knew they were the gods of fire.

I am Vorg, the male god told her with a bright, shiny voice.

I am Veva, the female god added.

Krea curtsied to the both of them. "I'm very pleased to meet you."

We greet you, fire-borne, Vorg told her solemnly, *we recognize you.*

"Are you sworn to Ophidian?" Krea asked.

No, Vorg responded with a laugh in his tone. *We are his younger siblings,.*

He is one of the Eldest, Veva added. *But we are all of the fire.*

The younger gods rule the elements, Vorg said. *Gods of water, fire, earth, and air.*

Krea groped for an answer. "And are there two gods for each element?"

Yes, Veva said. *Please excuse us, we must be elsewhere.*

The light of the two gods faded and the statues turned dull.

I've spoken with gods! Krea thought to herself, thrilled and terrified both. The frozen god must be Ametza's husband, she decided.

She moved on, pausing to curtsy before the gods of earth and the gods of air. They did not give her their names, although she thought that perhaps the gods of air might speak with her. Perhaps another day. In fact, on reflection, Krea hoped that it would be another day — speaking with gods was extremely tiring.

Well, go get some rest, then! A voice spoke inside her head, not hiding its irritation. Krea looked up and saw Ophidian.

"Wymarc, you've found another child, haven't you?" Ophidian said, not speaking to Krea but speaking for Krea's ears. Wymarc did not reply.

"She said that this meeting was mine alone," Krea told the god apologetically.

"Did she?" Ophidian said. "Always scheming, she is." The figure turned its head upwards, the stone glowing red-hot as it melted to accommodate the motions of the god. Finally, Ophidian turned the head back down to her. "And what is it you wish to say?"

"Is my father all right?" Krea said impulsively. Instantly she regretted her rash question but she decided that she had the right to ask — Ophidian had given her the chance.

The fiery red eyes twinkled and grew brighter. Then they closed for a moment. "What would you offer for his safety?"

"What would you have me do?" Krea asked. "I'm only a —" she stopped.

"A little girl?" Ophidian finished for her, not hiding the laughter in his voice. "But you're not, now, are you?"

"No," Krea said. "I don't know what I am."

She felt her lips start to move, but not by her own accord. Wymarc was speaking through her.

She is my savior, Wymarc spoke through Krea's lips. Krea could feel her intent turn to the god. *Without her, I would not be here and the Ferryman would have carried two souls onwards.*

"And what did you give her in return?" Ophidian asked, clearly hearing the words that seemed, to Krea at least, to be only spoken in her head.

A choice, a chance to save a life, Wymarc replied.

"I have already helped Rabel before," Ophidian said.

You will help him again, then, Wymarc said.

"Who are you to order me around?" Ophidian demanded, his tone growing irritated.

Because after all I have done for you, you owe me this at least, Wymarc said.

"I'll make him do it" Ophidian said.

No doubt you will, Wymarc agreed, *and charge him dearly for the honor.*

"Don't hurt him!" Krea cried and was suddenly aghast with the knowledge that she'd shouted at a god — she'd *ordered* Ophidian.

"If you survive the judgement, I shall do as you say, Krea Zebala, child of Rabel," Ophidian said, turning the head once more to point forward, unseeing. And then the god's spirit left and the statue cooled into a cold, lifeless figure.

"What judgement?" Krea asked out loud. No one answered her, not even Wymarc.

Chapter Three: Wymarc

"What did you learn?" Lyric asked as Krea closed the doors behind her. "Did the gods favor you?"

"My father is alive," Krea told her, "I was *so* worried about him!"

"Is that all?"

Krea wondered why Lyric was asking her these questions? Her father had taught her that her relationships with the gods were a private matter. Even the shaman at Ametza's temple let each person have time to pray to the goddess alone; no questions were asked after.

"It is more than enough for me," Krea said, deciding to heed her father's advice. She changed the subject, saying, "Is there anything I can get to eat? I'm hungry."

Lyric nodded and gestured for Krea to follow her. They went back down the long marble corridor but turned at the second right and continued a long way before Krea smelled marvelous scents coming toward them, the strongest being that of freshly baked bread.

"Not so fast!" Lyric said as Krea's feet picked up the pace. Krea turned back to her in apology but found that she couldn't slow herself.

She turned, in front of Lyric, into a large room which was sparsely filled with various peoples and arranged into a large dining hall. She stopped suddenly as a dozen pairs of eyes turned to her.

Krea froze, realizing that she wasn't wearing her hat. Her face was bare and exposed to the eyes of all these people. She wanted to turn back, shrink in on herself, turn invisible — anything to avoid the inevitable scorn heaped upon her because she was an albino. But the moment passed, the people turned to their food or back to their conversation, treating her as if she was nothing strange, just a normal person.

A normal person, Krea thought to herself. *To them, I'm normal.*

"Most of the people here came because of the gods," Lyric told her. She gestured and Krea followed.

There was a counter and behind it was a large, plump woman with bright smiling eyes.

"What can I do for you, dear?" the woman asked in a rich, warm voice. She was short voluptuous women with long blond hair in braided bun. She appeared to be in her thirties and wore a long white dress with a bright red apron.

"I'm hungry, is there something I can get to eat?" Krea asked politely. She turned to Lyric, "Is there something you recommend?"

"Oh, you're the one in the white room!" the woman said. She glanced to Lyric. "I'm glad to see her out and about."

"She's been to the room of the gods," Lyric said.

"Oh, and she's still alive?" the woman said approvingly. "Then I suppose we should feed you, at least this day." She glanced toward Lyric. "And you, dear? Did you visit the gods, also?"

"Of course," Lyric said, seeming affronted at the woman's question. "They were most useful."

"You brought her here," the woman said. The woman looked at Krea, then stretched a hand across the counter. "I'm Sybil. I manage the cooking here."

"It smells wonderful," Krea said, reaching up to grab the woman's hand. "I'm Krea Zebala."

"The new twin soul," Sybil agreed easily. She met Krea's eyes and seemed to peer through them, into a place Krea couldn't see. "Good to see you again, Wymarc," she said. "You've picked a sprightly one this time."

Krea didn't know what to say. This woman knew Wymarc? How?

"And you, dear," she said, looking at Krea once more, "you come from Kingsland?"

Krea nodded in surprise.

"So something fishy and spicy?" Sybil asked, turning back to the stove.

"What did Wymarc like?" Krea asked.

Sybil turned back again, with a bowl of something steaming in her hand and put it on the counter. "You'd have to ask her, dear."

Krea got the sinking feeling that she'd done something wrong and took the bowl with a nod of thanks.

"Same as yesterday?" Sybil said to Lyric. Sybil turned and prepared a quick tray. Krea was surprised to see that Lyric's tray was nothing more than cut vegetables, nothing warm or cooked. She kept her surprise to herself, nodding to Lyric who led them to a table.

As they sat, Krea noticed that the woman who had been tending her in her room was seated a few tables over. The woman had her knitting piled on a chair next to her.

Krea took in the light in the room, the carved ceiling, the decorations on the wall and said to Lyric, "I've never seen anything so beautiful."

"Of course not," Lyric said, picking up a raw carrot and munching it down.

"In your caravan we ate soup," Krea said. "Did you want to try some of mine?"

"I eat hot when I have to," Lyric said. She seemed to think for a moment, then said, "I eat when I have to."

Krea looked around. "What is this place?"

"The gods did not tell you?" Lyric asked. Krea shook her head. "Then I shouldn't tell you, either."

"How long are we going to stay here?" Krea asked.

Lyric shrugged. "As long as it takes." She picked up a radish and chomped on it ferociously, ending the conversation.

When they were finished, Krea picked up her tray and looked around. "Where do I take this?"

"Leave it," a voice called to her. She looked over and saw that it was the knitting woman who spoke. "When your turn comes, you'll be assigned to clean."

"Thank you," Krea said. "I didn't know." She tried a tentative smile out, saying, "I'm Krea."

"I am Hana," the young woman replied, rising from her seat and grabbing her knitting with one hand, stretching out the other hand to Krea.

Krea took it and shook it gladly. "Thank you for looking after me."

Hana gave her a nervous glance and said hastily, "It was nothing. I was told to do it."

"Well, thank you anyway," Krea said. "I'm sure that you gave Lyric much relief." Hana raised an eyebrow and looked at Lyric in confusion.

"We should go back to your room," Lyric said, tugging on Krea's sleeve. "I'm sure you'll want to rest."

Krea looked back toward Hana. "I hope to see you again soon."

Hana grabbed her knitting tighter and gave Krea a worried look.

#

Krea wasn't tired but Lyric insisted she drink a sleeping draught and closed the curtains in white room, leaving her in silence.

"Will Hana come watch me?" Krea asked as Lyric turned to the door.

"I don't think it's her day," Lyric said unhelpfully, shutting the door behind her quietly.

Her day? Krea thought. Was Krea just a duty, like clearing trays in the dining hall? She hoped that Hana thought more of her than that but she couldn't be sure. The girl seemed… lost.

Hana's . Her dark eyes had seemed to gleam with an intensity that almost frightened Krea, yet Hana seemed wary, confused, like her silence — and her knitting — were shields to protect her.

Krea turned over in her bed and closed her eyes.

The world was nothing like she'd imagined. She had taken her choice and now… she wondered what it would mean. She was here, in a place where she could talk to the gods and was watched by silent knitters.

She was just drifting off to sleep when Ophidian's words came back to her: *If you survive the judgement.*

What judgement? Survive what?

Krea tried to force herself back to wakefulness but the draught, and the food, were too much and she sank into dark, troubling dreams.

#

She was with Wymarc. She saw that the wyvern was crying, she looked devastated. Krea moved toward her, reached out a hand that wasn't, trying to offer the wyvern comfort.

"How can I help you?" Krea asked. "I am here for you."

"That is the problem," Wymarc said. "You are here."

Krea pulled her hand back, deeply hurt. "What, you don't want me here?"

Wymarc turned her gaze on her, tears burning down her brilliant white muzzle, over the white scales with the intricate gold filigree. "It is not you, dear. It is that I have you."

"What?" Krea was confused. "I don't understand."

"For thousands of years this has been," Wymarc said, almost as if to herself. "It has always been this way."

"This is all new to me," Krea said. "I have only sixteen years, not thousands."

"And that, my dear, is why I cry," Wymarc told her sadly, turning her head away from Krea's eyes.

The image of the crying wyvern faded from Krea's sight and the world turned formless, dark.

I was only trying to help, Krea wailed.

You did dear, that is the problem, came a reply.

Krea groped for words, for understanding, but her dream slipped away from her and sleep reclaimed her.

Chapter Four: The Chore

The next morning, Lyric came for Krea. She waited until she had dressed and led her down the corridors to the dining hall. Sybil greeted her cheerfully and offered Krea gruel but Krea pointed to the large golden brown stack of thin bread.

"Oh, you want pancakes?" Sybil said.

"Is that what they are?" Krea said. "They look like flatbreads."

"They're much more tasty," Sybil said. "Warm, with butter, and lavender syrup, they're food for the gods."

"They're too rich," Lyric said, nodding to Sybil who, with a frown, placed another plate of raw vegetables on the counter.

"We've got eggs, and bacon, if you'd like," Sybil said to Krea.

"What do you recommend?"

"The bacon, some eggs, and a stack of pancakes will start your day properly," Sybil said with a firm nod. She quickly assembled a plate and set it on the counter in front of Krea who put it on her tray with a quick curtsy in thanks. She gestured for Krea to wait, turned to the stove and assembled another offering. "And here's a pot of vanilla tea with a hint of rosebuds. I concoct this myself. It's also recommended for healing and recovering."

"Hana," Krea called as she picked out the pile of knitting on a table nearby, "can we sit with you?"

"I'll sit over here," Lyric declared, moving toward an empty table.

Hana looked up, her mouth full, and gave Krea a startled look.

Krea took a seat opposite her and glanced down at her piping hot plate of food. "Do you think I'm eating too much?"

Hana shook her head quickly.

"How old are you?" Krea asked as she sliced into the stack of pancakes, and put the food into her mouth. "Oh, by the gods, this is great!" she cried when she could talk once more.

"It is good," Hana agreed. She gave Krea a look. "Have you never tried pancakes before?"

"I never even heard of them," Krea admitted. She raised her fork with more food on it. "Have you? Did you want to try?"

Hana shook her head quickly and took a bite of her food. Krea recognized it as an omelet with bits of ham and cheese.

"Where do you come from?" Krea asked. "I came from Kingsland."

"I come from the far east," Hana said. She shivered. "I do not like the cold." She raised her knitting. "Which is why I'm making things to keep me warm."

"It's not cold!" Krea said, looking around the large room in wonder.

"Inside, no," Hana said. She gestured beyond the walls that surrounded them. "Outside, it is the bitter north."

"North?" Krea said. "I flew that way."

"For how long?" Hana said. "And you flew?"

"I gave an oath to a wyvern," Krea said. "And I turned into a wyvern."

"Of course," Hana said, sounding enlightened, "you are a twin soul of Ophidian's get."

"And you?" Krea asked.

"I am fleeing the gods," Hana said. "They are angry with me."

"Why?"

"I have not had the courage to ask them," Hana replied, lowering her gaze to her food in shame.

"I'm sure you will," Krea told her stoutly. "Who did you give your oath to?"

"I did not give an oath," Hana said, her lips turning down. "I was sacrificed."

"Sacrificed?" Krea repeated in horror. "By whom?"

Hana dropped her gaze and shook her head mutely.

Lyric rose from her table loudly. She came over to them, saying to Hana, "Is she disturbing you?"

Hana kept her eyes downcast and shook her head again.

Lyric turned her eyes to Krea. "You shouldn't cause trouble."

"I didn't mean to!" Krea cried.

Lyric paid her no heed, jerking her head toward the exit. "Come with me."

Krea gave Hana an apologetic look and rose from the table. A short, bustling woman approached them, eyeing Krea unfavorably.

"Is there trouble?" the woman asked, frowning at Krea. She glanced at Lyric. "You said there would be no trouble."

"It is not of my doing," Lyric said, waving toward Krea.

"I will not have trouble in my house," the woman scolded Krea.

"Your house?" Krea repeated in surprise. She dropped into a curtsy. "Please, my lady of this marvelous house, accept all my apologies for however I may have wronged anyone here."

"She did nothing wrong," Hana said quietly from where she still sat, head bowed.

"*I* determine who stays in my house," the woman replied frostily.

Hana rose from her chair and met the woman's eyes frankly. "I will take charge of her, if you wish."

"I have been given that task already," Lyric told the dark woman.

"You say Ibb appointed you," the woman said, turning to Lyric. She pointed at Krea. "She did not."

"She would have died in the snows without me," Lyric said, her face going cold.

"That is not known," a new voice — a boy's — piped up from behind Krea. Krea turned quickly and saw a young boy, perhaps ten. She smiled at him and he smiled back, then waved a hand toward the lady of the house.

Krea turned back again, and saw that the boy had disappeared. She stared at the empty space for a moment, then turned back to the lady of the house. "I'm sorry, the boy…"

"What boy?" Lyric asked, giving Krea a look like she'd lost her wits.

"Never mind him," the lady of the house said. "We're talking about *you*."

"I can watch out for her," Hana said again. She rose from her chair and turned to the lady. "Really, it won't be any trouble."

"Both of you have been here for *days* and neither of you has done any chores," the lady said waspishly.

"My lady," Krea said, curtsying once more, "please tell me how I can be of service."

"How remains to be seen," the lady said sternly. Then her expression relaxed and she sighed. "At the very least you can help Sybil with the dishes."

"A pleasure!" Krea said, curtsying once more and rising to grab her tray, ready to bring it back to the kitchen.

"The cleaning room is over *there*," the lady said, gesturing toward a door that Krea hadn't noticed before. Under her breath, she muttered, "Really! To even *imagine* mixing good food and waste together!"

"I'm sorry," Krea said. "Our kitchen had the only sink in our —"

"Please!" the woman stopped her with an upraised hand. "I don't care what was in your past, child."

"Yes, my lady," Krea said dutifully. She started toward the door, then turned back. "Is there any other way I may serve?"

"My name is Avice, as you should well know," the lady replied sternly. She waved a hand toward the door. "Just clean all the dishes, that'll be a sufficient start."

"As my lady Avice wishes," Krea said, ducking her head in acknowledgement. She walked swiftly to the indicated door, turned around to open it with her butt because her arms were full and entered. As the door closed, she saw Lyric speaking to Avice and Hana looking on in worry.

She turned around to head forward, discovering that she was in a hallway. She listened and heard sounds coming from the doorway to the left but none from the right. The sounds on the left were kitchen sounds, so Krea guessed that Sybil was there. To the right, she decided, must be the cleaning room.

She entered and found a room full of dirty dishes. *Had no one cleaned, ever?* Krea asked herself in outrage.

She looked around the room. There were two sinks — both full — and four tables piled her with dirty cookware, plates, bowls, forks, spoons, knives — it was endless. Several things had green mold on them, Krea noted in disgust.

In addition to the four tables there were three carts on wheels, all full of dirty cookware.

How could anyone ever hope to clean all this? Krea thought in despair.

A sound startled her and she looked up to find Sybil wheeling in another cart full of dirty dishes.

"Oh!" Sybil said. "You volunteered! I was hoping it would be you."

"There are so many dishes," Krea said, waving at the piles.

"I'm sorry," Sybil said, "it's just that I get so caught up in cooking that I forget that things need cleaning, too." She turned to leave, calling back over her shoulder, "Of course, all this is no problem for you."

"For me?" Krea said. "Why me?"

"You're a wyvern, dear," Sybil replied as though it was obvious.

"How does being a wyvern help with *dishes?*" Krea wailed. But Sybil was already gone.

Krea was no stranger to soap and water, being responsible for her father's kitchen from an early age, and, earlier, being her mother's helper. So she looked at the large sinks, at the jars of soap stacked on shelves above them and thought merely to add soap to one of the sinks, use the other for rinsing, and slowly —

— but the sinks were clogged with dirty dishes! And there were no towels to dry the dishes once they were washed!

The whole situation was impossible!

Krea turned at a noise behind her and saw Hana.

"Can I help?" she asked quietly.

Krea gave her a look, gestured at the dishes, at the sink and wailed, "I don't see how *anyone* can help!"

"Well, I'm pretty good at drying dishes," Hana allowed. She glanced at the sink. "I don't suppose you could use fire magic and heat the water?"

"Fire magic?"

"You're a wyvern," Hana said, as though that should explain everything. Krea gave her a blank look. "Wyverns are children of Ophidian."

"I've never tried anything like that," Krea said. But her expression changed as she remembered, years ago, when she'd tried to hammer a sword in her father's forge. She'd got it completely wrong and the sparks had flown into the kitchen, nearly setting the house on fire but… there was *something*. And her father was *always* good with fire. She bowed her head and took a deep breath. "Do you know how I would do that?" She frowned as she recalled Hana's words, "How do you dry dishes?"

"Wash one and I'll show you," Hana said, leaning back against the wall to the side of the door.

"How would a wyvern wash dishes?" Krea mused. She tried contacting Wymarc in her mind — her twin soul *must* know such things — but the old wyvern did not respond. Krea could feel the other's presence but it refused any contact. Perhaps the wyvern was sleeping? It didn't feel that way to Krea. It was like the wyvern was waiting, giving Krea the chance to find the answer on her own.

So how *does* a wyvern wash dishes? Krea wondered. *She gets her human half to do it.* The words weren't Wymarc's: they were Krea's sense of humor answering her.

"Heat the water," Krea said to herself. "Heat the water, set it to boiling, have it scrub the dishes, and have them —" Krea closed her eyes and imagined the water in the left sink boiling merrily. She moved her hands toward the sink, not putting them in but imagining the water hot, steaming. She opened her eyes when she felt the first tendrils of steam rise to bathe her hands.

"So I boil the water," Krea said, "and then get the dishes to fly into the cold sink to rinse and then —"

"I'll take them," Hana said, moving forward and raising her hands in a dancing gesture.

Krea jumped as a dish hopped from the steaming sink into the cold rinsing sink and she gave a shout of surprise as the dish leapt out of the second sink and into the air. She turned to see Hana waving her hands like she was using the very air to dry the dish — and then suddenly the dish was dry. "Where should I put it?"

"I don't know," Krea told her. As if in answer, an empty cart rolled through the door toward them. Krea shook her head and pointed. "I guess we're supposed to put the dishes there."

"Keep washing," Hana said, wafting the clean dish toward the cart and turning back for another.

Krea cried with happiness, causing dish after dish to jump, cleaned, from the boiling sink into the rinsing sink and out again into Hana's waiting waves of air.

"It works best with a song," Krea said aloud. But she wasn't sure if the words were hers or Wymarc's coming from her throat. Hana nodded and began to hum in a light, delicate voice that sounded a bit like wind through chimes on a windy day. Krea smiled at her and opened her mouth to add… a melody she'd never heard before.

It was quick, it was throaty, it was warm. It was like the crackling of fire or the flapping of wings. The waters of both sinks seemed to be encouraged by the song and the hot sink was soon empty. Hana's song changed and suddenly more dishes flew into the sink. Krea laughed and nodded to her, changing the pitch and the tempo of her song as she whisked the plates and silverware through the boiling, soapy water and into the cold rinse of the second sink. She turned to Hana, smiled challengingly, and shifted the tempo even more. Hana smiled at her and nodded in return.

And they began a race. Their songs intertwined, the sounds of carts entering and leaving the room began to change in time and tempo as more and more plates, dishes, pots and pans flew through the air in an orgy of cleaning.

Somewhere in their race, Hana gave Krea a look and pointed at the dishes flying into the cleaning sink, a look that said, *your turn*. Krea smiled at her and waved one hand toward the dishes, imagining them flying like a wyvern into the steaming sink of wyvern's breath. Hana gave her a nod and increased her efforts in drying and stacking the newly-cleaned cookware. Their tune and tempo changed again to meet the new procedure.

In no time at all, it seemed to Krea, the last pot was flying into the sink, the last dish was sinking to a cart… and they were done.

Krea laughed and rushed over to Hana, hugging her tightly. "Thank you, thank you, thank you!" she said, emphasizing each thanks with a squeeze of her arms. "I couldn't have done it without you!"

Hana stood still, seeming shocked. Krea pulled back, afraid that she'd insulted the other girl somehow. Hana was silent for a long moment, then one tear ran down her right cheek and she said in a very small voice, "No one has ever thanked me before."

"Well, they should have!" Krea declared stoutly. "You were excellent!"

Hana shook her head. "I only did what I had to."

"Did you have to come in here and offer to help me?"

Hana frowned for a moment, then shook her head.

"There you have it," Krea declared firmly. "You didn't *have* to. You *chose* to."

Hana had no answer for that.

A noise from the doorway distracted them. "Very good, girls," Sybil called approvingly, waving her hand at the last cart which obediently moved to her direction. "I have two bowls of soup on the counter, when you're ready."

Krea and Hana exchanged looks and Sybil laughed. "Don't worry, you won't have to do *these* dishes." They relaxed, sighing. Sybil laughed again, "At least, not until tomorrow."

Chapter Five: Wandering

After they finished their soup and thanked cook Sybil, the two looked around the large dining hall. Krea didn't know what to do. Lyric was nowhere in sight.

"Why don't you go to the gardens?" Sybil suggested. "Everyone finds them restful."

"Where are they?" Krea asked when a glance to Hana showed that the girl was as lost as she.

Sybil laughed. "Wander around! Find them yourselves. I've got work to do." And the cook walked back into her kitchen, out of their sight.

Krea shrugged and gestured to Hana who gave her a nervous look.

"You can tell them you were showing me around," Krea said.

"I don't know where anything is," Hana replied. She'd picked up her knitting and pocketed it in one of the large pockets sewn on the front of her dress. It was white and looked like it was a hand-me-down or found clothing — not something the girl brought with her.

"Where were you?" Krea said.

"I was in the healing room at first," Hana said. "And then you came and I stayed to watch you."

"Why?" Krea's brows creased with curiosity.

Hana shrugged and wouldn't meet Krea's eyes.

"You didn't want to go out, did you?" Krea guessed shrewdly. She was delighted when Hana's reaction showed that she'd guessed right. The girl seemed almost Krea's opposite. Krea grabbed Hana's free hand and tugged her along after her. "We're going to have so much fun!"

"We might get in trouble!" Hana wailed.

"You can blame it all on me," Krea told her with a wicked grin. They reached the doors to the dining hall and Krea looked left then right. She jerked her head to the right. "Come on! Let's go!"

It seemed, as Krea walked down the halls with a reluctant Hana in tow, that there were more doors than she recalled from the other day. Something inside her roused and she got the impression that Wymarc was amused.

"I can feel air," Hana said, pointing to the door at the end of the corridor.

"Outside?" Krea asked, tugging the other to the door.

Hana took a deep breath and shook her head. "It smells —"

Before she could finish, Krea and pushed open one of the two double doors and pulled the dark-eyed girl behind her.

They stopped in their tracks. The door closed behind them.

"It's beautiful!" Krea said.

"This must be where the food is grown," Hana said. Krea gave her friend a look and a nod — they were in a huge garden. Above them was bright clear glass which showed a world outside that was frozen, the ground covered in snow. Krea moved forward enough that she could crane her neck in all directions. They were in a valley surrounded on all sides by high ice-covered peaks. Krea wondered idly how a wagon, like the one she'd been in, could possibly have made it through those mountains to reach here.

A smell distracted her and Krea turned toward it. "Wyvern flowers!" She dragged Hana toward them and knelt to sniff at the marvelous honey scent from the small plot of the blue-hued flowers. "I met the wyvern in a field of wyvern flowers," she told Hana.

A short man, only shoulder-high to Krea's form, pushed a wheelbarrow down a path toward them, his expression intent.

"Are you the gardener?" Krea asked. The man stopped, eyed her from foot to head and frowned. A moment later he shook his head. She gestured toward the wyvern flowers. "Did you plant these?"

The man glanced at them and nodded.

Hana jerked and turned with a horrified expression on her face toward another patch of plants. There were red at the top, shading down to yellow. Krea thought they were beautiful. They seemed to have a hot, spicy scent that gave Krea energy.

"Foxbane," Hana said in a growl. She looked at the man. "Do you hate me?"

Before the man could respond or Krea ask what she meant, Hana ran out of the garden and back into the marble hallway.

Krea searched for something to say to break the awkward silence that fell. "We were washing dishes earlier," she ventured lamely. "I think she's tired."

The short man shook his head in disagreement and gestured for Krea to follow him. Dutifully, with one regretful look toward the door Hana had disappeared through, Krea followed.

They stopped in front of a plot of roses. Reverently the short man knelt toward the nearest bush, pulled a small set of shears from one of his pockets and gently snipped off a blooming rose. He held the stalk out to Krea who took it and sniffed the rose appreciatively.

"Thank — Ow!" Krea cried as the man grabbed her hand holding the rose and crushed her fingers against the thorns. "Why did you do that?" she said. "Was I being mean? Did I upset —"

The man shook his head quickly and pointed back toward the red foxbane plants. He gestured to the rose, mimed sniffing it, mimed jerking at the pain of the thorns just as Krea had done and then he pointed back to the foxbane.

"Oh!" Krea said, suddenly enlightened. "The foxbane hurts her like the thorns of a rose?"

The short man gave her a brief smile, nodded, then shook his head. He pointed toward the blue patch of wyvern flowers, smiled again and then brought up his hands to cradle his head against them, like he was sleeping peacefully.

"What?" Krea said, confused. "The foxbane is for Hana like the wyvern's flowers were for me?" The man shook his head. Krea tried again. "They say that wyverns come to the flowers when they die." The man gave her a sharp look, encouraging her to continue. "Are the foxbane like the wyvern flowers?" The man cocked his head: that was part of the answer. "Wyverns come to the flowers when they're dying, to find a new twin soul," Krea said now. She surprised herself with that — had Wymarc come in hope of finding Krea? Or someone like her?

The short man nodded and gestured for her to go on.

"But the foxbane… it's like wolfsbane, isn't it?" Krea said. "Something to keep foxes away?"

The man shook his head and pointed to Krea, making a "get on with it" motion.

"Not foxes?" Krea guessed. The man nodded and pointed toward the door where Hana had fled. "Twin soul foxes?"

The man wagged a hand from side to side: Krea was half-right.

"I'm sorry," she apologized, "I don't know all the names of the twin souls."

The man smiled at her, moved his wheelbarrow to one side and gestured for her to follow him. Puzzled, Krea followed.

They went back through the double doors. Outside the dining hall, the man raised a finger, telling Krea to wait and walked in.

"Terric!" Sybil's voice cried. "Are you coming to bring me more food? No?" Her voice grew quieter and Krea couldn't hear what was said until Krea heard Sybil call, "So you're going to show her? Does that mean you like her?" Krea couldn't hear an answer but heard Sybil say, "The two were good with the dishes, worked out things just right between them." A moment later, Sybil finished, "And a good day to you, Master Terric!"

Terric appeared around the corner, smiled to Krea, and indicated that she should follow him. They continued down the long hallway into the main corridor — the one that led to the gods — went down a ways and turned to the right down a hallway Krea didn't remember and went about halfway down without seeing any doors on either side until they were in front of a set of ornately carved doors in a frame surrounded with various creatures, and scenes.

The man smiled at her, opened one of the doors and gestured for her to go inside.

It was a library. The man led her to one section, pulled out a book, and handed it to her. He guided her to a table and sat with the book, gesturing for her to sit beside him. The man smiled at her as he opened the book, turned through several pages — all lined with illustrations that seemed so real that they appeared to be moving — she spotted one page with the image of a wyvern on it but Terric flipped past it until he found the page he wanted.

"Kitsune?" Krea said as she read the title. Terric nodded and gestured for her to read the page, rising from his chair, and moving toward the door. Krea got the impression that he was heading back to the garden and his work.

"Thank you for everything," she called to him as he turned back to close the doors. "Shall I come find you when I'm done?"

Terric raised an eyebrow at her and smiled ambiguously, raising a hand to wave his fingers in farewell. Krea waved back and then she was alone with the book.

Kitsune were fox-tailed twin souls. They were often found around rice fields. Krea had heard of rice but didn't know where it came from. It seemed that some kitsune were good with winds and kept the rice fields from flood and destruction. The page also indicated that some kitsune were less pleasant and could demand sacrifices — perhaps that was what had happened to Hana?

Krea turned the book to the passage on wyverns and read about them for comparison. She had only just started when the door opened and Lyric stepped in.

"What are you doing here?" Lyric demanded.

"Terric brought me here," Krea told her, looking up from her book.

"Terric?"

"The gardener," Krea explained.

"A gardener? And what right does he have to send you to the library?" Lyric said with a sniff. "Why aren't you working?"

"I'm done," Krea said.

"If you get in trouble, I won't be responsible," Lyric told her nastily, moving to the back of the library.

"I can take care of myself," Krea said, rising from her chair, and bringing the book back to where Terric had found it. She would have preferred to stay there, reading, but the emotions radiating off of Lyric were too distracting.

She closed the door silently and stood outside for a moment, wondering what to do next. With a smile, she turned and went back to the main corridor.

Sybil had said to wander. And Krea wanted to wander to the front doors, or any doors that would lead to the outside. After her encounter with Lyric, Krea wanted some fresh air.

Chapter Six: The Bite

Krea had nearly given up in her search when a head peered out from a door and turned her way. It was Hana.

"I'm going outside," Krea said, when she saw her, "do you want to come?"

Hana's eyes widened and she shook her head. "It will be freezing outside."

"We don't have to stay out for long," Krea told her, moving to grab the other's arm. "Come on, it'll be an adventure!"

"I don't like adventures," Hana said. She glanced back toward the room she'd been in. "I prefer knitting."

"Knit when we get back," Krea told her. She smiled at the dark woman, adding, "If you want, I'll teach you redwork."

Hana gave her a blank look which gave Krea the chance to tug her along behind her. They opened many doors, found many locked doors, and finally came to the end of the hallway where there were a set of double doors.

"This is not where the gods are," Krea said, pushing open the doors, "so this must be…"

She stopped as a cold breeze curled around her and her breath froze in her lungs. With a laugh, Krea pulled Hana along with her and the doors closed loudly.

"… outside!" Krea finished, turning to Hana and giving her a huge smile.

Hana took one startled look at the snow piled up around them, the fiercely brilliant sun, felt the harsh wind biting at them… and turned into a four-legged black creature that stood as high as Krea's hips.

"You're beautiful!" Krea said to her friend in her kitsune form. "I wish I could —" and Krea stopped, feeling suddenly very odd.

It's good to get out! Wymarc said happily.

And Krea Wymarc leapt into the skies, beating rapidly to climb into the cool air surrounding them. Below them, Krea heard a howl and looked down to see a black shape looking up at them with brilliant green eyes. Before Wymarc could react, Krea dove and reached with her legs to grab the fox form, beating her wings mightily to lift them up into the air.

"Isn't this great?" Krea cried to her friend. Below her, firmly held in her feet, the black fox howled. Krea got the sinking feeling that perhaps the black fox didn't like flying and, repentantly, glided back to the ground, depositing the fox gently.

A moment later she was human again, reaching down to cuddle the fox in her arms.

No! Wymarc's voice cried in Krea's head just before the fox opened its mouth wide and bit Krea's hand, hard. Krea pulled her hand back in surprise and pain just as the fox turned back into Hana who looked in horror at Krea's injuries.

"I'm sorry," Hana cried. "I didn't mean to! You scared me!"

"It's my fault," Krea said, cradling her injured hand. "I should have read the whole section on kitsune."

The doors opened and Avice and Terric rushed out, followed by Sybil and Lyric.

"What is going *on* here?" Avice shouted, glancing accusingly from Hana to Krea. Her eyes narrowed and she said to Krea, "What did you do to her?"

"She bit me," Krea said, holding out her hand as evidence.

"She was provoked," Avice said flatly. "What did you do?"

"I only took her flying when she transformed," Krea said defensively. "I wanted her to see —"

"You don't know anything, do you?" Avice shouted at her. "Whyever did you torment her?"

"Torment?" Krea repeated blankly. She glanced to Hana. "I'm sorry, I thought you'd like it!"

"You *never* take a kitsune from the ground!" Avice scolded. She jerked her head toward the doors. "Now get inside, both of you!"

#

Krea was sent to the infirmary on her own while Avice consoled Hana. Lyric glared at Krea before she tossed her head and stalked off in disgust.

Krea was halfway down the corridor to the dining hall when she realized that she didn't know where the infirmary was. Was that the room she'd first woken in? It hardly seemed like it, having only a bed, a table, and a chair. The infirmary must be nearby, Krea guessed and so, she turned around, tracing her steps back to where she remembered her room to be.

When she tried the door, she found it was locked. She glanced down the hall behind her and realized that she'd left a trail of blood, little red dots on the clear white marble. *Will I have to clean it all up?* she wondered miserably.

She tried the next door and the next, growing more frantic with each failed attempt. Finally, she moved to the opposite side of the corridor, trying the door that she thought was opposite the room she had slept in.

"Oh, about time!" Avice cried as she spotted Krea entering the well-appointed room. She stabbed a hand toward the counter beside her. "Come here! I can't imagine why you dawdled so much —"

"Please, I didn't know where the infirmary was," Krea confessed miserably.

"Well, why didn't you say so?" Avice demanded irritably. She motioned Krea to put her hand on the counter, continuing, "What did you think I'd intended? That you go wandering around lost and miserable?" Before Krea could respond, Avice continued, "Lyric told me that she'd given you an orientation."

"She showed me where the room of the gods was located," Krea said.

"Did she, now?" Avice asked in a suddenly different tone of voice. She looked down to examine Krea's torn hand, ran her fingers over it, and slipped them into her mouth with a smile. "Fresh blood," she cried. "Nothing like it!"

Aghast, Krea looked down at her hand — and all the wounds were gone. So was the blood.

"The blood you dripped outside is gone, too," Avice told her in a kindly voice. "So you needn't worry about cleaning it."

"How did you —?" Krea asked, startled.

Avice grinned at her. "I've heard the question a time or two," she told Krea. She took her fingers from her mouth, put her hand to her side and looked at Krea consideringly. "Terric told me that he'd taken you to the library —"

"It's beautiful," Krea cried, her eyes lighting up with excitement. "I've never seen so many books!"

"Of course not," Avice replied. "Where did you come from?" She waved her other hand dismissively. "Never mind, it won't have a library anywhere near as good as ours."

Krea nodded in firm agreement.

"So you've seen the library, why didn't you learn —?" Avice cut herself off, her look going thoughtful. "You're twinned with Wymarc, aren't you?"

"Yes, my lady," Krea told her with a quick curtsy.

"What sort of foolishness did she use on you?" Avice asked, although from her expression, she was half-talking to herself. "Wyvern flowers, right?"

"Yes, there was a field near to my house," Krea said.

"Near your house!" Avice cried in surprise. "What fool would plant a field of wyvern flowers near their house!"

"I think my father did father," Krea said in a small voice. "But I do not know for sure. I think it was because my mother liked them."

"And was your mother a wyvern, too?"

"No," Krea said. "She was human." She paused, frowning. "I think."

"Not, perhaps, as much as you should," Avice said acerbically. She raised an eyebrow at Krea. "And who was your father?"

"Rabel Zebala," Krea said.

"Rabel!" Avice cried in delight. She raced around the counter and grabbed Krea in her arms, giving her a huge hug. "Why didn't you say so? How is the old scoundrel? Still working deals with Ophidian, is he?"

"What?" Krea said in confusion. "Ophidian spoke to me, not my father."

"Oh, don't you believe it, child!" Avice chortled. "Rabel has cheated the Ferryman more than once." She glanced up to the ceiling but Krea had the impression that she was looking even further away. "Knowing this, I've no doubt he'll be offered some new temptation by Ophidian again, shortly." She cocked her head toward Krea. "How old is your father?"

"Very old," Krea said, feeling miserable. "He was feeble and I was supposed to marry his apprentice. Angus was going to look after us when father got old —"

"And what happened? How come you're here and not married?"

"I gave comfort to a wyvern," Krea said. "I took her offer —"

"Not hers, I'm sure," Avice interjected. "That'd be Annora, always looking out for her mate." She snorted. "So what happened then?"

"Jarin —"

"Jarin!" Avice exclaimed. "I hadn't realized *he* was involved in all this!" To herself she added, "Of course, Annora Wymarc were probably sent by Ophidian to make sure the fool didn't do anything *too* terrible." She raised her eyes to the ceiling once more and brought them back to Krea. "And *then* what happened?"

"Jarin stole the prince's jewels," Krea said. "And he found me when I lost one of my fingers —"

"You *lost* a finger?" Avice interjected. Krea gave her a hasty nod. "Go on, go on! I can't *wait* to hear this story!"

"And he told me that I was twice sworn, and I had to make a choice," Krea said.

"He was right enough there, surprisingly," Avice agreed. She saw Krea's look and added, "I'm surprised he had that much sense."

"Pardon?"

"Not his fault, really, he was frozen in the ice," Avice said, waving a hand in the air. She frowned at Krea. "He was frozen there until just a few years ago when Ophidian sent someone to find him."

"Wymarc?" Krea guessed.

"Not quite," Avice said. She waved a hand, pointing outside the house. "Somewhere out there is a frozen god who will be quite irritated with Ophidian when he's freed." She chuckled, then nodded to Krea. "So, child, tell me the rest of your story."

"The king and the prince sent a mob after us —"

"Us or Jarin?"

Krea shrugged. "And then Ibb and Angus caught up with us —"

"Angus?"

"My fiance, my father's apprentice," Krea explained.

"Ibb lives in Kingsford, so you must be from there," Avice said, nodding to herself. "Go on."

"Ibb told us that the only way to complete the transformation was for Angus to stab me with a hatpin —"

"Is that the same hatpin we found in your room?" Avice interrupted.

"You found it?" Krea cried eagerly, twisting her head in a quick scan of the room, hoping to see it.

"You didn't get it?" Avice asked, her brows crashing down. "That's odd," she said in a lower voice. "So you had your fiance stab you with a hatpin — it had to belong to someone special —"

"My mother," Krea said in agreement.

"Bet it hurt all the same," Avice murmured.

"It did," Krea agreed. "And then I was dead and then —"

"Wymarc bawled at you, told you to breathe, and you completed the transformation into a wyvern," Avice concluded. She eyed Krea critically. "Must be a pretty wyvern, there are not many made in winter."

"And with my complexion," Krea agreed, dropping her eyes from the other woman.

"There's nothing wrong with your complexion, my dear," Avice told her kindly. "You will no doubt meet many odder people here than you." She nodded her head briskly in confirmation. "And, because of who you are, you will doubtless treat them better than you were treated."

"Of course!" Krea said, surprised that anyone could think otherwise. "It's not the skin or the shape that makes a person."

"Well said," Avice agreed. She frowned. "Which means… that you really weren't trying to frighten the poor kitsune girl."

"No, I would never!"

"Ibb," Avice said, looking Krea in the eyes. "How do you know Ibb?"

"My father worked with him," Krea said.

"Oh, ho!" Avice laughed. "And you probably grew up with the old rustbucket."

"I like Ibb," Krea said in protest, "he was nice to me."

"I like Ibb," Avice told her with a wave of her hand. She shook her head, then her brows creasing once more. "But I can't see him sending you here. At least not immediately." She frowned. "Something is not right." She looked up at Krea. "I am not allowed to tell you much but I can say this — you have my permission to read in the library."

Krea's eyes widened and she broke into a huge grin. "Oh, thank you!"

"Thank me later, dear," Avice said. "In the meantime, I'd be careful if I were you." She nodded firmly. "There's still a judgement to be made."

"Ophidian said something about it," Krea said.

"What, exactly?" Avice demanded tensely.

"He said that he'd tell me something after the judgement," Krea said, wondering why the other woman was so worried.

Avice relaxed. "Good," she said. "At least he's not breaking *those* rules."

"What rules, my lady?"

Avice pursed her lips thoughtfully. Then, with a sigh, she said, "You have come to the House of Life and Death." Krea's eyes bulged in surprise. "The hatpin killed you. You should be dead."

"But — Wymarc!"

"Exactly," Avice said. "Your oath to Annora bound you to Wymarc, made a twin soul. But a life was lost. Death must be paid." She shook her head. "It cannot be any other way."

"But — I died!" Krea said. "Shouldn't that be death enough?"

"It would be," Avice agreed, "except that you're talking to me now, alive."

"So what will happen?"

"Judgement must be made," Avice said with a shrug.

"Judgement?" Krea asked. "Who makes the judgement?"

"Why, you've met him already, dear," Avice said with a smile. "He's the little boy."

"What little boy?" Krea said, her brows furrowed. A moment later, she said, "*That* little boy?"

"Hmm," Avice said. "You remembered. That's quite rare."

"*He's* the judge?"

"No," Avice corrected. "He's the god. Judgement."

Chapter Seven: Krea's Room

When she was satisfied that Krea's hand was healed, she led her out of the infirmary.

"Where is your room?" Avice asked.

"I was in one of the white rooms when I woke," Krea said.

"Yes," Avice agreed, "that was a recovery room."

"Hana was with me."

"She was watching you?" Avice asked. "That's very interesting. I thought Lyric —"

"Lyric picked me up when I fell out of the sky," Krea said.

"Because you were flying for the first time and didn't know how quickly you'd get tired," Avice said.

"Yes," Krea admitted.

"It happens all the time, dear, all the time," Avice said, patting her arm. Her tone turned acerbic, "Particularly with one of Wymarc's souls."

Krea couldn't think of anything to say.

"Well, your room should be around here, somewhere," Avice said. "Why don't you lead us to it so I know where it is?"

"But I don't know —"

"You will, when you find it, dear," Avice told her, gesturing down the corridor.

Perplexed, Krea turned in the direction indicated and started walking, examining the doors as she approached them. The first several seemed too close to the infirmary, she expected them to be recovery rooms, so she ignored them.

They came to the main corridor and Krea turned left, towards the hall of the gods. There were no doors. Worried, Krea picked up her pace. She went all the way down to the end of the corridor just in front of the hall of the gods and looked around wildly. She turned right and went to the first door on the left. It looked soft, its wood carved with gentle images of animals. Krea tried the knob.

It opened.

"Hello?" Hana called from inside. Krea pushed the door open and peered inside cautiously.

"Is this your room?" Krea said, eyeing the furnishings in surprise.

It was a surprisingly large room. Krea saw that there was a hallway beyond the first room and she saw three doors, with bright light coming from two.

"Is it yours?" Hana asked rising from the rocking chair she'd been sitting in, putting her knitting down on a side table.

"I just tried the door," Krea said.

"There's redwork over there," Hana said, pointing. "And a hatpin." She frowned. "I didn't notice them earlier." She looked appalled. "If I had, I would never have taken your room."

"I've never been here before," Krea said, shaking her head and holding up a hand to Hana.

"Interesting," Avice said, motioning Krea aside and entering the room herself. She closed her eyes and took a deep breath of air. "*Very* interesting."

"What?" Krea said, sniffing herself. The room smelled faintly of a scent that she'd learned to associate with Hana — and of trepidation, fear.

"I do believe that this is your room, dear," Avice said to Krea.

"Oh, I'm so sorry, I'll leave!" Hana said.

"You don't have to —" Krea blurted.

"It's *your* room, too, dear," Avice said smiling at Hana. She glanced to the hallway. "I believe you found two bedrooms and a bath, did you not?"

Hana nodded mutely.

"Aron!" Avice called out commandingly.

"I didn't do it," a boy's voice replied from the doorway. A moment later a ten year-old boy popped his head inside. He looked at Krea and smiled. He did not smile at Hana.

"But you would have?" Avice asked.

"It will speed things up," Aron said.

"There's no harm in it," Avice decided. She glanced to Krea and Hana. "Do you object?"

"I hurt your hand!" Hana cried miserably.

"I scared you!" Krea said in reply. "I'm so sorry." She held up her hand. "And my hand's all right. Avice fixed it."

Hana turned wide eyes to Avice who looked back at her with a shrug and grinned.

"I could teach you redwork," Krea said, pointing to the work on the wall. It was a good piece.

"There was twine and other things in that cabinet there," Hana said, pointing to the cabinet opposite the door. Shyly, she added, "Knitting things, too."

"Good!" Avice said. "So it's decided." She glanced at the two girls. "I'll leave you to it."

"Goodbye," said the boy.

"Who was that?" Hana asked a moment later.

"Who?" Krea said, walking to the hallway beyond the front room and glancing in each of the bedrooms.

"The boy," Hana said.

"What boy?" Krea asked.

Hana gave her a puzzled look, then shook her head. "Do you have a preference on rooms?"

"They both look the same to me," Krea said with a shrug. "Which one did you pick?"

"I haven't," Hana said. "I was too worried that I wouldn't be allowed to stay."

Krea's brows furrowed. "Weren't you in a different room earlier?"

Hana nodded. "That's why I was afraid," she said. "Someone came and told me to leave, that I was in the wrong room."

"Who?"

"That woman, the one who brought you here," Hana said. "The one who made me watch after you."

"Lyric?"

"That's the one," Hana said. With a frown, she added, "I don't think she likes me much."

"She doesn't seem to like anyone," Krea said. "She was nicer when we were in the caravan on the way up here."

"Caravan?" Hana said. When Krea nodded, she continued, "Was it on wheels?" Krea nodded. "How could anything on wheels get over the mountains?"

173

"How did you get here?" Krea asked. She frowned in memory as she added, "I'm sure you didn't fly."

"I was sacrificed," Hana said. She made a sad face. "They killed me —"

"Did they puncture your heart?"

Hana nodded.

"And then?"

"Then the *kami* said, 'How would you like nine tails?' and I said, I didn't know if I'd look good with them," Hana replied. "And the *kami* said, 'Try. If you don't like them, we'll see what can be done.'"

"What's a *kami*?" Krea said.

"It's a spirit," Hana said. She glanced toward Krea and said in a lower voice, "One with incredible power."

"Who punctured your heart?" Krea asked.

"My parents," Hana said, a tear forming in the corner of her eye.

"What's your *kami*'s name?" Krea asked. She pointed at herself. "Mine is Wymarc and before she met me, her human half was Annora."

"Human half?" Hana said. She closed her eyes and slowed her breathing. Krea could tell she was thinking deeply, perhaps communing with her soul. She opened them a moment later and said, "Meiko says I am the first."

What? Wymarc cried inside Krea's head. *First?* Her tone changed. *Be very careful, my little one. This is dangerous.*

"I like her," Krea said out loud.

She bit us, Wymarc said.

"That was my fault," Krea said. She saw Hana looking at her and explained, "Wymarc is talking me."

"Until you asked, I had never talked with Meiko," Hana said.

"Why not?"

"I didn't think she wanted to talk with me."

"I'd think," Krea said, "that if she took you as her twin soul, she must know that you're amazing."

Hana gave her a disbelieving look.

"Why don't you ask her?" Krea said.

Hana mulled the question over cautiously.

"You're going to have to talk with her sometime," Krea said.

Hana sighed and closed her eyes. A moment later, her expression changed into a smile. She opened her eyes again. "She was lonely, and she saw that I was lonely, so she picked me."

"There," Krea said, "you should talk with her more."

"Wouldn't that be rude?" Hana asked. "To you?"

Krea shook her head. She pointed to Hana's knitting. "Why don't you knit something? Whenever I do redwork, I get to think a lot. I imagine if you're knitting you get to think a lot, too."

Chapter Eight: Terric's Words

Krea was the first to admit that Hana's knitting was more interesting than redwork. Oh, Krea loved the results she could get with her needle and thread but watching Hana's knitwork grow larger and larger with each new row was amazing.

"Please teach me!" Krea begged, putting aside the redwork she'd started. She glanced at Hana's work and cocked her head. "What are you making?"

"I'm making a hat," Hana said, shivering. "It's cold!"

Under Krea's impetuous questioning, Krea learned that the easiest thing to start with was a scarf. Neither were surprised to discover that there were extra needles and yarn available in the cabinet where they'd found the other supplies.

It took Hana no time at all to, in her quiet, steady voice, explain to Krea how to cast on, how to knit and how to purl. Hana had her making a rib stitch for the first inch then had her switch to a stockinette stitch — "It's easy: you knit one row, then purl the next row and repeat."

In no time Krea had a four-inch wide scarf four inches long. And then her fingers cramped.

"That happens," Hana told her, "when you're beginning." She showed Krea how to massage the muscles and then suggested that they see if it was dinner time.

"If not, perhaps Sybil will have some soup," Krea said hopefully.

#

Outside their door, they started toward the main corridor. Hana stopped and glanced nervously at the stairs that led up to the hall of gods.

"What's wrong?" Krea said. "I went in and everything was all right."

"I was told that I would meet my doom in the hall of the gods," Hana said.

"Who said *that*?"

One of the double doors to the hall of the gods opened and an old man came out. He looked at Hana and sighed.

"He did," Hana said, pointing.

"You are Krea?" the man said as he spotted her. Krea nodded. "I have heard of you, too." A moment later, he added, "Of course."

"Me?" Krea blurted. "What did you hear of me?"

He shook his head and looked far off, as though reading the stars. He frowned. "I'm sorry, I've said too much."

He turned away from them, heading down the opposite corridor from their room and was quickly lost to sight.

"I met him before Lyric came," Hana said. "He took my hand and cried over it."

"He cried?" Krea said. She couldn't imagine how a man that old could have any tears.

Hana nodded. "He cried and said that he was sorry. So sorry."

"What for?"

"For what would happen to me in the hall of the gods," Hana said. She shivered and crossed her arms, grabbing her shoulders. "That's why I don't dare to go inside."

Krea frowned and shook her head. "Food, you need food!"

#

Dinner was being served as they entered. They nodded at Sybil who took one look at Hana and dropped her serving spoon. She rushed around the counter and hugged the girl tightly.

"He talked to you again, didn't he?" Sybil demanded. Hana hung her head and nodded glumly. "Don't you listen to him! He doesn't know everything!"

"Who is he?" Krea asked. She knew that Sybil was referring to the old man.

"Some shaman of Hansa's," Sybil replied sourly. "They're always predicting the worst."

Krea knew of Hansa, the god of fate. She had prayed to him as her mother was dying. Her prayers were heard, but not answered, her mother died anyways. Krea had no prayed to him since then.

"They think they always know what's going to happen," Sybil added. She looked at Hana and repeated, "But they're not always right."

Hana said nothing.

"Come on, I've got your favorite," Sybil said.

"What's her favorite?" Krea asked. "Can I have it, too?"

Sybil frowned. "It might not suit your tastes."

"I'll never know unless I try," Krea said.

"Very well," Sybil agreed. She waved them toward a table. "I'll bring it to you."

#

Krea guided Hana to a seat. The girl seemed almost in a daze, like Sybil's concern had frightened her even more than the shaman of Hansa.

"I'm glad that you taught me knitting," Krea said to fill the silence. Hana nodded glumly. "Do you want me to teach you redwork?"

"How long would it take to make a piece?" Hana asked.

"It depends on what you do," Krea said. "Some pieces can take months to complete."

Hana shook her head. "I don't think I can wait that long."

"Wait?"

"To see the gods," Hana said.

A thump on their table startled them and they looked up to see Lyric putting her tray down.

"May I sit with you?" she said, not waiting for a reply. She glanced over to Hana. "What's wrong?"

Something in the tone of her question bothered Krea. It seemed like she was enjoying Hana's unhappiness.

"Here we are!" Sybil called out, carrying two trays, one in each hand. She spotted Lyric and her brows rose in surprise. "I thought you were going back to the library."

"Changed my mind," Lyric replied tersely, munching loudly on a piece of celery.

"Hmmph," Sybil said, placing a tray in front of Hana, then the other in front of Krea. "Here you are, my dears. Food from Hana's homeland."

Krea examined the small pieces with concern.

"You don't have to eat them," Hana told her. She took a small jar of brown liquid and poured it into a little tray, adding some green paste and stirring it with two thin sticks. Satisfied, she picked up one of the pieces of — it looked like raw, thin-sliced fish — and dipped it in the brown liquid before putting it in her mouth and chewing blissfully.

"Fresh fish, caught this morning," Sybil told her. She smiled at Krea. "Terric has a pond he fished from every day."

"He catches the fish?" Krea asked, repeating Hana's steps with difficulty. The two sticks were hard to manage until Sybil explained the proper way to hold them. Once she got the piece into her mouth she chewed slowly before swallowing. Hana gave her a questioning look but Krea had already snagged another piece. "It's good!" she said between mouthfuls.

"It's raw fish, mostly," Sybil explained. Krea's eyes bulged. "I know, I know! You Kingslanders never think of such things."

"It's still good!" Krea said, snagging her third piece. She pointed to some thin white shavings beside the green paste. "What's that?"

"Try it," Sybil said, her eyes dancing. "You've probably never seen it this way but you've had it, certainly."

"Don't take too much," Hana warned.

Krea tried a small sliver with her next piece. "It's ginger!"

"Indeed it is," Sybil agreed. "In Kingsland it's used in some chicken dishes, mostly."

"With garlic, it's good with beef," Krea said.

"Ugh!" Lyric said. Krea looked at her. "Beef! Chicken! Raw fish!" She munched pointedly on a carrot, her disgust evident. "How can you eat living things and hope to live forever?"

Krea considered this question while eating yet another of the marvelous morsels. Finally, she said, "I don't know. I never wanted to live forever."

"The wyvern is *wasted* on you," Lyric said with a snarl. She rose from her place and moved away, leaving her tray. "I can't eat here."

After she left, Sybil picked up her tray and glanced at it thoughtfully. "She's not likely to live forever if she doesn't eat enough to keep soul in body."

"It will be a long while before she faces the Ferryman and Kalan's decree is met," an old man's voice replied. They all glanced up. It was the old man once more.

"Ah, Nevik," Sybil said, "I would expect no less from a servant of Hansa."

"You're welcome," Nevik said with a low bow. "My Lord said that it would be my fate to see Kalan served." His gaze settled on Krea disturbingly.

"Kalan?" Krea said, looking to Sybil.

"The god of justice," Sybil explained.

"Is he a little boy?" Krea asked, recalling a dim memory.

"No," Sybil said, "we call him Aron here, he is the god of judgement."

"What's the difference?" Krea asked.

"Aron works with Terric and Avice," Sybil said. "Kalan works alone."

"Aron is the god of judgement," Krea said. She frowned. "Terric and Avice are gods, too?"

"The gods of death and life," Sybil said.

"Terric is a gardener!" Krea said.

Sybil nodded. "He is death to plants, life to us."

"So he is just death to plants?" Krea asked hopefully.

Sybil shook her head. "Although only to some does he show his true face."

"People are dying all the time," Hana said. "How could he have any time for the garden?"

"He's a god," Sybil said. "Time does not control him."

"Do people stay here long?" Hana asked, glancing around at the mostly empty dining hall.

"No," Sybil said. She smiled at Krea. "That is why we waited so long to clean the dishes."

"What is the longest time a person stayed here?" Krea asked.

"The longest time is Hana," Sybil said. "She's been here for almost two weeks now."

"Judgement will come soon," a boy's voice piped up from right beside them. Krea turned, startled, to see the ten year-old boy she'd spotted — and forgotten — before.

"Lord Aron," Krea said, bowing her head.

The boy smiled at her and shook his head. "Just Aron, please." He waved at her and then he was gone.

"Who was that?" Hana said, looking dazed.

"Who?" Krea asked, looking to Sybil. "Was someone here?"

"No, dear," Sybil said in a sad voice, "no one at all."

#

Krea insisted on showing Hana the library before they went back to their rooms. She found the book Terric had shown her and showed Hana the pages on *kitsune*.

"Some are good and some are bad," Hana read, frowning. "I hope I'm good." She glanced at the picture. "Why is there only a white *kitsune*?"

"Someone drew the picture," Krea said, "they probably didn't know many *kitsune*."

"That's a new page," a man's deep voice spoke up. They glanced up in surprise. The speaker was Terric. He smiled at Hana. "Until you, there were no twin souled *kitsune*."

"What?" Krea said. "Why?"

"I have been told," Terric said, "that the *kitsune* have wandered their land for thousands of years looking for worthy souls."

Krea gasped and turned to Hana. "Did you hear? You're the first! And you're special!"

Hana paled, her face looking green. She pointed at Terric in terror.

"What?" Krea said.

"He spoke," Hana said when she could find words.

"Yes," Krea said, wondering why this would bother the girl so much.

"Death only talks to those he will see soon," Terric said sadly. He nodded to the two girls. "I am sorry. I have said enough."

And he was gone, leaving them alone in the suddenly chilly library.

Chapter Nine: Gifts

Krea paused at the top of the main corridor, outside the hall of the gods.

"Don't go in!" Hana pleaded. "You heard what Terric said!"

"I heard," Krea said. She stroked the doorknob on the right. It was smooth, warm, inviting. "But I've died once already —"

"So have I, and I don't want to do it again!" Hana told her. She tugged on Krea's sleeve. "Come on, it's late. We can do some more knitting before bed."

"Okay," Krea said, allowing herself to be hauled away by the smaller girl.

#

"There!" Krea said, casting off the final row and holding up her scarf in triumph. "It's done!"

The scarf was only four feet long and four inches wide but it was Krea's first. The yarn had been dyed in a gradient of color running from blood red to pale yellow. She stood up from her rocking chair and went over to Hana.

"What?" Hana said, glancing up from her own knitting — a hued blue hat — to see what Krea was doing.

"Here," Krea said, wrapping the scarf around the other girl's neck. "This will keep you warm the next time we go flying."

Hana's eyes went wide but her hand went to the scarf. "This is lovely!" She looked stricken. "But this is your first! I can't take it!"

"Of course you can," Krea said sternly. "In fact, I would be *hurt* if you don't take it."

Hana frowned, her hand still stroking the soft fabric. Finally she glanced up to Krea. "Okay, if you insist." She glanced down at the scarf. "It's beautiful."

"And it will go with your hat," Krea said.

"Oh, no!" Hana said with a laugh. "I was making this hat for *you!*"

"Well, hurry it up," Krea teased, "my head is getting cold!"

Hana smiled at her and waved toward the bathroom. "Take a bath and get clean. I'll have it ready when you get out." As Krea turned away, Hana added in a lower voice, "That is, *if* you get out."

Krea turned back and stuck her tongue out in a display of her exceeding maturity.

#

Heating the water with her magic was something that Krea delighted in doing, so it really *was* a long time before she got out of her bath. Krea wrapped herself in another towel and went to her room in search of clothes.

One of the great pleasures of the House was that it provided clothing whenever Krea needed it. She and Hana had discovered that when they'd each taken their first bath — the one after cleaning *all* the dishes. Krea's chest of drawers would magically contain clothes in her cut and size.

She was surprised when she got to her room to see a beautiful blue knit hat sitting on top the dresser.

"Oh, Hana, it's wonderful!" Krea cried, putting it on before searching for any other clothing. "It fits perfectly! I love it!" Krea pranced in front of the mirror, deciding that the range of shades were perfect for a winter look. It was only then that she realized that her mother's hatpin, which had been on the dresser, was missing. It had been right where Hana had left the knit hat. "Hana?" Silence. Krea dressed quickly and rushed out of her bedroom.

The living room was empty.

"Hana?" Krea called, heading back to Hana's room. The door was shut. Krea knocked on it lightly. "Hana? The hat is beautiful!"

Silence. Krea's heart pounded heavily in her chest, a sense of dread overwhelming her.

"Hana?" Krea called again. She tried the knob. It was locked. "Hana, are you okay? I'm worried, please talk to me."

Nothing.

"Hana," Krea said firmly, "I'm coming in." She twisted the locked knob, pushed against the door and grunted. Nothing. Krea pounded on the door. "Hana, Hana!" No response, not even a noise. Frantic, Krea grabbed the knob and pushed. "Open, damn you!"

Nothing happened. Krea took a deep breath, collected her thoughts… and closed her eyes. She knew how doorknobs were made, how the locks worked. She thought of the tongue that stuck in the door jamb.

Melt, Krea thought, imagining the tongue in the door jamb slowly turning bright white with heat, melting, flowing…. Krea pushed the door open, ignoring the white hot metal dripping to the ground.

"Hana, I'm sorry but —" Krea stopped.

The room was empty.

#

Krea burst into the hallway, shouting at the top of her lungs, "Hana!"

She raced down the hallway, toward the main corridor, frantic.

She paused at the top of the corridor, glancing down it. Maybe Hana had gone to the dining hall? Or the library.

Krea shook her head, turning to the double doors behind her. The hall of the gods.

"Hana?" Krea said in a small voice, turning the knob of the door on the right. She crept inside. "Hana?"

"Go away," Hana said in a strangled voice. "Please, go away!"

"Yes, Krea, go away," Lyric's voice echoed harshly in the huge hall.

"No," Krea said, moving forward with determination. Something was wrong.

"I've been reading," Lyric said. "I've been reading a lot, in the library." Krea followed her voice — it was deep in the huge hall, toward the back, a place where Krea hadn't ventured before.

"So have I," Krea said.

"Hah! You! You don't even know what to read!" Lyric said. "You would have read nothing had the gardner himself not shown you!"

"Terric was teaching me," Krea said, glancing from side to side — Lyric's voice was echoing around the hall now, it was getting harder to trace it.

"Teaching you?" Lyric taunted. "What does Death teach but how to end life?"

"Terric is not death until he talks to you," Krea said. Her words didn't quite make sense to her but she *knew* that was right.

Judgement is coming, Wymarc warned. *Be careful, child!*

"Who told you that?" Lyric challenged.

"Terric," Hana said in that same tight, choked voice. "Krea, leave me! It's my fate!"

"No," Krea said. "I do not abandon my friends!"

"Friends?" Lyric sneered. "What makes you think you can be *friends*? You're both here for judgement. Only one of you can live. Why do you think you ended up in the same room?"

"So be it," Krea said. "Hana Meiko is the first of her kind. Wymarc has lived long —"

"What about you, child?" Lyric interjected. "Just sixteen, aren't you?"

"Old enough to know," Krea said. She pinpointed Lyric. She was just around the corner. "I must see the Ferryman one day. Today will do."

Brave! Wymarc said approvingly. *But understand, she means to take your place.*

"Does she?" Krea asked out loud.

"Does she what?" Lyric said.

"Do you mean to take my place?" Krea asked her.

"Of course!" Lyric said. "Ibb lied to me. He told me that I could make myself a mechanical, that I could live forever." She snorted bitterly. "Then I learned about the twin souls." She chuckled. "Bound to a twin soul, I could live as long as the gods!"

Not quite, Wymarc thought to Krea. *And she cannot take you by force.*

Krea turned the corner and Lyric took a step back. She had Hana's throat grasped in one hand, Krea's hatpin in the other, the tip resting over Hana's heart.

"No!" Krea cried, lurching forward.

"Stop!" Lyric shouted. "Make one more move and she dies."

"You cannot take her by force," Krea said.

"No, but I can kill her and make you watch," Lyric said. "That will satisfy the gods."

"But you won't be immortal," Krea said.

"I will be," Lyric said with a hungry smile. "You'll remember what I did to your friend forever." She tensed her arm and the hatpin pushed into Hana's skin. Krea could see a line of blood darkening Hana's dress. Hana gasped in pain.

"Stop!" Krea said, raising a hand imploringly.

Lyric stopped. She gave Krea a triumphant look.

"Freely given," Krea said, bowing her head. "Take me." And she moved forward resolutely.

"Fool!" Lyric cried, pushing Hana aside and thrusting the hatpin deep into Krea's heart.

"Wymarc, I'm sorry," Krea gasped as the pain overwhelmed her. "I would have liked so much to soar with you once again."

No! Wymarc roared in Krea's mind.

With a snarl of victory, Lyric pulled the hatpin out of Krea's body. She stood back, waiting.

It doesn't work that way, Wymarc thought to Krea. Using Krea's voice, she said aloud, "It doesn't work that way."

"What?" Lyric said, glaring at Krea. "What did you say?"

Krea felt her hands moving and she touched her chest.

"*I* said: 'It doesn't work that way'," Wymarc said again with Krea's voice. *Watch and learn, friend.*

Krea's blood pulsed brightly as her hands — guided by Wymarc's will — moved over the puncture that was gushing blood.

"I accept you," Wymarc said out loud with Krea's voice, the sound subtly different. There was a flare of bright light and then — the hole was gone. Wymarc raised a bloody finger to Krea's lips and sucked on it. "Tasty."

That's what Avice said, Krea thought.

"You can't kill us," Wymarc said to Lyric. "We will not die."

"You won't," Lyric said, her jaw clenched. "You break the rules of the gods." She nodded. "Very well, try to stop me now." And she plunged the hatpin into Hana's chest where she lay, stunned on the ground.

"Hana!" Krea cried rushing forward, dropping to push Lyric away from her friend.

She was too late. With a harsh cry, Hana convulsed on the floor and lay still. Dead.

A flash of light surrounded Lyric who gave a cry of triumph — and turned into a bright white *kitsune*.

The *kitsune* howled in despair as it looked down at Hana's body. It knelt, licked the blood on the hatpin, and licked the girls' dead face.

And then it disappeared, leaving the room darker.

"Judgement has been made," the voice of a small boy echoed in the room. He did not sound happy. "Balance has been restored."

"No!" Krea cried, grabbing the limp form of Hana in her arms. "No, this can't be!" She shouted up to the empty hall, "She did nothing wrong!"

She gathered Hana up and stood with her, turning in a circle, crying to the walls of the hall of the gods. "You cannot allow this!"

"A life was paid," the voice of Aron, god of judgement, said. "What would you have us do?"

"Justice!" Krea shouted back. "I want justice!"

"The wheels of justice grind slowly but they grind exceedingly fine." Another voice spoke. It was a voice of steel, a deep voice.

"Then *I* will be the wheels of justice!" Krea shouted to the walls. She shook Hana's limp form in her arms. "*This* cannot stand! This is *not* justice! She didn't deserve to die. Her *kitsune* did not deserve to be stolen by a murderer!"

"You will be the voice of justice?" the steel voice asked.

"Yes," Krea said. "Just bring Hana back to life, let her have her chance and I will deliver her justice."

Do you know what you're saying? Wymarc cried in alarm.

Yes, Krea told her firmly.

I've never been a Voice, Wymarc said thoughtfully. A moment later, she said, *You are right. This calls for justice. I accept.*

"Heard and witnessed," Ophidian's voice boomed out from the statue in the distance. "Krea Wymarc have sworn to Kalan, god of justice."

"Witnessed," another voice called. It was Avice. She sounded pleased.

"I agree," Aron, god of judgement, said.

"As do I," the god of death, said.

"Well played," Ophidian said, turning his statue's head to a distant figure: Justice. "Well played indeed." He turned his head down to Krea Wymarc. "Well done, my heart. I accept this. You may proceed."

Krea felt a rush of immense power flow into her, through her and into the body she held in her arms. It wasn't just the fire of Ophidian, it was the life of Avice, the judgement of Aron, the end of Terric, and the power of Kalan's justice.

Hana's body convulsed in Krea's arms and she gasped for air. Krea leaned down and kissed Hana's cheek. "It's okay," she said, "we're going to fix this."

"She killed me," Hana sobbed. "She killed me and took me away from Meiko."

"I know," Krea said. "But we're going to find her and bring her to justice."

Hana looked up at her, eyes wide. Then she looked down to her chest and wailed, "Oh, your scarf! It's all bloody!"

"I'll make you another," Krea promised. She felt Wymarc's approval glowing inside her and smiled.

Wyvern's Wrath

Book 5

Twin Soul series

Chapter One: Find Your God

"Can you walk?" Krea asked as she held Hana in her arms. Hana looked up at her and nodded shakily. Krea understood the other's shakiness: it had only been moments before that each of them had been killed, in turn, by Lyric skewering their hearts with a hatpin. The same hatpin that Krea had used weeks before to complete her transformation into the winter wyvern.

"I'm so sorry about your scarf!" Hana repeated the words she'd said only moments before. When Lyric had stabbed her, Hana had bled on the scarf that Krea had knitted just hours before.

"It wasn't your fault, dear," Wymarc said through Krea's lips. Krea felt no surprise nor affront by Wymarc's actions — it seemed only right. After all, Wymarc had not begrudged her the use of her wings when they were in wyvern form; Krea could hardly do less when they were in her human form. It was, Krea suspected, all part of the give and take required to be a twin soul, particularly one of Ophidian's children.

"Has this happened before, Wymarc?" Hana said as she tottered on her feet. Krea's arm shot out to support her but Krea hadn't done it — it was Wymarc once again.

"If it has, I haven't heard of it," Wymarc said.

"We should get you to cleaned up," Krea said.

"Krea?" Hana guessed, smiling. She grabbed Krea's hand with hers. "I'm so sorry, I got you killed."

"I got *you* killed," Krea said. "If it hadn't been for Lyric —"

"Lyric got you both killed," Wymarc interrupted Krea testily.

Krea quirked her eyebrows and asked Hana, "Did that make sense?"

Hana nodded and took a few steps forward,, "I can tell which one of you is which now"

"Are you sure you can manage, dear?" Wymarc asked.

"Yes, ma'am," Hana said, clenching Krea's fist.

"Then, before we leave," Wymarc said, "we should let you find your god."

"My god?" Hana said.

"Your god," Wymarc agreed. She raised Krea's free hand and waved it around the hall of the gods. "Somewhere in here is the god who accepted your sacrifice and paired you with your *kitsune*."

"Meiko," Krea added. She felt her head nod as Wymarc relayed her understanding.

"Being a twin soul takes some adjustment," Wymarc said through Krea's lips as she caught Krea's surprise. "That is why I did not talk to you too much until now."

"Will I ever get a word in edgewise?" Krea though to Wymarc, half-joking.

"That depends, dear," Wymarc replied within Krea's mind, "on whether you have anything interesting to say."

"Ugh!" Krea groaned.

"Sixteen," Wymarc said. "It's been centuries since I was *sixteen*."

"We're finding her god, Wymarc," Krea reminded her twin soul. She turned her attention to Hana, speaking to Hana out loud, "Go on, Hana, get it over with."

"It's not like she can kill you again," Wymarc muttered in agreement. Hana shot Krea a worried look but Krea just shrugged. For once, Wymarc had said something Krea would have said.

"She's probably right," Krea told her friend. "After all, it's been centuries since she was sixteen."

Inside her head, Wymarc chuckled at Krea's jab but said nothing. Krea decided that if both of them were going to use her mouth, she'd have to be careful to avoid cramping her jaw muscles.

I'm always *careful*, Wymarc thought to her primly.

"Wymarc, is that you?" a woman's voice called from above them. "You're wearing a different body."

"A tragic accident, an encounter with a flying ship murdered my Annora," Wymarc said, bowing to the goddess above them. She raised her hand and gestured at Krea's body. "This is Krea, my new twin soul. She is sixteen." She pointed to Hana. "And this is her friend, Hana, once twinned to the first *kitsune*."

"We heard," a man's voice boomed above them. They could hear the groans of stone as it was forced to turn hastily from side to side by the god's will. "A tragedy, truly a tragedy."

"I am Hissia, dear," the goddess said to Hana. "This is my husband, Hanor."

"We would be honored if you let us touch you with our power," Hanor said.

"It won't *quite* be the same, by we could give you back *some* of your power over air," Hissia said.

"I — I —" Hana stammered, glancing between the two gods looming above her.

"Take it," Krea and Wymarc said simultaneously. Wymarc added, as Krea was speechless in surprise, "It is a gift of the gods. The highest of honors."

Hana curtsied to both gods. "Thank you, I accept your gift."

"It's the least we can do, under the circumstances," Hissia said, lowering her hand toward Hana. Hanor did the same and Hana bowed her head as soft white lights descended upon her from the two hands held over her.

Hana stood upright and glowed with the brilliance, her face splitting into a huge grin. "Thank you!"

"It was nothing," Hanor said.

"Nothing more than you deserve, young one," Hissia agreed. She gestured Hana forward. "Now go, dear, and find your mother."

"Mother?" Hana repeated fearfully.

"She means your mother god," Wymarc explained. "The god of the *kitsune*."

"She doesn't know, does she?" Hanor asked.

"No, dear," Hissia agreed. She bent her head to smile down at Hana. "I expect you'll be pleased."

"Normally your twin soul would tell you but…," Hanor said with a shake of his head.

"Thank you," Hana said, reaching to touch the hands of both gods in respect. "I shall never forget."

"Just go with Krea Wymarc, god-touched of Kalan, and deliver the justice that is required," Hanor said. He nodded down to Krea Wymarc and then winked. "You, too, will have the honor of our aid."

"Thank you, Lord, Lady," Krea Wymarc said with a formal bow of her head. "Our fathers thank you for your consideration."

"You earned it," Hissia said, waving them on.

Hana moved forward, now unafraid to glance up at the statues of the gods. She smiled and bobbed her head at each, wondering when one of them would react to her presence.

Wymarc bowed to each as well and named them, aloud to Krea and Hana.

Some Krea knew, many she'd never heard before. She glanced at the figure of Arolan who Wymarc said was Ametza's husband, missing now for centuries.

"As near as I can tell, Ophidian and Ametza trapped him somewhere," Wymarc said bitterly, "sending him on a some fool errand."

"Gods can be trapped?" Krea said, surprised.

"Yes," Wymarc said. "And worse." She shook Krea's head. "It's not easy being a god, as I have come to know."

"You?" Hana said, turning to look at Krea. "You are a god?"

"Of course not," Wymarc said with a chuckle, "But I understand their burdens. I have lived a long life and had many children. The world changes with time, and sometimes it is hard to catch up.

"You have children," Krea repeated out loud. Accusingly, she added, "You never said."

"Why wouldn't I?" Wymarc said dismissively. "And," she added with a sniff, "you never asked."

There wasn't time, Krea thought to her twin soul.

Hana raised her eyebrows and remained quiet.

"I have many, many children," Wymarc continued out loud. "And grandchildren, and great-grandchildren, and so on from different twin souls. "

Wymarc looked up at the last two statues and shook her head. "We must have passed your god, Hana," she said. "There's only the Sun and the —"

"Kahlas," Hana said, curtsying deeply, pulling her dress wide to either side as she knelt, "mother moon, I greet you."

"My child, I grieve for you," the statue of Kahlas, goddess of the Moon, replied. She bent down and brushed her stone fingers through Hana's black hair. "This should never have happened."

"We are oathsworn to bring justice," Wymarc said with Krea's voice, looking up to the serene goddess.

"So Kalan told me," Kahlas replied. She smiled down at them. "There is no mystery to me," she said, "Hansa warned me this might happen."

"The god of Fate warned you?" Wymarc said, shaking her head. "I thought —"

"Surely, Wymarc, by now you must know that Fate is only possibilities," Kahlas replied. "Hansa was never happy with surprises but he has learned to accept them."

"They're untidy," Hansa's voice boomed through the room. "I prefer certainty."

"Indeed," Kahlas agreed, her stone lips twitching up in a smile. She nodded toward Hana. "All is not lost," she told her. She gave Hana a sad look, adding, "Yours is a great tragedy but there are seeds of a great triumph, if you will fight for them."

"She'll fight," Krea said firmly. The Moon god looked her way and nodded.

"She certainly has fierce allies," Kahlas said. "Wymarc, accident or not, I think you have found yourself a worthy twin."

Wymarc said nothing but, deep inside her, Krea could feel the wyvern's quiet agreement.

"She died to save me, mother Moon," Hana said quietly. She reached for Krea's shoulder and grabbed it firmly. "I cannot imagine a greater friend."

"Much damage will be done before this wrong can be righted," Kahlas said. She nodded to Hana. "You will have to grow, my child, if you are to find justice."

"I can't leave Meiko…" Hana said, her voice trailing off.

"If you are truly bound to her, she will not leave you, either," Kahlas said. She closed her eyes for a moment, as though in pain. "Feel for her," she said to Hana, her eyes still closed, "and you will find her."

"I will find her, mother Moon," Hana said.

Kahlas opened her eyes again and bent down, low, to stare in Hana's eyes. "I claim you as my child, Hana," Kahlas said. She leaned forward and kissed Hana on the forehead. "You may call upon me in need."

Hana's face broke into a huge grin and she closed her eyes, humming softly to herself, overwhelmed by her god's gift, tears running down her cheeks.

"Do what must be done, my child," Kahlas said softly, rising to her full height. And then the god left the statue and it was just dead stone.

Krea rushed to grab Hana in a hug and held her as she cried out all her pain.

#

Wymarc insisted that rinsing the scarf in cold water was the first step in removing the blood stain that Hana's death had left.

"It won't really ever be the same," Wymarc said out loud, "but, then again, neither will you."

Hana nodded. They had returned to their room and had changed clothes, using washcloths to wipe away the worst of the blood. They had found new clothes to replace their stained ones and both were extremely tired.

"I know we are all tired but we should go to the dining hall," Wymarc said. "Sybil will have something for you and both Terric and Avice will want to know what happened."

"Don't they know already?" Hana said.

"From your lips, dear," Wymarc corrected, waving toward the door. "I should have said." They started to the front door of their rooms but Wymarc stopped Krea and grabbed Hana's arm. "This time, dears, I think we'll take the quicker way."

Before Krea could react, they were standing outside the dining hall. Wymarc could feel Krea's surprise and explained, "We can't do that often, dear, but sometimes, particularly in this house, the thought is the deed." Krea felt her lips quirking upwards with Wymarc's pleasure. "And I *thought* we should be here just now."

"Wymarc? Did you bring them?" Sybil's voice called from inside. "I've got something for them."

"Come along, dears," Wymarc said, setting Krea to motion and using her hand to drag Hana along.

"Is she always this pushy?" Hana asked, glancing toward Krea Wymarc with wide eyes.

"Only when necessary, dear," Wymarc replied, "only when necessary."

"Come in, come in," Avice's voice spoke from a nearby table. "Nevik is here with us, awaiting your words."

They entered just in time to see the old man leap from his chair in shock. "What? Did it happen? Did you meet your gods?"

Krea nodded.

"Yes," Hana said. She smiled. "I have the honor to be claimed by Kahlas, mother Moon, and have been touched by Hanor and Hassia."

Avice's eyes widened and she glanced over to Terric who was standing beside her. He moved over to Nevik and said quietly, "Things didn't work out quite as you expected."

"What?" Nevik cried, turning his head from Krea to Hana and back to Terric. "You spoke! I thought you mute."

"I only speak when the time has come," Terric told him.

Nevik's eyes widened and he licked his lips fearfully. "The time?"

"Your time," Terric said. "Hansa told you that you would witness something amazing."

"He said I would live to see Kalan served," Nevik said, his brows narrowing critically.

"And then you would meet your doom," Terric said in agreement. He glanced toward Krea Wymarc. "Do you wish to tell him?"

"You have been waiting for this your whole life, sir?" Wymarc asked the old man respectfully. Nevik nodded. Wymarc glanced to Terric. "May I tell him the whole tale?"

"He has lived his life for that," Terric agreed.

"Which is a pity, as there were so many flowers he could have smelled, sunrises he could have surveyed, so many magics missed," Avice said, shaking her head sadly. She glanced to Nevik sympathetically, "But you were persistent and loyal, I'll grant you that."

"The story begins with an airship," Wymarc said. She recounted the tale of her twin soul's death; how Krea had offered her life to save her; how Krea had died at the hand of her betrothed to be reborn as the winter wyvern; how they'd flown north and been rescued by Lyric; how Lyric had slain both Krea Wymarc and Hana Meiko in succession; how the gods had interceded; and how Krea had promised justice.

Nevik turned incredulously to Krea. "*You* are the servant of Kalan?"

"*We* are," Wymarc replied with Krea's voice.

Nevik bit his lip, shook his head sadly. Then he perked up and said to Krea Wymarc, "This is the tale I lived my whole life to hear. I wish you success in your oath, that justice be served on the murderer, that the twin souls be reunited as they should."

"Thank you," Krea said, bobbing her head and curtsying. Hana's lower lip trembled and she could say nothing, looking on the old man sadly.

"Come sir," Terric said softly, grabbing Nevik's arm. He pulled two gold coins from his pocket. "My son will escort you," he said. He raised the coins. "If you close your eyes, I'll set the payment upon them."

"You?" Nevik said, glancing at Terric in awe. "You are the god of death?"

"Yes," Terric replied, sounding neither happy nor sad, just resigned. "I am the ending," he nodded toward his wife, "Avice is the beginning."

A tall, shapely man appeared beside Terric and nodded. Krea could see the resemblance. Before she could react, she felt herself in motion, her voice crying, "Bryan! It's good to see you again!"

Bryan, the Ferryman, glanced toward Krea. "Wymarc?" he cried, grabbing her in a big hug. "You're not coming with me, are you?"

"This is Krea," Wymarc said, getting Krea to curtsy, "she's sixteen and we've sworn to Kalan for justice in this one's —" she gestured toward Hana "— name."

Bryan the Ferryman laughed, a huge, cheerful bellow. "Well done! Well done!" He said, pointing a finger at Wymarc. "Ophidian always said you were his best."

"Don't let the others hear that," Wymarc warned.

"Oh, that one!" Bryan chuckled. "I think I'll wait longer for him than for you." He glanced toward Nevik. "Sir, it is my pleasure to take you to the other side."

Before Nevik could respond, Bryan had touched his shoulder and the two disappeared.

"Beautiful," Wymarc murmured in appreciation.

Terric beamed at her, raised his hand and two gold coins appeared. He smiled and pocketed them once more. "The thing is done."

"I have soup for you two," Sybil said, bearing a tray and gesturing toward a table. She sat down and placed three bowls. "If you don't mind, I'll join you."

"With pleasure," Wymarc said. She glanced toward Terric and Avice. "Will you honor us with your presence?"

"Oh, you can be sure of that!" Avice said with a laugh. She dragged Terric along and glanced warningly at Krea and Hana. "He doesn't talk to many people but you two — being thrice-born — you're going to get an earful."

"I wouldn't say that, dear," Terric began slowly.

Krea found herself seated in front of a bowl of delicious smelling soup and scooping up a spoonful.

Krea glanced warningly to Hana who merely shrugged and smiled, dipping her spoon into her bowl and blowing on it coolingly.

A moment later, Krea noted that Bryan, the Ferryman had returned and was sitting beside her.

"It's not often that the whole family gets to dine with guests," Bryan said, smiling first at Krea and then Hana, to whom he added a wink.

"The family?" Hana asked, glancing up from her soup fearfully. She turned to Sybil.

"I'm their daughter," Sybil said, smiling.

"You're a god, too?" Krea asked in amazement.

Bryan chuckled. "Of course!" He beckoned to Sybil. "Hey, sis! I need some strength!"

Sybil sighed, waved her hand and another steaming bowl of soup appeared in front of Bryan, with a spoon beside it. Bryan beamed in appreciation and slurped up a mouthful with a groan of pleasure.

"You're the god of strength," Krea said with no doubt in her voice.

Sybil merely grinned at her and bobbed her head.

"Someone has to do the work around here," Avice said, nodding toward her daughter approvingly.

"Aw, Mom!" Sybil said, blushing bright red. Teric grinned at her and another bowl of soup appeared in front of him. Strangely to Krea's eyes, Avice ate nothing.

The bowls refilled until everyone had all they wanted.

Finally, Krea Wymarc leaned back in her chair. She glanced at Hana and caught the other's drooping eyes.

"The humans need their rest," Wymarc said to the gathering. She yawned. "And I'm a bit fatigued by the day's events." She glanced to Sybil. "If it wouldn't be too much trouble…?"

Sybil shook her head, waved her hand —

— and they were back in the living room in their apartment.

"Thank you," Wymarc said in the direction of the dining hall. "That was most gracious."

You're welcome, Sybil's voice echoed through their heads.

Hana gave Krea a startled look but Krea nodded in confirmation — they had heard the goddess of strength in their minds.

"Sleep now," Wymarc said, gesturing toward the bedrooms. "Wash in the morning. There will be much to do."

Chapter Two: Whole New Body

"Could you heat me some water?" Hana asked, ducking her head around into Krea's room the next morning. She held up a jug.

"Best put it in the sink," Krea said. "Tell me when and I'll heat it there."

"Not too hot, please," Hana said as she made her way back.

"I won't promise anything," Krea called. "This is all new to me!"

"Okay," Hana called back.

Krea closed her eyes. *Wymarc?*

You did just fine without my help the other day, Wymarc said testily.

I just don't want to hurt Hana, Krea thought.

Wymarc was silent for a moment, then responded, *Very well. Follow along with me so you'll know next time.*

Krea felt Wymarc reach out, find the water in the sink, and think it warm.

"Try it now, dear," Wymarc said through Krea's voice.

"Trying!" Hana called. "It's a bit too hot, I'm afraid."

"Well, you'll have to blow on it or wait until it cools," Wymarc said. "I can't make things cooler, you know."

Krea returned to her dressing and threw on a new, but identical white dress and the leather shoes. She heard a gentle sound from the bathroom and suddenly a huge gust splashed the water out of the sink all over the bathroom.

"Ooops," Hana said in a small voice.

Krea rushed out of her room to find Hana in the bathroom covered from head to toe with water and a rueful expression.

"I think I used too much force," Hana said.

Krea nodded her head, trying to keep from laughing. She moved into the bathroom, picked a towel from under the others — it was still dry — and started to wipe down her friend.

"Thank you," Hana said, moving away, "but I think I need to learn this myself."

"I suppose you're right," Krea said, moving out of the bathroom.

It took a good five minutes before Hana was dry, dressed, and ready.

You two may walk, Wymarc said in response to Krea's unasked question. *You need the exercise, it'll do you good.*

"Come on, Hana, let's get our breakfast," Krea said, cocking an arm out in invitation. Hana smiled and took it, trailing behind Krea but skipping when Krea skipped and humming when Krea hummed.

Krea paused for a moment as they came to the doors to the hall of the gods but Hana merely motioned her forward, saying, "I'm hungry. Let's explore later."

#

Sybil served them with a huge grin and joined them at their table. Terric and Avice arrived moments later and they had a friendly, leisurely meal where everyone ate their fill — except Avice who, once again, ate nothing.

"So what are you doing today, dears?" Avice asked as they finished the last of their pancakes and scrambled eggs.

"The library, I think," Krea said, seeking Hana's eyes for approval.

"For a bit, yes," Avice agreed. "But you can't stay here forever —"

"Do we need to leave now?" Hana asked in alarm, half-rising from her chair.

"No, no, nothing of the sort!" Terric said, waving her back down. "You're always welcome, both of you."

"It's just that the world doesn't stop and things will happen," Avice said.

"And the longer we leave Meiko with Lyric…," Hana guessed unhappily. She glanced to Krea but looked for Wymarc. "Will she forget me?"

"No," Wymarc replied firmly with Krea's voice. She curved Krea's lips up in a smile. "She could never forget you. You are her first." Her tone sounded wistful, recalling old memories.

"You're going to have to learn how to use your powers," Sybil said. She nodded at them. "I can teach you, both of you."

"Ahem!" Wymarc grumbled with Krea's voice.

"And *when* were you last sixteen, Wymarc?" Sybil asked the wyvern pointedly. "You and Krea are doing well together but how often have you flown?" She raised her eyebrows challengingly. "And *how* long?"

"You're right, of course," Wymarc said after a moment. She nodded an apology to the god. "One forgets these things."

"Indeed," Sybil agreed. "It would not do to have to re-learn them at an inappropriate moment."

"Of course," Wymarc agreed.

"And Hana needs to learn to ride on you," Sybil said, nodding toward the . "The *kitsune* was terrified, something you must learn to overcome."

Hana frowned fearfully but nodded.

"So the library for the rest of the morning, then lunch, then some training," Sybil said, rising from her chair.

#

They did as Sybil suggested. Krea found books on Hana's home country, far around the world and halfway down. She was both fascinated and horrified with what she learned — it was such a completely different world to the one she knew growing up.

"Travel broadens the mind, dear," Wymarc said out loud. "As no doubt our Hana has already discovered."

"It's *cold* here!" Hana said. She asked Krea, "Is it always cold?"

"We're very far north, here at the House of Life and Death," Wymarc said. "And this is the cold season as well. When summer comes it can get *much* warmer."

Krea stole her head long enough to nod emphatically at her friend. Hana giggled, saying, "I can *always* tell when it's you, Krea!"

"And that's a *good* thing," Wymarc said. "It can get quite tiring having to identify myself every time I open my mouth."

"There's no fear of *that*," Krea said with the same mouth.

Mostly, though, Wymarc left Krea and Hana to their own devices, merely suggesting a couple of books that might be of interest and making happy noises when they found something that triggered an old memory.

#

After lunch, Sibyl led them to a room off the corridor just beside the front door where they found all sorts of outdoors clothing and gear.

"Wymarc," Sybil said, "I'm going to need you to take your form as soon as we get outside and let me measure you."

"Measure me?" Wymarc asked. "Whatever for?"

"Hana," Sybil said, as if it were obvious. "We'll need to make a harness so she can fly with you."

"A harness?" Wymarc said archly. She jerked Krea's head back in horror. "Why, I've never *heard* of such a thing! Wyvern's don't *take* passengers!"

"Well," Krea said, grabbing her voice and turning to Hana, "*this* wyvern does." More to Wymarc than to anyone else, Krea continued, "We swore to provide justice, Wymarc. And that means we have to bring Hana back to her *kitsune*."

Wymarc sighed deeply and nodded slowly. She looked at Sybil. "But you know, if *I* do this, *everyone* will want all the dragons and wyverns to *carry* people!" She shook Krea's head. "Where will that end, I ask you?"

"Ask Hansa," Sybil said with a shrug. She grinned. "Or just try and see."

"Very well," Wymarc said with another deep sigh. To Krea she said, "Don't wear too much dear, it'll make it more difficult to change when we get outside."

"And we'll have to construct some sort of carrying sack for your clothes," Sybil said, nodding both to Krea and Hana.

"Food, too, I've no doubt," Wymarc grumbled. She glared at Sybil. "You'll turn me into a mule, you will."

"Exercise will do you good," Sybil said. "You need to build *your* muscles, too, you know."

"It's a whole new body," Wymarc said in agreement. Vainly, she added, "What do you think?"

"I like the look," Sybil said. "The white with the gold filigree is very refined."

Krea could feel Wymarc preen in pleasure.

"But now that you're all dressed," Sybil said, gesturing the way, "it's time to get to work."

The cold air struck them all the moment they stepped outside. All except Sybil who took in their looks and explained, "This is no colder than my ice box."

"Admit it," Wymarc said sourly, "this *is* your icebox."

"Well, of course," Sybil said. She drew a length of string from one of the pockets in her dress and said to Wymarc, "Change, so the poor girl doesn't freeze."

Are you ready? Wymarc thought to Krea.

Yes! Krea cried eagerly.

Then follow my thoughts, Wymarc said. Krea felt Wymarc lift her head, look to the far distance, take a quick step, leap —

— and then they were flying.

This is wonderful! Krea shouted to Wymarc as the wyvern's wings beat steadily in the cold, dense air, pulling them further and further into the sky.

The last time she'd flown, she hadn't had a chance to look around much before she'd dropped back to the earth with the frightened *kitsune*.

Now she could look all around —

No! First check your flight path! Wymarc shouted in Krea's head. *Only* then *can you afford to take in the sights!*

Sorry! Krea thought back, looking firmly ahead, glancing just slightly up and down, left and right, until she was certain that it was safe. Then she glanced to her right and felt herself banking in that direction. Krea felt a sudden terror as the ground appeared at an angle to her — they were going to fall!

Nonsense, Wymarc assured her, pulling them into a tighter turn. *This is natural. The rules of the air make it so that we won't fall unless we —* and Krea had just a barest hint of Wymarc's glee before they plummeted straight down to the ground.

Wymarc! Krea cried in terror.

Hang on, child! Wymarc replied, thrusting her wings out and nearly pulling them out of her body as she cupped air and slowed their plunge. One beat, two beat, three beats and then they were back flying once more. *That was nothing!*

Please, I'm going to be sick! Krea wailed.

Hold on, Wymarc told her, straightening them up and gliding gently upwards, reducing the effort of their wings until it almost seemed to Krea that they were gently rowing their way higher and higher in the air. *Annora lost her lunch the first time she let me fly,* Wymarc thought, sounding both sad at her loss and pleased with Krea's response. *You'll learn, my dear. In time, you'll grow to love this.*

Krea thought to her first flight, beating her wings high into the sky, into the sleeting snow, crying in triumph as her new-found wings took her higher and higher and further and further away from the town of her birth. *I think I love it already, Wymarc.*

I know, Wymarc said. *But you've only seen the least of it!*

Krea had no objection as they circled higher and higher. She noticed that Wymarc led them to a place where warm air boosted them upwards, like a waterfall in the sky — only backwards.

We call it a thermal, Wymarc explained. *Hot air is rises and we can rise with it.* Wymarc started another slow bank, taking them away from the thermal, allowing Krea a chance to look down at the house below.

It's a castle! Krea exclaimed. *It's tiny!*

Actually, it's rather big, Wymarc said. She turned them back toward the thermal and glided them further upwards.

While they were rising, Krea spotted the large glass enclosure of Terric's garden. There were three other gardens arrayed around the outside of the main building which had three stories and five turrets rising high into the sky — but still several hundred feet below them.

We can clear the mountain pass, Wymarc said, turning toward a gap in the snowy peaks.

I'm getting cold, Wymarc, Krea said. *And Hana isn't used to this weather.*

Wymarc accepted Krea's observations without comment, still beating their way toward the pass.

Just one more moment, and we'll turn back, Wymarc assured her. *Look to the horizon, tell me what you see.*

Krea looked through the gold-slitted eyes that were her wyvern's sight. She realized that she could see further than she could on the ground — or were her wyvern eyes sharper?

A bit of both, Wymarc replied with pleasure. *I want you to practice using our eyes so that you can help me spot —*

It's the airship! Krea cut across her. She felt Wymarc's surprise and doubt. *See, the colors, there! Those are the balloons!*

In an instant they'd turned back and started plunging to the ground.

Wymarc? Krea cried.

We must tell the others, Wymarc said, not halting their plunge.

Chapter Three: The Frozen God

"I reckon we'll stop in another hour, sir," Lieutenant Knox reported glumly to Captain Ford on the remains of the royal airship *Spite*.

"I imagine so," Ford agreed.

They had been flying for two whole days and nights after their encounter with the frozen god, Arolan. In response to their homage to the god, the god had broken free of his icy prison, and, in gratitude — or spite, Ford was now not quite sure which — had blown them away, further into the bitter north.

For two days they had flown over nothing. Now, just barely visible in the distance, was the smudge of mountains. Mountains that, to Ford's trained eye, appeared to tower well above *Spite*'s altitude.

"We'll either stop soon," Ford said, passing the telescope to Knox, who took it eagerly and put it to his eye, "or we'll crash on those mountains."

"Or — what was that?" Knox said, straining forward to get a better view.

The two of them were at the top of the highest balloon, out of earshot of the rest of the crew, where they could talk in private and look further ahead than anyone below.

"What?" Ford said.

"I thought I saw something," Knox told him, passing him the glass. "Just between the two peaks, a glint or gleam of something white."

Ford strained with his good eye on the telescope and pulled it away, frowning. "I see nothing."

"Could've been a cloud," Knox said with a grimace. "It doesn't matter, the way things are."

"Perhaps it doesn't," Ford agreed. He passed the telescope back to his first lieutenant. "When we get below, we'll beat to quarters."

"Sir?" Knox asked in surprise.

"It'll give the men something to do, burn off the last of our shot and powder, *and* it might signal someone out there in the distance," Ford said with a shrug. "It's the least we can do."

"Aye," Knox said, moving to follow his captain back down to the deck below. "At least it'll keep the men amused."

#

On the deck when Knox relayed Ford's orders, the men all grumbled until Angus spoke up. "If we just use the stern guns it'll help push us forward."

Ford nodded in agreement. "You heard him, men! Let's get those guns aft and fire them off!"

"And when we're done?" Sykes asked with a growl.

"When we're done, we'll throw the cannon overboard and you can watch them fall to the ground," Ford told him with a smile. He moved forward amidships, seeking out the purple-robed mage.

"And how are we today, Reedis?" Ford asked as soon as he got close enough to speak privately.

"Freezing, captain," Reedis told him honestly. He was shivering, his robes wrapped tight against the wind and hidden beneath three different layers of jackets.

"Yes," Ford agreed with a small nod. "I imagine we'll all wish we were gods before long."

"And then we'll just be dead," Reedis said, shaking his head sadly.

"But you can't say we haven't had a grand adventure," Crown Prince Nestor said, moving up to join them. Captain Ford gave him a nod and, a moment later, Reedis followed suit. He peered forward. "I don't suppose there's any aid forward, is there?"

Ford shook his head. "There's a mountain range but it's higher than we are."

Boom! The first gun fired on Knox's orders.

"Aim for that mound of snow, over there!" Sykes called to his gunners, the first to haul their heavy six pounder back to the stern. "And keep firing! Don't let anyone slow you down." Sykes turned to catch sight of Ford's eyes and shake his head sourly. Before Ford could react, Sykes' expression changed and he shouted, "Captain, Captain, look!"

Ford turned toward where Sykes was pointing and back again.

"What is it," he called back to Sykes but the mate was already racing forward, snagging the telescope out of Knox's hands and running past Ford. "Come on, you've got to see it! It's the best thing ever!"

"What?" Ford said, rushing after the mate.

Sykes didn't stop until he was all the way at the end of the bowsprit. He braced himself against the forestay and leaned into the telescope.

"We need to send a signal!" Sykes cried, sprinting down the bowsprit. "There's someone in the distance!" He was halfway down the ship when he stopped and called to his men, "Belay that! Cease firing, you sods! Unhook that gun and pull it forward, smartly now, we're going to send a signal!"

The cheer that went up from the stern of the ship overwhelmed any noise Ford made in complaint. He went to the end of the bowsprit and sighted in the distance.

There was something… a smudge… something in the clouds. It was moving rapidly toward them but Ford couldn't make it out.

"What is it, Captain?" Reedis' voice came from the end of the bowsprit.

Ford shook his head, "I'm not sure…"

"Lash it tight there, men!" Sykes called as the first six pounder reached the bow. "Tie her there on the port beam!" Sykes turned back to Captain Ford and grinned ear to ear. "They might not see us but you can be damned sure they'll hear us, sir!"

"That's what I'm afraid of," Ford said, glancing toward Sykes and the frolicking gun crew. Even as he watched, the second six pounder was hauled up to starboard and quickly lashed to makeshift rigging.

Boom! The first gun roared. Ford could see the ball arcing forward and slowly falling to the ground.

A moment later the second gun roared out. The men began cheering loudly, hoping that their voices would carry over the harsh sound of the guns.

"You can't say their heart isn't in it, sir," Knox said as he took position to Ford's left and rear. "At least we'll be going out in style."

"Indeed," Ford agreed glumly. "And if there's anyone out there, they'll soon hear from us."

Chapter Four: Fountain of Air

"Are you *certain*?" Sybil said, when Krea Wymarc returned to human form. "A flying ship?"

"Yes," Wymarc replied grimly. "That's what killed Annora."

"What is it doing here?" Hana asked, staring off toward the pass, in hopes of spotting it.

"It's after me," Krea said in a dull, dark voice.

"They tried to kill me once before," Wymarc added in confirmation, "I imagine they are hoping to finish the job."

"How did they kill Annora?" Hana asked with dread.

"They shot her with a cannon," Krea said.

"They shot *Jarin* with the cannon," Wymarc corrected. She closed Krea's eyes in pain. "I couldn't let them hurt him. He was so new, so lost…"

"So you pushed him aside," Krea said, opening their eyes again, pushing warm thoughts toward her twin soul. "You saved his life."

"And he found you," Wymarc finished with an upwards lilt in her voice.

"If he hadn't, I'd be dead," Krea said.

"We would *both* be dead," Wymarc said in fervent agreement.

"Who is Jarin?" Hana asked.

"Jarin is a dragon, new-found," Sybil said. She glanced at Krea, looking to Wymarc. "Annora Wymarc were tasked by Ophidian to help him grow and protect him from himself."

"From himself?"

"Have you never done something silly?" Sybil said to the young girl. She gave Hana a thoughtful look and shook her head. "No, I suppose you never have." She tried again, "Have you ever seen a boy doing something incredibly silly? Something they might die doing?"

Hana had no problem nodding her head vigorously.

"Jarin is like those boys," Sybil said.

"Only a thief," Krea said, "and a liar."

"And a dragon," Wymarc added, shaking her head. "He thought it would be fun to tease the airship but they fired on us and then Jarin got angry." She frowned Krea's face sadly. "He toyed with them until they got smart and then they shot toward him and the only thing I could think to do —"

"Was push him aside," Sybil said, nodding. "Very much your manner, Wymarc."

"He was just a child!" Wymarc wailed. "And because of him, Annora died." Her tone changed as she added, "But he killed one of theirs, threw him off the top of one of their balloons. He plunged to his death not far from where I fell."

"They have cannon?" Sybil said, glancing to Krea Wymarc for confirmation. She glanced back toward the castle that was her home. "With cannon, from the sky, they could destroy this place."

Boom! The sound carried faintly in the chilly air.

"They're too far away, we can't even see them," Hana said, frowning. "Why are they shooting at us?"

"They're challenging us," Wymarc declared.

"Can you take the ship by yourself, Wymarc?" Sybil asked.

Krea found her head shaking with Wymarc's response.

Sybil glanced toward Hana. "The gods of air have blessed you, would you like to learn what that means?"

Hana's eyes grew wide.

"What are you thinking?" Wymarc asked.

Sybil smiled at her. "Don't get jealous."

"What? Why?" Wymarc said crossly.

Sybil smiled at her and turned to Hana. "The gods of air have blessed you," Sybil said to her. "Are you ready to use their gift?"

"What do I do?" Hana asked. Krea could tell she was nervous.

"You used your air magic earlier," Krea reminded her.

"And drenched the whole bathroom!" Hana said.

"Good," Sybil said, "that's a good start!"

Hana and Krea exchanged looks.

"I want you to remember what you did but think it bigger and underneath you," Sybil said. "I want you to think of a funnel of air lifting you upwards."

"A funnel?"

"You'll be in the center, and it will lift you up like a fountain," Sybil explained.

"A fountain of air?" Krea said. Sybil turned to her. "Krea Wymarc, get aloft. Hana will join you."

Krea smiled at her friend encouragingly.

"Your turn now, I think," Wymarc told her. Krea nodded in agreement. She took a quick step forward, skipping, once, twice, and then she jumped —

— and flew upwards, crying with joy and excitement.

A funnel! Wymarc exclaimed tartly. *Wings would do the job better.*

If the funnel doesn't work, we can suggest that, Krea thought in reply, imagining giant air wings attached to Hana's shoulders and lifting her into the sky.

"Very well, Hana, go meet your friend," Sybil called from the ground.

Watch this! Wymarc said, turning their wyvern form in a tight circle, nearly hovering over Sybil and Hana one hundred feet below.

"You'd best be careful, Wymarc," Sybil called up to them. "This might be tricky."

From below, Krea Wymarc saw Hana frown in thought and then a swirl of air rose around her. It grew wider, forming a great circle easily twenty feet in diameter and closed in, tighter and tighter on Hana. And then, with a cry of shock, Hana surged up into the air.

We may need to catch her, Krea warned Wymarc, readying the talons on her feet.

Hana's eyes were wide with fright as she rose up toward Krea Wymarc and then she her head back and laughed.

"I can do it, I can do it!" Hana cried with joy. She saw Krea Wymarc and shifted her stance, moving one hand and causing a new funnel to grow from it, pushing her toward the wyvern. "Let me come to you!"

It's at times like these when I regret not having a voice, Wymarc thought to Krea. Krea understood the other's feelings but screeched in response to Hana's words, flicking her wings in a beckoning motion.

And then Hana was floating beside them, resting on a pillar of swirling air.

"Come back down!" Sybil shouted from the ground. "Hana first, then you Krea Wymarc."

Hana nodded and turned back toward Sybil. She turned green with horror as she looked down and suddenly Wymarc stooped, cupping her wings to her sides and diving towards the stricken girl, for Hana's fear had stripped her of her magic and she tumbled uncontrollably to the ground.

Krea Wymarc caught her just a few feet from the ground and gently lowered her. A moment later, Krea turned back into her human form, grabbing at the sobbing Hana and muttering soothing words.

"You're not hurt, just frightened," Sybil said, joining them. She caught Hana's eyes and said, "You did very well for your first flight."

"But the airship is out there —" Wymarc objected. Another *boom!* punctuated her words. "— we have to do something now."

"Perhaps we can go on our own," Krea said.

"I can't help you in the sky," Sybil said regretfully. "Nor can my family for that is not our power."

Krea stepped back from Hana and said soothingly, "It's okay. We'll be fine."

Hana looked up and sniffed, shaking her head. "I'm sorry, I know I can do it but —"

"No worries," Krea told her. She turned, skipped, jumped — and flew away in wyvern form.

#

We must be careful, Wymarc said as they flew higher and higher. *We have to be smart if we're to defeat this flying ship.*

Krea said nothing. The people at the House of LIfe and Death had befriended her. If they needed her and Wymarc to protect them, she would do it.

It is not *enough to have a brave heart,* Wymarc corrected her testily. *We are going to have to fight and no one has ever fought an airship before.*

What about you and Jarin?

Fought successfully, Wymarc said.

First, let's see what the ship is like, Krea thought.

They rose up level with the pass and Wymarc started them flying through. *We must be careful here* — a gust swept down from the nearest peak and suddenly flipped them on their side. Krea cried out in alarm but they straightened up again. *The air currents through passes are treacherous and can be frightening,* Wymarc finished sardonically.

Moments later they were through the pass and heading out over the great snowy plain below.

Boom! the airship's gun roared out. A moment later, another *boom!* marked the firing of a second cannon.

Let's climb above them, Krea said, adding her will to Wymarc's to cause their wyvern form to climb higher and higher. *Perhaps we can find a thermal,* Krea suggested when all their effort seemed to only inch them further into the sky.

The higher we fly, the harder it is to climb, Wymarc told her. *If we look for thermals, we can't watch the airship.*

Krea turned their head toward the airship which was now ahead and a bit to their left.

It doesn't seem to be going anywhere, Krea said. She turned, peering more closely. Another *boom!* confirmed her suspicion. *The guns are firing from the front.*

They fired all of them from the side when they hit us, Wymarc recalled painfully.

They can move the guns, Krea said. *If they see us, they may move the guns to the sides.* She looked at the strange ship, saw the balloons from which it was suspended. The top one at the front was a different color from what she remembered.

It is different, Wymarc confirmed when Krea brought her observation to the other's attention.

Something happened to it, Krea guessed, *and they replaced it.*

It's magic, isn't it? Wymarc said.

I wonder if it can be punctured, Krea thought.

What's that? Wymarc thought, turning toward a new sight. *There's fire.*

It's for the engines, Krea said, *to turn the propellers.* She realized that they hadn't been turning before and wondered what that would mean for them.

Chapter Five: The Wyvern's Shriek

"Sir, sir!" Knox cried running back to Captain Ford. "It's the wyvern!"

"What?" Ford said, turning to follow Knox's directions. He pulled up his telescope and quickly glanced through it. "By the gods, you're right!"

"The gods have smiled on us," Crown Prince Nestor said. "The wyvern is here. All we have to do is defeat it and our glory is guaranteed!"

"It won't do us any good unless we can return to Kingsland," Knox muttered grimly. He glanced up at Ford. "That's the same beastie that killed Lieutenant Havenam, sir?"

"No," Ford said, shaking his head. "That wyvern was gold. This is white with gold etchings. The colors of the one who flew away." He gave the prince a sour look. "The one who was reborn."

"My father told me to come back with the wyvern or not come back at all," Nestor said, glaring toward the white dot that flew toward them. "This is my only chance at the crown and my inheritance."

"It's no use killing the wyvern," Sykes said. He'd seen the others talking and had sprinted back from the bow to join them. "How are we to bring it back?"

"The head, surely," Knox said. "That'd be all we need."

"So, after we kill it, we're supposed to land, chop off its head and then sail back triumphantly to Kingsland?" Sykes said. He shook his head. "How are we going to kill it, anyway?"

"You can't kill her!" Angus Franck cried from his position by the useless steam engine.

"Well, I can hardly see how we can capture her," Sykes replied, gesturing toward the wyvern. He frowned. "She's getting closer, isn't she?"

"I can talk to her, if you let me get near enough," Angus said in a pleading tone.

"I don't see how we can go anywhere, we've got no power," Knox said.

Angus licked his lips, desperately trying to come up with a solution. Finally, in triumph he cried, "We could tear up the decking, or the wood in the quarters and use that to stoke the boiler!"

"And how do we get back?" Ford asked the apprentice smith ruefully.

Angus frowned for a moment, then looked up brightly, "She could tow us, sir!"

Ford stroked his chin as he considered this wild idea. He glanced up to Angus. "Very well, Mr. Engineer, you may use the ship's wood for your fires." Angus started to rush away but Ford stopped him with an upraised hand. "Take the bulkheads first and the galley tables. Try to leave us enough that we don't fall apart."

Angus nodded hurriedly and rushed off.

"Mr. Reedis!" Ford called loudly to the mage who stood amidships ready to do his job. Reedis turned to his call. "Can you warm the water for us? We're going to stoke the boilers with the ship's wood but it would be a great help if the waters were already hot."

Reedis walked quickly back to the captain, raising a hand in salute which Ford, in surprise, returned.

"If I do that, sir, I'll be no good for anything else," the purple-robed mage warned. "Not going up or coming down."

"If we can't move forward, we're doomed," Ford said. He nodded firmly. "Do it. We'll manage what comes after."

"I hope so!" Reedis replied with a grin. He turned to the looming shape of the metal boiler and, shaking his head regretfully, walked toward it. He turned to call back to Ford, "Have someone ready to catch me."

"Of course," Ford said, nodding to Knox who detailed a sturdy airman to follow the mage.

With the airman at the ready, Reedis put his hands on the boiler, drew himself up to his full height and threw all his magic into the cold, frozen water. With a gasp, Reedis dropped to the deck, caught by the airman at the last moment.

Angus came rushing hurrying a squad of airmen who were carrying bundles of wood. He had the men throw them into the boiler and hastily called up flames.

"I didn't know he could do that," Knox muttered to Ford, pointing to Angus.

"It's fire magic," Ford said. "Maybe Ibb taught him."

"No," Annabelle said as she approached them. "He had the need, so he found the power." She glared at Ford. "He tore all the tables and benches out of the galley, where are the men going to eat?"

"The wyvern!" Crown Prince Nestor cried, grabbing Annabelle's arm, "we found it!"

Annabelle jerked her arm out of his grasp. "You found the wyvern, so what?"

"I can go home!" Nestor said.

Annabelle shook her head and snorted. "How will that happen, princeling? We've no fuel — we're burning our own ship for power and we've no shot left for the cannon."

"What?" Nestor cried in alarm. He glanced to Ford. "No shot?"

A cannon fired and Nestor jerked his hand toward it. "What is that, then?"

"Listen to the sound," Annabelle told him testily. "That was charge of gunpowder, no ball."

"But we have to kill the wyvern!" Nestor wailed. "If we don't, I can't return to my father."

"Nestor," Ford said, with a sour look on his face, "I have something to tell you —"

"Tell me that we'll get that wyvern!" Nestor shouted back.

Ford's face flushed with anger. "Whether we get it or not, your father ordered me to return without you!"

Nestor's eyes went wide. "What?"

"Your father, King Markel, said that whatever happened, I could not return with you," Ford told him in a hard-edged voice. When he saw the lad's confusion, he persisted, "He wants you dead."

"Dead?"

"Dead," Ford confirmed. Ruefully, he added, "Your royal mother, on the other hand, told me not to return without you."

"Mother always liked me better," Nestor said in agreement. He glanced toward the white form in the distance. "But if that's the case…"

"It doesn't matter what we do with the wyvern," Ford said.

"You'll not be killing her, not while I have breath in my body!" Angus declared hotly, coming to the stern to join the others.

"I hardly think it's possible," Ford allowed mildly, "given that we've no cannonballs left."

"I'm not sure that she knows that," Annabelle said, pointing at the rapidly approaching figure of the wyvern. She cast a glance at Ford. "Do you suppose she is out for revenge?"

"I would be, in her position," Ford agreed grimly. He glanced around, toward the bow where Sykes and his crews were firing off the last of their powder, toward the stern where the propellers were deployed and had begun pushing *Spite* — however slowly — forward once more. "Cease fire!" Ford called. He saw Sykes turn back to him incredulously. "Mr. Sykes, cease fire, jettison the cannon!"

"No!" Sykes shouted back. "It's our only hope!"

"Mr. Sykes," Ford called back, keeping a firm rein on his temper, "we're out of shot!"

"We don't need shot to attract attention, *sir*!" The last word was said derisively.

"I'm rather afraid he's right," Annabelle agreed, pointing to the wyvern.

"What should we do with Mr. Reedis, sir?" Knox asked, gesturing toward the airman who held the unconscious mage in his arms.

"Take him below to my cabin," Ford said. As the airman started to carry out the order, Ford raised a hand. "When you get him below, remove his jackets and settle him on my bunk."

"Aye sir," the airman replied.

"Annabelle," Ford said, beckoning to her. She approached him warily. He beckoned for to lean her ear to his lips. Quietly he told her, "There's a belt on the back of my door. A blue one. Be sure to put it on. Reedis has a purple one." He motioned her eyes down to his waist and fingered his green belt.

Annabelle gave him a curious look but nodded. "It's a strange time to be giving presents, Richard, but thank you," she said with a smile.

"It might save your life," Ford told her. She gave him a surprised look but moved away, catching up to the airman carrying Reedis. "Here," she called, "I'll get his legs."

"He'll not recover in time, sir," Knox said to Ford as the trio disappeared below. "What will we do?"

"I think, Mr. Knox, that we'll just have to leave our fate in the hands of the gods," Ford said, glancing upwards and out toward where they'd last seen the wyvern. He turned his attention to Angus. "Make your best speed," he told him. He looked at Knox. "We'll steer toward that pass, there might be something beyond it."

Knox gave him a dubious frown but nodded and turned back to the helmsman, a look of resignation on his face.

Ford started forward to force Sykes to stop firing and jettison the dead weight of the guns when the world erupted in flame and *Spite* jerked the deck out from underneath him, sending him sprawling. He pulled himself up to a kneeling position and saw that the whole front of the bow had been shattered — torn away. A gun, Ford guessed. Sykes had been ramming power in so quickly, one of the cartridges must have exploded in the gun, shattering it.

He heard the wyvern's shriek and then *Spite* was falling, bow first at a tremendous rate.

Chapter Six: Let Them Die

What is that? Krea cried as the front end of the airship became one giant billow of smoke and fire.

They're trying to kill us! Wymarc replied angrily, plunging down toward the airship with all the power she could muster, her talons stretched and ready.

What are you doing? Krea thought. *I don't think —*

Well, I do! Wymarc replied, diving on the topmost balloon. *If we tear these apart, this cursed ship will plummet to its destruction!*

Krea could feel the wyvern's power, revelled in her grace and strength even as Wymarc screeched in triumph and looped back for another strike.

The airship was falling, the remains of its bow hanging lower than the rest of the ship as it sank in the air.

I'll show them! Attack one of Ophidian's get! Wymarc said triumphantly. *Watch and learn, my dear! We'll show them a wyvern's wrath!*

And the wyvern opened her mouth and flamed the front of the ship. Krea saw that the harsh wyvern's flames had set the remains of the bow on fire and flames were licking back toward the rest of the ship. Flames raced up the rigging to the first balloons and soon they were engulfed in flames.

There! Wymarc cried triumphantly. *Annora, you are avenged!*

"We surrender!" a voice called loudly from the ship. Krea recognized that voice. It was the Crown Prince Nestor, the same prince she had seen in the square before Ibb saved her from the fire.

"I fired on you, I killed you! Take me but please, for the love of the gods, spare the rest of the crew! They are blameless!"

Wymarc? Krea thought. She could feel the other's stubborn resistance.

"Don't listen to him!" Another voice boomed. "I am Captain Ford, I ordered the guns fired. If you must take someone, take me!"

Let them all die, Wymarc thought. *Let the ship burn and be a pyre for Annora.*

And what of Kalan? Krea asked. *Is this justice?*

But do you know of justice child? They killed my Annora, they deserve to die. Wymarc thought.

Krea was silent for a long while, then she thought *That is what you want, but is that what Annora would have wanted?*

Wymarc heaved a sigh that stretched through their wyvern body.

What would you have us do?

Save them, Krea said. She saw a man stumble and fall past the wrecked bow of the ship. *Save those we can, bring them to the judgement and justice of the gods.*

#

"Abandon ship!" Ford called as he found his feet. The explosion and the wyverns' attack were enough by themselves to ensure *Spite's* destruction but together, there was no hope. "All hands, abandon ship!"

"How are we going to do that, sir?" Knox asked, glancing at the snowy waste far below them.

"Throw ropes over the side," Ford said. "Let the men climb down them. Tell them to let go when the ship is near the ground."

"Aye, that might work," Knox allowed dubiously.

"See to it," Ford said firmly, turning to the stern.

"And you, sir?"

"I'm going to see to the mage," Ford said. He clapped Knox on the back. "And Knox?" The grizzled seaman gave him a look. "It's been a pleasure serving with you."

Knox broke into a grin. "Thankee sir. It's been a pleasure serving with you, too! And you can't say we haven't seen the sights, you can't say that, that's for certain!"

Ford nodded once, gave Knox one last salute and strode away quickly, leaving the first mate bellowing, "Throw ropes over the sides lads! Scramble down and cast off when we're near the ground! Come on you lot! Your lives depend on this! Jenkins, get the men moving! Mr. Franck! Have your men cease their work and prepare to abandon!"

Ford glanced back over his shoulder to see Angus Franck, stunned, looking at the wyvern rising above them.

"Never forget the fury of a woman spurned, Mr. Franck," Ford quipped to himself.

Surprisingly, the other man seemed to have heard him across half the length of the ship and over all the cries of the remaining crew. He gave Ford a quick salute and called back, "And never forget the flames of a wyvern in anger, sir!"

"Indeed!" Ford called back, diving down the hatchway and sliding down the ladder.

Inside the flailing remains of *Spite*, Ford was overcome with the sounds of his ship dying behind him as he grabbed handholds and pulled himself up the steep incline toward his cabin in the very rear of the ship.

"There you are!" Annabelle cried as Ford kicked the door open. She reached a hand back to him and helped haul him inside. Ford slammed the door behind him which fell rather than shut as bow became bottom and stern became the top of the stricken airship.

"Put your belt on and climb through the window!" Ford shouted at her. He moved toward Reedis who was moaning and struggling to regain consciousness. "We've got to get out of here!"

"And when we're outside, what then?" Annabelle asked him crossly. "Do we grow wings and fly?"

"No," Ford told her, dropping a hand toward his belt and nodding to Reedis. "We grow balloons and *float*."

Annabelle's brows rose and she gestured toward Reedis. "His work?"

Ford smiled and nodded in agreement. "Now get yourself out, I'll need your help with him."

"There must be a word or something," Annabelle said even as she started pulling herself through the narrow stern windows.

"There is but I'll have to spell it," Ford told her, gesturing toward his belt, "because saying it will kick off my balloon."

"So spell it," Annabelle said, pulling herself fully through the window and turning around to lean inside with one arm toward Reedis.

"A-L-T-U," Ford said, pushing Reedis upwards to the window. He could feel when Annabelle caught Reedis' arm and began pulling the mage out onto the ship's stern.

Spite lurched suddenly and fell faster.

"The balloons!" a voice on deck cried. "The fire's got the balloons!"

"Never mind, men!" Crown Prince Nestor cried. "Over the side, grab a line and climb down!"

Ford had a moment to be impressed with Nestor's calm and control before the ship lurched once more and he lost his foothold and crashed back onto the door.

"Richard!" Annabelle called back to him. "Richard, are you all right?"

"Never mind me!" Ford called back. He could feel that one of his legs was broken. "Just get him and leave."

"He's not through the window!"

"Just get him halfway through," Ford called back, moving painfully to push himself upright, limping on his good leg and searching for handholds that he might use to get up back to the window to help push Reedis.

Ford could smell smoke coming through the door. *Spite* was burning fiercely, the flames being fanned by her plunge through the air. Dimly he heard cries of men outside the ship and with a horrified thought guessed that their ropes had been burned through, leaving them to plunge thousands of feet into the frozen plain below.

"He's through!" Annabelle called. "Richard — "

"Say your spell!" Ford shouted back.

"Alt you," Annabelle said in a nervous voice. "Richard, Richard! What's supposed to happen?"

"You didn't say it right!" Ford called back. He'd managed to get himself to within a hand's width of Reedis' foot. He moved once more, his teeth clenched in pain as he took weight on his broken leg.

"I don't know how!" Annabelle wailed. "Richard!"

Richard Ford took a deep breath, pushed against Reedis' lower foot with all his strength and shouted, "Altu!"

"Ow!" Annabelle called in pain and surprise above him.

"What? What? No!" Reedis' voice came back faintly through the open hatch. "You fool! You've doomed yourself!"

Ford's belt burst into a huge balloon which filled his cabin and trapped him away from the window.

"No, Richard, no!" he heard Reedis' pained cry as the mage flew away from the wreck of *Spite*.

"Go with the gods, my friend!" Ford shouted back with the last of his strength. To himself, in a whisper, he said, "You cannot say it wasn't fun."

Chapter Seven: Have A Heart

We can't catch them fast enough! Krea wailed as another man fell beyond them to his death.

We have to try! Wymarc called back even as they swooped and caught two men in their talons. The sudden weight caused Krea Wymarc to screech in pain but then they were diving with all their ability down to the ground below.

Drop them! We're low enough! Wymarc ordered and Krea agreed. With despairing cries the two men fell to the ground even as Krea Wymarc strained her wings to get back to the plummeting ship.

We'll never save them all, Krea groaned in horror as they saw two more men falling, their ropes burnt through.

I realize now, these men could have been my children, Wymarc thought sadly even as the two of them, twin-souls, fought the air for height.

What's that? Krea thought as they spied something out of the corner of their eye coming quickly from the mountain pass.

Help, I hope, Wymarc replied, turning them so that they could have a better look.

It's Hana! Krea cried in surprise, causing the wyvern to screech loudly and triumphantly. Below them, the few remaining men on the deck cringed, expecting their doom.

Except one man. Krea watched in surprise as the man jumped up and down and waved at her.

Who is that? Wymarc asked.

It's Angus! Krea cried in surprise. And, suddenly, her heart felt like stone. *We have to save him!*

He's waving toward the others, Wymarc said. *I think he wants us to save them first.*

There are too many! Krea wailed, fighting with Wymarc trying to dive toward Angus.

We can't get him, Krea, he's still on the ship, Wymarc said. *We can get those who are on the lines. And they're in greater danger.*

No! And Krea fought for control of the wyvern. The white winged beast jerked back and forth between the burning deck and the flailing men hanging below.

Krea! Wymarc shouted. *You can't save him!*

Krea shuddered in despair. Wymarc was right. As a wyvern there was no hope of getting down to the burning deck and scooping up the man. Only those dangling below could be saved.

Angus! Krea wailed. *He made us, Wymarc! Without him, we wouldn't be here!*

I know, Wymarc said soothingly. *And we will honor his memory just as we honor his will now.*

Have a heart Wymarc! We share this body, my feelings matter too! Krea wailed.

Hana hove into sight and waved, grinning from ear to ear as she spied Krea Wymarc. "I did it, I did it!"

And — without warning Wymarc — Krea shifted back into a human.

What are you doing? Wymarc cried in alarm.

"Hana!" Krea called, her voice barely carrying over the fire and wind around them. "On the deck! That's Angus! Save him!"

You fool, Wymarc cried as they plummeted earthwards, *you've killed us both!*

"Nope!" Krea said smugly. And she shifted them back into wyvern form, their wings outstretched, breaking their fall, turning it into a dive — a dive which brought them under two more stricken men which they grabbed with their talons and lowered back to the frozen ground below.

#

Hana dove to the burning ship, craning through the smoke to find the man that Krea had begged her to save.

The airship was nearly perpendicular to the ground, held up by only the last three balloons.

"I'm going to get you!" Hana shouted over the winds that supported her. She saw the man — Angus — jerk his eyes toward her. Angus was moving back to the stern of the ship, climbing over the railing and standing on the stern. Hana moved herself closer to the plummeting ship, close enough to Angus to hear his breathing and reached out a hand. Angus smiled at her and jumped toward her. Hana gasped in surprise and horror as her fingertips brushed his but he fell away from her, plunging toward the ground below.

"No you don't!" Hana shouted, killing her winds and diving toward the man below. She forced a wind on her back, pushing her down faster and faster until she caught up with him and then she pushed herself closer, arms outstretched.

"Are you a god?" Angus cried to her in amazement.

"No, I'm Hana," she said, grappling him, clutching him tight in her arms and moving the winds under them to cushion them, slow them down.

"I'm very pleased to meet you," Angus Franck told her with a grin.

Hana was about to reply when a shout and a noise caused the two of them to turn back toward *Spite* in time to a man plunge toward the stern, shouting, "By the gods, I won't leave you!"

"He's going to miss the ship!" Angus cried in horror.

"No," Hana said, "I'll get him there." And she raised a hand, called on the gods, and sent a blast of wind toward the falling man, forcing him in the right direction.

#

Reedis looked up in alarm as the spell jerked him upwards, pulled by the safety balloon he'd half-expected to fail. Below him he saw *Spite*, flaming and plummeting to the ground below. His eyes widened as he took in the green of Ford's balloon — trapped inside Ford's cabin.

Frantically he looked around and up. There was a balloon above him. He recognized Annabelle by her boots.

"Annabelle!" he shouted up into the wind.

"Reedis, Richard is trapped!" Annabelle called back down. "I couldn't get to him."

"Your knife!" Reedis shouted. "Throw your knife into my balloon!"

"What?" Annabelle called back in surprise.

"Just do it!" Reedis bellowed.

"I don't want you to die," Annabelle said in worried tone.

"I don't plan on it," Reedis called back. "Now puncture my balloon, I've got to get back to Captain Ford!"

Reedis craned his neck upwards, trying to see around his balloon and then he peered downwards, trying to compute his aim. He felt rather than heard the knife hit the balloon and then he was falling, arms all akimbo, toward the burning ship below.

"I really must be mad," he muttered to himself as the horror below registered on his senses. "Oh, gods! And I'm going to miss!"

He had just a moment to spot the strangest sight — a young girl and Angus Franck hovering in the air — before the girl blasted him with a harsh burst of wind and he fell right onto the stern of the burning *Spite*.

"Ow!" Reedis groaned as he hit the hardwood with all of his body. Reflexively he grabbed on and slowly started pulling himself toward the captain's window and the green balloon. "Richard! Captain Ford, I'm coming!"

"Reedis?" Ford's muffled and pained voice came up to the mage's ears. "Reedis, what are you doing?"

"Rescuing you, captain," Reedis told him.

"Your balloon?"

"I had Annabelle puncture it," Reedis said proudly. "Fell right back down. Would have missed the ship except some remarkable girl pushed me with her winds."

"Reedis, you idiot, we're going to die," Ford grumbled.

"Some day," Reedis agreed readily. "Can you move? I propose to get you and that balloon out in one piece."

"My leg's broken," Ford told him. "The balloon pushed me back to the bottom." Reedis heard him groan in pain as he tried to move. Then Ford said hopelessly, "I don't think I can get out."

"We'll figure out something," Reedis said gamely.

"It'll have to be quick," Ford's voice came back. "I can feel the flames on the door."

Reedis realized that he could smell the smoke more strongly and glanced around. Flames had engulfed *Spite* almost completely. On the very stern of the ship still survived.

"If we can get the window wide enough, the balloon should pull you out," Reedis said.

"And you?"

"I'll grab on as you go by," Reedis said. "The balloon should hold us both."

"So all you need is a strong man with an axe," Ford said grimly.

"Will this help?" a voice boomed up from over the railing. It was Crown Prince Nestor. Reedis looked up and saw that he had an axe in his hands.

"Nestor?" Ford cried. "Why are you still here?"

"I had to get the crew off, sir," Nestor called back.

"You? What about Knox?" Reedis asked in surprise.

Nestor's face fell and he shook his head grimly. "It was Mr. Knox who gave me the charge. I'm afraid he didn't make it."

"What?"

"He went over with the last line," Nestor said with a catch in his voice. "I ordered him."

"Good man!" Reedis said, surprised that the prince had shown such mettle.

"I wish," Nestor said. "The wind shifted and his line caught fire. He fell without a word." He hefted his axe. "We're all that's left. What do I need to do?"

"Smash the window, widen it so the balloon can get through," Reedis told him, moving aside and gesturing the prince toward him.

Nestor grimly pulled himself over the stern and clambered down to the window. He raised his axe and started hammering away at the wood frame of the window. He struck grimly, quickly, and with more strength than Reedis would have guessed the prince possessed.

Nestor caught his look and grinned. "Sykes had me working hard," Nestor told him. "And you're the last of the crew."

"The captain goes down with his ship," Ford cried feebly.

"Not this captain," Nestor said, hacking steadily at the frame. "Your prince commands you to survive." In an undertone he added, "You can avenge those my father betrayed."

The frame grew weaker and weaker, Reedis could see the green balloon bulge through more and more, straining to grab the air and freedom.

"One more good hit, your highness," Reedis told him.

"I agree," Nestor said. He raised the axe high. "Be ready to grab — urgh!" Crown Prince Nestor cried in alarm, the axe falling from his hand as a pair of strong talons grabbed him and plucked him off the ship.

Reedis had one glimpse of the wyvern screeching triumphantly and climbing away before the window frame shattered completely and the green balloon burst forth.

"Grab on!" Ford cried as he flew by. Reedis lurched, leapt and —

— caught both hands around Ford's leg, plummeting the length of Ford's leg to halt, hard, his hands clinging desperately to Ford's ankle.

"Oh, gods! That hurts!" Ford cried. "That's the broken leg!"

"I don't know if I can hold on," Reedis cried, looking down to see *Spite*, fully engulfed in flames, falling below them. They were falling, too, but not as fast as the dying ship.

"By all the gods, you'll hold on!" Ford swore. He glanced down and saw *Spite* below him. "We need you."

"Need me?" Reedis said. "Whatever for?"

"To build more airships," Ford told him. "We're going back to Kingsland."

"Kingsland."

"To avenge Nestor," Ford said.

"Do you know," Reedis said after a moment, "I think that's a great idea!"

Chapter Eight: House of Life and Death

A screech in the distance alerted Hana to Krea Wymarc's presence. She waved and started moving in the direction of the wyvern with Angus Franck clutched to her chest.

Below them, *Spite*, in her death throes, crashed loudly on the frozen plains. Flames licked at the last of her wood, at the canvas of the twisted propellers at her rear, and soon there was nothing left but fire and ash.

Krea Wymarc circled the wreck once and then winged back toward the mountain pass.

"What will happen now?" Angus said to Hana.

"I suppose you'll be judged by the gods," she told him.

Angus gave her a fearful look then steeled himself. "I'm ready."

"No, you're not," Hana said, laughing at him, "you're just trying to be brave."

"How long?" Angus asked. He saw her look and added, "Before we get there?"

"Over the pass and down to the castle," Hana said, her green eyes glowing into his dark ones.

He nodded toward the wyvern who was pacing them. "Is that the winter wyvern?"

"It's Krea Wymarc," Hana confirmed. She gave him a look. "She turned human in mid-flight to tell me to rescue you."

Angus took this in slowly. "I killed her," he confessed miserably.

Hana nodded her head. "I know," she told him. "She said that you had no choice, that she would have died if you hadn't."

"We were to be married," Angus said.

Hana mulled this over. "Do you still want to marry her?"

Angus looked over at the wyvern, his face a mix of emotions. "I promised her," he said. "If she still wishes it, I will."

Hana said nothing until they reached the pass and she waved at the castle below. "This is the castle."

"It's beautiful!" Angus said. "Have you lived here long?"

Hana shook her head. "Only two weeks." She made a face. "And I'm going to have to leave soon."

"Leave? Where?" Angus asked with concern.

Hana shook her head. "Shh! I have to concentrate on landing."

"Do you do this often?" Angus asked, as the ground grew closer and closer to them.

"This is the second time," Hana admitted.

"I shall be very quiet," Angus whispered.

Hana smiled at him, glancing over his shoulder to see the ground below.

\#

Krea Wymarc lowered Crown Prince Nestor to the ground before alighting and turning back into her human form.

Nestor jumped back in surprise. "It's you!"

"Both of us, actually," Wymarc said coldly.

And then Krea let out a huge cry and sank to the ground. "My arms!" Nestor glanced around for someone and, when he realized they were alone, he rushed over to the girl, picking her up.

"What is it? What can I do?" he asked her worriedly. But she was unconscious. Nestor turned around, saw the huge doors of the castle, and rushed toward them with the girl in his arms. He kicked the doors, shouting, "Help! Help!"

When no one came, he turned around and pushed his back against the doors with all his remaining strength. Shivering in the cold, he nearly fell when the doors behind him opened. Inside, he glanced around the huge corridor of white marble, his eyes wide.

"Help! I've got an injured girl here, she needs help!" Nestor cried at the top of his lungs. "For the love of the gods, please help her!"

"Not so loud, not so loud!" a woman's voice called back to him. He saw the shadow of a person growing in the distance. "That's the trouble with the living, always so loud!"

"Please," Nestor said in a more normal voice. "This is Krea Wymarc and she just saved my life. She brought me here and she collapsed. *Please* can you help her?"

"She collapsed because she strained every muscle in her body," the woman replied crossly, as she closed the last of the distance between them.

"She changed into a human, called to her friend, and then back into a wyvern in time to pluck me off the burning ship," Nestor explained, his eyes wide with worry and fear. "Please, can you do anything to help her?"

"Hmph!" the woman snorted, turning back the way she came. She stopped to turn back to the bemused prince long enough to say, "Come along! Follow me if you want to help her." As she continued briskly back down the corridor, she muttered to herself, "No doubt there'll be more coming shortly."

"The air girl and Angus, at the least," Nestor called in agreement even as he hurried to catch up with the woman. The girl, Krea, weighed no more than an average girl in his arms. Before his trip to the bitter north on *Spite*, Nestor would never have considered carrying another body — it being both beneath his royal stature and outside the abilities of his body. But the weeks in the air and his time with Sykes had done much to change both his attitude and his endurance. Krea Wymarc felt as light as a feather in his arms. He glanced down at her, taking in her white skin, white hair — she was an albino, that much was obvious. But he saw the way her nostrils flared ever so lightly and she drew breath and exhaled. The curves of her lips were gentle, the shape of her arms beautiful, the —

"Stop ogling her and hurry along!" the woman in front chided him.

"I don't think I've ever seen someone as beautiful," Nestor said softly, surprising himself.

"That, young man, is because you never *looked*," the woman snapped. She pushed open a door, walked inside and held it for him. "There's a bed, lay her there."

The room was all white. The bed was white with white linens and blankets. Beside it was a white marble table, and a white rocking chair.

"Lay her down — no! Let me move the sheets first!" the woman told him. "*Now* put her in bed."

Nestor did as he was told and pulled the sheets and blankets up over the unconscious form.

"Turn away, there's a good lad," the woman said. Nestor did as he was told. He felt something — he couldn't describe it — rush behind him and a moment later the woman said, "You may turn back again."

Krea Wymarc was dressed in a nightgown, her clothes laid neatly on a bench at the end of the bed.

"Magic?" Nestor breathed, eyes wide in awe, as he gestured to the nightgown and the clothes.

"One should hope, dear," the woman said, "one should hope." She pressed a hand to Krea's forehead and straightened up again briskly, looking at Nestor. "Now, what about you?"

"Pardon?"

"What are you going to do, now?" the woman demanded.

Nestor gulped and gestured to the chair. "Can I stay with her? Until she wakes? I'd come tell you —"

"Stay," the woman said, pointing to the chair. "I'll be back in a moment with some herbals and then she'll need rest." She glared up at the young man. "You *can* keep quiet, can't you?"

Nestor nodded, moving to the chair and rocking it back and forth vigorously, all the while staring at the sleeping girl in the bed beside him.

"How can I thank you, lady…?"

"Avice," the woman said, smiling at him. "Why would you want to thank me?"

Nestor pointed to the sleeping girl. "For her," he said. "If you hadn't come, I don't what I would have done."

"Oh, I don't doubt you would have thought of something," Avice replied with a quirk of her lips. She moved toward the door.

"Avice…" Nestor said, his brows furrowing. She glanced back toward him, one eyebrow arched. "I remember the shaman telling me…" He fought to recall a dim memory and then, slowly, all the color drained from his face. "Are you the god?"

"Goddess, dear," Avice corrected cheerfully. "I am the goddess of life." She watched with glee as Nestor struggled to form words before adding, "And, yes, this is the House of Life and Death."

Before he could react, she opened the door and closed it behind her, walking briskly away.

#

"You're going to need to carry her," a woman's voice said as soon as Angus touched the ground.

"Pardon?" Angus asked, glancing around in search of the woman. He had just enough time to glance toward Hana before he saw her eyes roll back into her head and she slipped toward the ground. Reflexively, he caught her and picked her up in his arms.

"I said," the woman repeated tersely, "you're going to need to carry her." Angus caught sight of a woman at the front of the double doors, turning to push them open. "Really! Things would have gone *much* better if you'd just listened to me!"

Angus followed the woman who held the door opened for them as they entered and closed it quietly when they were inside. Without a word, the woman turned and began walking off briskly down the corridor to the left, muttering to herself, "I'm going to need a nap after all this excitement!"

"Is she all right?"

"She just fainted," the woman replied. "She over-exerted herself carrying *you*."

Angus looked down at the young girl guiltily and held her tighter in his arms. "It's only right, then."

"What?" the woman asked, not turning back but opening a door to the right of the corridor.

"It's only right that I carry her now," Angus said, following the woman into the room. It was all white, with a white bed and white linen, a white side table, a white bench set at the end of the bed and a white rocking chair. Without prompting, he laid the girl in the bed after the woman had pulled back the sheets.

"She'll be too hot in those clothes," Angus said worriedly.

"Turn around and I'll fix that," the woman said. Angus turned around. He felt a flash of magic and, when the woman told him to turn back, found that Hana was in a nightgown under the covers, her clothes neatly piled on the bench. Angus gave the woman a look of surprise. The woman said, "I'm getting rather *good* at this."

"Can you help her?" Angus asked.

"I already did," the woman replied. "She'll sleep and wake, rested."

"Can I stay with her?" Angus asked. He saw the woman's look and shook his head quickly. "Just to keep watch."

"Indeed," the woman replied. She smiled a moment later and nodded him toward the chair at the far side of the bed. "I would expect no less from Krea's killer."

"You know Krea?" Angus said quickly. He glanced around. "Is she here? Is she all right?"

"Yes, yes, and yes," the woman replied. She pointed to the door. "She's in the room across from yours." She gave him a wry look. "Someone is keeping an eye on her, you can see her when she recovers."

"She's not hurt, is she?" Angus asked, turning to the door with worry.

"No more than Hana here," the woman said lightly. She gestured Angus to the chair. "Sit with her, she'll appreciate the company."

"She saved my life," Angus said.

"Yes," the woman agreed, "there's a lot of that going around today." She turned to the door. "Now, if you'll excuse me, I've things to prepare."

"My lady?" Angus asked.

The woman stopped, sighed. "My name is Avice. I'm the goddess of life. This is the House of Life and Death." She waved a hand at him. "Now rest. You're going to need your strength."

Chapter Nine: Crown Prince Nestor

"Rest, you're going to need your strength," Reedis said as he lowered Captain Ford to the snowy ground.

"Pfah!" Ford said, making a face. "We're leagues from anywhere, we're going to freeze before the dawn."

"We won't freeze until our fire dies," Reedis said, surprising Ford by throwing a bunch of broken wood onto the ground and setting it alight with his magic.

"You should leave me here," Ford said. He pointed to his splinted leg. "There's no way I can walk far. You could, though."

"I didn't *come back* for you to leave you here," Reedis said testily.

"The fire's warm," Ford said thoughtfully. He glanced to Reedis. "I'd be safe here. You could go on, maybe find some help —"

"Richard, that's enough!" Reedis snapped. "We are either going to get through this together or we're going to die together!"

"Why —" Ford's brow creased. "Do you know, mage Reedis, I don't think I ever learned your first name."

"That's because I don't like it," Reedis said sharply. "It was my father's, I think —"

"Think?" Ford interrupted. An awkward silence grew between them and then Ford waved a hand at the mage. "Oh, I'm sorry. I didn't know."

"No reason you should," Reedis said. He stared at the fire for a moment before looking up. "It's Karol."

"Karol?"

"My first name," Reedis said.

"Oh," Ford said. He glanced to the fire. "It's not a bad name, all thing considered."

"I go by Reedis," the mage said curtly.

"Very well," Ford said. He raised his eyes to meet the mage's, saying, "It has been a pleasure working with you, mage."

"So what's next?" Reedis said. "You said we should avenge Nestor, I believe."

"We should," Ford said. He roused himself, leaning up on an arm, wincing as the movement jerked his broken leg. "I have no respect for a King who wants me to commit the murder of his own son."

"*His* son?" Reedis asked mildly.

"I've heard the rumors," Ford said with a wave of his hand. "If the prince is a bastard, I guarantee this — he's Markel's bastard."

Reedis snorted with laughter. "Yes," he said when he'd recovered, "I can see why you say that."

"You know," Ford said thoughtfully, closing his eyes to concentrate better on his words, "I could see how, with some training, some guidance, someone to mentor him, he might turn out to be a decent king, even better than his father."

"You do?"

"I do," Ford said. "In fact —"

"Richard," Reedis interrupted him in a frightened voice. A voice that didn't come from the direction of the last voice.

Ford opened his eyes and glanced toward the mage who gestured with wide eyes toward where Ford had heard the *other* voice.

"I'm glad to hear that," the owner of the voice said. "Because I have a job for you two. One that deals directly with Crown Prince Nestor."

Ford glanced at the speaker, frowning. He *knew* that face.

The owner of the face saw his confusion and smiled. "Imagine me with a beard. Older." He paused as he saw Ford's continued confusion. "Frozen."

"And as large as a mountain," Reedis said in a very small voice.

"Exactly," the god Arolan said with a nod and a smile. He gestured to the distance. "I think this conversation is better carried out —"

And suddenly there were in a white room, warm, and both of them were in adjoining beds as the god Arolan continued —

"— when you've had a chance to rest and recover."

About The Twin Soul Series

Currently spanning 19 books and over 200 characters, the Twin Soul Series keeps on growing!

If you'd like a list of characters, scan the QR Code below, it'll take you to the characters page on our website, http://www.twinsoulseries.com

Acknowledgements

No book gets done without a lot of outside help.

We are so grateful to Jeff Winner for his marvelous cover art work.

We'd like to thank all our first readers for their support, encouragement, and valuable feedback.

Any mistakes or omissions are, of course, all our own.

About the Authors

AWARD-WINNING authors The Winner Twins, Brit and Brianna, have been writing for over ten years, with their first novel (*The Strand*) published when they were twelve years old.

NEW *York Times bestselling* author Todd McCaffrey has written over a dozen books, including eight in the Dragonriders of Pern® universe.

http://www.twinsoulseries.com

Printed in Poland
by Amazon Fulfillment
Poland Sp. z o.o., Wrocław
25 August 2021

93de3236-47d6-40cd-96ed-fd049572cd82R01